Charlene Sands is a *USA TODAY* bestselling author more than forty romance novels. She writes sensual contemporary romances and stories of the Old West. When not writing, Charlene enjoys sunny Pacific beaches, great coffee, reading books from her favourite authors and spending time with her family. You can find her on Facebook and Twitter, write her at PO Box 4883, West Hills, CA 91308, or sign up for her newsletter for fun blogs and ongoing contests at charlenesands.com.

Cat Schield has been reading and writing romance since high school. Although she graduated from college with a BA in business, her idea of a perfect career was writing books for Mills & Boon. And now, after winning the Romance Writers of America 2010 Golden Heart® Award for Best Contemporary Series Romance, that dream has come true. Cat lives in Minnesota with her daughter, Emily, and their Burmese cat. When she's not writing sexy, romantic stories for Mills & Boon Desire, she can be found sailing with friends on the Saint Croix River, or in more exotic locales, like the Caribbean and Europe. She loves to hear from readers. Find her at catschield.com and follow her on Twitter, @catschield.

Also by Charlene Sands

Her Forbidden Cowboy
The Billionaire's Daddy Test
One Secret Night, One Secret Baby
Twins for the Texan
Sunset Surrender
Sunset Seduction
The Secret Heir of Sunset Ranch
Redeeming the CEO Cowboy
The Texan's Wedding Escape

Also by Cat Schield

Upstairs Downstairs Baby
At Odds with the Heiress
A Merger by Marriage
A Taste of Temptation
The Black Sheep's Secret Child
Little Secret, Red Hot Scandal
The Heir Affair

Discover more at millsandboon.co.uk

HEART OF A TEXAN

CHARLENE SANDS

LONE STAR SECRETS

CAT SCHIELD

MILLS & BOON

First Published in Great Britain 2018
by Mills & Boon, an imprint of HarperCollinsPublishers,
1 London Bridge Street, London, SE1 9GF

Heart of a Texan © 2018 Charlene Swink
Lone Star Secrets © 2018 Harlequin Books S.A.

Special thanks and acknowledgement are given to Cat Schield for her
contribution to the Texas Cattleman's Club: The Impostor series.

ISBN: 978-0-263-93613-1

0818

MIX
Paper from
responsible sources
FSC™ C007454

This book is produced from independently certified FSC™
paper to ensure responsible forest management.

For more information visit: www.harpercollins.co.uk/green

Printed and bound in Spain
by CPI, Barcelona

HEART
OF A TEXAN

CHARLENE SANDS

To my sweet daughter Nikki,
you are an amazing mother of
two precious daughters. Every day you
make us proud with your abundance
of love and kindness.

One

Francesca Isabella Forte was hiding out. Not from an evil stalker, an old boyfriend or even a shady loan shark. No, that would be too simple. It was her father. During their last argument, he'd been so furious with her, he'd disowned her. Out-and-out cut her off without a dime. Even worse, he'd threatened to take custody of her child. All because she didn't want to marry a man he'd chosen for her and she didn't want to run the Forte Foods empire.

So she'd packed up her belongings and headed straight out of San Francisco's elite Pacific Heights' neighborhood to Dallas. Using her middle name, shortened to Bella, and her married name of Reid, to all the world, she was just a young unemployed widow. Her best friend from college, Amelia Gray, had taken her in, no questions asked.

Now, Bella drove along the interstate in her rented Ford Focus, noting how different the flat Texas landscape was from her hilly hometown.

And Bella felt free.

"Hey, Bella," Amy said. "What did Cinderella say when her photos didn't show up?"

"Uh…someday my prints will come."

They giggled at the silliness and then Bella put a shushing finger to her lips. She didn't want to wake the love of her life, her twenty-two-month-old baby, Sienna, who slept peacefully in the car seat behind her.

Everyone said Sienna was the exact replica of her mommy, with shiny dark hair curling at the tips and pretty meadow-green eyes. Bella ate those compliments up, but always reminded people that Sienna was also bright, and sweet, and kindhearted, and she'd gotten all those traits from her father.

Sienna was the best thing she and Paul had ever done in their lives.

That's why she'd been so stunned when her father had threatened to sue her for custody of her baby. Marco Forte claimed she was an unfit mother. That she couldn't provide for her baby. That she'd had a mental breakdown after her husband died.

Marco had the money and influence to start the proceedings. But he couldn't do that if he couldn't find her. Her father would never get his hands on her baby. Ever.

They were fifteen miles outside Dallas proper, the road dark, the beam of her headlights the only illumination as they headed to Amy's brand-new high-rise condo. But just then a cloud of smoke billowing up from the side of the road caught Bella's eye. She blinked to make sure she was seeing correctly and, sure enough, she wasn't mistaken. A car was on fire. "Oh, no!"

She braked immediately.

"Bella, what?" Amy asked, looking up from her cell phone. "Oh, wow. You think someone's in there?"

Bella froze. Her husband's helicopter crash flashed

through her mind. Paul had died on the job, in a fire just like this one, while returning from an aerial excursion in the Bay Area that he gave to tourists. She'd lost her husband; Sienna had lost her father. It had been a year ago and she still couldn't believe he was gone.

Paul, I'm so sorry.

Popping sounds from the burning car shook her out of her own head. She had no time for self-pity. She needed to do something. She couldn't just sit there. And finally it all registered.

"Amy, watch Sienna. I've got to check it out. Someone might be in that car."

God, she hoped not.

Amy blinked her eyes as if making up her mind about something. "I'll go."

"No. I have to do this myself." She couldn't explain it, but a force was driving her on. Something told her she needed to be the one to check out that car. "Please, just watch my baby."

"Okay, but be careful and don't worry about Sienna."

"I'll be careful," she said, already out of her seat belt. She could hardly believe this was happening. But she had to go. She couldn't sit back and wait for help to arrive.

She *was* the help.

If someone had gotten to Paul in time, maybe he would've survived to see his baby take her first steps, to hear her beautiful babble that was beginning to sound like real words.

Bella's feet tapped the ground lightly as she raced as fast as she could. The car must've spun off the road at high speed; it was a good ten yards off the shoulder. By the time she reached it, she was out of breath. The vehicle was overturned and someone was sitting upside down at the wheel. A man. He wasn't moving.

She whispered a silent prayer. She needed as much help as she could get. "Amy, call 9-1-1," she shouted.

"Okay!" Amy shouted back. "I'm calling now!"

The fire hadn't reached the front seat yet; at the moment, the hot flames were still confined to the engine. Was she crazy to think she could pull the man out? Probably, but she had to try. The smoke was thick, burning her nostrils, blurring her eyes. She wiped at them and took the biggest breath she'd ever taken, filling up her lungs.

The door refused to budge no matter how hard she tried. Breaking the window was her only option. She wrestled herself out of her hooded jacket and wrapped it around her fist. She'd seen this done countless times in movies and hoped it really worked. Then she squeezed her eyes closed, hauled her arm back and punched the window with all of her strength. The window shattered and crumbled into tiny pieces, like broken ice crystals. She shook out her hand. It throbbed like crazy. She'd have to deal with that later.

Still praying, she wedged herself into the window and frantically used her fingers to find the button for the seat belt. It was strange working inside the flipped car, but finally she pressed her thumb down hard on the buckle button and the belt released. The man fell onto her like deadweight. God, he was heavy. Too late, she realized the belt had been preventing him from falling and now he was crushing her. A grunt rose from her chest as she strained to grab hold of his arms and pull him rather gracelessly out the window. He was cumbersome and it was awkward, but finally she yanked him free of the car.

Wonder Woman would've been proud.

The man's face was bloodied and bruised, yet even through all that she could tell he was handsome and young. He couldn't be much older than Paul had been when he'd died.

Only, this man wouldn't die today. Not if she had anything to say about it.

The heat was unbearable. She had to get him away from the fire. The car could blow at any second. She grabbed his arms and dragged the man closer and closer to the road, falling a few times, scraping her hands and legs over the bumpy terrain. She did her best to keep his head from further injury. Using every ounce of her strength, she finally made it a safe distance away. She gave a quick glance at the car; she could tell the blaze was traveling toward the gas tank. She held her breath and prayed. And then boom! The explosion echoed on the empty road, the blast like a rocket in flight. She sat back on her butt, immobilized as she watched the car go up in smoke.

"Oh, my God," Amy shouted. "Are you okay, Bella?"

She nodded and yelled back, "I'm not hurt. But he is."

"Paramedics are on the way!" Amy remained close to the car. Hopefully, baby Sienna was still asleep in the back seat. The little one was a great sleeper.

Bella got a grip then and looked down at the man she'd pulled from those flames. He would've died in that fire. Her body began to tremble uncontrollably.

She heard the faint sound of sirens off in the distance and her shoulders relaxed slightly in relief. But she had more to do. She couldn't wait. In this case, every second counted. This man wasn't conscious and she was pretty sure he wasn't breathing.

She knelt by his side, thankful for the summer lifeguard camp she'd attended as a teen.

I know CPR and I can help.

The scent of soot burned in Jared Stone's nostrils, putrid and strong. It felt like a big rig was sitting on his chest, making it damn hard to breathe. And something powerful hammered in his head. Everything ached and the hurt was wicked. He couldn't open his eyes. He probed his mind for clarity and…nothing. He was looping through a black hole of emptiness. What in hell had happened to him?

The last thing he remembered was driving along the highway and…

He searched and searched, straining to recall something, anything. His cell phone beeped and the beeping continued to drone in his ears. The sound grated on his nerves and then it hit him. It wasn't a phone at all. He fought to open his eyes but lost that battle. His eyes fluttered like a baby bird's but ultimately remained shut.

And then a delicate hand covered his. So soft, so gentle. The single touch comforted him in inexplicable ways, soothing his distress, taking away some of the pain. He'd never felt anything softer or more welcome. His skin responded immediately to those fingertips, feeling life again, feeling brightness where there had been only darkness.

"You're going to be all right." A woman's lilting, angelic voice seeped inside him, her tone as sweet, as memorable, as the hand that still held his. It hurt to move and his eyes wouldn't open, but that gentle voice gave him hope. Actually more than hope: *he believed her.* That serene voice wouldn't lead him astray.

"You've had an accident. I rode with you in the ambulance and now you're in the hospital. They are taking very good care of you."

He was relieved to know an angel sat by his side. Who was she? He had no clue, but she'd been with him at the accident scene and, man, he wished he could remember what had happened. The incessant beeping rang in his ears. Now he knew he was hooked up to a monitor and those beeps meant breath and heartbeats and all good things.

Jared remembered being attached to wires on a hospi-

tal machine once, after he'd been tossed off a wild stallion on the ranch. His father had told him not to go near
that horse, but the daredevil in him had decided dear ole
dad was being overprotective. And at the age of twelve, he
took on that wild stallion and...lost. Nearly broke his neck
trying to tame Balboa. He'd been unconscious for a little
while, but he'd wound up walking away from that ordeal
with big purple bruises all over his body, a slight concus-
sion and wounded pride.

His dad had sold Balboa the very next day.

That had hurt more than his injuries.

Now, Jared tried to acknowledge the woman with the
melodious voice by nodding his head. But the dizziness it
caused shut down his attempt.

"Don't worry," she said softly. "I won't leave you. I'm
here for as long as you need me to be. You were very lucky."

He didn't feel lucky. Every movement he made caused
some sort of pain. But he clung to the angel's words.

I'm lucky.

I'm lucky.

I'm lucky.

Bella opened her eyes as thin streams of sunlight filled
the hospital room. She'd asked for permission to visit the
patient last night and the staff had been lenient, letting her
since she'd saved his life. But she had fallen asleep in the
chair by his bed at some point. Stretching out her arms and
gently swiveling her head back and forth on her shoulders
helped remove the kinks. She rose, ran her hand through
her long hair and stopped midway when a thick wad of
gauze got stuck in the strands. The right hand she'd used
as a battering ram last night was bandaged past the wrist
and partway up the arm. She'd almost forgotten how she'd
broken that window to drag the man to safety.

She was certain everything underneath the bandage was bloodied and black and blue. She wiggled her fingers and felt the blood return to them, but she was pretty sure her knuckles would never be the same. It was a small price to pay. Last night the nurses had made a big fuss, insisting she have her hand x-rayed. They'd found out the patient lying in the bed nearby wasn't the only one who'd gotten lucky last night. Her hand was not broken. Hallelujah!

She grabbed her cell with her left hand and read a text from Amy.

Sienna is sleeping soundly. Not to worry.

Her baby was in good hands. Amy loved her dearly and Sienna was smitten with her mommy's best friend.

After the paramedics showed up at the accident scene, Bella had taken one look at the patient lying on the gurney and decided the man whose life she'd just saved wasn't going to the hospital alone. He had to know someone was there for him. When Paul died, he'd taken his last breaths alone. It had gutted her.

She'd asked Amy to put Sienna to bed for her. Her baby was a solid sleeper. Thankfully she hadn't inherited her mother's insomnia.

Now, in the light of a new day, she studied the man lying still on the bed. His forehead was bandaged, as were both arms. She'd overheard talk of broken ribs. She hoped the chest compressions she'd given him hadn't caused the damage. She hadn't heard or felt any breakage, but then she'd only been focused on getting the man to safety. All else had sort of blurred in her mind. Tests done last night showed no sign of internal bleeding. That news was gratifying. He would survive the terrible crash without any permanent damage. And, the nurse had assured her, no matter the broken ribs, her fast action had saved his life.

The man was handsome, almost to a fault. The dark bruises under his eyes and along his chin did nothing to hamper how striking he was. His jawline was angular and strong, covered by a light dusting of dark blond scruff. He was tall and lean, his arms muscular.

Just then, the patient moved, rustling the bedsheets. Her breath caught in her throat as his eyes fluttered open. Eyes that were intense and captivating and ocean blue. Eyes that at the moment appeared completely confused.

"Hello," she whispered. "I'm glad to see you're awake."

"You're the angel," he said, his voice weak and barely audible.

She smiled and shook her head. "I'm…not an angel. I'm very real. And happy to see you're better."

He winced and pain reflected in his eyes. "Not sure about better," he whispered. "Feels like I was hit by a bus."

"Well, I didn't see a bus. But something like that."

"What happened to me?"

"I'm not sure," she said. "I was driving along the interstate and saw your car in flames quite a distance from—"

"Jared, my God. You had us scared half to death." A blond man strode into the room looking too much like the patient not to be related. Up until this point, she had no idea of his name; the hospital wasn't sharing that information.

But… Jared? That was a good name for a strong man. It fit.

The man walked straight up to Jared, looking like he wanted to crush the patient tight in an embrace and at the same time rip him a new one. "Hey, bro."

"Yeah, hey, bro."

The man peered at the bandages covering Jared's body and shook his head, tears welling in his eyes. It was a touching scene and she felt like an outsider. She was ready to slip out of the room now that Jared had his brother here to look after him. "Sorry I wasn't here sooner. The authorities had trouble tracking me down. But, man, you almost died last night. You have no idea how close you came to buying the farm." He inhaled and paused, as if regrouping his emotions. "Are you in a lot of pain?"

Jared nodded gingerly. The movement was probably too much for him right now.

"You have two broken ribs and some contusions, but honestly, bro, if it wasn't for this young lady, you wouldn't be here right now." He turned to her and put out his hand, finally acknowledging her presence. "I'm Cooper Stone. Jared's brother."

"I'm… Bella." She gave him her uninjured hand.

"I understand you pulled my brother out of the car and got him to safety."

She nodded.

"And the car was on fire at the time?"

She nodded again.

"Thank you. You were very brave," he said, his eyes misting up again. "And you were injured, too." He glanced at the bandage on her right hand.

"It's nothing. Just some scrapes."

"You did that?" Jared's voice was a little stronger now. It contained a hint of disbelief. "You pulled me out of the car?"

She understood his surprise. She stood five feet five inches tall and wore a size five dress. Hardly a match for such a big man. "How?" he mumbled.

She shrugged, her face warming from Cooper's and Jared's awed expressions. She couldn't go into the whole Paul thing or the fact that she couldn't have left him to die in that car without trying to help. Her conscience wouldn't have allowed it. "Protein, every day."

Cooper smiled.

Jared tried to smile, too, but pain seemed to grip him and he frowned instead. "Thank you," he managed.

"I'd better let the nurses know you're awake," Cooper said. "Excuse me for a second."

Bella waited until he was gone before walking over to Jared. His eyes were clear and locked on her. Having his full attention gave her the good kind of chills, and she ignored them because the bond she had with Jared Stone would be broken now. He no longer needed her.

She covered her hand with his, careful not to cause him further pain, and gave him a smile. "I'm glad I was able to help you." She nibbled on her lower lip, thinking of Paul and somehow feeling that she'd evened out the score, in a way. Jared Stone would survive. "But since your brother's here…well, I'll be leaving you in good hands."

"You stayed because I had no one else." It was a statement not a question.

"Yes, and to make sure you'd survive."

"I did, thanks to you." He applied pressure to her hand, the squeeze only slight but enough to convey his emotions. Fatigue pulled the lines of his face down and his eyes began to close.

"I'll be going now. Have a good life, Jared."

She wasn't sure if he'd heard her goodbye. Yet when she walked out of his hospital room, an odd sensation stirred in her belly. As she approached the nurses' station, she noticed Cooper in a discussion with a floor nurse.

Looking out the window, she saw a news van from a local Dallas station pulling up to the hospital. It wouldn't do to be here when the journalists started doing interviews. She couldn't afford to be recognized. She slipped past Cooper without being noticed and then exited the hospital.

Two

Sienna sat in the middle of Amy's living room, stacking colorful plastic blocks on top of each other. "I make castle," she announced.

"It's beautiful," Bella said. The formation tilted far to the left, and as soon as Sienna's chunky little hand attached the last block—shaped like a blond-haired princess—the whole thing toppled over.

Sienna broke out in giggles and Bella laughed along with her. "Oh, no!"

"Do again, Mommy. Do again." Sienna's wide green eyes beseeched her.

"Okay, sweet baby. We'll do it again."

Bella took a seat beside her daughter on the floor and helped gather up the blocks.

Amy came out of her bedroom and plopped down on the sofa. Her home was the epitome of class and elegance, with its white furniture, glass fixtures and beautiful light-slate flooring. Amy had worked hard since their days at

Berkeley, becoming a successful real estate agent. Bella could fit her small rental home where she'd lived with Paul twice over into this big luxurious condo. Yet, she'd never minded living on Paul's salary alone. Her father's form of punishment in withholding her funds had backfired on him. She'd actually loved living on a budget, as long as she and Paul were together.

"No luck on that job interview, I'm afraid," Bella told her, grabbing a few blocks and starting to build again. "I won't be the new sous chef at the Onion Slice."

"Did you do as I said?"

She shook her head. "No, I didn't cover up my bruises with makeup. It wouldn't have worked anyway. They would've seen right through it. Literally."

"I bet you didn't tell them the truth, either. That you got those scrapes from saving a man's life two days ago."

"The subject didn't come up."

"You're too modest."

"I just don't see how telling them about the accident has anything to do with my culinary skills. If they don't think I'm qualified for the job, then I'll find someplace that does. I have another interview tomorrow." She placed a pink block over Sienna's lavender one.

"Good for you. With Christmas coming, I'm sure the restaurants are busier than usual. You'll find something. But you know you can stay here as long as you like. I love having Sienna and you here for as long as it takes. Makes this big place feel more homey."

"I do know that. You've been wonderful. But I need a job. I need to get back on my feet." What she really wanted was to open a restaurant of her own. She'd worked toward that goal for a while. Now that dream had to be put on hold until she could make sense of her life.

"Have you heard any news of your father at all?"

"No, thank goodness. I didn't leave a forwarding address with anyone I know in San Francisco and I have a new cell number. Your place is so brand-new that even if he wanted to find me through you, he wouldn't be able to. He's a stubborn old mule. And Yvonne is no help. She's probably grinning from ear to ear that we're out of Marco's life now."

"The evil stepmother."

"Hardly a mother. She's only thirty-eight, ten years older than me. The thought of that woman ever raising my daughter makes me sick to my stomach."

"Your dad would never take Sienna away from you," Amy said. "It's an idle threat, Bella."

"I don't know that for sure. He was eager to accuse me of having a mental breakdown when Paul died. I did my best to hang tough, but it was difficult for me."

"You were grieving. That doesn't make you unstable," Amy said. "And you bounced back, for Sienna's sake."

A sigh blew from Bella's lips. "We're better off now. Starting fresh. Starting over. At least I won't have to worry about Dad announcing my *engagement* in the society page to a man I'd barely dated. That was the last straw."

"That was pretty underhanded," Amy said, lifting up the *Dallas Tribune*. "But it seems like you made the newspapers again, Bella. I found this last night on page three and thought maybe you'd like to see it."

Amy handed her the newspaper. The black-and-white photo of the accident scene jumped out at her first. It pictured what was left of the hot red Lamborghini and next to it was an image of Jared Stone. She skimmed the article, learning that the victim was an entrepreneur and rancher who lived on Stone Ridge Ranch quite a few miles outside the city limits. It went on to say that Jared Stone had multiple holdings and companies in and around the Dallas area and shared his ranching business with his brother, Cooper. The piece hinted at a privileged lifestyle, portraying a man who courted danger with fast cars, racing boats and motorcycles.

"Seems like your guy *has a need for speed*," Amy said, grinning.

"Yeah, well. Hopefully he's learned his lesson. When I think about what could've happened to him, I get flustered."

"Oh, yeah, that was a pretty gruesome scene. But you pulled it off. That guy doesn't know how darn lucky he was that you were driving on that road at that exact moment. There's a mention of you in there, but they didn't print your name. You're the brave mysterious woman who pulled him to safety and saved his life."

"Yeah, well, I ducked out of the hospital before the news crew arrived, I guess." She tossed the newspaper aside. "I don't want to think about it anymore. I have enough trouble sleeping at night."

"Oh, man, Bella. I'm sorry. I didn't realize it was keeping you up."

"It's nothing new. I'm a terrible sleeper. I envy people who can lay their heads down and fall asleep. That's so not me."

She helped Sienna put the princess block on the very top of the castle and this time it didn't topple over. "Yay! You did it!" She clapped her hands and Sienna mimicked her.

"I did it, Mommy!"

She hugged the baby to her chest. Sienna was growing up way too fast. She deserved a good life in a place she could call home, with a dog or a cat or a goldfish, and a backyard instead of a high-rise elevator.

But for now, they had to make do living in Dallas.

* * *

Jared leaned against Cooper, his brother bracing him under the arm as they strode into the house. He was banged up pretty badly, but after two days in the hospital, he refused to enter his home in a wheelchair. He'd make it under his own power, with a little help from Coop, and that was that.

"Man, I wish like hell you would've let me take you to my place," Cooper said for the tenth time. "Lauren is a great nurse."

"Your new bride is also pregnant. She doesn't need me underfoot and neither do you. Besides, I'll be more comfortable here." The last thing he wanted was to be a burden to the honeymooners.

Jared's home was on Stone Ridge land, a good half mile from Cooper's place. They shared the stables and pastures and got along that way just fine. They were brothers and business partners, but they both needed their own space. "You can barely walk. And even if Marie could help you around the house, she's getting too old to keep up with everything. It's not fair to her."

"Don't argue with me, Coop. It's hard enough just to breathe with these cracked ribs, much less get in a pissing match with you."

"Fine, but think about Marie."

Their housekeeper shared duties between the two houses, splitting her time between both. Jared's injuries would make it much harder for her to keep up. "Don't worry. I won't let Marie tax herself. I'll think of something."

They left the foyer and Jared gestured toward the great room, wincing slightly. "Just help me to the chair."

His favorite leather armchair faced the back window, where he had a view of the vast amount of land he called his backyard. His home was modern in most respects, but this room with throw rugs over hardwood flooring and a massive flat-screen television was more lived in, a place he could unwind and not worry about disrupting the fine order of things.

With Cooper still supporting him, Jared slowly lowered himself into the chair. He felt a sharp jolt in his chest and it took a good few seconds before the ache subsided. "I'm…okay," he said breathlessly.

Cooper's lips pulled down in a stern expression.

"You look like Dad when you do that," Jared whispered.

"And you look like a man who's…in pain."

"Good observation. Sit a minute, will you?"

Cooper took a seat on a matching leather sofa facing him.

"Tell me about the woman." The angel, whose voice calmed him, whose touch gave him solace when he might've panicked. The angel who'd risked her life to save his.

Cooper immediately knew what he was asking. "The nurses told me her name is Bella Reid. She was driving on the interstate with her friend and saw the car catch on fire. Her friend called 9-1-1 and Bella rushed over to get you out of the car before…" Cooper let out a noisy breath. "You know."

Jared gave a tiny nod. He was aware of his limitations right now, what he could and couldn't do. Mostly, he couldn't do anything, but a nod he could manage. "I can't stop thinking about it."

"Are you having nightmares?"

Jared blinked. "No. I can't remember anything about the crash. Or after, really. Except that Bella was there, holding my hand, saying all the right things to keep me calm. I need to thank her properly. See how she's doing."

"She slipped out of the hospital after I showed up, Jared.

I didn't get her number. I have no way to find her. Maybe you should let it go."

"No," he said forcefully enough for Cooper's eyes to snap up to meet his. "I need to see her, Coop. My God, that woman saved my life. I need to talk to her. Just once. I can't let it go."

"What do you want me to do, ask the sheriff to give me private information. Or how about I hire a detective?"

Jared's lips quirked up. "Nothing that drastic. You have a wife. And she's a nurse. And if she happened to see Bella Reid's medical chart…"

"I can't ask Lauren to do that."

"You don't have to. I will. She owes me a favor."

"Paul, what am I going to do?" Bella mumbled under her breath, staring at the phone in her hand. She'd just hung up with the Beaumont Club. They'd needed a chef and she'd been a day late and a dollar short. They'd just called to inform her the job she hadn't even had a chance to interview for had been filled.

Whenever she needed guidance, she'd talk to her husband. If anyone heard her, they would understand. She was a widow with a beautiful child to raise, a woman whose heart was broken the day that helicopter crashed, and she liked to think that Paul was listening to her. That he would somehow see how hard she was trying.

Her dream of working as a chef in some capacity was slowly fading.

Yesterday she'd seen an ad online for a dental receptionist. Maybe she should apply for that. The salary wouldn't buy her a house, or rent her an apartment, but it would allow her some financial independence.

Her shoulders sagging, she walked in to check on Sienna. Her baby was napping peacefully, her little olive-skinned cheeks rosy at the moment. Bella was ready to slide in next to her child on the tiny bed and try to catch a nap.

If only.

She was still debating that, watching Sienna's chest rise and fall rhythmically, when someone buzzed from the lobby. She pushed the button before it buzzed twice. "Yes?"

"It's Cooper Stone. I'd like to speak to Bella Reid."

"This is Bella."

"May I come up to see you?"

Bella leaned her shoulder against the door. "What is it? Is everything all right with your brother?"

"That's what I want to speak to you about. I promise it'll only take a minute."

Her curiosity more than anything had her beeping him in. "Come up."

"Thanks," he said.

And just a few minutes later she was showing Cooper Stone to the sofa in Amy's living room.

"Hi," he said, taking off his black cowboy hat as soon as he sat down. Bella sort of loved that about Texans. They wore hats like other people wore shoes. And only took them off when absolutely necessary.

"Hello, Cooper." She sat, too. "I have to admit I'm a little bit shocked that you're here. How did you find me?"

"Don't be frightened," Cooper said sincerely. "It's nothing bad. It's just that my brother—"

"What about Jared?" She had a vested interest in his well-being and was anxious to hear about his recovery. It was sort of strange how she'd bonded with the person whose life she'd saved. She'd only been with him a few short hours, yet images of that night popped in and out of her mind at all times of the day and night. Thoughts of his health nagged at her.

"He's doing as well as can be expected," his brother said. "He's young and strong and he'll heal eventually."

"I see. That's good news. So then why are you here?"

"It's just that—" Cooper scrubbed a hand over his jaw "—he can't seem to get you off his mind. He wasn't all too coherent that first night and he can barely remember you at the hospital and…well… I think he needs to see you and thank you personally. It's important to him."

"I, uh, understand, but that's not really necessary."

"It is to him," Cooper said, his face somber. "Believe me, if it wasn't I wouldn't be here right now."

"You still haven't told me how you found me."

Cooper's mouth twisted and he let out a deep sigh, making it obvious he didn't want to divulge the information. "My wife…is a nurse."

He didn't have to say more. Though she was surprised that her personal contact information had been breached, she wasn't angry. She should be, but she just plain wasn't. Cooper wasn't there for nefarious reasons. He was there on behalf of his brother, who could've died a few days ago.

"Lauren, my wife, is a good woman," he began, "and she loves Jared, too. It took a lot of arm-twisting, if that makes you feel any better. I hope you'll consider coming to the ranch to see my brother. I can drive you myself or I can send a car for you."

Suddenly, Sienna ambled into the room, her soft black hair mussed. She clutched her stuffed bunny rabbit in one hand and rubbed her eyes with the other. "Hi, baby girl. Did you have a nice nap?"

Her child eyed the stranger cautiously, making a wide berth around him to get to her mommy. Bella knew the look; her daughter was wary and shy of strangers. She considered that a good thing and picked her up. Immediately, Sienna buried her face in her chest. "Sorry, she's a bit shy."

"She's adorable," Cooper said, a twinkle in his eye. "My wife, Lauren, is pregnant. Our baby is due in early spring."

Lauren, the wife who'd rifled through her personal files. "Congratulations. It's exciting. Is this your first?"

He nodded. "Yep, it's our first. How about you? Do you have any other children?"

"No, my husband died last year. It's just the two of us."

"I'm sorry to hear that. Must be hard being a single mother."

"It is. But I have great friends who help out. Amy, the woman who was with me the night of the accident, is letting us stay here until I can find employment. She's been wonderful."

"So this isn't your home?"

"It's where we live, for the time being."

His head slanting to the right, he studied her as if puzzling something out. "What kind of work do you do?"

I'm the disowned heiress of Forte Foods. "I'm a cook. Well, a chef really, but right now, I'd sling hash in the local diner if it would pay my bills." She smiled to wipe away Cooper's concerned expression and furrowed brow. That's all she'd say on the subject.

"Mommy, I hungry." The tiny voice echoed against her chest.

"Okay, sweetie. I'll make you something to eat."

Cooper rose from his seat and grabbed his hat.

She stood and gestured to Sienna. "So now you see why I can't just pick up and come to your ranch today?"

"I do see. But please consider driving out. Soon. And bring the little one. I bet she'd love to see the horses. We're at Stone Ridge Ranch. Here's my brother's card. It has his address and phone number on it." Cooper walked over to place the card in her hand. "And thanks for not freaking out about how I found you. It went against every shred of Lauren's sense of propriety, but at the same time she agreed that the only way Jared can heal mentally from the accident is to speak to you."

"That's putting a bit of pressure on me."

Cooper's brows lifted, his face the picture of innocence. "Is it working?"

She tilted her head and admitted, "Maybe."

You've got to go. I know you're dying to. Just go and satisfy your curiosity, Bella. See the man whose life you saved.

Amy's words burned in her ears as she stood on the doorstep of Jared Stone's home. There was a chill in the air and she cradled her bundled-up daughter even tighter. Mesquite trees surrounding the property were strung with big colorful ornaments. The door she'd just knocked on a moment ago was bedecked with twin pinecone wreaths reminding her that Christmas was just weeks away.

Funny, it didn't seem like Christmas. When Paul was alive it used to be such a fun time of year. Those four Christmases she'd shared with him had been the best. Now it was something she'd have to get through. But for Sienna's sake, she was going to make it special.

Her little girl was taking in the decorations in wide-eyed wonder. She pointed at an old-fashioned red buckboard wagon decorating the grassy portion of the front yard. The bed of the wagon was filled with buckets of thriving poinsettias. "Want ride, Mommy."

"Oh, sweetie, I don't think that wagon works."

"Why?" Everything lately required an explanation. Her little one was a curious soul.

"It's kind of old."

"O-kay. Is pretty," she said, still fascinated by the wagon.

"Yes, the flowers are pretty."

So was Jared's house, which was accented with thick beams of light wood and beautiful stone siding. It was modern with rustic flair. As she'd come upon it, passing stables and barns, horses and cattle along the way, somehow she could picture Jared living here. It fit. Which was a weird thing to think, since she didn't know the man. At all.

The door opened and a sixtysomething woman greeted them. "Why, you must be Bella Reid. Come in. We've been expecting you. I'm Marie, Mr. Stone's housekeeper."

Last night, after she'd made the decision to come by, she'd called Jared but the phone call had gone straight to voice mail. At least, she'd given him fair warning she was coming and was glad the message had been received. "Hello, Marie. Nice to meet you."

"And who is this little darlin'?"

"This is my daughter, Sienna."

"She's a beautiful child." Marie didn't waste time. "Please come inside. Jared's in the other room, waiting for you. He's very glad you came by." The affection in Marie's voice was unmistakable. "And I'm tickled to meet you. You saved his life. The entire family is in your debt."

Marie stopped outside a closed door and suddenly wrapped her arms around her and Sienna and gave them a hug. "Thank you." She pulled away quickly. "Don't mind me, I'm a silly woman," she said, wiping an unshed tear from her eye. "But I just had to do that."

"No, it's fine," Bella said. "It's obvious you care about Jared."

"Since he was a boy."

"Marie?" an impatient male voice called out.

"They're here, Jared." Marie swept an arm toward the door. "You'd best go inside. I left a pitcher of lemonade and a plate of cookies on the table. I sure hope you like chocolate chip," she said to Sienna. The toddler grinned at the mention of cookies. "If you need anything else, please let me know."

"Thank you."

Marie walked off slowly and Bella caught her grimacing, placing a hand to her back as she exited.

With a bit of trepidation, she entered the room to find the tall man slowly, carefully, unbending his body and rising from his chair, his expression etched with sheer determination. But there was no masking the pain he was in. "Bella Reid?"

"Hello, Jared. Please sit down," she said softly.

His face seemed to mellow, some of the strain melting away as soon as the words were out of her mouth. He wore comfortable clothes, black sweats and a T-shirt with Stone Corp printed over a graphic of a rugged mountain peak. Their company logo, she assumed.

"After you," he said. Texas manners being what they were, she wouldn't argue. She took a seat, holding her shy daughter on her lap.

"Thank you for coming," he said, his voice low and deep and much more commanding than when he'd been in the hospital. He winced as he lowered himself down. There was a bandage draped over his left eyebrow; some reddish scrapes peeked through his dark blond stubble. His longish straight hair seemed to fall in a natural part, Brad Pitt–style. His eyes were alert, deep blue and mesmerizing, the kind of eyes it was hard to turn away from. "Is this your child?"

"Yes, this is Sienna." Her daughter wouldn't look at Jared. But it was okay. She wouldn't force the issue. "She's in a clingy stage right now."

Jared smiled. His entire face brightened and she could see the man beneath the pain now. "How old is she?"

"She's twenty-two months."

"She looks like you. And that's a compliment."

"Thank you. How are you feeling, Jared?"

"I'm breathing and alive, getting by okay. I'll probably be laid up for a couple of weeks."

"You look…much better than the last time I saw you."

"I suppose I do." Again, he smiled. "I, uh, wanted to thank you properly for what you did. No, that's not entirely true. *I needed* to thank you. You dragging me out of the car and bringing me to safety saved my life. I can't thank you enough. I don't know if I'll ever be able to repay you."

"Heavens, you don't need to," she said on a breath. "I'm just glad we were coming down that road at that particular time."

"So am I. It was a lucky day for me. All I remember of that night was a soft hand covering mine, giving me comfort and soothing the panic that was building up inside. And then you spoke and the sound of your voice was like a gentle balm, an angel's call telling me I was going to be all right."

He inhaled and his face wrinkled up in pain.

"Does it hurt to talk?"

"No. Just to breathe," he said, his eyes half twinkling.

"I'm sorry."

"Don't be. I'm Texan. You know how we are."

She smiled.

"Cooper filled me in a little about you. You're a widow. I'm sorry for your loss, Bella." He spoke with reserved respect that made it seem less like prying, less like opening up old wounds.

"Thank you. It's been a bit tough, but Sienna and I are managing."

"That's good. I understand you're between jobs right now. Is that by choice?"

"Heavens no. I've been interviewing but…well, it's not

going—" She paused and shook her head. "It's not important."

"I think it is."

She blinked, gazing at his solemn face. "You do?"

"Of course I do." His gaze traveled over to Sienna, who'd begun to warm up a little. She was peeking at him through her spread little fingers.

"You don't owe me anything, Jared. Honestly." God, if he wrote her out a check, she'd be mortified. She hadn't saved his life for a reward.

"Well, the truth is, I'm thinking you can help me and I can help you."

"How?"

"You met Marie. She's a sweetheart, but she's getting on in age and my present condition is taking a toll on her with all the extra work she has to do. For years, she's worked part-time here and part-time at Cooper's place. Now I'm afraid the chores are too much for her."

"What are you saying to me? How can I help?"

"I understand you're good in the kitchen and it just so happens I'm in need of a personal chef."

She gulped air, totally surprised. "You need a personal chef?"

"Yes. I've been thinking about this for a long time. Marie's got too many chores around here as it is. She could use the break and…well, I'm offering you the job."

"To…be…your…personal…chef?"

He smiled, his eyes lighting up again, as if he was glad she was catching on. Oh, yeah, she was. He was indebted to her and this was how he was going to repay her. "Yes."

"But, you don't even know if I'm qualified."

"You can send me a résumé at your convenience. But I don't need one. I trust you're up to speed on your cooking skills."

"Oh, yeah? And how would you know that?"

"Because… I already know what kind of person you are. Besides, I'm not fussy. Just put a burger and fries in my face and I'm happy."

She laughed. "I'll remember that."

"So you'll take the job?"

"I didn't say that. There's a lot to consider."

"You need a job and I need a cook. What's to consider?"

"You're forgetting that you live way out here, miles away from Dallas. Working out babysitting arrangements would be difficult, if not impossible. I don't want to be gone from Sienna for too long during the day."

"That's the beauty of this great big ranch house." He spread his arms wide. The gesture cost him physically. Her heart went out to him, seeing him so bravely mask his pain. "You can have your own wing of the ranch house, two rooms just for you and Sienna upstairs. I'm basically living down here right now anyway since climbing the stairs is like a *Ninja Warrior* obstacle for me. You'd have all the privacy you'll need."

"My goodness, Jared. You want us to move into your house? I mean, that's generous and all, but I can't—"

"Don't say you can't. Think about it. You'll have a job where you won't have to leave Sienna at all. She'll be right here while you're working. She'll have a yard to play in and wide-open spaces to run at her heart's content. Don't get me wrong, I'm thankful that you saved my life, but I really do need some more help here. My solution is a good one, for all of us."

He had a good heart but her pride was getting in the way of her good sense.

"I don't know…"

"Give it a try, Bella." His voice cut into her senses. So deep, so sincere. He really wanted to help her and she appreciated that. "If it doesn't work out, there'll be no hard feelings. It'll be up to you."

He was offering her something better than she could ever hope for: employment, a home and a way to stay close to Sienna. Taking the job would buy her time to sort out her life and make some long-range plans. "Let me talk it over with my best friend. I, uh, just need a little bit of time."

"It's a deal," he said and then glanced at her daughter. "Would you like a cookie, Sienna? You can have as many as your mommy says you can have."

Sienna faced him and smiled, her sweet dimples lighting up her cheeks.

"One," Bella said in her mommy tone.

"Like I said," he began, "you can have *one* cookie. And I bet your momma would spring for some lemonade, too."

Sienna giggled, nodding at the man who could barely move on the chair opposite her.

He was in bad shape right now and seemed genuine in his job offer.

Could she take a leap of faith and accept the job? Could she go through with it, concealing her true identity from Jared Stone in order to keep Sienna safe?

Or maybe the real question was, could she afford not to take the job?

Later that night Amy plunked down on the sofa next to Bella and handed her a glass of pinot grigio. "Here, take this and sip at will. There's plenty more where that came from."

Bella stared at the wine bottle sitting on the cocktail table in front of her. She probably would need to empty it before she could come to a decision.

Amy crossed her legs under her, sinking into a conversational posture on the sofa and sipping wine. "Not that

I'm trying to get rid of you but, honestly, Bella, this man is offering you a golden opportunity. Why not jump at it?"

Sienna had fallen asleep an hour ago. And this was supposed to be Bella's Zen time. Where she could find some peace in the quiet surroundings and shut her mind down a little bit. But Jared Stone's offer kept interrupting her serenity. Amy was on board with the idea, but there was still a nagging notion that wouldn't go away. "Because I know why he's offering me a job. Or *making up* a job. He sees me as the poor widow, a single mom raising a baby all by myself. It's charity."

"For one, you are all those things and more."

Bella stared at her friend.

"What I mean is, he sees you as a widow raising a child alone, but also as the courageous person who saved his life. It's *so* not charity. If he was going to hire someone—and you said it yourself, his housekeeper really seemed like she could use the help—why can't he hire you? I'd bet he'd much rather hire someone he trusts, someone who really needs the work, than a total stranger."

"I am a stranger. He didn't even want to see my résumé."

"Lucky for you, he didn't. What would you put on there? Former heiress of Forte Foods."

"I did go to culinary school, you know. Even though I didn't finish, I learned a lot and what I didn't learn I taught myself. I have been around the food industry and chefs all my life."

Amy smiled. "There, you see, you just made a great argument for yourself. You are qualified for the job. My goodness, he's one man. You could cook for him with your eyes closed."

"I'd have to move to his ranch. And I'd be deceiving him the entire time. Could I really do that?"

"For Sienna's sake, you have to. It's a darn good reason."

"I don't know."

"What don't you know? It's perfect. What do I have here for you and Sienna? Concrete and glass. My balcony is too dangerous for Sienna, so the poor kid can't even get some sunshine or breathe fresh air. Sienna would love being in a place where she could run wild. She'd be around cattle and horses. Maybe a dog or cat or two. And how long do you think it would take your father to find me, if he really wanted to? He knows we're friends. If he came looking for you, you'd be out of luck. But this way…"

"I'd be on a ranch in the middle of nowhere." Amy's arguments made sense.

"Take the leap," her friend said. "I'll be right here if it doesn't work out. You have nothing to lose."

Bella finished her pinot in one large gulp. "Okay, I'm gonna do it. I'll take the leap and call Jared Stone tomorrow."

Three

On Saturday morning, three days after meeting with Jared Stone, Bella followed a good-natured Marie up to her new rooms at Stone Ridge. The woman seemed genuinely glad to have her there. "I'll be staying today to help you get settled in," she said with a smile. "If you need anything, or have any questions, be sure to ask. Mr. Stone is down in his study. He's anxious to get back to work. If you ask me, it's too soon, but that boy is determined. He said as soon as you feel up to it, he'd like to see you."

Jared Stone had arranged for her things to be moved into the house this morning. All she'd had when she'd walked out of her father's house in Pacific Heights was a few pieces of luggage and three boxes of baby gear. She'd traveled light…well, as light as she could with a toddler in tow. Sienna had toys and special blankets and dolls that she couldn't live without. Really, Bella could have boxed it all up and placed it in her car, but her new employer had insisted on sending someone to help move her.

"Thank you, Marie. I should be down soon. As you can see, I don't have too much to unpack."

Marie's kind eyes warmed as she took in the meager boxes and suitcases on the floor.

Oh, goodness, she didn't want to give the woman the wrong impression. She didn't mean she was so destitute that these were all the things she owned in the world. Too late. Marie turned her attention to Sienna. "How's the little princess today?"

"Sienna, say hello to Marie."

Sienna wiggled her fingers in a shy wave. She didn't want to cross the cookie lady.

"She's going to have a bit of fun here on the ranch. You be sure to take her around and explore. There's a lot to see through a toddler's eyes."

"I will. Thank you."

"I'll be off now," Marie said. "Remember to ask if you have any questions. I'm just tickled as can be you're here. You two will bring some life into these four walls."

"You may get more life than either of you bargained for."

"Nonsense. Children only bring the world joy," Marie said as she made her way out of the room.

With Sienna latched onto her hip, Bella looked around the second floor of the house. Two adjoining bedrooms, both with queen-size beds, and a good-sized bathroom would be her new home. The rooms were lovely and in shades of light blues and lavenders with bleached white-oak contemporary furniture. She was pretty certain no one had ever stepped foot inside these immaculate guest quarters. Sienna would give the place a lived-in look within a matter of hours. Poor Jared Stone didn't know what he was in for, inviting a toddler almost two years old into his home. And poor her, trying to keep Sienna's antics down to a minimum. Jared didn't know it yet, but his quiet existence would soon be replaced with chaos and noise.

Bella walked over to the window and peered directly down into a backyard full of thick green grass and a flowery garden. There was a pool with a rock slide and trickling waterfall. All of the pool chairs and tables were protected and covered, but she could just imagine how inviting the pool would be on a scorching-hot Texas day. Her gaze traveled farther out to a pasture. Those tiny specks across the vista had to be a herd of cattle.

She glanced around the room again and sighed. "Well, Sienna, time to unpack our stuff."

Fifteen minutes later she'd organized the bathroom, complete with an Elmo toothbrush set, child-safe shampoo and body wash and Princess Jasmine towels. Sienna would sleep with her, until she got acclimated, and one way to do that was to put all of her toys in the second bedroom. All of their clothes combined didn't take up one-tenth of the generous walk-in closet space.

It was weird coming to live here with a total stranger, though Amy had done a thorough Google search of Jared Stone and eagerly shared that he was a successful rancher, an astute businessman and a budding entrepreneur. Recently he and his brother Cooper had funded the building of a playground for the local community. And his charitable donations didn't stop there.

He's hardly an ax murderer.

Amy's words sunk into her skull and she immediately felt better about coming to live here. "Okay, baby girl," she said. "It's time to say hello to the boss."

Taking hold of Sienna, she climbed down the stairs and went in search of the study. The house wasn't hard to figure out; it was as sprawling as a two-story ranch home could be, and after stepping into the beautiful gourmet kitchen, excitement stirred as she ogled her new "office." Sienna babbled loudly in her own sweet language as she made her way past the kitchen to the hallway leading to the study. Sienna squirmed and fussed to be let down. She had yet to have her nap. "Here you go," Bella said, setting the baby on her feet, "but please don't touch anything." She knocked on the partially shut door.

"Come in." The pitch of Jared's voice was deep and welcoming.

She opened the door and found Jared sitting behind his desk, closing down his laptop computer. Color had returned to his cheeks, his bandages were off and the scrapes on his face appeared to be healing. He wore a black snap-down shirt and jeans, looking much better than he had just three days ago.

He was handsome, there was no denying that. He now had a healthier glow about him; his eyes, less shadowed by pain, were deeper, bluer, mesmerizing.

Her heart raced. She would be living with him now, in this house, and all the awkwardness she'd felt the other day came back in full force. This would be her new normal.

He began to rise and she gestured for him not to. He did it anyway. He had to be six foot two if he was an inch. "Welcome to Stone Ridge."

"Please sit down, Mr. Stone. If you get up every time I walk into a room, you'll make yourself dizzy."

He chuckled and then his face hardened and his hand automatically went to his broken ribs. Of all his injuries, that one must be the most painful. "I will, if you call me Jared from now on."

"Okay… Jared."

"Please, take a seat."

She did, sitting opposite him. Sienna stood next to her chair, looking all around, taking in the big room with windows facing the groomed yard and books stacked on a wall of shelves. But her eyes found and stayed on two packages decorated with pastel balloon wrapping paper on the floor beside the desk.

"Hello, Sienna," he said. "I hope you'll like it here."

Sienna took one look at Jared, forgot about the packages and climbed up on Bella's lap, hanging on to her neck with a death grip. Bella pried her off her neck as gently as possible and her baby settled into a fetal position in her arms. "She'll warm up. This is all so new for her."

"I figured," he said.

"You're feeling better?" she asked.

He nodded. "Every day gets a bit easier. I should be one hundred percent in a few weeks or so." He paused as if speaking of his injuries made him uncomfortable. "I hope you like your accommodations. If there's anything you want changed, anything you need, just let me know."

"Thank you. That's very generous of you. The rooms are lovely and we're going to manage just fine."

"Good to hear. Marie will be here today to show you around the kitchen and the rest of the property. Feel free to use anything on the ranch, including the horses, if you like to ride. And if you need something—"

"I'll be sure to ask," she said.

Jared smiled, a much easier smile than the one he'd attempted a few days ago. He wrote something down on a piece of paper and slid it over to her. "Here's your starting salary. I think it's in line with the going rate."

She glanced at the number and was relieved to see he wasn't overpaying her. "Yes, it's perfect." It was a fair sum considering she was also getting room and board. If that number was even slightly higher, she'd feel less legitimate. The salary he offered allowed her a measure of pride. And Jared Stone seemed to be sensitive to that. "Thank you."

"I don't expect you to work every day. You'll have Sundays and Mondays off, if that's okay with you."

"That's fine. I, um, have a few questions for you, though, if you don't mind?"

"I don't mind at all," he said.

She sat a little straighter in the chair; Sienna was happy as a clam to continue to cling to her. "Well, since I'm cooking for you, I'd like to know how you see yourself food-wise."

"How do I see myself?"

"Yes. What's your culinary landscape?"

"In English, please?"

She held back a grin. "Okay. Are your food tastes conservative, traditional, adventurous, exotic, selective…"

"I'm definitely adventurous. There's nothing I won't try. Except liver. No liver, please." He made a little-boy face, scrunching up his mouth, and she laughed.

"No liver, check. Spicy?"

"Yes, but not necessarily all the time."

"Do you drink alcohol?"

"Does the sun shine?" he shot back.

She laughed. "Okay, got it."

He was basically a cook's dream. He liked to try new things and he ate everything, pretty much. She'd put that to the test very soon.

The healthy cast on his face when she'd walked in was beginning to fade. How long had he been at his desk working? She knew the look of fatigue. Being a single mom, she'd had many a sleepless night. And even when she did catch some winks, it wasn't for very long. Not all of that had to do with Sienna. She had a classic case of insomnia, an inherited trait. *Thank you, Marco.*

Too late, she averted her eyes. She'd been staring at Jared. And he'd been quietly staring back.

"If there's nothing more—"

"Actually, there is," he said.

Gingerly, he rose from his seat to full height. When standing, he was a solid presence in the room, a man who commanded attention. She'd noticed that about Cooper, too. "I have something for you both. It's a little welcome gift."

"You didn't have to do that." Goodness, she meant it. How awkward was this? What could he have possibly gotten the two of them?

"Would you like to open Sienna's first. It's in the big box."

He moved over to the two boxes by his desk. "Sienna, this is a present for you. Do you want to help your mother open it?"

Her daughter's eyes went adorably wide and she eased off her lap, took her hand and pulled her over to the wrapped box.

"Christmas isn't for a few weeks," she told Jared.

Jared only smiled.

Sienna grabbed at the paper and Bella helped her the rest of the way until all the wrapping was off. When the box was open, Jared explained. "Some assembly required."

Sienna took one look at her gift and started flapping her arms like a little bird. "Bike! Bike!"

"I can see that," Bella said.

The balance tricycle was hot pink with streamers on the handlebars and a chrome bell. It was already assembled except for the long rod that attached to the back step, so that it could be pushed and guided from behind. The training bike of tricycles.

Sienna found the bell and that was that. The ringing lasted at least thirty seconds before Bella took her hand away. "Sienna, do you like the tricycle?"

She began nodding. "Me yike it, Mommy."

"Can you say 'thank you'?"

"Tank you," she said without hesitation. Her eyes were transfixed on her new trike.

Jared grinned. "You're welcome. Now you can ride around the ranch in style."

"It's very generous of you," Bella said.

"There's a helmet for her, too. Lauren, my sister-in-law, said she couldn't ride outside the house without one."

"Yes, that's true. Again, very thoughtful."

Bella took the trike out of the box and set it on the floor. Immediately, Sienna, thrilled beyond belief, lifted her leg and tried to climb up. Bella gave her a little push and then she was all set, her butt settled on the padded seat.

"Your feet touch the pedals. Oh, my baby is getting to be such a big girl."

"I'll attach this thing," Jared said, a screwdriver suddenly appearing in his hand. He lifted the rod out and bent on his haunches. His body creaked and his face went white, but his jaw was tight, determined. Bella bent, too, and suddenly she was inches from Jared, breathing in a light musk scent, seeing the tiny lines of pain around his eyes. And for a second, the briefest of moments, she saw not the victim whose life she'd saved, but a beautiful, bone-melting, blue-eyed man.

Amy would say he was a hunk to the hundredth degree.

"Can you hold this?" he asked.

"Oh, uh, yes." She secured the rod while he screwed it to the back step of the trike.

"There," he said, his breathing labored. He was taxing himself, but there was a gleam of accomplishment in his eyes that shouldn't be shot down. "That should work."

"Yes, it's nice and tight."

"And now for your gift." He began to rise and wobbled

a little. She was there immediately to catch him, putting her arm around his waist. He used his other hand to brace himself on the desk and then gazed at her. "I've got it," he said quietly, the sexiness in his voice playing tricks on her.

"Yes, you do. Sorry."

"For trying to rescue me again?"

"For—" She shrugged. "I don't know why." The words tumbled out of her mouth and, too late, she took her arm off his waist. Jared Stone definitely made her nervous.

He smiled. A killer this time, showing white teeth, handsome lines around his mouth and a twinkle in his eyes.

Sienna was patiently examining her new trike. Once again the temptation to ring the bell was too much for her and clanging filled the room. "A set of drums might've been less noisy," Bella remarked.

A chuckle rumbled from his chest, one that caught him off guard. He winced, but it was brief and soon replaced with a smile. "I'll remember that next time. This one is for you," he said, pointing to the other wrapped gift. "I'm told every chef should have a good set of these."

She stared at him for a moment and then carefully unwrapped her gift. It was an attaché case and inside she found a twenty-four-piece set of executive chef knives. They were beautiful, of the finest caliber, the handles made of rosewood.

"Oh…" A lump formed in her throat. She'd grown up with privilege and had had the finest of things, but this gift was special. It was the first time she'd been recognized as a legitimate chef. Other than by Paul. Her husband had believed in her and was awed by her talent, but her father and his wife had never taken her seriously. "It's too much. I love it but—"

"No buts. Marie told me our kitchen was sorely lacking in equipment, and you should have all the tools you need at your disposal."

"You mean for those burgers and fries I'm going to toss your way."

Jared laughed.

"Thank you. It's a beautiful set."

Sienna went for the bell again and the ringing echoed off the study walls. "Well, we'd better get out of your hair now. Do you have more work to do?"

"Actually," he said, running a hand down his face, "I'm getting hungry for lunch. I'm up early most days, so I'm usually hungry about this time."

It was a little after eleven in the morning. She made a mental note of Jared's timetable. "It's good to know. I can make up a simple lunch, if you'd like."

"No. That's not necessary. Marie's got it covered today. You can join me, or you can let the little one play on her trike."

"In the house?"

"Sure…it's fine. She can't hurt anything."

"Obviously you haven't been around a two-year-old before."

"Can't say that I have," he said good-naturedly. "But between Sienna and Cooper's kid, I'm gonna get a real fast education."

That much was very true.

She opted to let Sienna ride up and down the hallway, guiding her with the rod and praying she wouldn't take out anything super expensive in her wake.

Dawn popped its way into Jared's window much too soon to his liking. He usually wasn't a bad sleeper, but the afternoon naps he'd been taking since the accident had a way of messing up his schedule. Dr. Corona had told him to rest as much as possible, and by the middle of the day, he was too wiped out to disobey. Who knew broken ribs could cause so much grief to his body?

Feeling helpless wasn't his style. He was mentally ready to get back behind the wheel. He had a garage full of vehicles, two motorcycles and several cars, as well as a speedboat docked at the nearby lake. He wasn't about to let what happened scare him away. But he had to heal first, and all the tossing and turning during the night did nothing to help his busted-up body repair itself. Today, even if he had to pry his eyes open with miniature pitchforks, he was going to fight the nap, tooth and nail.

Slowly he hinged himself up from the bed and drew a lungful of air into a diaphragm that was tight and sore. Those first few moves after being bedridden during the night were the hardest. He managed to stand without the help of a cane. Call it ego, but he'd have to be on his last breath before he'd submit to using that thing.

He managed to get his jeans on, grunting with each tug burning straight through his rib cage. The sting lingered like an unruly drunken uncle on Christmas day.

He'd never take getting dressed for granted again. "Marie," he called out. He hoped like hell she was there. He hoped she'd heard him.

He heard the sound of footsteps approaching, down the hallway and just as he was zipping up his fly, help arrived. It was Bella. She took two steps into his room, and budding sunlight cast a circular light around her head like a halo... *His angel.*

He blinked.

And was struck by her absolute beauty. She wore white jeans and a silky jade blouse that made her soft green eyes really come alive. With all that blue-black hair cascading down her back in a braid and her face shining and free of anything unnatural, Bella made his breath hitch. His rib cage hurt like hell, but as he slowly released pent-up breaths his focus never wavered. He was totally aware of her now and a spark of excitement strummed inside him, obliterating the pain.

Why now? It wasn't as if he hadn't noticed how pretty she was before. Of course he'd noticed, but he'd never let his mind go there. She was an employee, a widow and a mother of a small child. Three very solid reasons why the thought hadn't entered his mind. But right now, in an un-guarded moment, when he wasn't expecting to see her, suddenly he'd become very aware of her appeal.

Her eyes seemed stationed on his bare chest and her face colored as red as an apple, a tough feat for a woman with olive skin. He'd shocked her, no doubt, but he also witnessed a glint of admiration in her eyes.

"Jared?"

"Mornin'."

"Good morning. Do you, uh, need something? I heard you call out for Marie. She's at your brother's today. But if you need her, she told me to be sure to call her."

"No. Not necessary. Guess I forgot it was her day with Coop."

Bella looked straight into his eyes, as if she'd be set on fire if he caught her staring any longer at his chest. He could almost smile at that.

"What did you need?"

"Nothin'."

"You called for Marie for a reason."

"It's not in your job description."

She glanced at the shirt on the chair. "You need help getting your shirt on?"

There was no sense denying it. "Yes. But—"

"Heavens, if you need help with it, I can do it." She

sounded slightly annoyed, as if she were scolding a child. She stepped farther into the room, picking up his shirt as she approached, keeping her eyes level with his. No more sneak peeks at his chest.

"Here you go." She held out one arm of the shirt. "We'll take it slow." Her angelic voice, soft and accommodating, came back. If only he could close his eyes and listen to her all day long.

She smelled like cookies, a sugary vanilla scent teasing his nostrils. And then he gazed at her mouth, heart-shaped and rosy-lipped. She'd given him rescue breaths with that mouth. Oh, man.

She guided his right arm into the sleeve first and scooted it up his arm as he ever so slowly pushed his arm through. "Now comes the hard part," he said.

She wound the shirt around his back and he had to stretch his left arm way out to push it through the sleeve. By the time they were through, beads of sweat trickled down his forehead.

"Maybe a T-shirt would be easier," she said, tilting her head, analyzing the situation.

"That would be a no. I tried that already."

"Are you okay?" Her green eyes held sympathy.

"I'm fine. Thank you." He sniffed the air. "Besides you, something smells wonderful out there."

"Besides me?"

He grinned. "Sorry, thinking out loud. You smell like a cookie."

An angel with a tranquil voice who smelled like cookies…good thing he had his head on straight about Bella Reid. She was a no-go. He was gun-shy anyway. He'd had his heart ripped out by Helene and some wounds just refused to heal.

"Thank you, I think," she said, standing in front of

him now, keeping her eyes on the snaps she was fastening on his shirt. She stood a few inches from him and as soon as she was through took a big step back. "The drawbacks of a being around food all the time. But smelling like vanilla is much better than smelling like garlic. Or, God forbid, liver."

He smiled. "So true."

He was glad she'd moved away. He was injured but he wasn't dead. If anyone could bring a man back from the dark depths, it was Bella Reid. She'd done that literally for him once already. He wasn't going to push his luck.

"So what is that delicious smell?" he asked.

"I made apple crostata this morning."

"Already?" He had no idea what an apple crostata was, but it sure sounded good.

She nodded. "I've got it cooking in the oven for breakfast or a midmorning snack. I bake while Sienna is sleeping. I hope I didn't wake you."

"I didn't hear a thing."

"Okay, great. So would you like eggs and bacon to go with the crostata? Marie already told me how you like your coffee. It's brewing now."

"You're efficient."

"It's easy when you love what you do."

"And how long have you been doing this?"

"Oh, all of my life. I learned to cook at an early age. Out of boredom maybe, but I found I had a great passion for it. I can't imagine not doing it. Bacon and eggs?" she asked again.

"Uh, yeah. Thanks."

"Give me twenty minutes."

"Will you and Sienna be eating at the same time?"

It grated on him how much he enjoyed having a conversation with her. Her voice was permanently ingrained in his memory, and every time she spoke to him, something sweet and pleasant filled him up.

"I don't think so. Sienna sleeps until eight. It gives me time to get a few things done before my little tornado hits."

"That precious child?"

"Just wait," she said as she walked out of his room.

He smiled, watching her go. He really didn't want to eat breakfast alone.

Again.

Four

At breakfast, Bella watched Jared wipe his dish clean, soaking up the last of his soft-boiled eggs with a wedge of sourdough toast. It was gratifying to see him eat so hardily. The crostata was nearly half gone. Granted, he'd made her sit at the kitchen table and have a bite with him, so she'd had a nibble, as well.

"I'll be three hundred pounds if you keep feeding me this way," he said, plopping the last of his toast into his mouth. "What's in that crostata that makes it taste so good?"

"That's a chef's secret," she said. "But if you promise not to tell…"

"I promise."

"Butter…lots of butter. Everything tastes better with butter."

"I thought that's what they say about bacon."

She smiled. "That, too."

She got up and poured him another cup of coffee. He liked it black with one heaping spoonful of sugar. "You must not eat what you cook," he said.

"I do."

He glanced at the waistline of her white jeans and then lifted his gaze to her chest before meeting her eyes, shaking his head the entire time. "How do you do it?"

"It has something to do with chasing around a toddler. Plus I make it a habit to eat bites of food instead of the entire dish."

"Ah," he said, "that explains it." He glanced at his completely empty dish. "Guess I failed at that. But it was delicious."

"Thank you. But, Jared, just so you know, I like to balance the meals, so that you're not eating heavy at every meal. Lunch will be light, I promise."

"Because you don't want a three-hundred-pound employer?"

"Because of the *H*-word. Some chefs don't believe in it, but I do."

His brows gathered and a question formed on his lips.

"Healthy eating. Emphasis on good health."

"Does that mean I can't have beef? You do know I co-own a cattle ranch."

She smiled. "It means there are leaner cuts of meat and ways to prepare them that are healthier than others."

"I do know that."

"Until you're back on your feet, it'd be best if I keep the food on the lighter side."

"No more crostata?"

She shrugged, feeling a bit guilty. "I wanted to make a good first impression on you on my first day."

"Darlin', you don't have to worry about my impression

of you. I already think you're a combination of Wonder Woman and Clara Barton."

She nibbled on her lower lip and a flush of heat raced to her cheeks. She couldn't look at him. He was too honest, too humble and too darn appealing. It made her hate herself a little bit to find him so attractive.

Images of Paul popped into her head and she quickly grabbed Jared's plate and walked it to the sink. "I think I hear Sienna. She's waking up," she said with her back to him. She wiped her hands on a dish towel. "I'll be back later to clean this up."

She moved past him, feeling Jared's striking blue eyes on her as she exited the kitchen.

Sienna was just waking up as she walked into the bedroom. The baby slept with her in the big bed, surrounded by lush pillows to protect her from falling. She was sitting up, rubbing her eyes. "Mommy."

Bella sat next to her on the bed. "Mommy's here."

The baby lunged for her and Bella's heart lurched. This little child was her life. She was dependent on her. And Bella vowed that she was going to make a good life for her. Every penny of her earnings would go into one day opening up her own restaurant. It had been a dream of hers since she was a child and it had stayed with her all this time. She wasn't the corporate type. She wasn't cut out for business. She wanted to create food, and maybe work on a cookbook one day, too. All of her lofty aspirations were for Sienna's future now.

An image of Jared in his bedroom, zipping up his pants, his chest ripped with muscles, popped into her head. He was one sexy man. A man she felt a bond to, because she'd saved his life, but a man who wasn't going to upset her dreams. She couldn't allow it.

She still loved Paul and as she hugged his child to her

chest, she was immediately reminded of the love they'd shared. Sienna was a result of that love. Bella wouldn't forget that.

"Sienna, it's time for your bath. Let's get the water ready in this nice big tub." The triangular tub was set at an angle in the corner of the room. It was big enough for four children. As she filled the tub and poured in child-safe bubble bath liquid, Sienna began lifting her princess nightie over her head. "Good girl, Sienna." Bella removed her soaked diaper and then set her little naked baby into the tub.

Sienna giggled her head off, splashing her mommy immediately, just like always. The power of a smiley-faced, lovable child made all things seem possible. Bella found herself relaxing for the first time since coming to the ranch. She told herself that this might work out after all, as long as her father didn't hunt her down and ruin everything.

An hour later, after Bella had managed a quick cleanup in Jared's kitchen and had planned the lunch menu for the three of them, she stood on the stone pathway that led around the entire house. The gardens were on their last stages of pretty, the flowers fading, threatened by colder temperatures and harsher weather.

"Ready, Sienna?"

The baby sat on her new trike with a hot-pink helmet on her head, chin straps securing it in place. "Red-dee, Mommy."

"Hold on tight." Sienna gripped the white handles and Bella began pushing her down the wide pathway. Sienna giggled as they moved forward, ringing the bell over and over until Bella was sure the cows in the distant pasture were covering their ears.

As they were coming back around, Jared stepped out

of the house and leaned against a pillar at the top of the steps. "Uh-oh," Bella mumbled.

Jared kept his eyes focused on the two of them as Sienna tried to steer her trike. They were both getting the hang of it, but it was clear they needed more practice.

"Are we too loud?" Bella asked, coming to a standstill in his line of vision.

He shook his head. "Not at all. Just needed a breath of air."

For a man who liked going fast and being active, it was clear Jared hated being cooped up in his gorgeous house. The outdoors looked good on him.

"Don't let me stop you," he said. "Sienna's doing pretty good."

Sienna recognized his praise and smiled, her chest puffing out.

"I think so, too. She's never ridden one of these before." Bella left Sienna's trike and put herself in between Jared and her daughter, whispering, "Um, do you think I should make the bell disappear?"

His mouth quirked and his blue eyes brightened. "Are you a magician?"

She grinned. "I can be."

"If you do, I have a feeling another bell would have to magically appear."

She blinked. "You're sure?"

He nodded. "Doesn't bother me. What would bother me is if that smile was wiped clean off Sienna's face."

Thank you, she mouthed to him, a sudden sting burning behind her eyes. She was touched by his acceptance. The two of them clearly were a disruption in his life.

A car pulled up and all heads turned as a woman in a stylish, body-hugging, neon running outfit exited the vehicle. She held a covered dish in her hands and as she approached, her eyes were all for Jared. She gave him a big smile, her cinnamon-red hair cascading down her back as she hurried up the pathway. Before Bella could scoot Sienna away and give them privacy, the woman was in front of them.

"Jared Stone, I am so glad to see you up and around. When I heard about the accident, I was worried silly about you."

Jared smiled at her. "Hello, Johnna Lee. It's good to see you."

"Same here." She walked up the steps and put one arm around his neck, giving him a gentle hug. "I made you some of my special mac and cheese. Just the way you like it, with extra breadcrumbs on top."

"That's awfully nice of you," Jared said.

She held on to the casserole dish and traded looks with Bella, waiting for an introduction.

"Uh, Johnna Willis, this is Bella Reid. She's new to Stone Ridge." Jared turned to her. "Johnna is my neighbor. She lives just up the road."

"Pleasure to meet you," Johnna said kindly. "And who's this little cutie pie?"

"This is my daughter, Sienna."

The woman bent a little and spoke directly to her daughter. "Hello, Sienna. I sure do like your tricycle."

Sienna put her face down on her handlebars.

"Sorry, it takes her a while to warm up to new people," Bella explained.

"I totally get it. I was a shy kid, too. If you can believe that." She chuckled at the thought and Bella smiled. "She's really adorable."

"Thank you."

"So what do you do here at Stone Ridge?" Johnna asked.

"I'm…" She glanced at Jared and he gave a nod. "I'm Jared's personal chef. Uh, while he's recuperating."

"Oh, I didn't know Marie finally retired."

"She didn't." Jared intervened. "I think Marie's going to outlast all of us Stones. But with my accident and all, Marie needed some help."

Johnna blinked. "Well then, that's a good thing."

The conversation could've gotten awkward, being that she went to the trouble to cook her special mac and cheese dish for Jared, yet she chose to be gracious.

"I think so. Johnna, would you like to come inside?" Jared asked.

She didn't hesitate. "I'd sure love to. I need to hear all about how you're doing."

"Excuse me, Jared," Bella said. "Would you like me to fix you all a drink?"

"No thanks. Let Sienna play," he answered. "I think I can handle this." After Johnna walked past him toward the door, he gave Bella a shrug, his gaze lingering on her a bit. It was an intimate look and she figured it had more to do with him preferring to stay outdoors than having anything to do with her.

She sighed. So Jared had a woman caller. He'd probably had many. And good for him.

Yeah, good for him.

The second the door closed, Sienna's face popped out of hiding. "Mommy, ride."

"Okay, baby. Let's go."

She had an hour before she had to start on Jared's lunch. Unless he wanted mac and cheese instead. With extra breadcrumbs.

Just the way he liked it.

Heavens, Bella. Don't be a nitwit.

After a thirty-minute visit, Jared bid farewell to Johnna. She was a friend and neighbor, but at times she pushed a little too hard, and he always tried setting her straight without hurting her feelings. It had been sweet of her to cook him a meal and to offer to help with Christmas decorating. But ever since his breakup with his ex, he'd pretty much given up on the holidays. He related Christmas to Helene. It hadn't been pretty the night he'd found out she'd betrayed him and taken him for a fool. They'd been planning a Christmas wedding before everything had blown up in his face.

This year, Marie had insisted on decorations to boost everyone's spirits. He'd had his crew get started on the exterior of the house, but he had yet to do anything inside.

His phone rang and Jared lowered himself slowly into a chair to take the call. "Hey, Coop."

"Hey. How's it going? What are you doing?"

"It's going okay. Actually, I just said goodbye to Johnna. She stopped by for a visit, brought me a dish of food."

"Nice of her. Did you tell her you have a new chef cooking in your kitchen?"

"Actually, I didn't have to. She met Bella and Sienna outside."

"How did she take it?"

"Take what?"

"Nothing, bro. Just that she's had her eyes on you for a while."

"She's just being neighborly."

"Neighborly? Is that what they're calling it these days?"

"Okay, I hear you. But I'm not interested."

"You haven't seriously dated anyone in two years. Maybe it's time to jump back into the pool."

"Or maybe I'll never swim again."

"No, but you could try putting your foot in the water to see how it feels."

"If I did that, a gator would come along and chomp my toes off."

Cooper laughed. "Okay, okay. I get it. Listen, the reason I'm calling, aside from going over some budgeting issues with you, is that Lauren would really like to see you and your new personnel. How's it working out with her so far?"

"Bella is very talented and having them here hasn't been a problem. I hardly see them, except in the kitchen during mealtime."

"That's good news. Marie seems to be lighter on her feet these days, too. She really needed the break. It's a win-win."

"Yep, took me almost dying to figure that conundrum out."

"Don't joke about that. Your accident shaved years off my life."

Jared sighed. "I…know. I'm sorry about that. No more jokes, I promise."

"I'd rather you promise you're not going to be reckless with your life. That's the real promise I want from you."

"I'm not reckless, bro. I know my boundaries. And I'm living my life my way." Hell, their father had died at a very young age, his life cut short by illness. It made Jared realize that he needed to live his life fully, do the things he yearned to do and experience life on his own terms, without fear, without regret. Carpe diem had sunk into his skull. Each and every day he was living his life to the fullest. That was why being laid up was wrestling with his patience.

"If you say so." Cooper didn't sound convinced. "Listen, can we invite ourselves over on Friday night, if you're up to company?"

"Sure thing. Come for dinner and you can taste Bella's cooking."

"Sounds good, thanks. Now, are you up for a talk about next year's budget for the ranch?"

"Yeah, I will be as soon as I get over to the computer."

"Why don't you call me back when you're ready?"

"I'm slow, Coop. Not totally useless. Hang on. It'll just take me a minute."

"Sure. I'm glad to see you're back to being a pain in the ass. Means you're feeling a lot better."

"Funny, Coop. Real funny."

Bella's eyes popped open and she glanced at the digital clock on the nightstand. Yep, 2:00 a.m. She'd gone to bed at ten and four hours was all the sleep goddesses allowed her these days. While her insomnia could be her downfall, she decided long ago that rather than lie in bed and toss and turn for hours, she would get up and do the thing she loved.

The baby slept beside her, all nice and snuggled up tight under the covers, her little head resting on a pillow. Bella bent down and blew an air kiss over her forehead. *Sweet girl*, she mouthed softly before gently sliding off the bed. She checked the video camera set on Sienna—the most valuable invention for a busy mom—and then donned a loose-fitting shift. Tiptoeing out of the room, holding the video monitor, she made her way down the stairs and into the kitchen.

Turning on the light, she set the video monitor on the counter and gave it a glance. Thankfully, Sienna was sound asleep, looking extremely peaceful. Bella sighed and began taking items out of the fridge and cabinets. She had an idea for a wonderful low-cal pizza, but it needed a bit of testing first.

She grabbed a head of cauliflower and quartered it using the chef knife from her new set she was still embarrassed about accepting. Next, she began grating a chunk of cauliflower against a stainless-steel box grater, and tiny pieces of the veggie showered down, covering the cutting board like fallen snow.

Just as she was picking up her second quartered piece, Jared walked in, his eyes blinking against the kitchen lights. He wore a pair of jeans. Period. They hugged his waist below the naval and showed off a washboard chest. Bruises caught her eye for a second, but the beauty of his physique wasn't lost on her, either.

He padded farther into the kitchen. "Hi," he mumbled, sleepy-eyed.

"Gosh, I hope I didn't wake you, Jared."

"That would mean I was sleeping." His mouth crooked up in a smile.

"You weren't?"

"No. I, uh… No. I toss and turn some nights. I figured I'd get up and get something to eat."

"Are you hungry at this hour?"

"A little."

"What can I get you?" She dropped what she was doing and came around the kitchen island.

Jared glanced at her shorty-short shift and then at her legs and suddenly she felt self-conscious. Especially when she could hardly keep her focus on his face while he was standing there bare-chested, his hair mussed, looking quite appealing in a devilish sort of way.

"Nothing. I'll just grab some bread and make a sandwich."

"I'll get it for you," she said, brushing by him.

He gently clamped a hand around her wrist and pulled her back a bit. She turned to find Jared's eyes on her, felt the warmth of his hand covering hers. "You're off the clock, Bella. You don't need to wait on me day and night."

His eyes were soft, his voice tender. And suddenly she was fully aware of Jared Stone, a sensation sweeping through her so raw, so impossibly alluring, that she lost her voice for a second.

He bent his head a little to get her full attention. Little did he know he already had it.

"Okay?"

She swallowed and nodded.

"So, what are you doing here?" he asked, letting go of her hand.

"I hope you don't mind," she said. "I have trouble sleeping, so I use this time to come down and test out some recipes. Don't worry, I eat my mistakes. So there's no food going to waste."

He smiled and sat on a stool at the counter. "Go on with what you're doing. Since I can't sleep anyway, do you mind if I watch?"

"Oh, uh, sure." She couldn't kick him out of his own kitchen. Not that she wanted to, but she wasn't about to analyze why that was. "I can't imagine it's all that interesting, but I don't mind."

She went back to her workstation and glanced at the video monitor. Sienna rolled over, but was still fast asleep.

Jared caught her eye and raised his brows in question.

"I keep an eye on Sienna while she's sleeping. This way if she wakes up, I'll know about it immediately. Lucky for me, she usually sleeps through the night."

"I imagine that monitor is pretty darn handy."

"It is. I'm sure a worried mom invented it."

He laughed. "Probably. So what are you experimenting with?"

"Cauliflower-crust pizza."

Jared made a face. "What?"

"Yes, cauliflower. It's the new kale."

He shook his head.

"It's very healthy for you, low in calories and…well, has many uses. Do you like cauliflower?"

He shrugged. "I suppose, but it's not one of my favorites."

"Well then, you're a good one to experiment on."

"Maybe I should go back to bed." But then he winked and smiled, and Bella relaxed as he leaned his arms on the counter to watch her. Keeping her eyes down on her task, she pretended not to notice his biceps, broad shoulders and muscled chest, but she was aware. Oh, boy, was she aware.

She finished grating the cauliflower and then poured it into the food processor, tossing in minced garlic, oregano and basil. She pulsed it for a few seconds, added one egg and decided to also add in a few tablespoons of almond flour she'd found in the pantry. A few more seconds of pulsing to bind it all together and she hoped she'd have a delicious beginning to her low-cal pizza.

She was beginning to roll out the dough when Jared got up and left the room. She looked up just in time to find Jared walking back into the room, gently pushing his arms into the sleeves of his shirt. His expression faltered but he managed it all on his own.

"You're doing better," she stated while writing down her recipe in her binder.

"A little bit each day, but yeah."

"I'm glad," she said, feeling his gaze on her.

"So what do you put on this pizza exactly?" he asked.

"Anything you like. Why don't you look in the fridge and bring me some things you'd like on the pizza. I've got mozzarella here."

She tipped the dough out onto the surface and began kneading it, over and over. Something swelled within her as she maneuvered the dough, making it flat and round and then patting it down. It was a thing. Maybe a chef thing, or maybe just her thing, but she loved getting her hands into the food, the way gardeners loved digging into the soil.

Jared poked his head inside the fridge. "Doughnuts?"

She made a face. "Eww, Jared."

"How about pickles?"

"I think not."

"Chocolate chips?"

"That could prove interesting," she said, crisscrossing the dough with a rolling pin. "But no for tonight."

"I give up," Jared said.

"Open the crisper. What do you see?"

He slid open the drawer. "Red and green bell peppers, string beans, tomatoes, onions, mango slices and three different kinds of lettuce."

Mango slices? "Pick three of those things." *And don't let one of them be mango.*

Jared carried over onions, tomatoes and red bell peppers.

"That's good for a start," she said. She left the workstation and walked into a double-wide pantry. "Let's see," she said, taking a quick tour of ingredients that might work. "Do you like olives?"

"Love them."

"And, oh, here, how about artichoke hearts?"

"Yep."

"Great, we have our toppings now."

"How about I put on a pot of coffee?" Jared walked over to the coffee machine. "We can have a cup while the pizza is cooking."

She blinked. She hadn't intended for them to eat the pizza now. But he had said he was hungry. "Uh, sure. I'll just chop up some of these veggies and then put the pizza in the oven. I hope it turns out okay."

"Me, too," he said. And then smiled again.

He was messing with her. He had been since he'd walked in here, but she refused to make anything of it. So what if he was charming, he was also her boss at the moment. And business and pleasure mixed like oil and water, to use a foodie phrase.

The coffee brewed as she cleaned the kitchen. Once it was done, Jared poured a cup for both of them and they sat facing each other across the granite-topped island.

The coffee warmed her up and went down deliciously. "Mmm, this is perfect."

"Yep. It's not too bad. Just about the extent of my talent in the kitchen."

"I bet that's not true."

"Oh, wait, I have been known to fry an egg or two."

"Really? How did you ever get by?" *And get to be such a glorious picture of a man.*

"My mama was a good cook. She fed me real good. And then came Marie. I never had to learn."

"Do you want to?"

He put his cup down and leaned forward, the twinkle in his eyes as blue as a sun-drenched lake. "You offering to teach me?"

She tilted her head. Was he flirting? She'd always loved dishing it up with other foodies, but was he serious? "Don't you already have a job?"

He grinned and her heart nearly stopped. "I do. But as you can see, I'm not exactly running to the office every day." He cleared his throat. "I mean my Dallas office."

She couldn't afford to return his flirting. She was out of practice, so much so that she wasn't even sure he *was* flirting. Besides, she had a gigantic wall surrounding her heart stamped with a No Trespassing sign. There was no room behind that wall for anyone other than Sienna.

Certainly not a man like Jared Stone.

Goodness, she still loved Paul. Her heart broke every day from missing him.

"Well, uh…"

"I was just kiddin'," he said. "You've got enough to do around here."

How awkward. She really didn't have a comeback for him. She was busy, but spending more time with a lonely, injured Jared Stone wouldn't be wise.

Because she liked him. It killed her to admit it.

Her nerves jumpy, she sipped her coffee and checked the monitor screen. Anything to avoid eye contact with him.

"How's she doing?" he asked.

"Sawing logs."

"So do you usually stay up the rest of the night?"

"Lord, no. I'll go back to bed in a little while. I might catch another hour or two, maybe three if I'm really lucky and Sienna doesn't wake up. What about you? You said you toss and turn. Is it because you're uncomfortable?"

He gazed at her from just above his mug of coffee and shook his head. "Not tonight."

"Oh, no?" She bit her lip. "So then I did wake you."

"You didn't. Honest. It's just that I'm having…"

"Nightmares?"

He shook his head. "Flashes of memory. I see my car sliding off the road and me losing control. I must've hit some loose gravel and spun out. That's all I remember." He shrugged and stared into her eyes. "It's weird, not knowing what happened. But it's even stranger to see it happen in my mind in sort of slow motion."

"Oh, Jared. I'm sorry."

"Don't be. I'm taking it as a good sign."

"But maybe with the trauma of it all, it's better not to remember."

"Maybe. But whatever happens, I'll deal with it."

He put his hand to his chest and rubbed at his sore ribs. Her gaze fell to that spot and when their eyes finally met, something warm and crazy stirred in her belly.

Immediately she put her head down and stared into her mug.

"What's wrong?"

She shook her head. "Nothing."

"Bella?"

"It's just that I'm feeling guilty." About betraying Paul with her thoughts, her lies to Jared about her true identity and something else entirely.

"What are you feeling guilty about?"

"I might've been the one who broke your ribs."

A speck of acknowledgment flashed in his eyes. "Oh, that."

"You know?"

"I was informed at the hospital that it could've happened when you applied chest compressions."

"If it wasn't for me, you wouldn't be in so much pain."

"If it wasn't for you, I wouldn't be breathing. Besides, there's every possibility the rib injuries were caused by the crash. Let's leave it at that. You shouldn't feel guilty about anything. My ribs will heal. So enough, Bella, okay? No more guilt about anything."

She glanced at his rib cage again, her heart fluttering wildly, and then met his eyes. "Okay."

The timer dinged and she rose instantly, grateful for the distraction. Pulling the pizza out, she was impressed with the results.

"How does it look?" he asked.

She showed him their sizzling veggie-topped creation. "Presentation is important, but what really matters is how it tastes."

"Well, dish it up. I'm dying to try it."

"Me, too."

She used a pizza cutter to slice it and soon they were digging into hot, crusty pieces.

Jared gobbled the first one up. "Oh, wow. It's pretty damn good."

"You really think so?"

"Don't you?" he asked.

She took another bite and chewed, aware of his eyes on her. "I, um, yeah. I think it needs a bit more salt, but it's pretty good. What do you think of the crust?"

"Delicious," he said, grabbing another slice. "You should add it to that cookbook you're going to write."

"I'm writing a cookbook?"

"You *should* write one."

She smiled. "Thank you."

"You made the pizza. I should be thanking you."

"I mean, because…well, it's nice to have someone to experiment on." Someone to encourage her.

"Hey, I'm adventurous, remember. Experiment away."

"As long as you're honest with me, I plan to."

"Yeah, Bella. I promise to always be honest with you. Honesty is something I value above all else."

Bella kept a smile in place but Jared's words seared into her.

And once again guilt replaced her sense of accomplishment over the meal. This time she was demanding something of Jared that she wasn't willing to give herself.

She couldn't be honest with him.

Keeping her secret safe had to be her first priority.

Sienna's future was at stake.

Five

On Friday evening, while Bella put the finishing touches on the meal she was creating for Cooper and his wife, Marie pushed Sienna around the kitchen on her tricycle. "Here we go again, Sienna," Marie said. "You're a good driver."

"I good, Mommy," her daughter parroted.

"Yes, you are, my baby."

"She's getting the hang of this thing." Marie had a note of pride in her voice.

"Goodness, thank you so much, Marie. I just need a few more minutes and I'll be through. Thanks for playing with Sienna for me."

"Nonsense. Anytime," she said, waving her hand in the air. "This little one is the bright spot in my day. I can stay a few more minutes."

Sienna climbed down from her trike and whipped her helmet off, marching over to the big bag of blocks sitting on the floor by the table. "Play bocks?"

Bella rolled her eyes. Sienna had a short attention span. Not that it was unusual for a child her age, but she didn't want to tax Marie overly much. She'd already spent the day doing light housework.

"I sure will, but how about we play them up here on the table?"

Marie hoisted the blocks up and then lifted Sienna onto her lap. The older woman seemed comfortable around children and Bella appreciated her kind nature.

"Thanks," she said again, but Marie was too engrossed in playing with the baby to comment.

Fifteen minutes later, with the dinner cooking and Marie gone, Bella stared at the clothes hanging in her bedroom closet. She didn't think it was fitting to wear jeans with Cooper and his wife coming over, but she didn't really want to dress up, either. Though Jared had made it clear she and Sienna would dine with them tonight, she was still the help. But he'd said Lauren was eager to meet the woman who'd saved his life. Being pregnant, his sister-in-law had been drilling everyone with children about pregnancy and labor and child-rearing and well, Jared seemed to think the world of his sister-in-law. Bella really couldn't argue. She remembered how nervous she'd been about motherhood, too, and she was happy to share her experiences.

She picked out a pair of black slacks and a white scoop-necked blouse with sleeves that billowed out at the wrist. It wasn't fancy, but it wasn't casual, either, and it made her feel soft and female. "How about this one?" she asked Sienna, who was busy crawling around on the floor. "What do you think?"

The baby glanced up at her.

"I'll take that as a yes. Now for you, Sienna-poo." Tonight she wanted to show off her daughter to Cooper and his wife, so she picked out a jumper dress, the top made of light blue denim, the skirt a frilly flare of white voile decorated with bursts of gold.

Bella kept her hair down, wearing it straight. For Sienna, she found an elastic wraparound headband with a big blue bow. She dressed the baby first and then quickly donned her outfit. She was all set to go downstairs and check on dinner when her cell phone chimed.

She smiled when she looked at the screen and answered. "Amy! Hi. How are you?"

"I'm doing just fine. Missing you guys. How's our little girl?"

"Enjoying ranch living, I think. She's being treated very well here. Jared and Marie have been very welcoming. So far, I've managed to keep her happy. If all goes well, tomorrow I plan to take Sienna out to look at the horses. But, oh, we really do miss you. When are you coming to visit? I have Sundays and Mondays off."

"I'll come soon. I promise."

"I'm gonna hold you to that."

"Listen, Bella, I have something to tell you…it may be nothing at all but—"

"Amy, I hate to cut you off," she said, glancing at the digital clock on the nightstand. "Can you tell me later tonight? I'm about to serve dinner and I don't want to burn my first meal for Jared's family."

"Uh, sure. If you're in a rush. Just be sure to call me tonight."

"Amy, is everything okay?"

"Yeah…probably."

"I don't like the sound of your voice. Should I be worried?"

"Bella, I'll tell you later." Her voice brightened. "You go and wow the family with your cooking."

"All right, I'll call you."

Amy had her curious and a bit concerned. But she couldn't dwell on it. She had enough to worry about right now.

She hung up, putting Amy's ominous call out of her mind, and then scooped the baby up. "Here we go. I want you to be a good girl tonight at dinner, okay?"

Sienna laid her head down on her shoulder. "O-tay, Mommy."

Bella beamed inside. For all the bad things that had happened to her in the past, having these sweet moments of absolute joy helped heal her grieving heart. She cherished her baby and would do anything to protect her.

Jared was dressed in a tan snap-down shirt and a new pair of jeans. He'd lost weight since the accident and had ordered new clothes online, but had been a bit skeptical about the whole thing. And damn if the clothes didn't fit him well. He was as groomed as he could manage, a close shave being the least of his worries. He'd done his best trimming his beard.

On his way to the kitchen, the sound of giggles coming from the second floor stopped him cold. He stood at the base of the staircase looking to the top. Bella held Sienna in her arms as they were about to descend. Bella looked beautiful. Correction, she was beautiful, and he might as well stop denying it. His savior, his angel, the woman who'd started his heart on that dark road that night was *stopping* his heart right now. He inhaled deeply and his ribs rebelled.

Damn.

"Hi, Tared." Sienna waved and he was struck again by the vision of the two of them coming down the stairs.

"Hey there, Sienna. Don't you look pretty tonight."

"I pretty?"

"You are," Bella said. "I have to agree with Jared."

As Bella reached the bottom of the stairs, he took a step back. "Hi."

"Hi."

Bella's olive complexion and flowing dark hair made her soft green eyes stand out even more. He couldn't stop staring.

"I, uh…" she said, "I have everything under control. Dinner should be ready in thirty minutes."

"Great. You look nice, too."

"Thank you. I wasn't sure how to dress. I mean, I…"

"We're not formal here, Bella. Anything would've been perfect on you."

Jared blinked. Geesh, did he just say that?

She moved away from him. Like she was scared, or worse. Maybe she was feeling the same attraction that he was. "I'll go in and check on dinner."

"Need some help?" he asked.

"Not really." She walked past him, heading for the kitchen. "But thanks for the offer."

The doorbell chimed and Jared moved slowly to the door to greet Lauren and Cooper.

Once inside, Lauren gave him a big but gentle hug. "You look really good, Jared. How're you doing?"

"Hanging in. Every day I get a little better. My ribs hurt, but that's gonna take time to heal."

Cooper shook his hand. "Hey, bro. Good seeing you." He put his nose in the air. "Wow, smells really good in here."

"Bella's cooking." Pride registered in Jared's voice and once again he was baffled by the intensity of the feelings he shouldn't be having.

"Where is she?" Lauren said. "I'm dying to meet her."

"She's putting the finishing touches on the meal."

Jared led the way into the kitchen. He made the introductions and Lauren walked directly over to Bella and took her hand. "I'm so sorry about…you know. I apologize for my little indiscretion. Do you think you can forgive me?"

Bella blinked. Lauren wasn't usually so abrupt, but this had obviously been weighing on her.

"I was sort of stunned by it," Bella said earnestly. "But your husband explained your reasons and…well, I do understand why you did it."

"So you forgive me?"

Bella glanced at him and then nodded slowly. "Yes."

"Thank you," Lauren said breathlessly. "I appreciate it so much." She turned to Sienna, who was on a quilt on the floor, deconstructing her block house. Lauren bent down. "Hello, Sienna. My name is Lauren. What do you have here?"

"Bocks."

"Aren't they pretty? I like the purple ones. Which one is your favorite?"

Sienna grabbed one. "Dis one."

"That's a great choice."

Lauren turned to Bella. "She's every bit as cute as Jared said she was."

Bella smiled. "Thanks. Congratulations on your baby. Cooper told me you were expecting."

"Yes, we're excited. And nervous and scared and every emotion under the sun."

"Yeah, I remember that overwhelming feeling. It does get better. How far along are you?"

"Four months. I have a tiny baby bump." She put her hand on her belly.

"Enjoy that tiny feeling while you can."

Lauren laughed. "You're not the first woman to tell me that."

"Don't get me wrong, I loved being pregnant. Just knowing that Sienna was thriving and growing inside me was enough. It's miraculous."

"I agree."

Lauren glanced around the kitchen. "Is there anything I can do to help you out in here?"

"I think I'm good right now. But if Sienna acts up, I might ask you to entertain her until I get the dinner on the table."

"I'd love to."

"Thanks."

"I've put a dish of appetizers on the dining room table. You all can give them a try and let me know how you like them."

"Sounds good to me," Lauren said. "I'm always famished these days."

"Give a holler if you need anything, Bella," Jared said. "You know where to find us."

Jared led his family to the dining room. Lauren took a seat and then popped a stuffed cherry tomato into her mouth. "She's darling."

Jared grinned. "Sienna's a cute kid."

"I was talking about Bella. And don't pretend you didn't know who I meant."

"Uh, oh, bro. Lauren's got that look in her eye." Cooper sat and grabbed a mini veggie frittata.

"What look?" Jared asked.

"The matchmaking kind," Cooper answered.

Lauren downed another appetizer. "Mmm, these are delish. And I'm not matchmaking. But what do you know about her? Is she dating? Does she have someone in her life?"

Jared shrugged. "Hell, I don't know. I don't talk to her about personal stuff like that. But she's never mentioned anyone. She's got her hands full right now with working and raising a child on her own."

"She's beautiful," Lauren said softly.

"I've noticed…"

Lauren grinned. "I was talking about Sienna this time."

Jared rolled his eyes. His sister-in-law was messing with his head.

"But now that you mention it," she added, "you haven't met anyone quite so nice in a long while."

"I didn't mention it."

Cooper chimed in. "Johnna's been dropping by."

"Coop, please… I'm not interested in Johnna. I'm not interested in anyone."

Lauren covered his hand with hers. Now he was in deep trouble. "It's just that you're a great guy, Jared. You deserve to be happy."

"I am happy. Or I will be as soon as I get the okay to drive again."

Coop sighed. "You can barely walk."

Jared glared at his brother. "I'm walking just fine."

"You know what I think?" Lauren squeezed his hand. "I think that Bella may have been sent here, especially for you. Maybe your angel's not through saving your life."

"It sure was a blessing you were driving down that road that night," Cooper said after forking a piece of chicken into his mouth. "Where were you coming from, Bella? I don't think I've ever asked."

Bella dabbed at Sienna's mouth. The baby sat beside her in the dining room on a makeshift booster chair she'd concocted from a square pillow covered with a towel. The juice from the chipotle peach dressing was dripping down the baby's chin. Her peach chicken dish was messy, but also very delicious. All three of the Stones had already praised the meal. "My friend Amy and I had taken Sienna to the Winter Wonderland festival off Highway 12. We stopped for a late dinner and Sienna had fallen asleep as soon as she got into the car."

"Your lucky day," Lauren said to Jared.

"I'm not disagreeing," he replied, darting a glance at Bella, the gratitude in his eyes making her a bit uncomfortable. Or was it the heat she saw there that flustered her so much?

"How did Sienna like the festival?" Lauren asked. "She's what? Two years old?"

"A bit younger. She's twenty-two months and I think she liked all the colors and seeing Santa's reindeers. She kept calling them horsies."

"We'll have to remedy that," Jared said. "Tomorrow, I'll show her the stables. She can see our string of horses."

Bella blinked and bit her lip.

"Are you up for that?" Cooper blurted.

Jared's lips twisted and blood rushed to his face. Bella was glad she hadn't said anything. You'd think by the look on Jared's face his brother had emasculated him with that question. Clearly, Jared didn't like limitations of any sort.

"Hey, before you two get into a pissing match— Whoops, sorry, Sienna," Lauren said, turning an apologetic eye to Bella.

She nodded. "It's okay, she didn't hear you."

Lauren went on, "Before you two go at each other, remember that walking is a good form of exercise and if Jared is feeling up to it, he should do it."

"Thank you, Nurse Lauren," Jared said, giving his brother the stink-eye. "I'm feeling much better every day."

"Glad to hear it," Cooper said.

"Your brother is concerned about you, Jared." Lauren

spoke in a conciliatory tone. "You're his baby brother. So will you cut him some slack please…for me?"

Jared looked at Lauren and relented. "Yeah, I guess so. I'm just anxious to get back to my life."

"You will, in time. The Stone men aren't known to be patient," Lauren said to Bella. "But they are smart."

"Got that right," Cooper and Jared said in unison.

Everyone laughed and that was that. Immediately the tension in the room disappeared.

"So then, Jared, I suppose we're still on for our annual Christmas party. It's a week away and coming up fast. We didn't want to bring it up until we were sure of your recovery. We can host it this year."

Jared blinked as if he'd forgotten all about Christmas. A few seconds passed, Jared deep in thought. "No, I'll host it," he said unequivocally. "It's my turn."

"Are you sure? We don't mind," Lauren said and then turned to Bella. "The Stones always throw a holiday party for their crew. Family and close friends are invited, too."

"Yes, I'm sure," Jared replied. "You're pregnant and don't need the added work. I'll have the house ready, don't worry."

"That means a tree, and ornaments and decorations, not to mention food," Cooper said.

Jared eyed his brother. "I got it covered."

"I'll help, too," Bella chimed in. "Of course. I'd love to help with the party."

"That's very kind of you, Bella," Lauren said. "We'll all pitch in this year."

"Fine," Jared said grudgingly, looking like he'd rather tangle with a ferocious tiger than plan a holiday party.

"Well, if you're all finished with the meal, I'll get these dishes out of the way." Bella rose.

"Let me help," Lauren said.

"Oh, uh, Lauren, I was hoping you could entertain Sienna for a few minutes while I clean up and serve the dessert. That would be the biggest help. I keep a box of toys for her in the family room."

"If you're sure, I'd love to."

"I'll help Bella," Jared said and this time no one dared question him. "You and Cooper have fun with Sienna. She loves playing with her dolls. And jumping on the sofa. But that's off-limits. It's too dangerous."

Suddenly, Jared was an expert on Sienna? It was strange that she didn't mind the thought. Not at all.

After she got Sienna situated with Cooper and Lauren, she headed back to the dining room. Jared had already cleared the plates from the table. She only had to pick up the glasses and utensils. She met him inside the kitchen. "Thanks for helping."

"Anytime," he said.

"I like your family." She began rinsing off the dishes and arranging them in the dishwasher.

Jared leaned against the counter, next to her. "Even Cooper?"

"Especially Cooper."

"Why?" Jared's sincerely puzzled expression almost made her laugh.

"Because—" she turned to him, meeting his eyes "—he cares so much about you."

Jared's gaze softened and dipped to her mouth. "You're sweet to say that," he whispered.

She was locked in on him, unable to look away, though every bone in her body warned her to step back, to finish her chores and forget about how much she liked this deadly handsome, blue-eyed man standing so close. "You think I'm sweet?"

Jared's lips twitched. "And talented and smart and so beautiful I can hardly pretend not to notice."

"Jared." Was she warning him away or simply sighing his name? She was dizzy from his nearness and unable to figure any of this out.

"Bella, you're my angel." He touched a strand of her hair then, the gleam in his eyes filled with admiration and maybe something more.

"I'm no angel," she whispered.

"To me, you are." He bent his head and she froze.

But Jared's kiss landed on her cheek. "Thanks for a wonderful meal," he said quietly, smiling and then exiting the room.

Disappointed, she touched the spot where he'd just kissed her. She'd been telling herself all along she wasn't attracted to him. She couldn't be. So then why on earth was the skin on her cheek flaming so hot right now?

And why was her heart cracking open a bit when she'd believed it was locked good and tight forever?

Later that night, after getting Sienna down to sleep, Bella walked into the second bedroom to call Amy back, and her friend picked up right away.

"Hi, Amy."

"Hi. How'd it go over there tonight?"

"It went really well. Jared's got a nice family. Dinner for Cooper and his wife turned out pretty great, but I'm beat and—"

"Sorry to interrupt, Bella. I have something to tell you. I hope it doesn't ruin your sleep."

"What sleep? I don't usually indulge. So what's up?"

"Today the car valet at my condo building said some guy approached him with a picture of you. I got Travis his job at the parking garage, so out of loyalty he didn't say a word, even though the guy offered him a hefty bribe for any information regarding your whereabouts."

"Oh, no." Bella's heart pounded hard.

"Yeah, I know. Crazy, isn't it? Travis is going to get a nice bonus from me, that's for sure. But there's more. Your father has been personally calling my office. He's left a few messages today and I finally had the receptionist tell him I'm out of town. I don't know how long I can get away with that. But even if he finds me, I'll play dumb. He has no idea that we've been in touch. But I'll say one thing—it's a blessing that you're way out there on the ranch, Bella. It's probably the last place your father would ever look for you."

"I hope so." But she wasn't entirely convinced. Her father didn't give up on something when he wanted it badly enough. And now she felt the walls closing in on her. She didn't know if she should leave town or stay put for a while to see if things died down.

She bit her lip hard to keep tears from falling. Except for baby Sienna and her best friend Amy, she didn't trust a soul in the world, and that was a very lonely place to be. "Thanks for letting me know."

"Oh, Bella. You're upset. I'm sorry, honey."

"No, I'm glad you told me. I'll have to be very careful from now on."

"Honestly, I think it's going to be okay. There's no way he can trace you to Stone Ridge Ranch. And I'm certainly not going to tell him what I know. But just to be extra careful, I don't think I should visit you. We probably shouldn't see each other for a while."

"No, probably not." Her heart plummeted. She'd been looking forward to seeing her best friend soon, but Sienna had to come first. Bella had to be beyond cautious now. "I'm bummed about that."

"Me, too."

"Amy, thanks for everything. I don't know what I would do without you. You're the best friend a girl could have."

"Ditto to you, Bella. We'll talk soon. Now, try to get some sleep, okay?"

"Okay."

"'Bye for now."

Three hours later Bella was downstairs in the kitchen. She'd fallen into an exhausted sleep and now she was wide-awake and jittery, Amy's call a few hours ago having thrown her into a tizzy. The best way to remedy her anxiety was to dive right into work. When she was cooking and planning out new recipes, she'd get caught up in the moment and forget her troubles.

From the refrigerator, she grabbed a big loaf of sourdough bread, two cheeses, a slab of bacon, a slice of thick ham and a carton of eggs. She was grateful Marie had stocked up on the groceries she'd requested the other day. She had plenty to work with now.

She buttered a casserole dish and then, wielding her new chef's knife, began cutting off the crust on six slices of bread. At the sound of footsteps approaching, she lifted her head, and her stomach did a little flip as Jared walked into the kitchen. He was rubbing his head, making chunks of his blond hair stick up at odd angles. His mussed, drowsy-eyed look did a number on her already raw nerves.

"Hey," he said quietly. "Didn't think you'd be up tonight. You seemed pretty tired after dinner last night."

After she'd served dessert and said goodbye to Cooper and Lauren, she'd dashed upstairs with Sienna. That kiss, though chaste, combined with Jared's compliments, had ignited something in her that could spell trouble. And she had more than enough trouble right now.

"I was. But my body clock said it was time to get up and so here I am. How about you?"

"Same old. Can't seem to get comfortable in bed." He glanced at her workstation. "What are you making tonight?"

"Your breakfast."

"Really? What is it?"

"Kind of a cheesy egg soufflé. It's really rich, but I'm trying to cut down on the fat content."

"With bacon and ham? Sounds like my kind of dish."

"Hold on, buster, I'm not putting *all* of this into the dish. Bacon and ham will be added for flavor. And I'm going to cut the eggs down to three whites and three whole eggs."

"Okay, so burst my bubble. Want some milk?" he asked, heading to the refrigerator.

She shook her head. "No, but please leave it out. I need some for the recipe."

Jared poured himself a tall glass of milk and then took a seat across from her at the workstation to watch her. It was getting to be a thing, these after-midnight meetings.

He sat quietly for a while, sipping his drink. She was fully aware of his eyes on her. "Am I disturbing your quiet?" he asked.

As in, was his presence here making her nervous? Heck yes. But she didn't mind him being here. He was a nice diversion after that disturbing phone call from Amy.

"Actually, if I'm totally honest, I don't mind. Sienna is always interrupting my thoughts and I love her beyond belief, but sometimes it's nice to be able to have a conversation without being disturbed."

"I get that. You can turn off being Mommy for a little while."

"Something like that."

"You know, Cooper and Lauren were impressed with you," he said. "And Lauren's amazed at how you keep it all together, work and baby and single parenthood."

She kept her eyes on her task. Was she keeping it all together? She was on the run, trying to protect her baby and lying through her teeth to some very decent people about who she really was.

During dessert, she and Lauren had had a long talk about babies and pregnancy, and she'd shared with her a little about her life with Paul. But she'd had to omit so much from that conversation to keep her identity a secret.

"To tell you the truth, you impress me, too," Jared said.

She shrugged. Normally, Jared's compliment would have gone to her head, but tonight she was trying to keep things real. And nothing was more real than learning her father may have sent his henchmen out to find her. "I'm doing what I have to do. Sienna's the most important thing in my life. And as you can see, I can survive on very little sleep, so I have that over other women. I have a few more hours in my day."

"I guess so," he said, polishing off his milk and setting the glass down with a soft thud. "Can I help with anything?"

He was a gorgeous hunk of a man—how could she not notice?—but that wasn't why she was drawn to him. The bond of her saving his life would always be there, but more than anything she truly liked him and enjoyed talking to him. He was easy and nice and…well, she needed a friend so badly right now. "Can you cut up bacon and ham?"

"I can do that."

He came around the granite counter and she handed him a knife. "Just call me your sous chef."

"Do I have to?"

He laughed and it was the first time she'd seen him

laugh without visible pain. It soothed her heart to witness him healing. "Yes."

"Okay, if you say so. You're the boss."

"Not in the kitchen, I'm not." Jared smiled. "You're in charge in here. From now on, I'm gonna call you the Midnight Contessa."

Contessa? She actually liked the sound of it. Deliberately, she hadn't made reference to her Italian heritage to Jared, and it was just one more thing she felt guilty about. But the name had a nice ring.

"Feel free to use it as the title of your cookbook."

She could only return half a smile tonight. He had more faith in her than she had in herself. The cookbook and her dream of opening a restaurant had been put on hold indefinitely. She couldn't think that far into the future. She had to take one day at a time right now.

She hoped Jared didn't notice her anxiety. It would only lead to questions that she couldn't answer.

"Maybe someday, Jared."

They worked together, cooking up the diced bacon and ham, lining the casserole dish with bread and then adding the rest of ingredients. When it was all assembled, she put the dish into the oven and set the timer.

"What now?" he asked.

"Now I clean up the kitchen and wait. But you don't have to, if you'd rather try going back to sleep."

"Not on your life. This is my first sous chef creation."

"It'll take at least half an hour."

"Hey, I have an idea. Wait right here."

"I'm not going anywhere," she said, dumbfounded. "I'll just start cleaning."

But Jared was already out of the room. Not three minutes later he came back holding a suede jacket and a plaid wool shirt.

"What's all this?"

"We need some fresh air." He picked up the baby monitor and then grabbed Bella's hand and tugged her to the French door leading out to the large stone patio area. "Here, put this on," he said, handing her the suede jacket.

He left her to fiddle with knobs and buttons on a fire pit and the next thing she knew, she was sitting on a comfy outdoor sofa in front of a blazing fire. Jared sat beside her and warmth surrounded them.

"I haven't come out here in a long while," he said. "I've forgotten how beautiful the stars were. Look at that sky, Bella."

She glanced skyward. "It is quite amazing. So why haven't you come out here? Is it because of your injuries?"

"No, happened way before that. It used to remind me of…never mind."

"What?" she asked softly. "What did it remind you of?" She was really curious. Jared usually didn't speak much about himself and she was eager to learn more about him.

"Just a girl I once…cared for."

"Oh, so you would come out here with her?"

"Yeah, and we'd talk for hours about our future."

"I take it it didn't work out."

"No, it didn't."

"I'm sorry, Jared."

He took his eyes off the stars to glance at her. "I'm over it. Just kicking myself for being stupid."

"I doubt you were ever stupid."

He scratched his head. "No, I was. I trusted her, believed in her, even when I should've been more wary. Things weren't adding up and I was too damn blind to see it. She lied to me over and over, and it was her betrayal that really did a number on me."

Bella shivered. She could put herself into that equation

and the results would be the same. Lies and betrayal and abuse of his trust.

"Hey, you're trembling." Jared rose and sifted through a patio box, coming up with a soft gray woolen blanket. He sat beside her and tucked her into the blanket. "Sorry, didn't realize you were cold."

"I…shouldn't be." Her trembling had nothing to do with the temperature.

"Better now?" he asked, his eyes filled with genuine concern.

"Much."

Satisfied, he leaned back and put his arm around her. Cushioned by his warmth, she gazed at a sky full of twinkling specks of light. She sighed and her guilt about lying to Jared was immediately replaced by a soothing calm. "Thank you for bringing me out here tonight. It's just what I needed."

"Welcome," he said, smiling. He seemed pleased that he'd pleased her. A girl could let that go to her head. "You seemed a little… I don't know, sad? Or upset. I thought the fresh air and bright stars might brighten your mood."

He'd picked up on her anxiety? Here she'd thought she'd covered it so well.

"I'm…okay, Jared. Some days are more difficult than others."

"I get how hard this is for you. You being a *widow* and all," he said ultra quietly, as if the word would somehow set off a whirlwind of emotion. "And if you ever need anything, I'm here, Bella. All you have to do is ask."

She turned her body slightly, looking him in the eyes. She lifted her hand to his cheek and the fine stubble tickled her fingertips. "Thank you."

She leaned forward and placed a kiss on his cheek. And then he turned toward her and their mouths brushed, a gentle, tender caress that felt as natural as the sun shining. His lips were warm and firm and she waited for guilt to summon her, for a backlash of forbidden emotion to warn her off, but none of that happened. Instead she relished the kiss, savored the taste of him, enjoyed the sweeping sensations her body was experiencing.

She'd been wound tight lately and Jared coming to her rescue tonight soothed her nerves. And now kissing him was…well, putting only wonderful thoughts in her head.

"Bella." He called her name reverently, his tone humble and seemingly surprised. His hand cradled her face as his lips became more demanding. Kissing him was like a balm to her internal wounds, a safe haven where she could forget. "Tell me to stop, Bella. If you don't want this."

"Don't stop," she whispered.

A pent-up groan rose from Jared's throat and he took her into his arms, wrapping her in an embrace. The glow of the fire, the twinkling stars and the fresh bite in the air together gave her a sense of amazing peace and comfort.

She felt safe with Jared. It was as simple as that.

And she ignored all the warnings screaming at her to be careful. To be wise. To be smart.

She'd needed solace and Jared was providing it. Her body was slowly awakening from a yearlong slumber. How good it was to feel alive again.

Jared kissed her deeper now and she accepted him into her mouth. The touch of his tongue on hers changed from sweet sensations to pulse-pounding heat, and she gave in to the yearnings to touch him. She wrapped her arms around his neck and the blanket separating them slipped away, bringing her body up against his.

Her breasts crushed his chest.

"Oh, man, Bella," he muttered. "I wanted to be conscious if you ever brought your mouth to mine again, but this is better than I'd ever imagined."

It amazed her that he'd been imagining kissing her. She sighed into his mouth, the temptation to touch him further, to unsnap his shirt and feel the heat pulsing in his chest was battling with her sense of decorum. So far, they'd only kissed, but if she was bold enough to undress him, it would be an open invitation for him to do the same and she didn't know if she was ready for that.

A buzzing rattled in her ears.

The timer to her soufflé was going off.

They both froze and Jared backed away first. "My breakfast," he said, heat glimmering in his eyes.

"Your breakfast," she repeated, the burn of his lips imprinted on her.

Jared rose first and gave her a hand up. She took it and they faced each other. "Bella, promise me you won't be sorry about any of this."

He stared into her eyes, her answer important to him. "I promise. I won't be."

He nodded and took a gulp of air. "Okay, I'll see you in the morning."

"Good night, Jared."

And as if he meant to hold her to her promise, he bent his head and kissed her once more before opening the door for her to reenter the house.

The next morning she and Sienna strolled hand-in-hand along the path next to Jared. Good on his word, he was taking them to see the horses. "Cooper's got a bigger string of horses at his place, but I kinda like our stable. And we've got a new foal, a filly to show Sienna. I think she's gonna like Pumpkin Pie."

Sienna's ears perked up. "Punkin."

"Yes, baby girl. That's the horse's name," Bella said. "It's a little one, just like you."

Sienna stared up at the tall rancher. "Tared's horsie."

"That's right, Sienna," he said to her, smiling.

Sienna smiled back and reached for Jared's hand, her fingertips touching his knuckles. Jared's blue eyes melted for an instant as he folded her daughter's hand into his. He glanced at Bella, shrugging, an awed expression on his face.

Her instincts were telling her this wasn't a good thing, but she couldn't dismiss seeing the joy in Sienna's eyes as they approached the corral.

"Here we are." Jared stopped at the fence, where half a dozen horses were frolicking around the perimeter of the corral.

"Let's take a better look, Sienna." Bella lifted her daughter up, setting her little boots on the second rung of the fence to give her a better view of the animals.

"Mommy!" Sienna pointed to the filly, the smallest creature in the corral with a reddish-bronze coat.

"That must be Pumpkin."

"It sure is," Jared said. "She's sticking close to her mommy."

Sienna took it all in, fascinated.

"It's a big corral," Bella said. "How many horses do you have here?"

"About a dozen. Make that thirteen," he said, tipping his hat back on his forehead. "If I'm counting the new filly."

"Do they all get along?"

"Seem to. But we build our corrals oval, which keeps the horses from bunching up in corners and getting too territorial. Makes everyone happy."

"If only people were like that," she said, thinking aloud. Her cryptic comment brought Jared's head up and he stared at her, his brows raised in question. She swallowed hard, condemning herself for letting down her guard.

"You all right, Bella?"

She looked into his eyes, wishing she could tell him the truth.

As much as she thought things might've gotten weird between them this morning, they hadn't been at all. Jared had been as earnest and forthright as usual and she'd sort of fallen into a sweet ease with him. Slowly her qualms about the kiss they'd shared had disappeared, though it helped that she had Sienna as a buffer.

Bella was still wondering what that kiss had meant to Jared.

For her, it was a gentle release of anxiety, a grasp at something solid and real amid the lies she'd told. It was a way to relieve her fear about her father finding her. But a part of her felt as if she'd been cheating on Paul. She was not all right, but she couldn't tell Jared that.

How had her life become so complicated?

"Sure, I'm good," she said, nodding, doing her best to convince him.

He nodded back. A beautiful black-and-white mare strolled over to the fence and Sienna began flapping her arms. "Horsie! Horsie!"

"I see it."

"Say hello to Jubilee, Sienna," Jared said. "She's just a little older than you. She's a sweetheart, just like you. You want to pet her?"

Before Bella could stop him, Jared lifted Sienna higher and leaned over the fence. Her daredevil daughter didn't protest at all. Jared's hand covered Sienna's as he carefully guided her toward the horse's flank. "There you go, Sienna. How does that feel? You just have to treat her nice."

"Nice," Sienna parroted as she stroked the horse over and over.

"That's it," Jared said. "Maybe one day you'll get to ride one of these sweet girls."

"Not on your life," Bella said, her inner mama bear coming out.

Jared slid her a sideways glance. "Don't worry, Sienna. Your mama will change her mind."

"I don't think so. She's too young."

"I was one when I took my first ride."

"You grew up on a ranch."

"What difference does that make?" he asked.

"I don't know. It doesn't, I guess."

"Where did Sienna grow up anyway?" he asked. "I don't think you've told me."

"Not on a ranch." Bella reached for Sienna, taking her out of Jared's arms, rattled by his question. She didn't want to lie to him. As far as he knew, she'd been living in Dallas.

Jared flinched.

And she felt like an uncaring jerk for being abrupt with him. "Did she hurt your ribs?"

"No, she didn't." Jared thought about that a few seconds. "She didn't hurt my ribs," he repeated, looking stunned by the revelation. Then he grinned, the smile consuming his entire handsome face. Again, a little jolt of joy streamed through her system at Jared's healing. Each day he was getting stronger. "I can lift this little peanut without any pain."

Bella put her hand on his forearm and squeezed. "That's good."

Jared glanced at her hand on his arm and his eyes shuttered closed as if relishing her touch. She was suddenly self-conscious, her mind instantly flashing back to being in his arms last night, however briefly, and kissing him.

"It's not just good, it's damn near amazing. A few days ago, I was having trouble breathing."

The hopeful gleam in his eyes chipped away at all her internal warnings.

"I'm glad, Jared. That's wonderful news."

"Yeah," he said, ruffling Sienna's dark mop of hair. "It is."

Six

Sienna giggled as Marie wrapped shimmery gold garland around her body all the way up to her neck. And Bella plopped a big red bow on top of her head. "You're just about the cutest Christmas tree I ever did see, little one," Marie said.

They were in the middle of the living room surrounded by Christmas boxes. Garland and lights and snowmen, almost life-size reindeer as well as different variations of Santa Claus filled the room. There was a whole shed full of decorations sitting on the living room floor brought in by some of the Stone Ridge crew.

She and Marie had decided to start in here first, and were both getting a kick out of Sienna's enthusiasm. Not that she knew much about Christmas yet, but she loved being in the middle of the decorations, or rather, being a *part* of the decorations.

"Let's sort these all out and decide what room to put

them in," Bella said. "And once Sienna goes down for her nap, we'll be able to decorate."

"That sounds like a fine plan," Marie said. "Maybe Jared will be able to lend a hand, too, that is if he wants to. He's not been keen on the holidays ever since…"

Marie buttoned her lips, but the sentence she'd left hanging stirred Bella's curiosity too much not to ask. "Why doesn't he like the holidays?"

"It's just that…that woman broke his heart right after Thanksgiving. They'd been planning a Christmas wedding."

"Really? I had no idea." She bit her lip, remembering the conversation they'd shared on the patio last night. He'd opened up to her a bit about his love life, but he never mentioned he was to be married.

"He doesn't talk much about it, but ever since then, Jared's been an ole Scrooge about Christmas."

"Like he's going through the motions for family and friends, when he'd rather be anywhere else in the world?"

Marie sent her a thoughtful look. "I think that's exactly it."

Bella could relate. Ever since Paul's death, nothing seemed right. No holiday was the same. And his accident had happened right before Thanksgiving, so she really understood the pain and heartbreak he'd gone through at a time when everything was supposed to be jolly and bright.

"What happened between them?" Bella asked.

Marie shook her head. "It's not for me to say, but I will tell you that woman really deceived him and messed with his emotions."

Bella squeezed her eyes shut briefly. "That's awful." And it was also awful that she'd been lying to Jared since the moment he'd set eyes on her. Bella sat on the parlor sofa, shaken.

"Dear? Are you all right? You just turned pale as a bowlful of oats."

Jared came into the room and glanced around, smiled at silly Sienna and then studied Bella from head to toe. "What's wrong?"

"Nothing," she said, sitting straighter in her seat.

"All of a sudden the color drained from her face," Marie said. "Jared, maybe you should take her outside. I think she needs some fresh air."

"Will do," he said.

"No, don't be silly. I'm…fine."

Marie shook her head adamantly. "You need air, Bella. You two go on. And while you're outside, Jared, please take a look in the shed for the nativity scene. I don't see it here. I'll take Sienna into the kitchen for a snack. Come on, little one," Marie said gently, unraveling the garland surrounding her and taking her hand. "I think I found some animal crackers just for you." Sienna followed Marie out of the room.

Bella stood to face Jared. "This is not necessary."

"Marie says it is and I learned a long time ago not to argue with a force of nature. C'mon, I need your help anyway. The nativity scene is the one decoration that must go up. It's a Stone family tradition."

"Okay, Jared. But only to help you search because there's nothing wrong with me."

Jared grinned and led the way, saying over his shoulder, "I've noticed."

His compliment went straight to her head.

She sighed and exited the house. They walked side by side, Jared commenting on the cooler weather to come. She was used to San Francisco fog and clouds and cold winter nights. It was nothing new to her. But Jared believed she lived in Dallas with Amy, so she wasn't going to say too much. "So what do you do when you're not working with your brother?" she asked.

"I have a few other enterprises and an office in Dallas, which I've been neglecting lately. But I have a good team that's covering for me while I'm out. I tend to get restless just being on the ranch, so I became a novice entrepreneur."

"Must keep you really busy."

"I like the challenge."

"You're not a homebody?"

"Me? No. That would be Coop. He's happy on Stone Ridge."

"And what makes Jared Stone happy?" she asked.

"Let me show you," he said, leading her into a five-car garage attached to the house. It was dark inside until Jared flipped on the overhead lights. Squinting at first, she focused her eyes. They were standing in a showroom of expensive cars and motorcycles. "I guess you could call this my hobby."

"Wow. This is amazing." She turned to face him and smiled. "So, you're in the new car business."

His eyes lit up. "Funny girl."

She smiled again and strolled around the garage, taking in a white Corvette convertible, a jet-black Jaguar, a souped-up Jeep and two motorcycles. One she recognized as a Harley-Davidson. Everything represented speed and danger. That's what made Jared Stone tick.

Jared followed directly behind her and she was keenly aware of his presence. There was something incredibly intimate being in here with him, as if he was revealing his true self to her. As she turned to him, she found pride in his eyes and a boyish eagerness. Her nerves began to tingle.

"It's all really nice," she said, holding back her reservations about the danger these cars represented. Jared was a grown man and she couldn't very well lecture him when she'd married a man who'd flown helicopters for a living, sometimes under extreme conditions. "Do you have a favorite?"

He stood close, very close. "That would be the pile of ashes I left on the road."

"Oh…sorry." But a car could be replaced. Jared had been lucky to walk away from that accident without any permanent damage to his body. The memory of that night still made her queasy. The bond she had with him was growing stronger every day.

"I'm getting over it," he said, taking a strand of her hair in his hand. She swallowed hard, seeing this man so close up under the bright lights and noticing not one flaw on his handsome face. "I wouldn't have met you otherwise."

"Jared," she said on a breath.

"You're my angel, Bella. And I can't stop thinking about kissing you again."

"We shouldn't," she whispered without too much resolve because inside she was melting. Inside, her heart ached for a bit of tenderness to help her forget her terrible grief. Inside, she wanted the comfort and, yes, the excitement of being in Jared's arms once again.

He cupped her face in his hands. "I know you're still hurting, Bella. Tell me to back off and I will. I promise." His reverent tone tugged at her heart. "But I need to hear you say it."

She stared at him and no words formed on her lips. No refusals. She couldn't tell him to back off. She couldn't walk out of there and turn her back on him.

"Bella."

She heard desperate desire in his voice and a vulnerability that washed away her doubts.

His hands wrapped around her waist, his fingers inching her closer. She put up no resistance as he bent his head. The first brush of his firm lips on hers sent her flying and she moved closer to him and wrapped her arms around his neck. He was tall and she stood on tippy toes to reach his mouth more solidly.

His kiss was more demanding than last night, more powerful, and her heart fluttered wildly in her chest now, her body melding to his with less hesitancy. Their tongues did a mating dance amid her moans and his groans. Jared woke her body from its doldrums, making her feel free and alive and vital.

His hands slid underneath her butt, his fingertips pressing into the soft cheeks as he lifted her up and set her gently onto the hood of his Jaguar. Thrills raced through her belly and she became instantly aware of where this could lead as Jared's dizzying kisses kept coming.

He pulled away to stroke a finger down her cheekbone, his eyes blazing blue heat. "Angel," he said and then smiled and kissed her again.

She lay back against the hood of the car, taking him with her. "Jared," she whispered.

That one word gave him permission to take what she offered, and Jared only hesitated for a brief, maybe surprised, moment before he brought his hand to the dip in her blouse. His fingertips scraped the top rim of her breast and shock waves erupted from the sheer pleasure of his touch. If she reacted like this from one touch, she could only imagine what making love to him would be like. Suddenly, awfully, she wasn't as opposed to that notion as she should be.

He was unbuttoning the first button on her blouse when his phone buzzed.

Their eyes met.

"I don't have to get that," he said, sighing.

"You do. It could be about Sienna."

He squeezed his eyes closed briefly, acknowledging that fact. He moved away to reach into his pocket and pull out his phone. "Yeah, hi, Marie."

Bella sat up and then jumped down from the Jaguar's hood, her heart racing for another reason now. She listened to Jared's conversation.

"Yeah, you're probably right. Okay, I'll go get it from Coop's house."

"Ask her how Sienna is," Bella chimed in.

"How's Sienna?"

Jared listened and nodded. "Okay, I'll tell Bella. No problem. Thanks."

She waited patiently for Jared to hang up. "What?"

"Sienna's fine. She actually conked out after her snack and Marie put her down for a nap. She's staying with her."

"Okay, good. Jared listen…uh, about—"

He folded her into his arms. "Shush," he said, kissing the top of her forehead. And she felt so safe, so cherished, in his arms, she didn't say the silly platitudes she was going to say about not knowing her own heart, about not reading too much into this, about how this wasn't a good idea. Honestly, right now she didn't know if she truly believed any of it anyway.

"Marie remembered that the nativity scene is at Coop's house," Jared said softly. "Come with me to pick it up?"

"I don't know. Sienna—"

"Is sleeping. Marie's watching her and it's only gonna take twenty minutes. I promise."

Bella blinked, debating. Jared grabbed her hand and tugged her toward his Corvette. "C'mon, Bella. I want to take my first ride with you by my side."

"You can't drive, Jared." She pulled him to an abrupt stop, hardly realizing her own strength. "Tell me you didn't mean that."

"I'm not going to drive. You are."

She blinked, catching his meaning after a second or two. "I certainly am not!"

"Why not?"

"Because…because…"

"See…you can't come up with a reason."

"I don't want to," she said. Wasn't that reason enough?

"Okay…then you leave me no choice. I'm gonna have to get behind the wheel." Jared made a move toward the driver's side of the car.

"Oh, for heaven's sake. Move over," she said, angling her body between him and the car. "I'll drive."

Jared grinned. "That'a girl."

It wasn't as if she hadn't driven a sports car before. She'd been given an Alfa Romeo on her seventeenth birthday. It was a beautiful car, but she'd hated driving it. She wasn't showy or status-conscious and she didn't have a need for speed. The car had been impractical and made no sense for a college student. After a year and some arguing with her father, she'd traded it in for a much more sensible sedan. It was just another way she'd disappointed Marco.

"I'm only doing this to keep you from reinjuring yourself. You haven't gotten permission to drive from your doctor yet, have you?"

"That'll happen soon enough. It's just a formality now." He put out his arms. "I'm fit."

Glancing over his solid body, she couldn't argue that point. "You sure are."

He grinned and opened the Corvette's door for her. "I like you, Bella Reid. A lot."

"Call me crazy, but I like you, too." A lot.

Just minutes later Bella's hair was blowing in the breeze, the car kicking up all kinds of dust behind them. It was a short drive on Stone property to Cooper's place. Gosh, he looked totally at home in this car, and happy. She smiled. She'd kept Jared from driving and breaking all kinds of speed laws.

She, on the other hand, was breaking all sorts of laws of her own making.

And Jared Stone was at the heart of it all.

Jared was definitely sleeping better, his wounds healing and his sore ribs not so restrictive anymore. Yet his internal clock still woke him anyway at precisely half past one. As he lay in bed a couple days later, his first thoughts were of Bella, her soft lips under his, her body meshing against him as he'd kissed her. It was no use pretending he could wish these feelings away. The more time he spent with Bella, the more he wanted her. Kissing her filled all the voids in his body, corking up his heartache over Helene and filling the emptiness in his life.

She was preparing a meal in his kitchen right now and was careful not to make much noise, but he'd heard her come downstairs ten minutes ago because he'd been listening for her. Now he was in bed battling his conscience and warring with the lust he had for her. She was his employee, a woman whose heart had been broken just one year ago. He admired her, liked her, cared for her. She was the whole package of beauty, talent and sweetness all rolled up into one.

Something was happening between them and it was stronger than his willpower to just let it be. It was stronger than his internal warnings not to get involved with her. She was just steps away and it was killing him to hold back, to keep his distance.

Who knew what would've happened the other day if Marie's phone call hadn't interrupted them.

The digital clock flashed. Another minute had gone by. Eleven minutes. Was that all his willpower could afford?

Hell yeah.

He tossed off the covers and rose from bed. Moonlight streamed into his room. He slipped his arms through the sleeves of his shirt, ignoring the slight ache to his ribs, and slid on a pair of jeans. He strode out of the bedroom, padding toward the kitchen, eager to see Bella. He found her hard at work at the counter, surrounded by bowls and equipment and ingredients, jotting down her recipe on a piece of paper.

It made him smile. And suddenly he felt selfish for disturbing her and had a good notion to hightail it out of there. Just as he was about to turn around, she spoke up. "Ready for some milk?"

He glanced at the milk container sitting out next to an empty glass on the counter. Had she been waiting for him? Joy surged in his gut and he wasn't going to second-guess it. "The Midnight Contessa is hard at work again." He walked farther into the kitchen.

"That would be me. Can't sleep?"

"No. Not too much." Technically it wasn't a lie. But he wasn't going to admit he loved these late-night meetings with her.

"Sorry to hear that. But you seem so much better lately," she said, keeping her eyes on the flour and butter she was measuring.

"I'm getting better every day. Nights are harder to relax."

"Speaking from one night owl to another."

He laughed. "I guess. Hey, how about putting me to work, I'm too antsy to just sit here."

"I can do that. Help me get this dough together. Pinch and squeeze the flour to the butter like this," she said. He watched her over his shoulder as he made his way to the sink to wash his hands.

When he approached, she slid over and made room for him at the workstation. He dipped his hands into the large bowl of what would be dough soon and every so often her hand would graze his. Just a simple touch from her swelled his chest and put illicit thoughts in his head. He enjoyed working with her, seeing her make decisions, putting great thought into what she was doing. "I hope this is gonna be blueberry pie."

"Nope, not even close."

"You're not making pie?"

"*We're* not making pie. Sorry to disappoint you, but this is an experiment. I'm attempting to make a meatless pot pie using veggies and tofu."

Tofu? Jared blinked, trying to think of a tactful response. "Good Lord, why?" was all he could come up with. "I mean, hasn't someone already invented it?"

"Yes, but I'm trying to make it better."

Jared shook his head, cautious not to hurt her feelings. "Uh, that explains it." He stood close enough to see her long lashes flutter, her expression becoming thoughtful while their hands brushed against each other in the mixing bowl.

A chuckle rumbled out of her mouth. "You hate the idea."

"Not hate."

"And you're trying to spare my feelings."

"I have simple tastes, Bella. But you've already impressed the hell out of me. With your cooking," he added. And with a whole lot more.

"Really?"

"Really," he said emphatically.

Her shoulders slumped and she sighed. "You're right.

I wasn't exactly inspired, and you have to be when you're developing recipes. This is one adventure we won't go on together."

"Bella," he said quietly, "I'd go on any adventure with you." He laced their dough-covered fingers together and brought their hands out of the bowl. Her soft green eyes lifted to his.

"I'll make you blueberry pie, Jared," she whispered.

"Suddenly I have an appetite for something sweeter." His gaze dipped to her mouth as her lips parted and he wasn't about to miss the opportunity to kiss her. He'd been consumed with it since the very first time they'd kissed.

He touched her lips again, taken by her softness, by the tantalizing taste of her. She gasped—a swift inhalation of breath. He hoped he was reading her correctly. Stuck between deep desire and hopeless honor, he couldn't go on without knowing one thing. "Bella," he whispered over her mouth. "I can't seem to stay away from you. Tell me to stop. Tell me and I'll leave you alone. Your job will never be in jeopardy, I promise."

"I know that," she whispered back, relieving his innermost fear. "You're not harassing me, Jared. Just the opposite. When I'm with you, some of the sadness goes away." She cupped his face in her hands and gave him a sweet kiss on the mouth. "I don't know any more than that."

It was enough. Hell, it was everything he'd needed to hear.

She smiled at him. "You've got flour on your face."

"Thanks to you," he said.

"Let me just wipe it away," she said, rising on tiptoes and using her mouth to brush it away with tiny, moist kisses.

The woman was killing him in small doses, but he wasn't complaining. His heart was fuller than he could ever remember. "I like the way you clean."

"Do you?" Her head tilted coyly, all her lush black hair falling out of its clip.

Jared swallowed hard, loving the sight of her in her apron smudged with flour, her hair freely flowing.

He dipped his hand into the flour and touched her face, marking her, and then began sprinkling flour along her neck and throat and onto the luscious hollow between her breasts. "Looks like you could use a little cleanup, too."

Bella looked down at herself and giggled. The sweet sound brought a grin to his face and he reached for her, his hands circling her waist. He bent her backward in his arms and started his cleanup, licking the deep valley between her breasts. His heart beat like a sensual drum, deeper, harder, and as he kissed her soft, smooth skin over and over, the drumbeat slid lower, pulsing at his groin.

He touched her breasts through the material of her apron and groaned, making his way up her throat, kissing her chin and finally finding promise at her lips.

The little noises erupting from her throat relayed her pleasure and suddenly that was all Jared wanted to do— to give her pleasure. He kissed her again and again until the flour smudges on her body were good and gone and the noises she made became gasps and moans.

She trembled in his arms. "Bella," he whispered in a plea. "I need you."

He'd said *need* and not *want*, and it dawned on him immediately that he did need her, more than he'd ever needed a woman in his life. She was his angel and he'd be a damn fool to screw this up. "God." He stopped kissing her and put his head down, gently bumping his forehead to hers. "Tell me you feel it, too."

Bella didn't hesitate. "I feel it, too. I don't want you to stop, Jared. Maybe I should, but I don't."

"Come to bed with me, angel."

"I'm no angel, Jared," she insisted softly, grabbing the baby monitor and taking his outstretched hand.

"That's not true, sweetheart, but I'm not opposed to you proving me wrong…in the bedroom."

Bella set the baby monitor down on Jared's dresser, her heart beating in her ears. Her first priority always had to be Sienna, and fortunately her baby was sound asleep. Jared glanced at the baby monitor, too, and nodded. A big part of her wanted to believe Jared Stone cared about her and her baby, and not just because she'd saved his life, not just because he wanted a temporary bed partner.

He began unsnapping his shirt and she caught herself watching him as if she was floating in a dream, mesmerized by his elegant, swift motions and partly stunned that she was here in his bedroom in the first place.

Thoughts of Paul strummed in her head and she had no choice but to shove them aside or she'd start running. She couldn't live in the past. She'd been through a lot this year, and if being with Jared would help her get over her heartache, she had to take the chance.

She focused on him. He was nothing short of perfect, even in his slightly bruised state. Moonlight touched his profile and the sharp angles of his jaw looked hard and dangerous, but she knew he wasn't. She knew what kind of man Jared was and that's why she was here with him.

His shirt off now, he reached for her hand and laid it on his bare, muscled chest. She inhaled deeply, her fingertips scorched by his heat. His whole body seemed on fire and the flames spread to her like wildfire. His eyes closed as she slid her hand over him again and again, absorbing his rock-solid feel. It was as if he was absorbing her touch, as well.

"Jared," she murmured.

He claimed her mouth again and his hands wrapped around her back to untie her apron and lift it off her. From there, her shift easily followed as he gave it a tug at the shoulders. It slid off her body, circling her feet. She took a step out of it, fully aware that she was standing before Jared almost naked but for the tiny white bra and panties she wore.

His eyes burned into her as he reached around her again, this time flicking the fastener of her bra. He guided the straps down her arms, until she was free of the garment. Her long hair tickled the tips of her breasts, covering her from his view. Gently, he moved her hair aside, grazing her nipples with the back of his hands. She gasped.

And so did he. "Bella. Your name suits. You're...beautiful."

His eyes locked to hers, he cupped her breast, gently weighing and rubbing it with the palm of his hand, his thumb circling the aroused tip. Ribbons of heat flowed down her belly and a tiny moan escaped her mouth. He kissed away her next moan and the next and, before she knew what was happening, she was lying across Jared's bed, her head against a fluffy pillow, and he was over her, his erection pressing her belly through his denim jeans.

He was thorough in his kisses, making sure she was satisfied, and then he backed off for a few seconds, adjusting his position. The flat of his hand traveled from her breast down her torso, past her navel. Jared worked her panties down her legs and her heart rate escalated in anticipation.

When his palm finally touched her folds, she parted her legs for him and he stroked her over and over, his fingers working magic on her body. The painful pleasure shocked her and soon jolts of electricity streamed through her body. Her breaths came in short bursts, her hips arched and trembled, and a low unavoidable whimper escaped her mouth. Her release shattered, sending pieces of pleasure to all parts of her body. It was complete and abundant and so freaking amazing.

"Jared… Jared."

"I'm here, angel."

"That was so…"

"I know. I'm glad," he said, giving her a smile right before he kissed her.

She lay naked on the bed, fully exposed to him after having a mind-blowing orgasm, and there was no shame, no guilt, which sort of baffled her. Nothing about this night seemed wrong.

But she knew there should be plenty wrong with this scenario: namely that she was lying to Jared, deceiving him about her true identity. And for Sienna's safety, she couldn't do a thing about it.

His next kiss caused all thoughts and doubts to vanish from her head. She was in Jared territory now, a place she craved to be.

"I've got protection, Bella," he said, rising quickly to remove his jeans and briefs. She watched him sheath his erection and took a big gulp of air. Good Lord, he was magnificent and, for the night at least, all hers.

"Somehow, I knew you would."

He smiled a killer smile, cocking his head to one side. "You'd be surprised."

"I'm hoping to be."

He laughed, joy and lust filling his eyes. "That's a lot of pressure."

"I'm pretty sure you're good. Judging from what happened just a minute ago, I have no doubts."

He came back to bed, hunching over her, bracing his arms by her shoulders on the mattress. "I live to please you," he teased.

And then Jared got serious. He was definitely an overachiever. Within minutes her entire body had been touched, kissed, caressed and set aflame. She was breathing hard, tingling from head to toe and practically begging for mercy.

Finally, Jared came up over her and settled between her legs, joining their bodies, inching into her cautiously, almost reverently. "Oh, man, Bella. You feel...*so damn good.*"

She relished his comment, unable to reply, her heart and her body too caught up in the moment.

And then he began to move. Sensations deep and satisfying filled her, and all she could do was move with him, taking up his rhythm and cadence. They were fluid in motion, striving, pushing, giving to one another. Bella could easily let herself go, but she held back, held on.

Waiting for Jared.

"Are you ready, Bella?" he whispered finally.

She nodded. "For quite a while now."

A chuckle rose from his chest. "Maybe you're not such an angel after all."

"And maybe we're not as different as you'd like to think."

"You could be right."

Then Jared swept her away, taking her to a no-think zone, a place where he proved to her once and for all who the real devil was between the two of them.

And thank goodness for that.

Seven

The morning came quickly, too quickly for her to absorb all that had happened last night. She lay in her own bed, her body sore in all the right places. She'd hated leaving Jared last night, and though he'd begged her to stay, she couldn't leave Sienna alone all night. Besides, it was safer with him downstairs and her living upstairs. It gave her some space, some time away from him to gather her thoughts.

Mostly, she wished she'd met Jared under different circumstances. She wished to high heaven she hadn't had to lie to him and everyone here at Stone Ridge. She wished she wasn't in hiding, that she could've had a normal upbringing with a reasonable father who wasn't always trying to run—and had nearly ruined—her life.

But wishful thinking never got her anywhere.

Instead she turned to the one glorious thing in her life. Sienna. Her daughter's eyes fluttered and she tossed around in the bed. She'd be waking up soon, ready to take on a new day. Sometimes Bella felt it was just her and Sienna against the world.

It was enough. It had to be.

A minute later Sienna's eyes opened and she immediately smiled. For Bella, these waking moments were precious, seeing the light on her baby's face when their eyes connected. "Morning, baby girl."

"Mommy."

Sienna rolled over, nearly on top of her, and squeezed her neck.

"I'm here, Sienna. I always will be."

A tear dripped from Bella's eye. She was emotional today, overly so, and it was fear and doubt and confusion about her future all wrapped up into one tumbling snowball that was picking up speed and growing larger every day.

Being with Jared last night had made all the bad things go away. For a short time he'd made her forget about her problems. But this morning reality set in and she had no idea what to expect when she went downstairs to cook his breakfast.

Fifteen minutes later, after a quick shower for both of them, she dressed Sienna in her favorite cartoon character outfit and put her damp hair up in pigtails, while Bella donned a pair of jeans and a red-plaid shirt. She pushed the sleeves up, ready for work. The two of them headed downstairs to the kitchen.

It didn't appear that Jared was awake yet, which gave her time to implement her plan. She set Sienna on a blanket on the floor with her ABC blocks and a few of her princess dolls. Cinderella was her favorite. Bella thought it odd that she was in the same situation as the blond-haired fairy-tale princess. With the clock ticking, Cinderella came to the ball magically and quite by accident to spend time with the handsome prince, hiding her true identity and knowing full well her time with him was limited. When would Bella's clock strike twelve?

If there was even a hint her father was closing in, Bella would have to pick up and run. She'd have to leave Stone Ridge, a place where she felt welcome and safe.

She shook those thoughts off, convincing herself she was well hidden at the ranch, and set about making breakfast. In a matter of minutes she had all the ingredients ready and set the oven to bake. Next she cleaned up the mess from last night, washing dishes at the sink.

Suddenly she heard footsteps approaching and before she could turn around, Jared's strong arms wrapped around her from behind and his lips nestled her throat, planting soft kisses there. "Mornin', Bella."

She leaned against the wall of his chest and sighed. "Good morning."

"Did you sleep well after you left me?" he asked quietly.

She nodded. "I did."

"Me, too. Though I missed you."

She'd missed him, too. This was happening so fast and she should be frightened, but right now, pressed against him and feeling his strength, hearing his voice, she felt safe. "I hope you understand why I—"

"Of course I do. Sienna comes first. She always will."

She turned to him then and met his eyes. There was genuine understanding there and something else: the tiniest hint of the future. Or was she reading too much into his comments? "Thank you for—"

His mouth came down on hers for a beautiful good-morning kiss and she forgot her deep thoughts and simply enjoyed being in his arms.

When the kiss ended, she smiled. "I'm glad this isn't awkward or anything."

"Honey, nothing about me and you is awkward. We're kinda seamless, don't you think?"

Before she could absorb that, Jared turned away and hunched down next to Sienna on the floor. "Mornin', sugar plum. What're you playing?"

"Dollies. Pay, Tared?"

"Of course."

Bella scratched her head. Where had Jared Stone come from? He was like a gift from heaven. Was it possible she could be so lucky twice in one lifetime, first with Paul and now Jared?

She walked over to the two of them. "Can Mommy play, too?"

Sienna kept her focus on her doll. Jared was helping her put tiny shimmery shoes on Cinderella's feet. "Pay, Mommy."

Ten minutes later the air filled with a sugary aroma. Jared lifted his nose in the air. "Something smells awfully good."

"It's a surprise."

"A surprise breakfast? Does it have tofu?"

She shook her head. "I promise it doesn't."

"Then I'll be sure to love it." His blue eyes twinkled and her heart sort of melted.

"Prize, Mommy?"

Sometimes she forgot how astute Sienna was. She soaked up knowledge quickly. Her daughter was learning in leaps and bounds. Every day she understood more and more. "Yes, there's a surprise for you, too, Sienna."

When the timer dinged, Bella rose from her spot on the floor. "I'd better get that."

Jared rose, too, and picked up little Sienna. As he held her, Sienna's arm circled his neck and Bella stared at the two of them as if…as if…

"Sienna wants to see the surprise, too. Right, Sienna?" Jared asked.

Her daughter bobbed her head up and down.

Scary joy bubbled inside her at the sight of the two of them. She sighed. "Well, okay then." She grabbed two thick pot holders and opened the oven. Gratified to see how well the surprise had turned out, she lifted the pan from the oven and turned to her audience. "Ta-da!"

"Blueberry pie," Jared said, a big, wide grin on his face.

"Pie, Mommy. I have some?"

"Yes, we're all going to have some. With ice cream, too."

Jared's dark blond brows rose.

"Why not?" She could be adventurous, too, and Sienna deserved a treat after all she'd put her through lately. "We can have dessert for breakfast once in a while, right?"

"Absolutely. It looks delicious."

"I... I hope so. Blueberries aren't in season, so I had to use canned fruit." She set the pie down on the counter to cool.

"I would never know," he said. "Can't wait to dig in."

He leaned over and gave her a kiss on the cheek. "Thank you."

Immediately she glanced at Sienna to see if she had any reaction to Jared kissing her. She did. She leaned forward and, with Jared's guidance, kissed her other cheek. "Tank you."

Sienna grinned. "You're both welcome."

As it turned out, Sienna ate her piece of blueberry pie with French vanilla ice cream while sitting on Jared's lap. He spoon-fed her small bites like a pro.

"I can't remember having a better breakfast," Jared said when they were all finished. "And I'm certain little Sienna here hasn't, either. Pie was delicious."

"I'm glad you both liked it. The thing is, Sienna might be bouncing off the walls soon. Sugar tends to fuel her up."

"Does it now? I might have a solution for that."

"I'm all ears."

He grinned. "Do you trust me?"

She nibbled on her lip. She was having a hard time trusting people lately, other than Amy, who knew all of her secrets. She really had to delve deep to answer him. "What are you planning?"

"Can't tell you. This time, I'm gonna surprise you."

"Me?"

"You and Sienna."

"Well?" He was waiting, his brow furrowing. He seemed to think his question was a simple one. One she'd be able to answer without hesitation. Last night she'd trusted him with her body and he hadn't hurt or disappointed her. Just the opposite: it had been thrilling and crazy-good. But Sienna was a different story. Sienna was the most precious thing in her universe.

Yet she had to admit, Jared had been nothing but gentle, caring and kind to Sienna. She'd be safe with him. "Okay, yes. I trust you."

"Great, meet us outside in ten minutes."

She blinked. "Outside?"

"Yep, and no peeking."

"Jared, what are you doing? Get Sienna down from there this instant." Bella's heart raced, thumping against her chest. She bit down hard on her lower lip as she approached the fence.

Jared sat tall in the saddle on a chestnut mare inside the corral, holding Sienna with one hand wrapped around her body, the other hand on the reins.

"Bella, just look at her. Sienna loves it up here on Sundae."

Her daughter was smiling and, with Jared's encouragement, was stroking the horse's thick mane. "Come on over here, Bella."

Her heart in her throat, Bella stepped up to the fence, noting the joy on Sienna's face and Jared's big, strong hand locked around her. A war battled inside her head. Was she too protective of Sienna? As if *there* was such a thing as being too protective for a first-time mom. Or was she projecting all of her fears and anxiety on her baby girl?

"Breathe," Jared said to her.

"I am breathing. Hard."

Sienna giggled when the horse twitched and fluttered her mane. Jared's eyes met with Bella's. "Are we good here?"

She nodded, biting her lip once again.

"I'm gonna circle the corral with her. Okay?"

"Be extra careful," she warned.

He tipped his hat, Sienna waving to her as they moseyed off at a slow pace. Bella lifted her hand and wiggled a finger or two, keeping her gaze locked on Sienna, her trembling beginning to disappear as she noted Jared's obvious expertise on the horse.

By the time they reached the far end of the oval corral, Bella was breathing normally. But just as she let down her guard, a gigantic hawk flew out of the trees and swooped down, winging its way just over Sundae's head. The startled horse reared up, her front legs circling the air as she balanced on her hind legs. Jared and Sienna were thrown back on the horse and Sienna's panicked screams pierced the air. Bella shot over the fence and raced toward Sienna. By the time she reached the two of them, she was out of breath. Jared held her crying daughter in his arms, trying to sooth her.

"Give me my baby now," she demanded. She was spitting mad, but didn't want to frighten Sienna so she held her anger inside. "She's scared to death."

Bella reached up and the second Sienna saw her, she nearly flew out of Jared's arms to be comforted by her mother. "It's okay, baby. It's okay." She kissed the top of Sienna's head over and over, holding her close.

"I can't even talk to you right now," Bella said to Jared, unable to look at him.

Jared climbed down off the horse and followed her as she began walking away.

"We were never in any real danger. I would've never let anything happen to her, Bella."

"Jared," she said through clenched teeth. "Please shut up and let me take my baby inside. I don't want to cause a scene and frighten Sienna any more than she already is."

She heard Jared let out a big sigh but, thankfully, he stopped following her. The darn man hadn't even thought about his own injuries and the damage he could've sustained.

She'd been a fool to trust Jared Stone. What the heck had she been thinking?

Jared paced in his study, unable to keep his anger in check, unable to get any work done this morning. Did Bella really think he'd put Sienna in danger? The horse had been spooked, but Jared had never lost control. He'd clamped onto Sienna like a vise until Sundae settled down. It was all over in a split second. He was sorry Sienna got frightened, but she'd stopped crying the instant she was back in her mother's arms.

Yet he'd never wanted to cause Bella any more grief. He'd never wanted to hurt her. She was becoming important to him and this little rift between them wasn't setting well.

His cell phone rang and he grabbed it off his desk to look at the screen. It was his mom. Veronica Stone Kensey wasn't one you could put off. She'd been calling every day or so to check on his recovery while on a trip to the Mediterranean.

Pinching his nose, he let the phone ring one more time before answering. "Hi, Mom."

"Hi, honey. We're finally back from our vacation. I'm in love with the Italian Riviera. And I think I've gained ten pounds. But more about that later. How are you today?"

His mom was sleek and pretty and she never really put on any weight. Her Floridian friends said it was a blessing how she could eat and eat and never gain an ounce. "I'm doing well, Mom. Every day is easier and easier."

"So, you're up and about?"

"Pretty much. I'm working, and today I took Sundae out for a ride." He wouldn't go into details but his mother deserved to hear his progress. He and Cooper had insisted she not come home from her trip when the accident happened. Things could've been a lot worse, but Jared had been lucky and there wasn't much she could have done to help his broken ribs. So as a compromise, they'd agreed to give her updates every day or two. Cooper and Lauren's pregnancy was also a subject of these conversations.

"You're not overdoing it, are you?"

"No, Mom. I know my limitations."

His mother seemed skeptical. She'd never approved of his daredevil streak.

"Okay." She sighed. "I guess I'll be able to see that for myself. I'm coming home for the holiday party at the end of the week." Even though his mom lived in a ritzy retirement village in Florida, she always referred to Stone Ridge Ranch as home. "I'll spend a few days with you, if that's all right?"

His eyes slammed shut. He loved his mother a lot, but her timing wasn't good. "Sure, Mom. I'd love to see you. You're welcome here anytime."

"Thanks, honey. Gosh, it's always so good to hear your voice."

"Same here, Mom. I'm glad you had a good time on your trip."

Jared ended the conversation and ran a hand down his face. With Bella angry at him, he felt at odds with everything, and now he'd have his mother to contend with. She was astute in matters of the heart; one look at him with Bella and his mom would figure out that something was going on between them.

Around lunchtime, he heard Bella being unusually quiet tinkering in the kitchen and he knew what that meant. She didn't want him popping in to watch her cook. That was too damn bad. He needed to iron this out with her or this uneasy feeling in his gut would never go away.

He took a few calming breaths and then marched to the kitchen. Standing in the doorway, he found her at the island chopping onions with a vengeance. "I bet you wish that was my head."

She glanced up and eyed him. "No. Maybe. I don't know."

"Where's Sienna?" he asked, walking into the room.

"Napping. She had quite a morning."

"Blueberry pie and a wild horse ride."

Bella put the knife down. They stood with the granite island between them. "It's not a joke. She was really scared…and so was I."

"I'm not making a joke. I'm sorry, Bella. I never meant for you to be frightened."

"You have no idea what it's like being a single mother. I'm all Sienna has. And she's all I have. I love her beyond belief. And it's my job to protect her."

"Protect her, Bella. Not stifle her."

"Jared, for heaven's sake. She's not even two years old."

"I know that. But I also want you to know that I'd never put her in danger. She was safe the entire time. I'd die rather than have anything happen to her. I can protect her, too."

"You almost did die not too long ago. You can't protect her, not the way I need. You don't see the danger in things. You drive fast, race motorcycles, take too many chances. Almost dying in that accident didn't change you."

Jared put his hands on his hips and stared at her. This conversation was going nowhere.

"Listen, I'm really sorry for making you worry. For scaring Sienna. It won't happen again. I can't take us being angry at each other, Bella. Not after last night. Not with the way I feel about you."

Bella put her head down and her arms braced on the counter began to tremble. Tears dripped from her eyes.

"Ah, Bella." He came around the counter and turned her into his arms. "Don't cry."

"It's the…o-onions," she whimpered.

"It's not the onions," he said softly, brushing away the soft strands of hair falling into her face. "I'm sorry, sweet angel. So sorry. I promise to be more cautious with you and Sienna. Just don't cry anymore."

His plea had the opposite effect and she broke down completely, sobbing into his chest. It was as if all of her troubles had come crashing down on her and all he could do was hold on to her tight, absorb some of her pain. Make her feel safe again.

"Let it out, sweetheart. It's okay. I'm here."

A nibble of curiosity about Bella's background was beginning to grow in his mind. She seemed to be hiding more than her grief, but he wasn't entirely sure about it and now was not the time to question her. Or maybe Jared really didn't understand what she was going through. Maybe, unintentionally, he was making things worse for her.

Finally after a minute, she quieted to a sniffle. "I'm... sorry. I messed up your shirt."

She patted his chest and lifted her soft, sad eyes to his. His heart squeezed tight. "Anytime, Bella. Ruin all my clothes, I don't mind."

The tiniest smile graced her face. She was so pretty, red-nose, swollen eyes and all. Or maybe he was such a goner when it came to her.

"You always say the right thing," she whispered.

Her voice was sweet, touching him in a dozen amazing ways. "I think we had our first fight."

She nodded. "I think we did."

"Kiss and make up?" he asked. He had Bella in his arms and she was soft and pliant and, unless he'd missed something, ready.

She gazed at his mouth, deep longing in her eyes, and he let out a quiet groan. She was vulnerable right now, and he wouldn't take advantage of that, but everything about her seemed to need the exact same thing he needed. To touch, to kiss, to forgive.

"Bella," he whispered right before he claimed her mouth. Both sucked in a breath at the joining of their lips. His heart raced and his body pinged. This woman made him ache. He deepened the kiss, unable to stop, unable to release his hold on her.

She kissed him back gently and then, as if something snapped inside her, desperation seemed to take hold. She gripped his shirt, nearly climbing up his body, demanding more of his kisses, more of him. There was a spark, a connecting energy that couldn't be ignored. It demanded. It crusaded. It conspired to bring them together.

"Forget lunch," he said between fiery hot kisses. "Come with me, Bella." If his ribs had been slightly more recovered, he'd have lifted her into his arms. Instead he put his arm over her shoulder. Her head automatically rested against his chest as they strode to his bedroom.

This time there was no hesitation. No quiet, intimate words. Once inside the bedroom, they climbed upon the bed fully clothed. The clothes were a minor nuisance, something that could be taken care of later. All that mattered right now was touching each other, kissing, bringing their need and desire to be together, to make up, to give in, to ease the pain that seemed to scar them both.

He touched every part of her through her clothes, kissed her lips, cheeks and chin. The need inside him was strong and potent and so very real, it half scared the life out of him. Nothing much did, but this…this thing between him and Bella was driven and wild and blissfully uncontrollable.

Soon kissing wasn't enough and their clothes were off quickly. He couldn't describe what it was like being skin-to-skin with Bella. It was off-the-charts good. She tasted like sugar all the time, her body so sweet and delicious. He cupped her perfect pert breasts, not large by any standard, but luscious, and suckled one then the other. The little cooing sounds she made were so damn enticing he was halfway to oblivion already.

She nearly finished him off when she circled her hand around his shaft. His hips jolted upward. Surprised and pleased, he leaned back, absorbing the feel of her hand on him, the way she moved, the beautiful vision she made in the minimal light coming into the room as her long black hair streamed down her body.

She *was* his angel, because he was surely in heaven.

"Bella," he breathed. It was on the tip of his tongue

to tell her what he was feeling inside, but he held back. It wasn't the time to claim her as his. She deserved better than a bedroom declaration, but he knew in his heart where this was heading.

"Jared, please. I need you."

Oh, man, he needed her, too. It took only a few seconds to sheath himself with protection, and then Bella was straddling him, her olive-skinned body glowing above him. The sight of this woman straddling him, ready to make love to him, would be forever embedded in his mind.

"I'm ready, sweetheart," he said, placing his hands on her hips and guiding her onto him. Their joining stole all his breath. He couldn't utter a sound. She was breathtaking and he was about as turned on as he'd ever been in his life.

They moved in unison, giving and taking. Her pulse-pounding erotic movements spurred his endurance. He never wanted this to end.

But when they'd finally reached the pinnacle of their desire, Jared wasn't sorry. They splintered apart at the same time, drawing out the last fragments of pleasure for each other. Unselfishly giving whatever they had left to please each other.

For Jared, it had been the best, most satisfying, sex in his life.

It was also something else, as well. Bella was systematically erasing Helene's betrayal from his mind and perhaps giving him a second chance at hope and faith and trust.

A little later, Bella lay in Jared's arms. The baby monitor he'd so thoughtfully brought into his bedroom showed Sienna napping soundly. Jared stroked Bella's hair, absently weaving his fingers in and out of the strands.

She cuddled up closer to him, breathing in the scent of his skin, feeling the steady, solid beat of his heart under her palm. She was in a different world when she was with Jared. He made her forget the bad things. It amazed her how quickly she'd become attracted to him, how quickly his presence in the room brightened her day.

Even though she'd been totally pissed at him about his recklessness on the horse, he'd managed to appease her with an apology that had come straight from his heart. Bella believed him to be sincere and earnest. There wasn't a deceptive bone in his body. He was the real deal. Score one for Jared.

Too bad she couldn't say the same about herself.

But she wasn't going to think about that now. These precious moments with him would soon be over when Sienna woke up. Right now, she just wanted to concentrate on being with him, guilt-free. "This is nice," she murmured as he absently stroked her arm, his touch creating tingles.

"It is. The best way to spend an afternoon."

She could hear his smile. "For me, too."

"I never thought…"

He stopped himself from finishing the sentence and she got the feeling it was going to be profound. "You never thought what?"

He sighed deeply and held her a bit tighter. "I never thought I'd ever feel this close to a woman again."

"What does that mean?" she asked quietly.

"It means that my ex really screwed me for relationships. I've been with a few women since, but it was never like this. It never lasted."

She didn't want to think about Jared with another woman…ever. But she needed a few answers. Was he telling her he thought they would last? That his feelings for her were strong enough to overcome whatever his ex had done to him? "She must've hurt you badly."

He kissed the top of her head. "She did."

"How? What did she do, Jared?"

He hesitated a long while and she thought to retract her question. Tell him it didn't matter. Tell him he didn't have to reveal his secret, because she couldn't reveal hers, and already the guilt she experienced was piling up.

But before the words were out, Jared began. "I met Helene in Dallas more than two years ago. She was working as a secretary in my friend's construction office. She was new in town, from this little country in Eastern Europe, and we hit it off immediately. We began dating that summer and things spiraled from there really quickly. I mean, I thought she was the one. I met her brother, she met mine. We were happy. You know, looking back, I see all the red flags, but at the time I was sort of blind. I fell hard for her and asked her to marry me. We were to have a Christmas wedding."

"And then what happened? Did she break it off?"

"No, I did. I surprised her one day at her apartment and walked in on her and her *supposed* brother in bed together. God, I felt like a big idiot. She'd set me up. She'd needed permanent entrance into the country and the man she'd introduced as her brother had really been her lover."

"Wow. That must've been a shock."

"You have no idea."

"Jared, I'm sorry." She lifted up enough to reach his mouth and kissed him.

He smiled. "Don't be. I'm fine, other than it's been sort of hard to trust anyone, you know?"

Pricked by guilt over her lies to him, she sighed. "I do know. Thanks for sharing that with me."

"Hey, I'm okay. But I know you're struggling about some things, too."

She froze. Oh, God, had he picked up on her lies? Was he suspicious? Because she'd saved his life, he'd taken her at her word about who she was. She still didn't think she knew him well enough to reveal her secret. She trusted him with her body, yes. But, she couldn't possibly trust him with Sienna's safety. He was a good guy, but his judgment at times came into question. What had happened today with the horse had sealed her stance on the matter. So as much as she wanted to share her burden with him, her instincts were telling her it was too soon.

"I mean, you've been through so much, losing your husband and raising Sienna."

Her shoulders fell in relief. "I won't lie. It's been difficult. But it's getting better."

"Am I part of your healing?"

"Maybe. Am I part of yours?"

"Hell yeah, you are. The day of the accident, I remember you telling me how lucky I was. I didn't think so at the time, when everything in my body ached. But now I do. Now, thanks to you, I'm lucky enough to ache in different ways."

He kissed her lips quickly and laughed.

"You!" She tossed a pillow at his head and he dodged it.

"Pillow fight," he announced.

"Not right now. I've got to get upstairs. Sienna's restless and bound to wake up soon, but I'll take a rain check on that pillow fight. It could get really interesting." She rose and donned her clothes rapidly. Jared snagged her arm and pulled her in, claiming her lips in one last kiss. A doozy.

And then she was off to see about her daughter, smiling wide in direct contrast with the hefty dose of dread draining into her stomach.

To say she was conflicted was a gigantic understatement.

Eight

The sun was just setting on the Christmas tree farm, the temperature brisk. The whimsical laughter of children filled the air as Bella shopped for the perfect Christmas tree. Jared followed directly behind her, holding a bundled Sienna, the two thick as thieves now.

"How about this one, Sienna?" Bella asked. She pointed to a Douglas fir that rose eight feet in the air.

Sienna tugged on her red-and-white knit cap and giggled. "No."

It had fast become a game.

"No, we don't like it, Mommy," Jared said.

"*You* don't." Bella stomped her feet and pouted. "But I think it's perfect."

Sienna giggled again and shook her head, joy twinkling in her eyes as she and Jared conspired and both chorused, "No!"

Bella laughed at the silliness and they moved on.

They came upon a giant open-air shed decorated with all sorts of multicolored lights, blow-up Santas and snowmen, and pretty wire reindeer. The owners were selling ornaments and tinsel and trees, of course. Hot cocoa and snacks were also available to make the shopping experience even more fun. "Hey, let's get some hot cocoa," Jared suggested. "And maybe a Christmas cookie or two."

"Sounds great," Bella said.

"Okay, I'll be right back." He handed Sienna over to Bella but the baby left his arms quite reluctantly.

"Tared be right back," her daughter repeated.

"Yes, he's coming right back with cookies, sweetie. Don't you worry."

She found a hay bale to sit on and cuddled up next to Sienna, keeping them both warm. But when Jared didn't come back right away, Bella began scanning the grounds, wondering what was keeping him. She spotted the woman first; the neighbor she'd met not too long ago. Johnna stood close to Jared, holding on to his forearm like her life depended on it.

Ripe, unwelcome jealousy slashed through Bella and she took a hard swallow. The two seemed to be laughing about something, the mists of their breaths mingling, and it was like a knife slicing her heart. But she had to come to grips with the fact that she had no real claim on Jared. They hadn't spoken of matters of the heart. What was happening between them was all so new and…and…her life was such a mess right now.

Watching Jared with a woman who wasn't lying to him, a woman who seemed genuinely nice, a woman he had known most of his life, not only confused her but brought her reality back to the forefront. What was she doing with Jared Stone?

Having an affair?

Hiding from her real emotions?

Jared returned shortly after, holding a box of goodies, and noticed her mood immediately. "Sorry, it took longer than I thought," he said, breaking off a small piece of cookie and giving it to Sienna. "Here you go, sugar plum. I ran into my neighbor," he added.

"Hmm, Johnna."

Jared handed her a foam cup of hot chocolate. "Yeah, Johnna. She's all excited."

"I could tell."

Jared shook his head, a cocky smile lifting one side of his mouth. "Hey, no need to be jealous."

"I'm not jealous, for heaven's sake. I have no right to be."

"You have every right to be. I mean, you have no need to be. I mean, what the hell, Bella? You're making me crazy. Before I met you, I wanted nothing to do with Christmas ever again. And now look at me. I'm here having a Christmas experience with you and Sienna, and enjoying myself. Doesn't that tell you something?"

Bella couldn't keep her lips from twitching. "A Christmas experience?" A chuckle escaped.

The heat in his eyes mellowed and he smiled. "Yeah, that's what I said."

"So what's the big news with Johnna?"

"She's getting back with her ex. He's been trying to make things right with her for months and they've finally worked things out. There might be a wedding soon."

"That is good news." Now she felt like Scrooge.

"Bella, you have nothing to worry about. I'm not… going anywhere."

"Because you live here."

He rolled his eyes. "Woman, don't you know how much I care about you?"

She inhaled deeply. "I'm…beginning to."

"Where's mistletoe when you need it?" he asked, leaning in.

"You don't need it, Jared."

And then his lips came down on hers. She closed her eyes and relished the feel of his kiss and the tiny bursts of joy popping around inside her. But too soon it was over and he lifted Sienna and kissed her cheek, too.

Sienna hung her arms around his neck and a glimmer of something beautiful entered his eyes.

He reached into his jacket pocket. "Here, this is for you," he said, handing Bella a gift wrapped in red paper and tied with raffia.

"For me?" she asked.

He nodded. "I just saw it and it reminded me of you."

He took out another gift, one much smaller, and handed it to Sienna. "One for you, too."

Bella untied the bow and opened the paper on the first gift. It was a Christmas ornament. A gold-rimmed, white-porcelain angel holding a basket of red-and-green flowers in her hands. Written on the angel's wings were the words Joy and Faith.

"This is beautiful, Jared."

"Sienna's is a smaller version. She's an angel, too."

"Thank you," she said, tears welling in her eyes. She helped Sienna open her little package. "Look, Sienna. A baby angel. Can you say 'thank you' to Jared?"

"Tank you." She held on to the angel like it was the most precious gift she'd ever received. "Pretty."

"It is pretty. Let Mommy take care of it for you while you drink your milk." She took the angel out of Sienna's hands and replaced it with a milk bottle.

"Bella, you've brought me joy and helped to restore my

faith in life. I know you don't like me saying it, but to me, you and Sienna are angels."

"Jared, you give me too much credit." Holding the ornament in her hand, touched by his generosity and thoughtfulness, she still felt as though she didn't have any right to him, not in a way that mattered.

"You know what?" Jared said, ignoring her comment. "How about we finish our cookies and find a nice big tree to bring home to Stone Ridge."

"I think we can do that."

And they went in search of the perfect tree to decorate with their new angel ornaments.

"Don't let me distract you," Jared said, sitting on a kitchen stool facing her workstation.

Was he kidding? He was a total distraction. It was almost 2:00 a.m. and Bella was hard at work perfecting a new recipe. "That's like saying don't let the sun shine."

She looked away from her notepad to gaze into his gleaming blue eyes. The twinkle in them sped up her heartbeats. Jared, barefoot, wearing a pair of dark sweatpants, filling out a white T-shirt with a solid chest and muscular arms, his hair sleep-tousled... All combined, it was enough to make her forget to add tomatoes in her tomato soup recipe. Not good.

"I can leave, Bella," he said, as if it was the last thing he wanted. "Let you do your work."

It was the *last thing* she wanted, too. "Actually, stay."

"Because I inspire you?" He was teasing.

She smiled and nodded.

A groan lifted from his chest. "Bella."

"I mean, uh, I like having the adult company."

"And I like *being* your adult company."

She smiled, not allowing her mind to go there. If she

did, she wouldn't get any work done tonight. "It was awfully nice of you buying a little Christmas tree for the kitchen." She took her eyes off him to view the five-foot Douglas fir sitting in the corner of the room, waiting patiently to be decorated. They'd actually left the tree farm with two trees.

"Sienna spends so much time in here, she should have a tree to enjoy all day. And she can help decorate it."

"That sounds like fun. I think we'll do it in the morning."

"Coffee smells good. Want some?" he asked, rising from his seat. Earlier, she'd set a pot of decaf brewing.

"Sure, thanks."

After a minute he delivered a cup to her. It was amazing how wide-awake they both were. She was used to waking up and cooking during the night. But this would all change soon for Jared. Once he got back to work full-time and began commuting to Dallas, these special nights would probably end.

Jared sat and sipped his coffee. "Tell me about your childhood, Bella."

She stiffened and averted her eyes, pretending to peruse her notes. "Uh, nothing much to tell really. I don't remember my mother. She passed away during childbirth. My baby brother didn't make it, either. At the time, I was just a tot, not much older than Sienna is now, and I had no clue how it had affected my father. Until I got older, that is. I don't think he ever got over the loss. He had trouble being both mother and father to me. We don't get along."

"Sorry. That's rough. My dad died young, too. It sort of made me want to branch out and do everything I've ever wanted to do, like, right away. Before time runs out."

"But maybe, Jared...doing so could actually cause your time to run out faster."

He scratched his head. "You sound like my brother. And mother."

She walked over to him, wrapped her arms around his neck and brought her mouth to his, giving him a solid earth-shaking kiss. "Do I?" she whispered. He reached for her but she swiftly moved away before he could reciprocate.

"Okay, point taken. So tell me more about your life, Bella."

"First, you tell me what sort of extreme sports are waiting for you once you heal completely?" Her question was meant as a diversion, a way to take the focus off her life.

"They're not extreme, Bella. I ride motorcycles. I like fast cars. I race boats during the spring and summer. I've been on long endurance runs on my bike. I've river-rafted and skydived. As soon as I get the word from the doc, I'm gonna take flying lessons."

"Yeah, all normal everyday stuff as safe as, say…going to a movie or hiking a trail."

"You don't approve? Hell, Bella, if you want to go to a movie, I'll take you anytime."

She rolled her eyes. Was he serious? "Jared, you're forgetting I have an investment in you. I'd like to see your life continue, preferably without injury."

"I'm not going anywhere, Bella. You don't have to worry."

Sadness filled her heart. "That's what Paul would tell me. I don't have to worry. And then he died and it hurt for a really, really long time. It still hurts, Jared."

"I know, Bella. I hate to see you hurting." He rose and approached her. "Fact is, it's the last thing I want for you," he said softly. This time when he reached for her, she flowed into his arms. His solid strength surrounded and settled her. It amazed her how easily his touch could do that. Being tucked into Jared's broad shoulders cocooned her in warmth and heat began to grow in her belly.

He tenderly kissed her forehead and lifted her chin. She looked into his blue eyes, blazing with heat and hunger, and she couldn't fight it any longer. She knew what it was like to be with Jared now, to be joined with him flesh-to-flesh. He was a beautiful man, flawed in only one way: his love for speed and danger. Could she overlook her doubts and open her heart fully to him?

A deep plea rose from her throat. "Jared."

It was a call to him. To take her. To be with her. To make love to her the way he had last night.

"I'm here, angel." And then he lifted her into his arms. The move didn't seem to strain him or to hurt him in any way. "And you don't have to worry."

Jared held her tight, her head resting on his bare chest. They'd made love just a few minutes ago and Bella's body was still humming like a sweet bird. There was nothing selfish in the way they pleasured each other. Jared worked his magic on her, hitting all her sensitive points, making her whimper. And she was beginning to discover what he liked her to do to him, with her mouth, her hands. Which seemed to be pretty much anything she wanted. His wild responses to her, his deep guttural groans, gave her a sense of power and command in bed. She loved pleasing him.

Earlier, Jared had mentioned his mother's visit, but she hadn't had a chance yet to ask him about it. "So, your mother is coming on Friday?" Bella whispered, wondering what her role would be once she got here. She stroked Jared's chest with the palm of her hand, absorbing the feel of him. Already, tingles of awareness were plotting against her tranquility.

"Yeah, she's anxious to see me. I've spoken with her on the phone, but with the party and all, she wants to be here."

"I can understand that. She has to see you for herself. You may be all grown up and resilient, but you're still her boy."

"Boy?" He grinned. "I'll show you boy," he said, rising up. He planted his mouth on hers and kissed her senseless. The heat of his palm covered her derriere and he gave it a long, proprietary squeeze.

She could easily give in to him again—she wanted to—but this was important. She gave him a shove, startling him, and he landed back on the bed. "Jared, we're having a serious conversation here." She smiled.

"We are? I thought we were going to—"

She covered his mouth, stopping his next words. They turned her on and he knew it. "Later. Right now, tell me about your mother."

Jared sighed. "She's as good a mom as we could've ever asked for. Cooper and I put her on a pedestal, continuing in my father's footsteps. He adored her and made us see how wonderful she was every day of our lives. We always knew our mom was on our side when it came to the really important things. She's smart and fun to be around. I guess that's why, when she met Grant six years ago, Cooper and I didn't stand in the way of her getting remarried. Once we scoped him out, that is, and figured out he was worthy."

Bella was floored by his admission. The Stone boys were protective of their mother. "Wow. She's lucky to have you both."

"Yeah, I guess so."

What would it have been like to have a mother who loved you unconditionally and a father who supported your wishes and stood behind your decisions? She'd had neither, but she wasn't going to have a pity party over it.

She'd come to grips with her situation a while ago, but still, every so often, she would fantasize about growing up in a normal, loving household.

That's what she desperately wanted for Sienna.

She touched Jared's cheek, scrutinizing his profile. Was he the man who could make that happen? Was Jared Stone the one?

He lifted her hand to his mouth and kissed it. "My mom's gonna like you, Bella."

"I hope so."

"I know so."

"I've been working with Marie and Lauren a bit on the party. Now that I know your mom is coming, I'm getting a little nervous."

"Why?"

She shrugged. "I don't know. I guess if I were in total control, it might be different. But I wasn't asked to cook anything."

He turned his head to look into her eyes. "Are you upset about that?"

"No. Just curious."

"We've used the same caterers every single year. And…well, to be honest, I don't want you working that night."

"Because the party is mainly for your employees?"

Jared's eyes grew wide. "Is that what you think? Hell, woman. I don't want you behind the scenes because I want you by my side. You and Sienna."

"Like a date?"

"Yeah, like a date."

She stared at him for a long while. Was he dense? And then finally he shook his head, as if shaking out cobwebs.

"Uh, sorry. I should have asked you formally."

"Well?"

"Bella, will you be my date for the Stone Family Christmas party?"

It was really ridiculous how giddy she was about this. Here they were, buck naked in each other's arms after having mind-numbing sex, and Jared was asking her on a date.

"Yes, of course. Sienna and I would be happy to be your date."

"Great. It's settled then."

"Yes, settled."

Jared's hand wandered to her backside again and this time she didn't shove him away. This time she was eager and ready for whatever pleasure they could bring each other.

The next morning, in the privacy of her bedroom, Bella picked up her phone and texted her friend.

Miss you, Amy. How are you?

Amy was attached to her phone by the hip and she texted back right away.

I'm good. What about you? Any news? How's the hunky cowboy?

She made a goofy face at the reference. Jared was fine. As in FINE. She smiled.

All is good here. No problems. What about you? Has anyone else come around looking for me?

No, thank goodness. But I did speak with your father. He's persistent. I led him astray, I think. Told him you might've

gone to Oregon to visit Miranda Davies. He shouldn't
think you're in the Dallas area. I hope.

Oh, wow. Miranda was a high school buddy. Her father
barely knew any of her friends. He'd never taken an interest. He'd always been too wrapped up in his company.

Brilliant. Thank you. Call you when I get a minute.

She ended the message with half a dozen purple-heart
emojis and released the breath she'd been holding. If Amy
was right, her father wouldn't be looking for her in Texas,
which bought her a good deal of time.

Marco thought her an unfit mother, but if she held down
a job long enough to prove she was providing a good life
for Sienna, his case against her wouldn't stand a chance.
At least, that's what she believed after doing extensive
research on the subject. And then with that issue settled,
she could look to the future and dream her dream again of
opening up a restaurant. She was taking baby steps now,
but with larger leaps to come.

A few minutes later she put Sienna in a pale blue jumper
and pulled her hair back in two big bows, getting her ready
to go down and decorate the Christmas tree. Sometimes
she'd look at Sienna and simply melt. The maternal need
to protect her overpowered Bella at times. She was living
a big fat lie to keep her safe. It was necessary, but along
with it came tremendous guilt. It had crossed her mind
several times to trust Jared. Would she have the nerve
to tell him the truth? God, she wanted to. She didn't like
lying to anyone, especially Jared. He was becoming truly
important in her life.

She was scared…about losing Sienna, and that fear kept

her mouth buttoned up tight. She kept telling herself when the time was right, she'd tell him.

Bella dressed in a pair of black slacks and a flowery blouse to offset the cold, dreary day outside. She put her hair half up and secured it with a pretty clasp to keep the strands out of her eyes while she cooked breakfast.

Halfway out the door with Sienna in her arms, she stopped up short. "Whoops. We can't go down without our angels." Bella opened the dresser drawer and handed Sienna hers. "Here you go. Hold on to it carefully. It's very special. Mommy's got hers, too."

"Angel, Mommy." She grasped her ornament with as much care as an almost-two-year-old could possibly manage.

As they descended the stairs and approached the kitchen, the sound of female voices reached Bella's ears. She slowed her pace and stood in the doorway. She found Marie serving coffee to a pretty brunette woman, her eyes as deep and blue as Jared's.

"Come in, Bella," Marie said, waving her inside the kitchen. "Come meet Jared's mother."

The woman stood and smiled. Dressed impeccably in beige slacks and a soft, silk blouse, her face sunny and bright, she put out her hand. "I'm Veronica. So glad to meet you."

"I'm Bella. Very nice to meet you, too," she said, hiding her confusion. Jared's mother wasn't due until tomorrow.

"Yes, Bella. And this must be Sienna." Veronica focused on the baby with delight in her eyes. "Hello, Sienna. I hear nothing but sweet things about you."

Sienna turned away, burying her head on Bella's shoulder. "She's a bit shy with new people."

"I understand. Gosh, it's been years, but Cooper was like that, too. She's adorable."

"She's a good girl," Marie added.

"Thanks, Marie. She has her moments, though."

"They all do," Veronica said. "You never know what little bits of mischief they will get into." She glanced at the ornaments in their hands. "Were you going to decorate the tree?"

"Oh, uh, yes we were, after I make breakfast."

"No need," Marie said. "I made Veronica some toast and coffee when she arrived. That's all she ever likes to have in the morning."

"I'll remember that."

"Jared has no idea I'm here," Veronica said. "After speaking to him last night, I got overly anxious to see him so I changed my flight. Booked a red-eye and well…" She threw her arms up in the air. "Here I am."

Bella smiled.

"Tared?" Sienna asked, looking around for him.

"He's still sleeping, little one," Marie said. "He'll be down in a few minutes, I'm sure."

Bella set Sienna down and she wandered over to the unadorned tree. "Are you sure I can't get you something else to eat?" she asked Veronica.

"Not a thing. But what you can do for me, if it isn't too strange, is let me give you a big hug. You saved my son's life."

She blinked. "Oh, um, sure."

Veronica stepped up and brought her into a gentle embrace. "Thank you from the bottom of my heart," she whispered. "I can never repay you for what you did, but if you ever need anything, please let me know." Veronica backed away, giving her a sincere look. "Okay?"

"Okay, but you don't owe me anything. I'm only glad I was there to help."

"So am I. When I think of what might have happened…

never mind. I won't nag him…much." Veronica wiggled her brows and Bella laughed.

Veronica scrutinized her face for a second. "You kind of remind me of someone I know. But I can't quite place it."

Bella froze. Her heart began to pound. "Do I?"

Veronica nodded. "You do. Maybe it'll come to me." She turned her attention to Sienna, who was munching on a cracker Marie had given her. "So tell me, how old is Sienna?"

They spent the next ten minutes talking about babies, the joys and frustrations of raising children. Veronica was super excited to become a grandmother for the first time. She was planning on surprising Cooper and Lauren next this morning. She was so easy to talk to, Bella passed off her earlier comment. She knew for a fact she'd never met Veronica Stone, so it was probably nothing. She was being too paranoid about things. She had to lighten up. Amy had pretty much assured her she had nothing to worry about with Marco.

"Angel, Mommy."

"Yes, I know, sweet girl. Excuse us," she said to Marie and Veronica. Sienna ran over to the tree and just then Bella spotted Jared in the kitchen doorway, his shirt undone, his jeans riding low on his waist, the face she'd kissed a hundred times shadowed with a day-old beard. She gasped as his eyes found hers and then his mother stepped into her line of vision.

"Hi, honey."

"Mom, you're here." He blinked a few times. "Am I dreaming?"

She glanced at Bella and then back at him. "Actually, you do look a little dreamy-eyed."

His mother was astute. A warm rush of heat climbed up Bella's throat.

Veronica walked into Jared's arms. "So good to see you, son. I've been worried about you. I hope you don't mind me surprising you this way."

"No, Mom. It's good to see you, too." They separated after a few seconds and Jared stepped back, buttoning his shirt. "Have you met Bella and Sienna?"

"I have. We were getting to know each other when you walked in."

"That's good. Did you travel all night?"

"Just half the night. But it's worth it to see you looking so healthy. I bet Bella has something to do with that."

"Bella?" Jared nearly croaked.

"Marie tells me she's an amazing chef, all healthy food apparently. Is that right, Bella?"

"Yes, uh, that's right."

"Well, I'm happy you're here," Veronica said. She gave her son another glance, one he may have deliberately ignored.

Walking farther into the room, he picked up a piece of toast from the table and chewed for a moment. "You want to put your angel on the tree, sugar plum?"

Sienna nodded.

"Let's do it." He smiled at his mom, then strode to the tree and bent next to Sienna. "Where do you think it should go?"

Sienna looked at the tree then ruffled a few branches until she found her spot. "Tere."

"I think that's a very good place for it."

Hand in hand, he helped Sienna hook the ornament onto a branch. "Wow, Sienna. You did it."

"I did it," she parroted.

Bella clapped her hands. "Good girl. I'm so proud of you."

Sienna's face beamed.

Veronica and Marie smiled, too.

"Babies bring so much joy into the home," Veronica said.

Then she looked straight at Jared with knowing eyes.

Jared sat for dinner at Cooper's house, breaking bread with his brother and his wife and, of course, his mother.

"Too bad Bella couldn't come," Lauren said. "I invited her and little Sienna."

"You did? She didn't mention it." It was news to Jared. His mother had insisted on all the family being together. It happened too rarely and he hadn't been about to disappoint her by not showing up.

Lauren was feeling great these days, having passed some pregnancy milestone that meant no more nausea or exhaustion. She was almost five months along now. And to think Coop had almost blown it with Lauren, plotting a scheme to stop her wedding to her sleazy fiancé. All during that time, Coop never planned on falling in love with her. Now Coop was married and going to be a father. There was no doubt he would make a damn good one.

"Maybe Bella needed a night off," Cooper said.

"It sounded more like she didn't want to impose," Lauren said. "Even though I insisted she wouldn't be. She did me a big favor today and I feel bad I didn't press her harder to come by."

Jared scratched his chin. He wanted Bella here and was at a loss without her. But it hadn't been his place to invite her. "What did you ask her to do?"

"You'll see. It's a surprise," Lauren answered.

He'd spent a good amount of time catching up with his mother today, and while she'd rested this afternoon he'd finished up on the day's work and hadn't seen Bella after that.

"She seems like a lovely girl," Veronica said, giving Jared another one of her expectant looks.

What did she want him to say? That he was falling for his personal chef? Hell, it was true. Bella was unlike any other woman he'd ever met. And that was a good thing. Instead of revealing his feelings, he simply nodded. "Seems to be."

Lauren put a delicious rib roast on the table with white potatoes, creamed asparagus and biscuits and gravy. No salad, no fresh fruit. And the veggie that was smothered in heavy sauce.

He smiled. Bella would be analyzing this meal and figuring out a way to make it healthy, substituting things and completely removing others. He was getting used to eating her way…healthy with cauliflower everything.

"Are you in la-la land or something, bro? You're smiling silly."

"Am I?"

Lauren eyed him. "Yes, you are."

"I'm feeling fit. Got an appointment on Tuesday with the doctor and I'm hoping he'll give me the okay to get back to my life as usual."

"That's wonderful, Jared," his mother said. "I hope so."

"Yeah, it's been hard doing all the heavy lifting with the company," Cooper added, winking at his wife.

"Don't be an ass, Coop. You know darn well I've been holding up my end." He'd been putting in some useful hours in his office and keeping up his part, when he wasn't playing with Sienna or admiring her mother.

"Is that what you call it? I thought you were playing house."

"Boys!" His mother was only half kidding in her reprimand.

"Playing house? Coop, watch your mouth." Jared's pitch elevated. "You have no idea what Bella has been through."

Everyone's head snapped up and three pairs of eyes stared at him. His protective instincts had kicked in. When Bella and Sienna were involved, he couldn't seem to help it. But now he faced the more than curious scrutiny of his family. How could he answer their questions about his relationship with Bella when he still had so many of his own?

"Hey, sorry," Cooper said. "I meant no disrespect. Bella's great and that kid of hers is a doll."

"She is that," Veronica said. "I like them both, Jared."

"I do, too," Lauren added. "She's doing a great job as a single mom. Actually, I don't know how she does it, balancing work and raising a child without having a husband around to pick up the slack. It's got to be hard. But Bella seems to be working it all out." Lauren placed a hand on her belly bump. "I only hope I can do as good a job."

Cooper leaned over and kissed her forehead. "You'll be a great mom, Laurie Loo. I have no doubt."

"Neither do I," his mother added. "You're a nurturer by nature, Lauren. I only wish you'd tell us what you're having, so Grammy-to-be can do some fun shopping."

Cooper gave his wife a cocky smile. "Shall we?"

Lauren nodded. "We've kept you in suspense long enough."

"Yeah, we wanted the family together when we do our baby's gender reveal."

"Oh, my, you're gonna tell us tonight?" His mother's face lit up.

Lauren rose from the table. "As soon as I clear up the dishes."

"Sit down and don't touch a plate," Cooper said. "I'll clean up."

"I'll help," Jared said.

The two of them made fast work of clearing the table

and bringing everything into the kitchen. As they were setting the plates down, Cooper turned a serious eye to him. "You really like that girl, don't you?"

Jared nodded. "I do. She's…she's…"

"I get it. You know, I was just teasing you earlier. You're my kid brother and I want to see you as happy as I am. You deserve it."

"Wouldn't know it by the way you harp on me."

"Nah, don't worry about that. It's my way of getting back at you for scaring the skin off my hide. Man, that accident was really bad. But promise me one thing, Jared. You won't go confusing your gratitude to Bella for the real thing. I mean, we're all indebted to her, but you've got to work through your issues before you can commit. You know what I mean?"

"What if I told you I'm working through those issues with Bella's help?"

"You're sure?"

He nodded. "I'm getting there."

Cooper slapped him on the back. "Then I'm happy for you, bro. Like I said, you deserve it. Now, let's get back inside. We've got the baby's gender to reveal."

Jared walked into the dining room, Cooper behind him holding a chocolate cake on a pedestal server. "Dessert," he announced, "compliments of Bella Reid."

"She made that? It's beautiful," his mother said. "But when do we get to find out if it's a boy or a girl?"

"Right now, Mom." Cooper handed his mother a long cake knife. "Do the honors. The color of the cake inside will give you the answer."

Tears welled in his mother's eyes. "I consider it an honor." She glanced at everyone first, then put the knife into the center of the cake and drew out the first piece.

"Pink!" His mother exclaimed. "It's a girl!" She bounced

up and down in her chair like a small child and then rose to kiss both Cooper and Lauren.

Jared grinned and shook his brother's hand and then walked over to hug Lauren. "Congrats, you two."

"Thanks," she said. "It's finally out in the open. We're having a girl!"

"Yeah, too bad your mom couldn't be here. Cooper said she was out of town this week."

"She's in Louisiana for the week visiting a friend, but we found a way. She's on FaceTime now." Lauren looked into the cell phone and waved. "Hi, Mama. Wish you were here with us."

"Me, too, honey. Oh, sweetheart, you're having a girl. I'm very excited. Be sure to save me a piece of that pink cake."

"We'll do that, Mama."

When all the hoopla died down and the final details of the Christmas party were discussed, Jared and his mother said their goodbyes and drove off. He was dying to see Bella, to tell her how sweet it was of her to bake the cake for Lauren and Cooper. To tell her he'd missed her. He glanced at his mother behind the wheel of his car, and shook his head.

With his houseguest, this evening, there would be no rendezvous with his Midnight Contessa.

Instead it was going to be a long, lonely night.

Nine

Bella stood at the top of the stairs, dressed in a snow-white, knee-length, tailored dress adorned with a red-ribbed belt with a matching poinsettia bow to her side. Her shoes matched, too. The only jewelry she wore was a pair of sterling-silver chandelier earrings. Sienna was dressed in Christmas plaid, the dress flaring out in poufy layers, shiny black Mary Janes on her feet.

They were ready for the Christmas party.

"Okay, Sienna. Remember, best behavior, sweet girl. This is your first Christmas party," she said as she held Sienna's hand and started down the staircase.

Jared stood at the bottom of the stairs, dressed in a black suit, looking sharp and crisp and deadly handsome.

She'd missed him these past couple of nights. And she was eager to be his date for the party. Veronica sidled up next to Jared at the bottom of the staircase, and she also watched them descend. There was a point when Jared's mother looked at her and flinched, and then she seemed to recover, leaving Bella with an odd sensation before Veronica walked off.

"You look beautiful, Bella," Jared said. He touched her hair, a sweet, innocent touch that sent shivers up and down her spine. "I like your hair like that." She'd pushed all of it to one side, letting it drape down her chest. It was held in place with a long silver clip.

Then Jared bent to Sienna. "Sugar plum, I don't think there's a prettier girl here. Give me five."

Sienna giggled and slapped at Jared's hand. Sometimes she made it, sometimes she missed. Tonight she made it and her chest puffed out.

"That's my girl."

Jared rose and took Bella's hand.

"This place is really transformed," she said.

"Thanks in part to you."

"Just a small part. I helped with the decorations."

They strolled around the warm, cozy house, two big, blazing fires in the fireplaces keeping the cold December air away. The two trees were decorated with colorful bulbs and ornaments and garland. Christmas music played and Sienna danced about.

Jared introduced Bella and Sienna to many of the ranch hands, workers and their families who kept the ranch going. There were many small children present and Sienna made fast friends with a few of them. Bella also met some of Jared's associates from his Dallas office. All in all, there were about fifty people.

"Champagne?" he asked, grabbing two flutes from one of the wait staff.

"Sure, thanks."

He put his arm around her waist and brought her up

close, so they were hip to hip. "God, I miss you," he whispered in her ear.

She swallowed hard. It was the first time he'd touched her in public like this for all the world to see. Heat rose up her neck. She was his date, but she hadn't expected any real show of affection from him in front of his crew and friends. After all, she was his employee.

She whispered back, "Do you really think this is wise?"

"Wise? I think we're beyond being wise, Bella. I'm falling for you and I don't care who knows it. Do you?"

His declaration caught her off guard. God yes, she was falling for him, too. She was too floored to do anything but nod.

"Good. Look up."

She lifted her eyes to find a thick bunch of mistletoe hanging from the ceiling. And when she tilted her head back down, Jared's lips were there, kissing her lightly but with enough potency to set her body on fire.

She scanned the room to see if anyone noticed and found Veronica's eyes on her for a split second before she shifted her attention to the person she was conversing with. Bella's gut clenched and she was suddenly ice cold inside. She shivered.

"Hey, if you're cold, let's go stand by the fire," Jared said. "I think Sienna would like it, too." Jared gathered up her daughter, tempting her with a candy cane, and the three of them entered the parlor and stood by a crackling fire.

"The caterers will be putting out dinner soon," he said. "Are you two hungry?"

"I hungry," Sienna said, sucking on the candy cane.

"Not just for candy, sugar plum." Jared tickled her and she burst out in sweet laughter.

The sound was enough to put joy back into Bella's heart,

even though her stomach felt queasy. "I could eat a little something," she said, plastering on a smile.

"Good, because later we might just have Christmas carolers come by the house. And who knows, maybe one of Santa's elves might be stopping by, too."

"Sounds like fun," Bella said, reaching for Sienna and taking her out of Jared's capable arms. She needed to hold her daughter tight to help the uneasy feeling in her gut disappear. Holding Sienna tight always seemed to work.

Yet her mind kept going back to Veronica. Bella scoured her memory, trying to think if she'd said anything to Jared's mother that would upset her. They'd been on friendly terms these past couple of days as they got the house ready for the party. And Veronica had been complimentary of the dishes she'd cooked for all of them.

So what was going on? And why was Veronica avoiding her?

The last of the partygoers was gone now and the caterers and cleanup crew were working hard to get the house back in order. Sienna had managed to keep her eyes open during the festivities, fascinated by the lights and activity, the carolers who'd come inside the house to sing their Christmas tunes and, of course, seeing one of Santa's helpers. Sienna hadn't been brave enough to sit on his lap, but she did receive a toy, a baby doll she'd clutched in her arms the rest of the night. Now Bella was heading up to bed with Sienna fast asleep in her arms.

"Bella, wait." Jared approached the staircase. "Let me take her up for you."

She hesitated only a second. "Okay, thanks." She made the transfer easily and Jared followed her up. She walked into the adjoining bedrooms and quickly turned down the sheets on the bed. She and Sienna had been sleeping together and, at some point, her little girl would get a bed of her own, but these conditions were fine temporarily.

Jared laid her down and Bella carefully removed her shoes and changed her into her pajamas. She tucked her in and kissed her forehead. Jared bent to do the same, and Bella blinked back tears. It was a ritual she and Paul would do together. She wasn't saddened by the gesture but rather hopeful and touched that Jared cared so deeply about her daughter. She walked him to the door and whispered, "Thank you. It was a lovely party."

"Our first date." She smiled and he wrapped his arms around her waist and pulled her close. "I'll miss you tonight."

He nuzzled her hair and then claimed her lips, the kiss going long and deep. They were both breathing hard when the kiss ended. "I'd better go." He sighed and backed away from her.

"Yes, you'd better," she whispered back, feeling the same longing she witnessed in his eyes. They were both aware his mother's room was just down the hall.

"Good night."

"'Night," he said and then he was gone.

Bella walked around in a daze, her heart spilling over with emotion, her lips still tingling from Jared's kiss. She was in love with him. She had no doubt. In the short time she'd known him, he'd become important to her. Every time he walked into the room, her heart just about stopped. She had come to cherish their midnight encounters, as well. Making love with Jared was amazing, but it was more than that. She shared her love of cooking with him, and had his full support. Those late nights had come to mean so much to her.

Five minutes later, as she was brushing her hair, a soft knock woke her out of her thoughts.

Her heart pumped faster at the thought of seeing Jared again.

She opened the door quiet as a mouse and found Veronica standing on the threshold. She gave Bella a small smile. "Can we talk?"

"Uh, yes. Sure. Just let me get the baby monitor."

Veronica waited and then led Bella to a sitting area, a little alcove in the hallway comfortable for two. "Is this all right?"

Bella nodded, her stomach beginning to ache. So she hadn't been wrong, something was up with Veronica and she was about to find out what it was.

"I won't beat around the bush, Bella. Or should I say Francesca? I know who you are. What I don't understand is why you are lying to my son."

Bella bit her lip and put her head down. Her eyes burned and she struggled to keep from crying. "You're right. I am lying to Jared. But it's not what you might think."

"Honestly, I don't know what to think. When I saw you coming down the stairs tonight, dressed like you are now, I remembered a brief meeting with a young woman who wore her clothes with poise and grace, whose long, dark hair was styled like yours tonight. A beautiful young woman with striking green eyes."

"We've met? I don't remember."

"You wouldn't really, I suppose. You see, before Grant retired, my husband owned a small chain of restaurants and we were at a charity dinner in San Francisco. It must've been…oh, about five years ago. Your father, Marco, was one of the main benefactors and you were with him. I know I'm not wrong. I've since checked you out on the internet. Granted, you weren't in the public eye much, but I did find a link between you and Forte Foods."

"I'm sorry, Veronica. I'm not hiding my identity for any nefarious reasons. I'm trying to keep Sienna safe."

"Care to explain?"

Bella had no choice. She'd been caught red-handed and a big part of her was glad to unburden her secret. For some reason Veronica, although a mother hen with her boys, also had a compassionate streak and seemed willing to hear her out. "Yes, of course. You see, I didn't have a traditional childhood. My mother died when I was just a tot and my father…"

Bella explained everything, leaving nothing out. She told Veronica of her struggles with her father from an early age, of his smothering her, trying to run her life. She explained how she'd defied him when she'd married Paul and then refused to work at the company. Then, while she was still grieving, her father had pushed Ben Tolben on her. He was a very nice man who worked for Forte Foods. They'd had a few dates, but it was never serious and it never could be, yet Marco leaked to the press that they were getting engaged and it had all escalated after that. She concluded with describing the fight that had driven her from San Francisco, fearing that she'd lose her child.

Veronica asked a few questions and seemed satisfied with her answers, but she still wasn't ready to dismiss her lying to Jared. "Why didn't you tell Jared this?"

"I… I couldn't. I haven't been able to trust too many people in my life, especially when it comes to Sienna's safety. She's all I have in this world right now. The thought of her being taken away from me, well… I can't even think about it without feeling sick to my stomach. I…was too scared. So, yes, I'm hiding out here, but I can assure you, what I feel for Jared is very real."

"Yet you couldn't trust him?"

"T-this hasn't been e-easy for me," she whispered. "I'm

not a liar by nature." Bella glanced at the monitor she held in her lap. Sienna was sleeping soundly, and tears formed in her eyes seeing her beautiful child looking so peaceful. There wasn't anything she wouldn't do for Sienna. If it meant leaving Jared and Stone Ridge Ranch, she'd do it. She'd pack up her belongings and go, because keeping Sienna with her was her first priority. "I'm protecting my daughter."

"And I'm protecting my son. You understand. I assume you know about Helene and the number she did on Jared?" She shook her head. "I can't let that happen to him again. He's a good man."

"I know," Bella said. "He is good. I care for him very much."

Veronica closed her eyes briefly and drew a breath. "You have to know how appreciative I am that you saved my son's life. And because of that, and the debt I owe you, I'm not going to tell Jared what I know."

"Thank you," Bella said softly, overwhelmed with gratitude and relief.

"But I am going to insist that you do. Bella, you have to promise me you will tell him the truth, the sooner the better. If you don't, I'll be back here next week for Christmas and I won't keep my mouth shut. You understand as a parent, I can't let my son be led astray."

"I'm not doing that. And yes, I promise you, I will tell him."

"Sooner rather than later?"

"Yes, I'll… I'll try to find the right time."

Veronica took her hand and gently squeezed. Her eyes softened in understanding. "Bella, don't wait too long."

"I promise, Veronica." Several tears trickled down her face. This wasn't an easy conversation and she surely didn't want Jared's mother to think the worst of her. She'd keep her promise and tell Jared the truth—and hope she wouldn't lose the man she loved. "I'll tell him soon."

Bella hardly got a wink of sleep, and in the morning rose from bed exhausted and perplexed. She caught her reflection in the dresser mirror and groaned. It was not a pretty sight. Her body ached, probably from tossing and turning. All night, she'd rehearsed what she would say to Jared and how she would implore him not to see what she'd done as a total betrayal. She'd have to make him see that, just like him, trust didn't come easily to her. He should understand that.

She'd lay it all on the line and tell him what was in her heart and hope that would be enough. Up until this point, he seemed to be a reasonable man. Well, except for his crazy need for speed and danger. While he was recuperating, she really hadn't seen that side of him, but she'd heard enough from his mother and brother about it, and how could she forget the accident?

She shook off the image and glanced down at her baby daughter on the bed. Just gazing at her angelic face was enough to make her forget all the bad stuff in her life. But Sienna's nose was running and she looked pale and clammy this morning.

Bella immediately climbed back on the bed and laid her palm flat on Sienna's forehead. The baby felt warm. Sneezing in her sleep, she nearly woke herself up, but Bella immediately tucked her in more cozily with the blanket.

Once she was sure Sienna was asleep, she walked into the other bedroom and texted Jared.

Sienna isn't feeling well this morning. May have a fever. I won't be down to make breakfast. Sorry.

She climbed back into bed with Sienna to keep a good eye on her, and not two minutes later heard soft knocking at her door. She padded to the door and opened it only inches.

Jared stood there, dressed in his usual jeans and blue chambray shirt, face unshaved and hair unruly. Her heart skipped but she was too concerned about Sienna to think about anything else. Still, Jared's presence just had a way of disrupting her normal breathing patterns. "What's wrong with the baby?" he whispered immediately.

"I'm not sure," she answered, keeping her voice low. "She was fine last night. And this morning her nose is running and I think she has a fever."

"You think?"

"Yes, she's warm, but my baby thermometer is broken, so I'm not sure. Sorry about breakfast."

He waved her off. "There's enough leftovers to feed my entire crew. Don't worry about cooking today."

"Thank you."

"So besides a baby thermometer, what else does she need?"

"That's it. I think I have everything else."

"Let me see what it looks like. I'll make sure you get a new one."

"Okay," she whispered. "Give me a sec."

She went into the bathroom and returned right away, showing Jared the thermometer. "This is it."

He took it out of her hands. "I'll have a new one delivered from the pharmacy in town."

She stared into Jared's concerned eyes. Gosh, he really cared about Sienna. If Bella blew it with him, it might be the biggest mistake of her life. "Thank you."

He nodded. "Just keep that sugar plum healthy, will you?"

* * *

The baby slept most of the day and Bella managed to get some rest, too. Sienna had no appetite really, only munching on baby crackers and sipping from her bottle. The thermometer Jared had delivered from the pharmacy registered a low-grade fever, which meant Sienna's body was fighting off an infection.

Bella got up to shower and change her clothes. She took her computer to the other room and began going over her notes. She was in the middle of designing a different version of a Christmas morning soufflé when Sienna began coughing. The cough was rough, coming from deep in her chest, and nothing Bella had ever heard before. She raced over to her and sat her up immediately, holding her until the coughing fit was over. And then Bella touched her face. "Oh, no, Sienna." The baby was burning up.

She raced to the door and called down for help. "Jared! Marie!"

Sienna's hacking returned. It was deep and guttural, like barking.

Bella heard Jared's footsteps on the stairs and the sound put her a little bit at ease. She needed him right now. "What's wrong, Bella?"

"It's Sienna. She's burning up and the cough...it's horrible. I think she's wheezing. She's not getting enough air."

He walked over to Sienna and the frightened look in his eyes added to her own fear, but his voice was calm as he picked up the phone. "I'll call Lauren. She'll know what to do."

Bella stayed with Sienna, encouraging her to drink between her coughing fits. The wheezing got worse, and raw panic seized Bella's stomach. Her baby wasn't breathing right.

Jared hung up the phone and strode over to the bathroom. "Bella, while I get the shower going, you get Sienna and hold her on your lap on the toilet seat. We need the room to steam up real fast."

She didn't have time to question him. She did as he asked, picking up the baby and bringing her to the bathroom. He closed the door behind them.

"We need Sienna to breathe in the steam until she's back to normal. Lauren is pretty sure it's croup. It means a ride to the hospital later, but only once we're sure the steam is reducing the swelling in her throat. That's what's causing the wheezing."

"Should we call the paramedics?"

"We could but, honestly, Stone Ridge is so remote, it'll be faster to drive her to the hospital ourselves. And Lauren says not to be scared. She's calling ahead to our local hospital. It's small but efficient and this way they'll be waiting for her."

"Okay, okay." Her own breathing nearly stopped, but she trusted Jared's instincts on this.

"Encourage her to breathe in and out."

The room steamed up pretty fast and they sat there for long minutes as the baby began to breathe easier and easier.

Sienna seemed confused about all of it, but her cough wasn't as bad as before and her breathing seemed much better. It was time to go.

Jared helped dress the baby in warm clothes and then tossed Bella her jacket. "Put this on. Mommy doesn't need to get sick, too."

Jared picked up Sienna. "You ready?"

"Yes, let's get her checked out."

Outside, as they approached her car, a light rain started to fall. Jared put his hand out for her keys.

"You can't drive," she said.

"I'm driving, Bella. You need to get in the back seat

and see to your daughter. There isn't time to argue. It's raining and, besides, I know where I'm going. I'll get us there faster."

She stared at him.

"Safely."

He'd read her mind. But, honestly, her nerves were too jumpy for her to drive anyway. She dumped the keys into his hands. "Okay. Let's go."

Jared paced back and forth outside the triage room. Bella was in there with Sienna and he wanted so much to be with them. He wanted to comfort Bella and to keep her calm—well, as calm as she could be with her daughter in the hospital.

His phone rang and he took it out and answered quickly. The hospital waiting area was quiet and he didn't want to disturb the silence. "Yep," he whispered.

"It's Coop. How's the baby?"

"She's in with the doctor now. Lauren saved the day, I think. Bella didn't know what to do and neither did I. But the steam seemed to work. Sienna's breathing was pretty good by the time we got here. Good thing, too. Bella was frantic."

"I can imagine. That sweet baby is all she has."

Jared took exception to that. She *had* him. Only he'd never told her. He'd never said the things nearest to his heart. That she'd helped him overcome his trust issues. That she was all the woman he would ever want in his life. That he was a goner when it came to Bella Reid.

He loved her.

Grateful he was alone in the waiting room, he grinned like a silly fool just thinking how hard he'd fallen for her. And how, because of her, everything else in his life seemed to fall into place, too. He had to tell Bella he loved her. But now wasn't the time. She was distraught over her daughter's illness, and he couldn't blame her. Sienna was a special kid.

"Hey, you still there?"

"I'm here, Coop."

"It was all I could do to keep Lauren from running out in the middle of the night to meet you at the hospital. Will you talk to her? Assure her about Sienna?"

"Sure, no problem."

"Hi, Jared," Lauren said. "Nurse Lauren needs to know how the patient is doing."

"Well, Nurse Lauren, according to the initial diagnosis, you were right. Sienna has croup. Bella is in with her now."

"They'll give her something to reduce the swelling in her throat. She'll probably stay overnight, just because of her age and the late hour. I would've met you there, but Cooper is being overprotective of me right now."

"As he should be."

"I'm glad you were there with her, Jared. Bella must've been so scared."

"Yeah, she was." So was he. But she'd turned to him for help and the significance of that pumped him up.

The exam room door opened and Bella walked out. "I gotta go, Lauren. Thanks again."

"Of course. Give the baby a hug for me."

"I'll be sure to."

Jared hung up and stood to greet Bella. "How is she?"

"She's sleeping. The doctor says she's going to be fine. The swelling is down now. And they're giving me some medication for her. I only came out to tell you they're keeping her overnight. You don't have to stay. I can—"

"I'm staying, Bella."

When he expected an argument, she slumped into his arms. "Thank you," she whispered.

"Come here, take a rest. You're exhausted." He led her over to a chair and they both took a seat. Wrapping her snugly in his embrace, he kissed her forehead and stroked her arms up and down.

"That feels good," she said softly.

"Feels good to me, too."

She chuckled and a soft glow lit her eyes. "You're so bad."

"You like me that way."

Slowly her eyes closed and she nestled closer into his chest. "I like you any way I can get you."

Jared smiled, totally knocked out. She was soft in his arms and smelled like a sugar cookie. He lifted her chin and placed a soft kiss to her lips. "Me, too, Angel. I like you any way I can get you, too."

Ten

Tuesday morning dawned gloomy and gray, with a light drizzle coming down. After growing up in San Francisco, Bella wasn't bothered that much by the lack of sunshine, and especially not today because Sienna was up and happily singing a silly song along with the cartoon characters on her favorite morning show.

The ordeal with Sienna over the weekend had taken a toll on her nerves. She'd never been more frightened in her life. Yesterday they'd stayed in all day and Sienna had recuperated fast, the meds and the nourishment giving her the boost she'd needed to get better. She hoped to high heaven Sienna wouldn't get croup again, but if she ever did, now she knew how to recognize it and what to do about it.

"Are you ready to go downstairs?"

"See Tared?"

"In a little while. We'll make him a nice lunch for when he gets back." Jared had a doctor's appointment early this morning. She hoped he'd get a clean bill of health. Not that he'd observed his doctor's warning about not driving. But Bella had understood his need to take control and help her. She'd actually appreciated his taking her to the hospital. And though he had driven fast, he hadn't broken any speed laws.

"Come on, let's go."

By the time they got downstairs, the rain was coming down hard. "Looks like we're in for a storm, baby."

They entered the kitchen and she spotted a note at her workstation.

I'll be back before noon. See ya then. Love, Jared.

She smiled at his reference to love. Things were happening quickly between them and she wanted to clear the air, to talk to him from the bottom of her heart. She hoped that he would accept her reasons for not telling him the whole truth. To make him see that it wasn't him she didn't trust, but a fear of her father learning her whereabouts that had kept her lips sealed good and tight.

She glanced at the clock. It was almost noon now. "Okay, well, let's get started," she said, rolling up her sleeves and putting her apron on. She set Sienna down in front of her brand-new dollhouse, a gift from Jared, taking up space right next to the kitchen Christmas tree. *Because she's been sick*, he'd explained. He teased Bella that he had an even better gift for her, but she had to wait until Christmas.

As she was putting the finishing touches on a vegetarian chili dish, with enough kick to knock Jared's socks off, she glanced at the clock. It was already half past twelve and no Jared. She checked the messages on her cell. Nothing. She was about to text him about his delay, a little knot of tension working its way into her system, when she heard his footsteps at the front door.

Thank goodness. He was home. She picked up Sienna and walked to the door. "Let's surprise Jared," she said. She opened the door with a big smile. And came face-to-face with her father.

Oh, no. She froze and then backed away, her mind racing. She could hardly believe her eyes. "What are you doing here?"

"That's a nice greeting for your old man." He appeared every bit as stately and entitled as he'd always been, but there was sadness in his expression and maybe a few more lines around his eyes than she remembered.

"You mean the father who threatened to take my baby away? *That* old man? The man who cut me off and caused me to run away in fear? I don't think you deserve any sort of greeting from me."

"Francesca, please. Do you know what I've gone through looking for you? The least you could do is let me inside. It's brutally cold and I'm getting soaked."

She hesitated, but finally, because they needed to resolve this, she mustered her courage and stepped away, allowing him entrance. She had no right letting a stranger into Jared's house, but what else could she do? Her father wouldn't just go away. She knew him all too well. He'd stake out the house until Jared got home and then cause a big scene.

"How did you find me?"

"I'll tell you later, but first, let me see Sienna." He turned his attention to her baby. "Hello, sweetheart. Grandpa's here now. How pretty you look this morning." He reached for her to ruffle her hair and Bella stepped back. She wouldn't allow him to touch her baby.

He sighed heavily, looking a bit defeated. "I've missed you. In fact, I've missed both of my girls."

A lump formed in Bella's throat. "Marco, what do you want?"

"I want…a chance to speak with you, Francesca. That's all."

She squeezed her eyes closed briefly. "Ten minutes."

She led him into the parlor and offered him a seat.

Keeping a steady hand on Sienna, she lowered herself down at the far end of the sofa facing him.

"You weren't easy to find, Francesca."

"That was the idea."

"Yvonne says I've been overly harsh with you. She says you believed me when I said I'd cut you off."

"Yes, I did believe you. And you did cut me off. You made my life…unbearable," she admitted, her voice sinking. "I just couldn't take it anymore."

"Yvonne told me as much, too. She's been your advocate, Francesca. I know you two never got along."

"You married a woman only ten years older than me. Hardly a mother to me."

He pointed his finger at her. "Nobody could ever replace your mother, you remember that. The truth is," he said, "I never really got over losing your mother and brother. It was very hard on me and I think, in a way, I placed all my hopes and dreams in you. Maybe unfairly."

"Extremely unfairly."

"I felt you were throwing your life away."

"You tried to dictate my life, Father. You told me what school to go to, what boy to date, what man to marry, where I should work, where I should live. I'm twenty-eight years old. While you weren't looking, I grew up, but you never saw that. You never understood me, never supported my passion for cooking and creating. You wanted me in corporate America. That's not me."

His shoulders slumped. "I was doing it for your own good."

"And look how well that turned out."

He blinked, and anger sparked in his eyes. "Francesca."

"No way, Marco. You have no right to be angry. Not after what you put me through. How do you expect me to trust anything you say?"

"I know, you're…right."

"What?"

"I said, you're right. I admit it. I was overbearing. The truth is, I recently had a health scare. My heart was acting up. I'm going to be okay with diet and a change of lifestyle. But you know, that trip to the hospital got me thinking about my life and what's important to me. Yvonne says I've finally gotten my priorities straight. She's been helping me with my issues.

"Believe me when I say she cares about you. She wants us to be a family. I came to tell you I'd never take Sienna away from you. It was an idle threat, Francesca. You're a good mother and I never meant for any of this to escalate."

"Are you saying it was all your wild temper?"

"I'm saying I was bluffing to get my way. I'm…sorry."

"You're sorry?" She squeezed her eyes closed briefly. "How did you find me?"

"Apparently a Sienna Reid had been in the hospital overnight. I've had a team of detectives checking all the hospitals, making calls all around the country and…well, we got lucky. Not that Sienna being hospitalized is a good thing. But she looks fine now. What was wrong with her?"

"You mean your henchmen didn't find out?"

"Francesca, please. I love my granddaughter."

"She had a breathing problem due to a virus. Her throat swelled up, but she's much better now."

"Croup?" her father asked.

"How did you know?"

"You're forgetting I was a single father for quite a few years. You had a bout or two of it yourself."

Bella stared at him, stunned. She'd never related what she was going through with what he'd gone through when her mother died. Her father had always seemed larger than life to her.

He gazed at his granddaughter and smiled. "She's a beauty. Just like you, Francesca. I want you both back in my life."

"Things have changed for me, Father."

"I heard you're working here as a chef."

"How did you— Never mind." She didn't want to know the nefarious ways her father found things out. "I am. I have a job and I've been happy here."

"You can be happy in San Francisco, Francesca. Please consider coming home. Christmas won't be the same without you and Sienna."

Bella glanced at her watch. Jared was late, but he'd be returning soon. She didn't want him to find Marco Forte here, not before she had a chance to explain the situation to him. It was time. And she'd promised Veronica she would. "Father, you have to leave. I have...duties."

He frowned and inhaled a breath, giving her a long stare.

She was ready to ask him again but he beat her to it. "Okay... I'll go."

"You will?" She was astonished. Her father usually never backed down. Maybe Yvonne was a better influence on him than she'd ever given her credit for. And maybe, just maybe, that health scare softened up his heart a bit.

"Yes, as long as you promise to call me. We'll talk some more."

"Yes, we'll talk some more. I do promise."

Marco stood and put out his arms. And when she stood

her ground, he walked over to her. Again, she'd triumphed. People always catered to him. She'd never seen this side of her father before.

They embraced, the three of them, Sienna breaking out in giggles.

Her father kissed them both on the cheek and then he was gone. Bella stood with Sienna in the living room, dumbfounded, watching his limo pull away. She couldn't believe what had just happened. Had her father really capitulated? Had she just seen a big change in him? He was actually behaving like a caring father. Well, almost. Or was it all part of a grand scheme to get his way? It was hard to place her trust in him, but his tone, the sincerity in his voice and the genuine look in his eyes had swayed her.

Was her life finally turning around? Did she dare hope?

Bella needed a few minutes to absorb all that had just happened with her father. She sat next to Sienna on the floor and watched her daughter touch some of the shiny ornaments on the Christmas tree as a hard steady rain came down outside. "Careful, baby. We don't want to break them."

Just then the front door burst open and Cooper walked inside, bracing Jared with an arm across his shoulder. Jared's leg was dragging behind him and blood dripped down his face. Cooper guided him toward his bedroom. They were both drenched.

"Cooper?" she called as they passed the living room.

"Jared decided to take his bike out in the rain," Cooper said over his shoulder as he continued moving. "The roads were slick and he took a curve too fast."

"I told you why," Jared lashed back. Bella gasped and plucked up Sienna, taking her into the kitchen and handing her a baby cracker. "Here you go, sweetie. Play with your dollhouse and Mommy will be right back."

Bella approached the bedroom and saw Cooper facing Jared, who was half sitting, half leaning against his pillows on the bed. "You get permission from the doctor to drive and your first decision is to hop on your bike in the middle of a storm?"

"It wasn't storming when I left the house," he said through gritted teeth. "What was I supposed to do? Johnna called in a panic. Her dog knocked loose a steel pipe in the barn and it fell on top of him. The dang thing would've crushed Rusty to death if I hadn't gotten there fast enough. I had to take the back road shortcut and that meant taking the Harley."

Cooper closed his eyes and shook his head. "Man, bro. You don't get it. You went out on slick roads and nearly got yourself killed. This is your second crash this month. When are you gonna learn?"

"Don't lecture me, Cooper. I'm gonna be fine."

"Yeah, once again you defied the odds. How many more chances do you think you'll get?"

Bella stepped up then. "Jared, are you all right?"

"I'm just a little banged up. I'll be fine," he assured her.

"Someone should look at your leg." She glanced at his ripped pants. Blood was already drying on the wound.

"I'm bruised. That's all. No big deal," he said.

She walked into the bathroom, soaked a towel with hot water and antiseptic soap and then returned to the bedroom. "Here," she said, handing him the towel. He appeared startled. Did he expect her to nurse his wounds? He could've been killed today. Did the man have a death wish? "For your face. You'll frighten Sienna if she sees you like that."

She glanced around the bedroom, the place where magic happened between them, the place where she'd felt safe and sheltered. But she didn't feel that way anymore. Now, her eyes were open wide, seeing Jared as he really was, perhaps for the first time. The healthy version of Jared Stone was a man who loved to test his limits. He had a garage full of vehicles to pursue his pastime and he'd never tried to hide his true personality from her. In fact, he'd been only too happy to share his love of speed and danger with her.

He'd said it himself. He wanted to live his life fully before time ran out, the way it had for his father. Jared, once free of restrictions and physical limitations, couldn't wait to hop on his motorcycle and race the storm. And she had been too busy falling in love with him to think this through. Now the cold slap of reality hit her hard.

Jared Stone wasn't father material. He wasn't husband material. He was a man who had been kind and caring to her, but that's where it had to end.

Bella had already lost one good man. She couldn't stand to lose another. Not to death. It was too final, too heart-wrenching. And she'd learned one lesson from her father, if only one, and that was she'd never try to change a person who didn't want to change. If this was the way Jared wanted to live his life, she wouldn't stop him.

"Cooper, will you check on Sienna for me? I need to say something to Jared."

"Uh, sure." He gave her a knowing look, bowing his head to her, his eyes seeming to plead with her to be gentle. "Take your time."

Once Cooper left the room, she had Jared's full attention. Her heart pounded in her chest, her eyes stung and the words were hard to come by. "Jared, I'm…sorry. This isn't going to work."

"What isn't?" His hand froze where he'd been cleaning the blood off his face.

"You and me." She managed a tiny smile.

"Bella, you don't know what you're saying."

"I do know what I'm saying. I'm saying…we're over."

"What, because of this?" His voice rose. He tossed the towel aside and stood, but his wounded leg gave way. He collapsed back on the bed.

Her heart bled, seeing him that way. He braced his elbows on the bed and stayed put. "I can't do this again," she said. "I've been down this road before. I've already lost one good man."

"Bella, come on. You're not gonna lose me. I'm here. I'm fine. I couldn't let that dog die."

"But you could've taken your car and driven a little slower. You could've been more cautious with your life. Every time Paul went up in his chopper, I worried. But he was doing his job, supporting his family. It's what he knew. And when he died, I was crushed. He left me a lonely widow with a child to raise on my own. It's taken me a long time to get to this place in my life."

"I'm not going to let you go."

"You can't stop me. I'm not one to criticize anyone's life choices. Lord knows my father did that to me to the point of suffocation. He tried to run my life and take away my own dreams, my own passions. I won't do that to you. No matter how much I care about you, we're not a good fit."

"I say we are."

"No. You're not what Sienna and I need."

His gaze burned right through her. "Not true, Bella. You know how good we are together. All three of us."

Oh, God. His words destroyed her. She wanted to believe him, to trust him, but she had Sienna to think about. She had to protect her from another loss. It was better to end it here and now. "There's more I have to tell you and you'll be less inclined to want me around once you hear it."

"There's nothing you can say—"

"I've been lying to you."

He blinked and gave her a dubious look. "What are you talking about?"

"I promised your mother I would tell you. And I meant to right away, but then Sienna got sick—"

"My mother?" His brows furrowed, his expression growing dim. That and the blood caking on his face made him appear dangerous. He was, to her well-being. "Bella, what does she have to do with this?"

"My name's not Bella. My real name is Francesca Isabella Forte. I'm heiress to the Forte Foods empire. Your mother recognized me. I'd met her once, a long time ago."

"Where?" he demanded.

"In San Francisco…where I grew up. I only came to Dallas to spend time with my friend Amy. And then I met you."

He pushed a hand through his hair. "I can't believe this."

It killed her to see his utter disappointment, the admiration he held for her rapidly fading. The loss hit her in the pit of her stomach and she felt the blood drain from her face. How would she ever get over Jared Stone?

She went on to explain. "I'm estranged from my father, and I've been… I've been hiding out here at Stone Ridge Ranch. Trying to make a new start."

His eyes shot fully open. "So you've been lying to me about everything?"

"I'm terribly sorry, Jared. But my father cut me off, or so I thought, and I needed to—"

He stood now, on his own. Pain lined his face and she cringed. He could barely hold himself up, yet he remained standing, favoring his wounded leg. "You needed what? To lie and deceive me? Give me a run for my money? Oh, no, maybe not that. Since you're loaded," he said, raising his voice. "Here I thought I was giving you a home, a job, a place to raise Sienna and all the while…what? You were playing a sick game with me."

"No, it's nothing like that. It's about Sienna. I really thought she was in danger."

"From who?"

"My father. He threatened to take her away from me, to sue me for custody. I panicked and ran. I've been through a lot this past year and I—"

Jared stared at her and began shaking his head. "Are you really a widow?"

"God yes, I wouldn't lie about something like that. Everything I told you about my life before was true."

"You lied about everything else. You didn't trust me. You didn't tell me the truth. And you know how much I *hate* liars."

A shudder ran through her. He was comparing her to Helene, a woman who'd broken his heart and made him wary and closed off. Now he equated her with that awful, cheating woman.

Her emotions high, tears spilled down her cheeks. She never wanted to hurt Jared. She still loved him, but now, even friendship would be too much to ask of him. "I… I couldn't take the risk."

"I'll never be able to trust you." His eyes grew cold, hard. She'd never seen that look on his face before. "I thought you were perfect. My perfect angel."

She didn't have to say she wasn't. That had become abundantly clear.

"You saved my life and I'll always be grateful…" His voice trailed off and he fell back onto the bed, his shoulders slumped. "We were never meant to be."

"No, I know that now. But, Jared, I really didn't want it to end this way. I had planned to tell you the truth."

He snorted in disbelief.

"I really did." Her daughter was her primary concern, and she couldn't subject Sienna to Jared's reckless ways. Even if he could ever forgive her, they wouldn't work. They wanted different things in life. Heartbroken, she had to face facts.

There was no way back from this.

Dread pulsed in the pit of her stomach. "I guess we'll be moving out."

He put his head down and nodded. "Do you have a place, *Francesca*?"

Hearing her real name fall from his lips stymied her. She prayed for strength. "I don't know what I'll do, but I have to go back to San Francisco. I can't hide away any longer. I have to make some hard decisions."

He nodded again. "I'm only concerned for Sienna's sake," he said, unable to hide his bitterness. "I'd like to say goodbye to her."

A lump formed in her throat. "Of course."

She stared at him for a long while. He refused to meet her eyes. There was nothing left between them, and it hurt like hell to admit it. "I'm terribly sorry," she repeated. "Goodbye, Jared."

He said nothing as she walked out of the room.

A loud crashing sound startled her. It was glass breaking against a wall. Jared's vivid curses reached her ears.

She cringed but kept on walking, putting one foot in front of the other, feeling just as shattered as the lamp Jared had just destroyed.

Bella glanced out the study window at her father's mansion. The day was gloomy and gray, matching her mood. Christmas was three days away, but she wished like crazy it would be over already. She put on a happy face for Sienna, making a big deal about her "gampa's" Christmas tree, all snowy white and flushed with beautifully wrapped presents underneath.

She'd agreed to spend the holidays with her father and that they'd mutually try to patch up their differences. After that, she intended to find a place of her own.

Poor Sienna was confused. She'd settled in nicely at the ranch and though they'd only lived there a few weeks she still mentioned "Tared" often.

And it broke Bella's heart.

She still remembered Jared's near tearful goodbye to Sienna. He'd given her her Christmas gift early, a stuffed toy palomino horse with a thick golden mane and a saddle. Sienna slept with the darn thing at night.

Now they were back in Pacific Heights, yet her heart was in Texas with a handsome rancher with dark blond hair and incredible blue eyes.

"How're you doing?" Yvonne said, coming into the room.

"I'm…okay."

Yvonne glanced at the papers strewed around her desk. "You're still at it? I'm glad to see you haven't given up on your dream."

"Thanks, Yvonne." They'd had a nice long conversation the other day and cleared the air. Yvonne wasn't a threat to her, as Bella had once believed. She was in her corner, and Bella found she'd been overly hard on her father's wife over the years. She'd apologized, hoping it was enough. Yvonne had a good heart. "I'd go crazy if I didn't have something to do right now."

"Marco says tomorrow he's taking you out to look for a place to lease…for your restaurant."

"Yes, he is. He's actually being quite good about it. But I doubt we'll have much luck, being so close to the holiday and all. People have other things on their mind." Now that her trust fund was available to her, she had the resources to pursue her dream.

"I can see that you do."

"I do. It's just that… I'm not sure of anything anymore. I've been going over my recipes and all. But am I ready to open up my own restaurant? I doubt it."

"You're hurting, Francesca."

"Yes." She wasn't going to deny it. Yvonne now knew everything. "It was hopeless from the start, but I can't deny my feelings. I'm in love."

"Nothing's hopeless when there's love involved."

She shrugged. "Jared was furious with me. He practically kicked me out of his house."

"After you broke up with him."

"I know. I did. But…but…"

"You know you can try to speak to him. See if he's cooled down yet."

"No, I can't. He's not a good fit for me. I need stability in my life. I need a man I can count on. I told you about the incident with Jared taking Sienna on that horse. It shaved years off my life seeing Sienna so frightened. No, Jared and I are too different. We want different things in life."

Yvonne took her hand and squeezed. "I think you'll find a way. You're strong, Francesca. Just like someone else I know."

Bella smiled. Maybe Yvonne, with the shapely figure and long blond hair, wasn't a mother figure to her, but they could be friends, and that went a long way in making her feel better. "Thanks. I want to make this a good holiday for Sienna. I'm trying…"

Jared sat in the great room in Cooper's house, watching a football game. Lauren had taken pity on him and invited him over to dinner. His face was a mess, but he'd let his beard grow to hide the scrapes. His leg still ached like a son of a bitch from his most recent crash. But nothing compared to the emptiness in his heart. He was hollowed out inside and pretty bad company.

Lauren sat next to him, offering him a plate of home-made cookies, while Cooper helped Marie with the dishes.

"No thanks," Jared said.

"Hey, when a pregnant woman works all afternoon baking, you need to humor her."

"Okay. Thanks," he said, grabbing one chocolate-chunk cookie. His appetite lately was on the blink. He wanted a Bella-original meal and every time he would think it, he'd cuss himself out for being a fool. If only he could stop thinking about her. Bella, Francesca, whatever the hell she was calling herself lately.

"Coercing you into eating a cookie wasn't the reason I invited you over," Lauren said. "I have news."

"What kind of news?"

"Bella called me. We had a long talk. She's concerned about you. Wanted to know how you were feeling."

"Like crap. But she doesn't need to know that. I'm… not interested."

"You don't want to know what she had to say?"

"No."

"She put Sienna on the phone and she asked for Tared."

Jared's eyes squeezed shut. He was on his third bottle of beer and ready to gulp down the whole damn six-pack. "That's hitting below the belt."

"Yeah, a real sucker punch to your gut. I'm that good."

Jared eyed his sister-in-law. "And I thought you liked me."

"I do. I want you to be happy."

"I can't get over how she deceived me, Lauren. It's like

déjà vu all over again. But I thought Bella was different. I called her my angel. I thought…we had a chance."

"She is different. Think about this. She didn't deceive you to cause you harm. She didn't want anything from you. She actually had to be talked into taking the job. With her father threatening to sue her for custody, her back was up against the wall. Can you imagine how frightened she was? Marco Forte is a powerful man and she didn't know who to trust. She was protecting Sienna. I can understand that. I haven't met my baby yet, but I'm already a protective mama bear when it comes to my child." Lauren put her hand on her baby bump. "There isn't anything I wouldn't do for the ones I love."

"It doesn't matter anyway. She doesn't approve of me."

Lauren laughed, a hearty chuckle that rankled his nerves. "I can't blame her for that. We're all down on your hobby. Why can't you just build things, like Cooper does?"

"I'm not Cooper, that's why."

"But you're not stupid, either."

"I'm not too sure about that," Cooper said, walking in and handing him another beer.

"Shut the f-up, Coop."

Lauren shook her head. "Cooper you're not helping."

His brother plunked down on a chair and faced his wife. "Did you ask him yet?"

"I haven't gotten to that," Lauren answered.

"Gotten to what?" Jared asked.

"To asking if you're in love with Bella. Because Lauren is sure she's in love with you."

"Cooper!" Lauren shot Coop a hot glare.

"God, you two. Of course I love her. Why else would I be so damn—"

"Idiotic?" Cooper's brows lifted.

"Hurt?" Lauren suggested.

"Pissed off. Yeah, I'm pissed off, because…damn it. She broke up with me and left."

"You didn't stop her."

"How could I? She betrayed me."

"That again," Cooper grumbled.

"If you really believe she betrayed you, then there's no sense talking any more about it," Lauren said. "But if there's wiggle room inside your head, maybe you should rethink it."

That's all he had been doing lately…thinking. God, he missed Bella and that kid of hers. His house was like a morgue and it'd only been a few days.

Cooper's cell phone rang and he answered it. "Hi, Mom."

Jared began shaking his head. He didn't need a tongue-lashing from his mother tonight. But Cooper looked straight at him and smiled. "Yeah, he's right here." He tossed him the phone. "Mom wants to talk to you."

Jared mouthed a curse at Coop and then answered the phone. He was in for it. His mother wouldn't mince words. She'd been on his case since the first accident. It didn't matter that he was a grown man, worth millions, he was still her little boy worthy of a scolding. Crap. He got up from the sofa and walked out of the room. Seeing his brother gloating was too damn much to take right now.

An hour later, after downing two cups of coffee at Coop's house, Jared drove home at a snail's pace, needing the time to gather his thoughts. When he pulled into the garage, he cut the engine on his Jeep and sat there. Thinking. Special white-tile flooring and all the tools he'd ever need to work on his cars made this a very special place. His vehicles had all the bells and whistles, the finest money could buy. Though his Harley was being repaired and his

Lamborghini was gone, all the rest of his collection shone sterling-bright, beckoning him to take them out.

Pick me and I'll give you the thrill of your life.

His phone rang. It was Blake again, manager of his speedboat race team, and Jared knew what he wanted. It was time to pay the entry fees for the upcoming spring races.

Jared let the call go to voice mail for the third time today.

Then an idea popped into his head and he strode over to his hot red Corvette.

Bella finished wrapping Sienna's final Christmas present and hid it in her bedroom closet. Her daughter understood that Santa would be arriving first thing tomorrow morning, with his special gifts to her, as much as a twenty-three-month-old child could understand. Yet she delighted in the spirit of the holiday, the decorations, the holly and a Christmas tree with lights that changed colors with the click of a remote control.

Bella and Yvonne baked cookies and fudge with Sienna's help. Her daughter mostly licked the spoons and grinned like a monkey afterward. Seeing Sienna enjoy herself so much, a tiny bit of holiday cheer seeped into Bella. Things weren't perfect, but her father had really come around and, for now, she would take it as a small miracle.

Bella descended the stairs and found her father in the parlor, playing blocks on the floor with Sienna. Yvonne had just come in holding a wrapped Christmas box. "This was just delivered. It's something for you, Francesca." She handed her the box.

"Thanks."

She sat on the sofa and turned the box around on all sides, shaking it a bit, curious who had sent it. She lifted the lid carefully and moved the wrapping paper aside. A copy of the *Dallas Tribune* was inside. She shook her head and lifted it out. "See Page Three" was written diagonally across the front page in big, bold letters.

"What is this?" she muttered, turning the pages. And then she found the headline: Dallas Tycoon Jared Stone's Charity Auction.

She blinked, her hands trembling. She continued to read on.

"What is it?" Yvonne asked after a few impatient moments.

"It's an article about how Jared is auctioning off all his cars and motorcycles and will be developing a new foundation to benefit children's causes. All of the proceeds of the auction will go to the foundation."

Bella continued reading and then she gasped. "Oh!"

"What is it?" Yvonne asked. Her father's eyes were on her, too.

"Jared's naming the new f-foundation..." Bella choked up, unable to speak for a second. She held back tears. "He's naming it... Sienna's Hope."

"Sounds like the man's got some smarts after all," her father said.

"That's...amazing, Francesca." Yvonne smiled. Then she glanced at Marco and the two seemed to have some secret communication.

"What?" Bella asked, still shaking.

"There's another gift waiting for you and Sienna outside."

Emotions roiled in the pit of her stomach. "There is?"

"Yes, and it's pretty cold out there, so put on your coats and hurry."

"What's going on?" Obviously it was something Yvonne and Marco were privy to.

"Christmas comes early sometimes," Yvonne said, ushering her into her coat while her father put on Sienna's quilted jacket.

They nearly shoved her out the front door. She glanced back and Yvonne grinned and shut the door in her face. Bella took Sienna's hand. "Apparently, little one, there's a surprise waiting for us out here."

She climbed down the steps and walked along the path leading to the front gate.

Outside her father's house stood a living, breathing Jared Stone next to a pearl-white SUV.

Her heart pounding in her ears, she absorbed the sight of him. Oh, how she'd missed him. Before she could utter a word, Sienna let go of her hand. "Tared!" She raced toward him and lifted her arms. "Up."

"Hello, little angel." He picked her up and kissed her cheek. It was a solid sight, the two of them together. It seemed so right.

Bella walked up to him. "Jared?"

He set Sienna down and immediately came closer to graze her cheek with the palm of his hand. It was cold outside, yet the contact sizzled, warming her up inside. Was she silly to hope?

"God, you're beautiful. I've missed you like crazy, Bella."

"I've missed you, too. But what are you doing here?"

"I came for you," he said as naturally as breathing. "I realized once you left, nothing much mattered to me. I don't need to catch up to life. Or race toward it. I need a life. With you."

"So…you've forgiven me for lying to you?" This was all so unbelievable. More than she could've ever imagined, but she had to ask.

"Let's say I understand why you did it now, Bella. I

can't fault you for wanting to protect little Sienna. I just wish you'd trusted me."

"Oh, Jared. If I could do it all over again, I would. I know the kind of man you are. You would've protected us. And what you did, naming your foundation after Sienna, just about destroyed me. It was incredible and thoughtful. It means so much to me."

He took her hand and held it tight. "I'm glad it made you happy. That's all I want to do. I love you, Bella. You *are* my angel. No matter what, I don't want to live without you. I've given up my race cars for this. There's a car seat already installed."

Tears rimmed her eyes as she gazed at the SUV. "There is?"

He nodded.

"And you won't be sorry later?" she asked.

"No, never. I've realized how that part of my life is over, Bella. I'm gonna live my life in the present and not try to outrace the future. I swear to you. I only want you and Sienna in my life. The two of you are all I need. I called and explained that to your father and his wife. I think they know I only want your happiness."

Jared and her father had spoken? She was a little stunned. "And Father…agreed?"

"He wasn't thrilled, but yes, in the end, he wants what's best for you."

"I love you, Jared. And you're all I need, too."

"You do? You love me?" He grinned, a daring, blue-eyed pirate's grin. How could she have ever thought of living without this man?

"Will you come home to the ranch with me, Bella? Be my wife?"

"You're asking me to marry you?"

He nodded. "Will you, Bella?"

Joy consumed her. She had no doubts anymore. "Jared, yes. Yes. I'll be your wife."

His mouth came down on hers in a fiery all-consuming kiss and she moaned from the sheer pleasure. Oh, how she'd missed him. How she couldn't wait to marry him.

"Best Christmas present ever," he whispered and then lifted Sienna up again, the three of them huddling together.

"For me, too," she said, squeezing him tight.

He pulled away slightly to look into her eyes. "Bella, I don't want you to give up on your dreams. If you want to write a cookbook or open a restaurant, I'll support your decision."

"You will?" She beamed inside. Jared would always be by her side. And she wanted to do both, but not right now. Now she just wanted to go home to Stone Ridge. "You mean you'll still let me experiment on you with my new recipes?"

"Are you kidding? Secretly meeting up with the Midnight Contessa is the favorite part of my day. I look forward to it."

She laughed. "Me, too."

Those late-night encounters with Jared were scorching hot. She couldn't wait until they could be together that way again, meshing their bodies, melding their minds, making incredible love.

"Promise me one thing, Bella. You'll always be my own personal chef."

"Always, my love."

It would be an easy promise to keep.

* * * * *

LONE STAR
SECRETS

CAT SCHIELD

One

Will Sanders blasted through the glass doors of the sheriff's office and squinted as he emerged into the bright sunlight. The September heat rising off the pavement was nothing compared to the anger boiling inside him. Still no word on Richard Lowell's whereabouts and, with the manhunt showing no signs of ending any time soon, Will was fed up with the lack of progress.

The son of the bitch had tried to kill him. Then, while impersonating Will, Rich had taken advantage of four women—that they knew of—robbing them of their money, dignity and leaving two of them pregnant. Lowell had murdered Will's great friend and trusted confidant, Jason Phillips, stolen millions and continued to roam free. How many more lives was he going to ruin before getting his just deserts?

Hands shaking with rage, Will ripped the keys from his pocket and hit the button that unlocked his white Land Rover. For a second the color red glazed the landscape around him. Will lost his balance as his left foot caught on an uneven bit of pavement and the stumble cleared his head somewhat. He paused with his hand on the SUV's hood and sucked in a deep breath. Losing control wasn't going to help. As reason began to reassert itself, he released the air from his lungs, letting it hiss between his teeth. Another calming inhalation and his vision began to return.

Since waking up in Mexico with a blinding headache and scattered memories of what had occurred, his emotions had become volatile. Some days when he looked in the mirror, he didn't recognize himself. Before leaving on that fateful trip with Rich, he'd had everything a man could ask for. And it had taken that huge wakeup call to realize he'd taken his friends, family and good fortune for granted.

That period was over, he reminded himself again and again, hoping the litany would keep his demons at bay.

He needed to stay calm because logic and clear thinking would win the day. He couldn't afford to allow his runaway emotions to lead him to act in ways that would be counterproductive.

Sliding behind the wheel, he pulled out his phone and queued up his favorite contacts. His heart gave a little bump as Megan's name appeared at the top of his list. Speaking of letting his emotions drive his actions...

Things between them had grown strained since they'd shared that explosive night of passion in the aftermath of Jason's memorial service. They continued to talk a couple times a week, but their conversations veered from anything personal, revolving around the lack of progress in finding Lowell or how Jason's daughter, Savannah, was doing now that she'd lost her father. Megan loved her seven-year-old niece dearly and tried to spend as much time as possible with the little girl. Will knew it broke her heart whenever Savannah asked for her daddy.

For about a week now Will had been waiting for Megan

to open the door to them finally hashing out what had happened between them, but she was staunchly avoiding the topic. It was as if she wanted to forget it had ever happened. Will hoped that wasn't the case. It sure wasn't for him.

Maybe if he'd treated the encounter differently. Megan deserved to be wooed with expensive dinners and slow seduction. Instead, he'd come at her like a freight train, overwhelmed by the raw, primal need to comfort her as she grieved for her brother. They'd come together in a rush of heat and shared pain before establishing any sort of framework they could build a relationship on.

That was on him. Will hadn't been thinking clearly or logically as she'd torn at his clothes and he'd slid his fingers up her thigh. Instead, he'd succumbed to his body's call. The sensuality of her lithe body as he drove her wild with his mouth or the sounds she made as she came. She'd been glorious in that moment, and reliving it made him want more. Made him want to take her every way his overactive imagination could conceive. Hard up against a wall, gently in the deep tub in his master suite. In the backseat of his car like a couple randy teenagers.

Blood pooled in his loins as the list grew and he slammed his fist against the steering wheel to distract himself from the beginnings of an erection pressing against his zipper. It didn't work. Hands shaking with need he closed his eyes and surrendered to the heat burning through him like a wildfire.

Yet even as his body was battered by desire, Will recognized the need to be cautious as he ventured forward. Just because lust had brought them together in spectacular fashion didn't mean they could make a lasting relationship work.

Their situation was beyond complicated. Two strangers who'd been requested by law officials to maintain the legal aspect of their marriage for as long as Rich remained at large. They didn't live together and, except for occasional phone conversations and encounters among family and friends, hadn't spent all that much time together.

Yet each time he saw her, Will grappled with a growing ache to be with her, to have her intimately tangled in his life. A shift in his perception had taken place. He no longer viewed her as merely Jason's beautiful younger sister, but had started to think in terms of *my wife*.

Unfortunately, she wasn't really his. Not in the way he was coming to want her to be.

She'd married an imposter, and Will continuously wondered if the sight of his face, so similar to the man who'd stolen his identity, was one she despised. She refused to discuss Rich. No doubt she felt the same humiliation and fury at being tricked that weighed on Will. Would she forever glimpse his face and be reminded of all the terrible things that had happened?

The truth was, he had a ton of things he wanted to discover about Megan. Putting aside his urgency to glide his hands over her naked flesh, feast on her mouth and plumb her richest fantasies, he wanted to learn about her dreams and aspirations, to explore her goals for her company and figure out why he couldn't stop thinking about her.

So what tied his hands when it came to puzzling out these and many other questions? Why except for that frantic, passionate encounter following Jason's memorial service, hadn't he acted on his irresistible attraction to Megan? In part because the fierce physical pull between them threw his emotions into a tailspin. When he'd first returned home, he'd intended to bide his time until Rich was caught and then secured a divorce or annulment and never looked back. But long before the night of stormy passion, when he'd held her in his arms and tasted her hunger, he begun dreading the time when he'd have to let Megan go. She'd slipped beneath his skin and ignited his lust in a way no woman had ever done before. At the same time, he wasn't sure how to hold on to her or even if he *should*.

Whatever else Will wanted, foremost was for Megan to be happy. Already he'd been too late to save her from a sham marriage, and Jason's death was a burden he'd never put down. He'd trusted Lowell. He'd believed they'd been *friends*. Will's bad judgment left a tainted residue in his psyche that couldn't be washed away by wishing or throwing money at the problems Rich had created. People had been hurt. And it was all Will's fault because he'd been responsible for Rich coming to Royal.

His phone came to life in his hand. Startled, he glanced down at the screen before answering.

"Hey, Lucy, what's up?"

"Just wanted to remind you that I'm heading out of town for a few days to deliver a couple horses and to check on some rescues in Houston."

His stepsister was a talented horse trainer, specializing in rescues. She and her four-year-old son shared the main house at the Ace in the Hole with Will.

"I hadn't forgotten," he lied, realizing how preoccupied he'd become in the week since Lowell's secret stash had been discovered.

To make the millions he'd plundered something he could easily conceal and move, Rich had converted the money to gold bars and hidden them outside Royal. No one understood why he hadn't taken them with him when he'd fled months ago, but everyone agreed that he'd be back for the loot.

For many days Will had been convinced the discovery meant the imposter's capture was imminent, but as the days dragged on with no sign of Rich, Will grew more and more frustrated.

"Are you still taking Brody?" he asked.

"The trip is going to go longer than I originally thought, so I decided it would be better if he stayed in Royal."

"Sounds good. He and I will have a blast while you're gone."

"Ah…" Lucy began, sounding reluctant. "Actually, I was going to have him stay with Jesse and Jillian. Brody really loves being around Mac and you've got a lot going on…"

Jesse was Lucy's older biological brother and Will's stepbrother. He'd dedicated himself to running the family ranch, providing Will the freedom to pursue his passion for the family business. Since returning home, Will had watched Jesse fall in love with another of Lowell's victims, Jillian Norris. A former Las Vegas showgirl, she'd become pregnant with Mackenzie after a one-night stand with Rich while he'd been impersonating Will. It had been her emails and phone calls to Will in the weeks before the fated fishing trip to Mexico that had led to his being attacked and nearly killed by his former best friend.

"Sure," Will said into the awkward silence, making sure none of the gut-hit he'd just taken came through in his voice. "I understand. Tell Jesse and Jillian that I'm available if they need any help taking care of Brody." Although even as he made the offer, he doubted anything would come of it. "Have a safe trip."

"Thanks. I'll see you in a week."

He hung up the phone, trying to shake off the rejection that fouled his mood like cobwebs. In the months he'd been in Mexico, his whole focus had been on what he'd had to do to return home. He'd been eager to return to his life, focusing on close relationships with family and friends, the success he was having with his business ventures and general satisfaction with how great his life was.

Now, after spending months staying out of sight, watching those around him live their lives to the fullest—falling in love, being actively engaged in the world—he was feeling more isolated than ever. Once again, Will queued up his favorite contacts and stared at Megan's name.

He wanted to reach out to her. She'd become important to him these last few months that they'd been thrown together while Richard Lowell was on the loose. Will's brows came together. Why was he lying to himself? Playing it cool about his feelings for Megan to others was one thing, but denying the fierce desire that lashed at him whenever she was around was just plain idiotic.

Pain bloomed in his chest as he recalled their lovemaking after Jason's memorial service. She was a fire in his blood, an addiction he never wanted to be free of. The desperate hunger in their kisses and near frantic coupling had transported him to a whole new level of passion.

Was he getting in over his head with her? Obviously. His emotions were all over the place where she was concerned. Nor did he have a good idea how she felt about him. That heated, wild encounter had been about coping with a loss neither one of them wanted to face alone. He shouldn't expect that something born of grief could be the start of anything.

Yet for him it had been.

His intimate connection with Megan that night had launched a drumbeat of longing. Will wanted to have what his brother had found with Jillian. What Cole had found with Dani. Of the five women invited to his funeral as his supposed heirs, only Megan wasn't with the love of her life. Had that man been Rich Lowell, pretending to be Will? Would she have fallen for Rich himself? He'd not asked any of these questions of her, unsure how her answers would affect him.

Before he could question his motives, Will pulled up his app and typed a message.

Cora Lee planning BBQ at the ranch next Saturday. We'd love to see you there.

As soon as he sent the message, he was overwhelmed by a sense of anticipation. No matter what his jumbled emotions, he and Megan were stuck with each other for the time being. In an ironic twist, Will realized that part of him hoped Lowell would continue to elude the authorities for a little while longer. Because until he was caught, Will could enjoy as much time with Megan as he could handle. He caught himself smiling for the first time in hours because when it came to the stunning Megan Phillips-Sanders, Will could handle a whole lot.

The sky outside her office windows was well on its way to becoming a vivid midnight blue by the time Megan finished looking over the numbers for this year's fall shoe collection. Her staff had outdone themselves, and pride bloomed in her chest as she contemplated yet another triumphant season.

The success of her company had startled everyone in her family, herself included. Megan had started Royals Shoes to get out from beneath her brothers' shadows. When she'd voiced her intention to get into the luxury shoe business, they'd initially been stuck on their perception of her as the tomboy who'd spent her childhood trying to keep up with her older siblings. That, she could understand. They were her big brothers, after all. But that they'd doubted her ability to start a company and make a success of it had stung.

In a state like Texas and a town like Royal, bigger was always better. Ranches, fortunes, personalities. It was hard to stand out in an environment where achievement was the norm rather than the exception. Striving to be noticed by her family had preoccupied Megan from the time she was old enough to recognize that her brothers were her parents' pride and joy. Aaron and Jason had been at the top of their respective classes. And, as if that wasn't enough for her to keep up with, they'd both excelled at sports, as well.

Megan sank into the leather couch in her office and lifted her feet onto the glass coffee table. The sight of her company's stiletto pump with its wallpaper-inspired, broad black-and-white stripe and crystal-embellished buckle made her smile. Recognizing that to do well Royals Shoes had to stand out in a crowded luxury shoe market, Megan had decided that every single pair of her shoes would have a wow factor.

Her cell phone buzzed. A glance at the screen revealed a text from Dani Moore. The two women had struck up a friendship in their teens when Dani had been a freshman and Megan had acted as her senior buddy to smooth the transition into the academic and social challenges presented by high school. Despite the difference in their ages, they'd stayed friends through the intervening years separated by distance and time.

Can't make it tomorrow at 2.

Megan read the text and heaved a disappointed sigh. Between Dani's work schedule at the Glass House, her new relationship with Cole and her active role as a parent to twins, her free time was slim. In anticipation of enticing her friend to take a little time for herself, Megan had recently gifted Dani a pair of shoes, hoping it would inspire her to come dress shopping for something to wear to the engagement party for Megan's older brother Aaron and Kasey Monroe, Will's former assistant turned nanny to seven-year-old Savannah.

Megan had been a little surprised at how fast the brilliant, driven Aaron had adapted to being solely responsible for his brother's child. Of course, it was quite possible that Kasey had been the driving force behind his abrupt domestication.

She gave a little sigh as she pondered the recent spate of romances spawned surrounding the shake-up in their community thanks to Rich Lowell's impersonation of Will. In fact, Megan and Will were the only two who'd proved immune to love in the months since his return. Not that she was interested in having a love life after what Rich had put her through. Plus, it was a little challenging for either of them to succumb to a new romance when she and Will had been asked by the authorities to maintain the appearance of being married.

As soon as she responded to Dani, explaining that she understood and soliciting other times later in the week, Megan opened the text she'd received earlier from Will. Her pulse gave a familiar start as she read the simple message.

Cora Lee planning BBQ at the ranch next Saturday. We'd love to see you there.

Megan stared at the words for several minutes, wishing she knew how to respond to what appeared to be a casual invitation. Obviously he was being polite and it infuriated her that it annoyed her. She didn't want to recognize that what she wanted was for him to indicate his interest in resurrecting their passionate encounter from a week earlier. As electric as that night had been, Megan had become self-conscious around him, making their interaction seem overly polite and awkward.

Or maybe she was just imagining things. Will wasn't behaving differently. He was the same solicitous man he'd been since discovering he had a wife. He recognized that she'd been duped by Richard Lowell and, although neither of them understood the legal ramifications of their sticky situation, he'd understood that she was as much a victim as he was.

With a heavy sigh, Megan stood and gathered her purse and briefcase. It was late and she needed to go home. She hated returning to her big empty house on the edge of town. What had once felt like a symbol of her success now reminded her of the biggest mistake she'd ever made. Some days she wanted to set a torch to the place and burn it to the ground, but the memories of her marriage to a man who'd lied and manipulated her were deeply embedded in her psyche and there was no escape.

After setting the alarm, Megan let herself out the front door. Since the building was accessed by electronic locks, she could sail through the door without pausing to secure it. Before her, the small parking lot lay in deepening shadows. Near the far edge sat her Porsche, its carmine red darkened to a maroon blob. She loved the sporty car and drove with the top down as often as possible. Tonight, however, she wasn't in the mood to let the hot Texas wind blow her long brown hair into knots.

A sudden wave of weariness assailed her, brought on by a dip in her blood sugar. She'd neglected to eat dinner again and had not had anything since breakfast fourteen hours ago. No wonder she was feeling tired.

Her steps slowed as she dug into her purse for her keys. The damned things were always getting lost in the bottom of her bag. Finally her fingers closed around them and she eased a relieved sigh from her lungs. A second later her breath hitched.

"Megan."

Her head swung toward the familiar voice. *Rich*. Heart hammering, she stopped in her tracks and rotated her gaze in his direction. He was dressed in dark tones, gray or perhaps black, the color making him barely distinguishable from the shadows filling the parking lot. From the way his clothes fit his powerful physique, she guessed he wore one of the expensive suits he favored. Leave it to Richard Lowell to be impeccably tailored while on the run.

She was struck once again how much his features matched Will's. Yet after getting to know the real Will Sanders these past few months, Megan couldn't believe she'd ever been taken in by this monster. And yet the proof that she had occupied her finger. How could she have been so stupid?

Shame flared, attacking her confidence even as her "husband" advanced from her right, moving to get between her and the Porsche. Too late she realized her danger. Terror blazed. What a fool she'd been to stay so late and then leave on her own.

"What are you doing here?" Despite her bone-chilling fear, she was proud of her strong tone. "What do you want?"

"I want you. The only reason I came back is to convince you to come away with me."

His words sent a spasm of revulsion through her. She rocked back, knowing there was nowhere to run. In her five-inch heels she'd never make it back to the building before he overtook her.

She stood her ground and made sure he couldn't see her fear. "What do you mean?"

"You're my wife. We belong together."

The deepening twilight made his expression hard to read, so Megan wasn't sure if he actually believed this or if he was enacting some twisted game to terrorize her.

"I'm not your wife."

Yet as bravely as she declared the words, she wasn't sure that was true. She'd married him. Richard Lowell. She might have sworn to love, honor and cherish Will Sanders, but she'd stood before this man, looked him in the eye and pledged to be with him forever. The reality had crippled Megan's confidence these last few months.

"You are," Rich countered, his tone harsh. "You love me."

"I fell in love with Will Sanders."

Was she imagining the rage transforming Rich or had she picked up on subtle body language, clues that made her brace for an act of violence. It wouldn't be the first time he'd put his hands on her.

Looking back over their time together, Megan wondered how she'd ever believed he could be Will. The two men were nothing alike. Yet she'd made one excuse for another for his mood swings and quick temper. She'd been a fool to avoid looking past the surface resemblance and not recognizing that this man's soul was tainted with poison.

"You fell in love with me. I was the man in your bed. The one you couldn't get enough of." He took several menacing steps in her direction. "Do you remember how you gasped my name as you came?"

Summoning her waning bravado, Megan declared, "I called Will's name. Not yours."

"I was Will. *Your* Will." His right hand balled into a fist but his arm remained rigid at his side. "The only Will Sanders who would have you."

Even as she absorbed Rich's verbal blow, Megan's instincts warned her to keep her attention on Rich's hands in case he made any sudden moves in her direction. She carefully shifted her stance and put her feet shoulder width apart for better balance. If he tried to grab her, she wanted to make sure she was ready to dodge.

"But you aren't Will Sanders," she declared, standing her ground. "And you're nothing like him."

Her instincts screamed at her to shut up. He was a murderer and she was alone in a dark parking lot with no one to come to her rescue.

"No. I'm better." Bragging about his superiority caused the tension to ease from Rich's posture but his tone remained razor-sharp. "I was always smarter than him. The difference between us was that I didn't get a fortune handed to me on a silver platter. I had to work for everything I got."

And Megan suspected that was where Rich's obsession began. Maybe this was something they had in common. She had endured her own bout of fascination with Will during high school. Only, in Rich's case, admiration had twisted into the darkest sort of jealousy.

"Why did you kill my brother?" While bringing up his crime was the height of foolishness, Megan needed answers.

"Jason asked too many questions and discovered too much."

"So you killed him." The declaration rasped from her raw throat as grief nearly overwhelmed her. "Are you planning on killing me, too?"

"I could never harm you. You belong to me."

"I don't *belong* to you," she shot back, the very idea filling her with dread. But then curiosity got the better of her once more. For months she'd brooded over why he'd picked her. Had he glimpsed some weakness and exploited it? "Was it all just a big game for you?"

He didn't answer but she sensed she'd surprised him. Whether by her question or the bitterness with which she'd delivered it, Megan didn't know.

"Come with me and I'll show you how important you are to me."

His cajoling tone transported her to those first days of their courtship when he'd swept aside her reservations with a barrage of romantic words and sweet gestures. Her treacherous heart began to pound. She knew her feelings for Rich were based on a farce, but opening herself to love had transformed her.

Where once she'd avoided romance and sentimentality, falling for "Will Sanders" had been magical and had filled her with wonder. To have it all eventually turn to dust had returned her heart to a Popsicle.

Megan shook her head. "You've lost your mind if you think I'd leave town with you."

Little by little during their exchange, Megan's right hand had been making slow progress toward the side pocket in her purse where she kept the pistol she'd bought in case of an encounter just like this one. Neither its compact size nor its pink-pearl grip detracted from the gun's reliability and stopping power. She'd bought the pistol in the days following Will's reappearance in Royal. Living alone and working late, she'd imagined this scenario hundreds of times, but now that she was here, Megan wondered if she was equipped to shoot Rich in cold blood.

"My life is here," she continued, thumbing off the safety and curving her fingers around the grip as Rich took a step in her direction.

"Your life is here…or is it all about Will?" Rich sneered. "You're a fool if you think he could ever love you. I've seen you with him and know why you haven't filed for divorce. You're hoping he'll eventually come to love you. But that won't happen."

"You don't know anything." Driven by emotions she couldn't define, Megan pulled out the gun and pointed at him. "Don't come any closer."

Rich's eyes widened satisfactorily before he began to laugh. "You're not seriously going to shoot me with that tiny thing?"

"I won't if you back off and let me go." She tried to ignore how badly her hands were shaking and hoped Rich wouldn't notice. "I'm not going anywhere with you."

"We'll see about that."

He took another step forward and, without thinking, she pulled the trigger. The explosion shattered the quiet night and shocked Megan. There was only ten feet between her and Rich—she'd consistently hit the target at the range from twice that distance—but she hadn't been aiming for the center of his body. When he spun to the left and before she could wonder if she'd struck him, Megan bolted for her car.

She didn't look back as she slid behind the wheel and fired up the engine, but as she put the car into gear, her door jerked open. Rich's wild eyes blazed down at her. Megan's heart hammered in her throat, blocking a cry. Instead of pulling the door closed, she shoved it away, banging it into Rich's lower half as she gunned the car. The scream of tires on pavement drowned out her panicked keening.

For a heartbeat Rich held on to the door as Megan pushed down on the accelerator and then he was gone. Panting from fright and exertion, she made a right-hand turn out of the parking lot, the momentum causing her door to slam shut.

Fortunately there was no traffic on the side road that led to Royals Shoes because Megan's only concern was to put as much distance between her and Rich as possible. She glanced at the pistol resting on the passenger seat. Thank goodness she'd bought the gun and practiced shooting it. Still, she couldn't believe she'd actually used it against Rich. And she'd hit him. Not badly, since he'd been able to chase her down and try to pull her out of her car. But she'd demonstrated her ability to take care of herself.

Megan couldn't settle on an emotion. Part of her rejoiced that she'd gotten away from a madman unscathed.

Yet another was shocked at her lack of remorse for having fired a gun at another human being. And deep down inside was the fear over what sort of monster Rich had turned her into.

As if on autopilot, her car negotiated the roads that led to the sheriff's office. She'd spent far too much time around police lately, but couldn't imagine heading home where she ran the risk of encountering Rich again before reporting that he'd tried to accost her.

"Call Will," she commanded to her car. As ringing poured through the expensive speakers, she fought to swallow the lump in her throat.

"Hey, Megan, I was just thinking about you." His deep voice penetrated the final thread holding her emotions under control and she started to shake.

"R-Rich…"

"Are you okay?" His concern came through loud and clear.

"He came after me."

A sharp curse and then, "Are you hurt?"

"No." She dragged in a ragged breath and shook her head. "I think I shot him."

Silence followed her declaration before Will spoke again. "Where are you?" The question came briskly, filled with impatience.

Ahead of her were the familiar downtown stores and the Royal Diner. Except for the diner, the buildings were dark, enhancing Megan's isolation.

"In my car." Her jaw was so stiff she was having trouble speaking. "Heading to the police station."

"I'll meet you there." A pause. When he next spoke, his tone was soft and heavy with worry. "You're sure he didn't hurt you?"

"Yes."

"I'll be there in ten minutes."

"Okay." Megan disconnected the call, shocked by how much better she felt. Will's support during this difficult time had never wavered. He was the rock she clung to in the whitewater that had become her life and she found herself relying on him more and more.

To her relief, a visitor spot was available right in front of the door leading into the sheriff's office. Megan came to an abrupt stop, the Porsche's front tires bumping against the curb. For a second she stayed where she was, car running while she scanned the sidewalk to make sure Rich wasn't moving to intercept her. Deciding he'd be a fool to track her to the station, Megan exited the car and hurried toward the building.

When she burst through the front door, tears burned her eyes. Damn. She hated giving in to the weakness. Her emotions were running away with her again and she must have looked a sight as she set her hands on the reception desk.

"Is Sheriff Battle here?" she asked the woman manning the front desk. "Richard Lowell just attacked me outside my office."

The woman's eyes widened but her voice remained calm and professional. "He's not, but Special Agent Bird is in the conference room. I'll get him for you."

Megan took a seat on one of the cold, plastic chairs in the reception area and clasped her purse on her lap to keep her hands from shaking. At this hour the sheriff's office was nearly deserted and a dull despair swept over her as adrenaline ebbed from her system. Chills racked her body. With each minute that ticked by, her muscles grew stiff until she doubted she could stand without falling over.

What was taking the FBI guy so long?

The front door opened and Will stepped into view. A strikingly handsome man whose height and powerful physique commanded attention, his features were set in granite as his vivid green eyes scanned the immediate vicinity with feverish intent. A small, incoherent noise vibrated in her throat an instant before his gaze swung in her direction.

"Megan."

A single word. Just her name. But relief erupted like a fireworks display and suddenly everything was all right now that he was here with her.

Two

Will's entire world had narrowed to razor-sharp focus the instant he'd heard Megan's shaky voice on the phone. When she'd called, he'd been working in his office at Spark Energy Solutions, combing through the financials for more missing money.

Now, as he stormed through the door of the police station and spied Megan sitting whole and unharmed in the reception area, the knot in his gut slowly began to unravel. But when she glanced his way and her expression shifted into delight, it was as if a series of explosions began in his chest.

"Are you really okay?" he demanded, moving to kneel before her. He reached out and trailed his fingers gently over her pale cheek.

She caught his hand and drew it away from her face. "I'm fine." Her steady tone warned him not to coddle her. "Really. He never touched me." A smile ghosted her lips. "If anyone was damaged, it was him."

"Did you really shoot him?"

"Yes."

"I didn't realize you owned a gun."

As Will shifted onto the seat beside her, Megan opened her purse and gave him a peek at the contents. Sure enough, resting between her wallet and a polka-dot makeup pouch was a small pistol with a pink-pearl grip. He couldn't help himself. Will grinned.

"It's a 38-caliber Sig Sauer P238." Seeing his amusement, her eyes glinted combatively. "Wayne at the gun range describes it as a ballistic bauble."

It was hard to take the deadly weapon seriously when it was tricked out in such a way. No doubt Rich had underestimated the gun—and the woman who'd wielded it—and that had cost him.

"How does it handle?"

"Nice. There's not much recoil and the pull is about five pounds. I've gotten to where I can put nine bullets in a three-inch target at twenty feet."

"Impressive."

"Mrs. Sanders," Special Agent Bird said, coming toward them, his hand extended.

"Special Agent Bird," Megan murmured, getting to her feet and taking his hand.

The FBI agent was a thin man with a thick mustache who looked more suited to pursuing cases involving money laundering and cyber crime than getting his hands dirty with terrorism or murder. After spending long hours with the agent in connection with the funds stolen from SES and the Texas Cattleman's Club treasury, Will knew the man was well versed in the intricacies of Rich's money trail.

"I hear you had an encounter with Richard Lowell tonight."

"In the parking lot outside my building."

Will had risen at the same time and stood at Megan's

back, scowling at the special agent. Despite his ever-in-creasing irritation, Will stayed silent. He'd already spoken his piece earlier in the day and venting wouldn't help anyone at this point.

"Why don't you come to the conference room and tell me what happened," Agent Bird said, gesturing toward the hallway that led deeper into the building.

Megan nodded and began to move in his wake. She hadn't done more than shift her weight forward, however, before reaching back for Will's hand.

"Will you come along?" she asked, biting her lip in an uncharacteristic display of uncertainty. "I can't do this without you."

Mascara smudges and rubbed-off lipstick were testament to Megan's upset. Only one other time had Will seen her so out of sorts. Jason's memorial service. The night they'd made love. Then, like now, glimpsing her vulnerability made him long to pull her into his arms and kiss her worries away, but this was neither the time nor the place for a display of affection.

Too much remained unspoken between them since that fateful night. Will had to be satisfied with the fact that she'd called him, chose him to be with her tonight.

"I'm not going to leave your side."

With a satisfied nod, she squeezed his fingers and together they made their way toward the conference room Sheriff Battle had set aside as a command post for tracking down Lowell. As they entered the room, Megan glanced around at the whiteboards, taking everything in.

Will, who had been in this room several times in the months since he'd returned home, was frustrated by the lack of progress.

Bird gestured toward a chair as he said, "Mrs. Sanders, you told the receptionist that you shot Richard Lowell?"

"Yes. With this."

Before she sat, Megan withdrew the small pistol from her purse. Beneath the fluorescent lighting, the gun's small size and fanciful handle made it look like a toy and Will glanced at the FBI agent to gauge his reaction.

"You're sure you hit him?"

"I think so. He spun to his left, but I may have only grazed him because he chased me to my car and tried to stop me from driving away."

From his seat beside her, Will regarded Megan, stunned by her bravery.

The FBI agent nodded, his expression impassive. "How long have you had the gun, Mrs. Sanders?"

"A month, but I only started carrying it recently after I received my conceal and carry permit."

"Did you mention to anyone that you'd bought the weapon?"

Her lashes fell before she answered. "Dani Moore came with me to the firing range. I didn't go public about the gun. When no one is supposed to know what's going on, how could I explain my sudden need for protection?"

Special Agent Bird nodded. "That probably explains why Lowell approached you."

"Why can't you figure out where he's staying?" Will demanded.

The agent's gaze flicked in Will's direction before he said to Megan, "Perhaps you could walk me through to-night's events."

"I was working late and everyone had left by the time I headed out to the parking lot."

As Megan spun her story, Will clenched his hands into fists and held them on his knees out of sight. Tonight's in-cident had been stressful enough and she didn't need his anger mucking up the interview.

Still, it was a struggle to keep his frustration in check. Especially as she explained how Lowell had grabbed at her car door as she'd tried to make her escape. He didn't like what he was hearing. Lowell stalking Megan, watching her, waiting to make his move.

At the same time, Will was astonished by her quick, clear thinking in pulling out her gun and shooting him. He doubted anyone could've done better.

"He acted like he expected me to go away with him," Megan concluded, her energy trailing off as her story wound down.

"Did he say where he was headed?"

"No." Her eyes went wide and her voice vibrated with dismay. "I should have asked him that. I'm sorry I didn't. I was just so shocked that he showed up." She stared at the gun sitting on the polished dark wood of the conference table. "All I could think of was getting away from him."

"You did the right thing," Special Agent Bird said, sounding kinder for a second.

Megan visibly relaxed. Had she been worried at the agent's reaction to her actions that night? Could she have thought for a moment that she'd done something wrong? Will covered her hand with his and gave a light squeeze in support. The grateful smile she shot his way struck his nerves like a gong and reverberated through him long after she grew serious again. More than anything he wanted Megan to be happy.

"Is there anything else that he said that might help us find him?" Bird asked.

A crease formed between Megan's brows as she considered the question. At last she shook her head. "I'm sorry. I can't think of anything more. It all happened so fast."

A knock sounded on the conference room door. A moment later Deputy Jeff Baker poked his head inside and swept the room with troubled eyes.

"Any luck?" Agent Bird asked.

"Lowell was long gone by the time we reached the parking lot."

"Any sign of blood?"

Baker shook his head. "If Mrs. Sanders shot him, it must've been only a graze."

"I see," Bird said. "Were you able to get ahold of Sheriff Battle?"

"He's on his way in."

When the FBI agent nodded, Deputy Baker withdrew. Bird returned his attention to Megan. "Do you have somewhere safe you can stay tonight? I don't think it's a good idea for you to go home."

"Do you really think he'll try again tonight?" Will thought Megan had given Lowell something to think about. She wasn't going to go without a fight.

"I doubt it, but the guy has a tendency to act impulsively. I don't want to take a chance of losing him again if he does."

He could see it in the agent's eyes. They wanted Lowell to try again. Now that he'd demonstrated he wasn't going to leave town without Megan, she became their best hope for catching him.

Bait.

Will ground his teeth together in irritation. Part of him understood the agent's perspective, but the thought that Megan was in danger triggered a powerful need to protect her at all costs.

Setting his hand on Megan's upper arm and feeling the tremors vibrating through her, he said, "I'd like to take Megan back to the Ace in the Hole tonight."

"I'm not sure—" Megan began, only to be interrupted by the FBI agent.

"I think it's a good idea. We can send someone to watch her house in case he tries to contact her again. And we'll park a squad car near the entrance to your ranch."

"I could call Aaron," Megan offered without much conviction.

"I'm your husband," Will reminded her, overriding the beginnings of another protest. "I should be the one taking care of you."

Megan opened her mouth, glanced toward the FBI agent, and made her next protest in a low growl. "I don't need to be taken care of."

Both Will and Bird ignored her claim.

"We'll want to keep the gun for a few days," Agent Bird said. "As soon as we get a look at the parking lot and run some tests, we'll get back to you."

Megan nodded and got to her feet. "I hope you can find him. I'm not sure how much more of this I can take."

"I know this is a difficult time for you. If there's anything you need or if Lowell contacts you again, please let us know."

"Thank you." Megan's gaze flicked to Will as she headed toward the door.

"Do you want to run by your house and pick some things up?" he asked her.

She shook her head. "I know he's probably long gone, but I don't feel safe going there tonight. I don't suppose there would be a pair of pajamas I could borrow?"

Her half smile zinged through him like a lightning bolt. The thought of her spending the night in his house tempted Will. A little too much.

"I think I can find something for you to sleep in," he said, surprised by the effort it took to keep his tone casual. The memory of her wearing nothing at all flashed through his thoughts. He nearly winced as his body stirred. Sharing the ranch house with her was going to be challenging.

"I really appreciate what you're doing for me."

"Do not thank me. What you're going through is my fault."

She stopped in the doorway and turned to face him. "How do you figure that?"

Will slipped his fingers around her arm and guided her to the front door. "Look, it was my life Rich wanted. If I'd paid attention to the signs, maybe he wouldn't have gotten the jump on me in Mexico."

"You can't take responsibility for his actions. No one saw him coming and you aren't the only one whose life he messed up."

Will nodded, thinking of all the women Rich had lied to and manipulated. The lives he'd damaged. And the one he'd ended.

Megan's brother, Jason, who'd investigated the discrepancies surrounding imposter Will and had lost his life because of it. No one blamed Will for what had happened to his good friend because no one knew that Will had called Jason from Mexico and possibly set him on the path to his death.

"But you have to admit that I was his obsession," Will said. "He wanted my life and he got it." Silence fell between them as they left the sheriff's office. As they reached the sidewalk, Will paused in front of Megan's Porsche. "Do you want to come with me? I can send a couple of the boys back for your car." He let his gaze drift over the sporty vehicle. "They'll probably fight over who gets to drive it to the ranch."

Megan wrapped her arms around herself and regarded the car. "I'm okay."

"You've had a major shock tonight. I'd be surprised if you weren't rattled."

"Really, I'm fine." Megan scowled at Will, but he wasn't fooled.

"You've been through a lot." He followed her to her car. Her shoulders drooped. "I'm not the only one."

"That doesn't diminish your experience tonight." Once

again he had to bite back myriad questions dancing in the back of his mind. Ever since coming home and finding out she'd married "Will," he'd struggled to contain his tumultuous feelings for her.

"We have a lot to talk about," she said unexpectedly, keying the remote and popping her door locks.

"Such as?" He wholeheartedly agreed but wondered if they were on the same page.

"For the last few months we've been dancing around each other. Being polite and skirting the reality of our situation."

Will flashed back to the night of Jason's memorial. Nothing about that encounter had been polite. It had been raw and emotional. Naked. Panting. Clinging to each other in an effort to feel alive amidst the day's crushing sadness. Taking support and pleasure in each other's arms. They'd needed connection and oblivion.

The trouble for Will was that he still needed her. In his bed. At his side. Making love with Megan had blown a hole in what Will believed he wanted in his life. Now he recognized that he wanted more. He just wasn't sure she felt the same. Or that she ever would.

Will held on to her open door, preventing her from getting away. "You're right. We haven't talked much about the emotional ramifications of Rich taking over my life."

He had dozens of questions bubbling in his brain, but with curiosity came caution. How many of her answers would tell a tale he didn't want to hear?

"How about we drink a few shots and you can ask me anything with no repercussions?" she offered.

"I think that sounds like a great idea. We really should get to know each other better."

"The feeling is mutual," she said, her smile creating more confusion than clarity as she pulled her door out of his grasp.

* * *

On a dark patch of Main Street between two street-lights, Richard Lowell sat behind the wheel of a nonde-script pickup truck and watched Will Sanders disappear into the sheriff's office. Inside were dozens of people who had been actively seeking him for months and sitting here in the open like this was a grave risk to his freedom.

He shifted on the seat and pain blazed in his side where Megan had shot him. Before following her to the police station, he'd checked the damage and determined that the bullet had merely nicked him. It didn't stop the graze from hurting like a son of a bitch, but he used the discomfort to fuel his determination.

Who would've guessed that his wife would've grown claws in the months since they parted ways? He'd never imagined she'd buy a gun to defend herself against him, much less use it. This turn of events meant he'd have to plan more carefully if he intended to take her with him across the border into Mexico. Or he could say screw it and take Vanessa with him instead.

The stripper was younger, prettier and more to his taste in bed. Not to mention she did whatever he asked. As long as he indulged her craving for designer fashions and fed her opiate habit, she'd be decent enough company. At least until he wearied of her.

So why wasn't he putting the truck into gear and head-ing for Vanessa's dumpy apartment? He was already weeks past when he should've collected the gold and gotten the hell out of town. To linger invited capture. In fact, he would've been long gone if Sanders hadn't showed up at his funeral.

Rich hadn't foreseen that development and would've given anything to see the expression on people's faces that day. Of course, at the time Rich had been too pissed off to find any humor in the situation. And he still couldn't be-

lieve Will hadn't died in the explosion. Nor could he figure out where Will had been in the year since. He struck
the steering wheel with the heel of his hand. It was just
like that bastard to survive and make a triumphant return
to Royal.

At least a dozen times in the last few months Rich had
thought about going to the Ace in the Hole and finishing
the job he'd started off the coast of Mexico. But the ranch
security was more than a match for him. Instead, he had
settled down to wait, knowing Will would eventually make
a mistake. Only, he hadn't. He remained frustratingly vigi-
lant. Which was why Rich had decided to grab Megan, go
after the gold and get the hell out of town.

But Megan refused to go and now Rich thought he knew
why. Given the speed with which Will had showed up at
the police station, no doubt she'd called him. Had Megan
transferred her love to the real Will Sanders? The thought
twisted in Rich's gut like a knife. Should he be surprised?
She'd confessed to having an unrequited crush on Will in
high school. It was what had made it easy for Rich to seduce her.

As for why he'd decided to marry her when so many
other women appealed to him more? Rich had noticed
Will's attraction to her, yet he'd never acted on it. He hadn't
been convinced by Will's denials that there was anything
to it and gotten a rush out of moving in on someone Will
coveted but had never had. Even better, he liked the idea
of destroying every good thing in Sanders's life from his
solid family relationships to his reputation as a businessman and community leader.

But the best part? After he'd finished dismantling Will's
life, he could collect his plundered millions and head somewhere tropical to live like a king for the rest of his days.
Or that had been the plan before his dear old friend had
turned up alive.

Now, with Will back in Royal, working behind the scenes to fix all the damage Rich had done, it wasn't good enough that he had stolen millions from Spark Energy Solutions and the Texas Cattleman's Club. Nope. His hatred ran so much deeper than that. It was about revenge. Payback. Taking what should have been his in the first place. Bottom line? Rich refused to allow Will to be happy. So he had been hanging around, looking for a way to cause the maximum amount of mayhem. Now, seeing his old buddy come to Megan's rescue, he had an idea how to make Will pay.

Three

Megan smoothed her damp palms along her skirt and eased her foot off the gas as the brake lights on Will's Land Rover flared ahead. They were nearing the road that led to the Ace in the Hole entry gates. Moments later, her Porsche followed Will's luxury SUV onto the driveway.

Was coming here a huge mistake? Driving for half an hour had calmed Megan's nerves and allowed her to think clearly instead of just react. When she'd agreed to Will's suggestion that she spend the night at his ranch, she'd been anxious that Rich might show up at her house. Now, however, she had a whole new set of concerns to consider.

The last time she'd felt this vulnerable, she and Will had fallen upon each other with no thought to the consequences. She shuddered at the memory of his lips sliding over her skin and the way he'd filled her.

She cursed as an insistent ache began between her thighs. The craving to be possessed by him again consumed her. And this time it had nothing to do with grief or loss. The strength and confidence he exuded was like an aphrodisiac, turning her thoughts lusty and her impulses wanton.

Earlier she'd suggested they drink shots and get to know each other better. How shocked would he be to discover she'd made the offer while imagining herself pouring whiskey over his chiseled abs and licking the strong liquor off his skin?

Megan blew out a shaky breath as the wide iron gates, adorned with the ranch's brand, slid aside, offering them passage to the road beyond. The enormous ranch house had been built on a rise nearly a mile down the curvy driveway and couldn't be seen from the road.

Although she'd been to the Ace in the Hole many times, she never lost her appreciation for the main home's long, low profile with its white paint and expansive windows, placed to best enjoy the sweeping views. Chairs and a swing stretched along the broad wraparound porch. Against the dark sky she could almost make out two chimneys poking up from the roof.

Megan parked her car beside Will's and walked beside him up the wide steps to the porch. A soft glow spilled through the side panels on either side of the center-set, double front doors. After her wedding to imposter Will, she'd been disappointed to learn he didn't want to live at the ranch. She loved it out here. The wide-open spaces, the scent of rich soil and grass, and the intermittent lowing of the cattle from far off in the fields.

"You're smiling," Will said as he ushered her into the main living space. "That's good."

He didn't ask her why as his gaze roved over her expression, but his curiosity was palpable. After gesturing to the couch, he crossed to the bar and poured shots of whiskey into cut-crystal tumblers for each of them.

Megan kicked off her shoes and tucked her feet beneath her. Propping her head on her hand, she observed his smooth, economical motions. Damn, she enjoyed looking at him. All broad shoulders, muscular thighs and rock-solid abs. Tonight he was dressed in jeans and a white button-down shirt. He wore his black hair longer these days and the untamed style gave him an edginess that Megan found exciting.

"I feel safe when I'm with you," she explained, accepting a glass from Will and feeling a shivery tingle run up her arm as their fingers brushed. "And I like being here at the ranch."

"Can we talk about what you did tonight?" He dropped beside her on the couch and cradled his glass in both hands, staring at it for several seconds as if searching for answers in the amber liquid. When his gaze switched to her, anxiety and respect warred in his electric green eyes. "You are incredibly brave."

Heat suffused her from head to toe and she basked in Will's admiration. "I can't believe I shot him."

"I'm sure he can't believe it, either."

"Do you think it will make him more or less determined to get to me?"

There was a significant pause before Will answered. "I'm not going to let anything happen to you."

His fervent declaration swept over her, igniting her blood. He sounded possessive, like she was his to protect. It made her want to curl up in his lap and show him just how much she liked the idea of belonging to him.

"I hope they find him soon," she said. "I can't wait for this nightmare to be over."

"That makes two of us." A lengthy pause followed his words during which they both sipped their drinks.

"You know, we should talk about what happens when Lowell gets caught."

Her heart gave a little jump. "What do you mean?"

Despite what Megan had said earlier about answering whatever questions Will might have, she was nearing her last sip of whiskey and too drained to guard what she said.

"For now, while Lowell is still at large, the FBI wants us to act as if we're married. But once he's caught, we need to consider how to go forward. Legally, I mean."

Megan knew what he was getting at, but how did she divorce someone she hadn't actually married?

"Technically," she began, "I married Will Sanders."

Will's lips twitched. "And he's a lucky man."

His playfulness gave her the courage to ask, "Are you wondering if I'm going to ask for alimony?"

He grew immediately somber. "I'm happy to pay you whatever you want."

"I was kidding." She frowned at him. "You don't seriously think I expect financial remuneration."

"I think you're entitled to some sort of a settlement. After all, your entire life has been turned upside down because of Lowell pretending to be me. That makes me responsible for you."

"That's a terrible…" She didn't want to insult him but his assumption that she should receive money from him annoyed her.

"Terrible what?"

"I'm not some gold digger who needs or expects to benefit from marrying you," she huffed. "You might have a lot of money, but I'm not exactly destitute." In fact, she was doing better than she'd ever imagined.

"Of course not, but legally—"

"Stop right there," she said, throwing up her hands. "We are going to end up in our first argument if you keep on that way."

Will's quicksilver grin was back. "But think of the makeup sex we'll get to enjoy afterward."

To her horror, Megan's cheeks went hot. So did other

parts of her. The whiskey had dimmed whatever qualms she might've had about tearing off her clothes and throwing herself at him again. She shifted on the couch all too aware of the ache between her thighs.

"Then by all means," she said, her voice sounding odd to her ears, "let's get to it."

They stared at each other in silence while Megan's heart pounded so hard she couldn't imagine how Will didn't hear it. What would it take for them to come together in this moment? If she got to her feet and started unbuttoning her blouse, would Will stop her or meet her halfway?

Will blinked, breaking the spell. A grin slowly brightened his expression.

"You know," he murmured huskily, "I've enjoyed being married to you."

Disappointed that neither one of them had stepped up, Megan finished the last of her drink and held the empty glass to him. "It's been nice being married to you, as well. I'll have another, if you're pouring."

Will tipped the balance of his drink down his throat and got to his feet. Taking her glass, he crossed to the bar once again. For a moment there was only the sound of the top coming off the bottle and the splash of whiskey into the glasses.

"It was a pretty major shock to walk into my own funeral and realize I had a wife," Will said, returning to the couch.

"I'm sure you had several major shocks that day." Megan took the refilled glass and peered at the level. Had he given her a healthier dose this time? "Discovering you were dead, for example."

"It's weird, you know." Will turned sideways on the couch and watched her through half-lidded eyes.

She surveyed his features, pondering the edgy intensity he sometimes displayed since returning to Royal. Where once he'd been easygoing and wholly confident, these days she sometimes glimpsed discontent. He wasn't as perfect as he'd once been and that made him more human and less godlike. More like a man who might be interested in a woman like her with flaws and insecurities she worked hard to hide.

"What's weird?" she echoed.

"That Lowell was able to step right into my life and nobody questioned it. Was he so much like me?"

"He was a poor man's Will Sanders," she said lightly. "Everyone remarked on the differences, but we all put it down to the accident."

"Well, he must've done something right to get you to marry him."

Megan considered what Will hadn't asked and remembered that she'd agreed to open up. "Frankly, I was so thrilled that he—you—finally noticed me that I got sucked in." Megan noticed Will's surprise and forged ahead. With everything she'd been through tonight, why not take a chance and let Will know about her past crush on him? "Back in high school I would have given anything for you to smile at me, but you didn't know I existed."

"That's not true. I knew." He released a rough breath. "I'm just sorry I wasn't ever smart enough to appreciate you. We've known each other for a long time, but I never wised up and took my shot."

"I didn't help you out any," Megan said. "I was always so awkward around you. I guess it came from having such a huge crush on you when we were young and assuming you could never be attracted to me since I was such a tomboy back then."

Will shook his head. "I don't want you to think I wasn't attracted to you. Then…or now. You are an intelligent, beautiful woman with drive and passion…and I find that extremely appealing."

"That's really nice of you to say—"

Will interrupted her with an impatient snort. "Why do you think Lowell picked you out of all the women in town to pursue?"

"I don't know."

When she'd first learned that she was married to an imposter, Megan had suspected Rich had zeroed in on her because she'd never really gotten over Will even though her heart had been broken when she'd heard that Will married Selena Jacobs in college. One thing about Rich, though, he was good at preying on vulnerable people and had probably decided her unrequited love made her an easy mark.

"He wanted my life," Will continued. "Maybe he thought that should include a woman who I admired and lusted after."

"You lusted after me?" Megan shook her head. "I don't believe it."

"You can't be serious. After what happened between us the night of Jason's memorial service?"

"That was…" Oh, hell. What had it been? She knew what it had been for her. Had it been more than grief and a need to connect for him? "I just thought we were both upset and needing comfort."

"Don't do that."

"Do what?"

"Whenever I pay you a compliment, you wave it aside like you don't believe I'm telling you the truth."

"I do." But in truth she had a hard time accepting his claim that before he'd gone on that fateful fishing trip, Will had noticed her. Seeing his doubt, she amended, "I want to."

"What's stopping you?"

"There's a critical voice inside my head constantly telling me that I need to do better, work harder. It's as if I can't enjoy my success because it's never enough."

"If that's because you're constantly comparing yourself to Jason and Aaron, then you're doing yourself a disservice. What you've built at Royals Shoes is fantastic and I know both your brothers are...were very proud of you."

A spasm of pain crossed his features. Jason's death had packed a double whammy for him. Not only had he loved Jason as a brother, but he also felt guilty that his friend had died at the hands of the imposter.

"I know that's true," Megan said, reaching out to cover Will's hand with hers. "I guess I continue to be the product of two older brothers. Competitive older brothers. They rarely took it easy on me because I was a girl."

"They should've cut you some slack. Not because you're a girl, but because I know how they could be, and I'm sure they ganged up on you. That wouldn't have been fair regardless of your gender."

"It made me tough." At least on the outside. "I've learned to smile through every meeting I've ever taken."

"You don't have to be strong for me. Or with me." Will set his fingers beneath her chin and turned her face until their gazes met. "In fact, I like riding in on my white steed to rescue you."

"Having you as my knight in shining armor sounds really nice," she said, leaning the tiniest bit into his space, hoping he'd see that she really wanted him to kiss her.

"That's good because I intend to be there if Lowell shows up again." Will's somber vow sent goose bumps chasing over Megan's arms. His fingers stroked along her cheek, leaving tingles in their wake. "I couldn't live with myself if anything happened to you."

To her dismay, when the longed-for kiss came, Will's lips brushed her forehead, not her mouth. She sighed at the contact, anyway, impressing a memory of the scent of his cologne and the softness of his breath against her skin.

"Now," he said with a wry smile, "can we talk about the pistol with the pink grip?"

Megan rolled her eyes, accepting the ribbing but still feeling like she needed to explain herself. "I did my research and the gun had great reviews."

"But it was pink."

"It was the only one they had in stock and I wanted to get it as soon as possible." She made a face at him. "And it did the trick. I shot Rich, didn't I? Or, at least, I grazed him. In any case, I surprised him and that's what enabled me to get away."

"You did a stellar job defending yourself. No one could have done better. I just wish I'd been there to see his expression when you pulled out that gun and pointed it at him."

"It was pretty funny," she admitted. But her satisfaction was short-lived. "And most of the reason he was probably surprised was that I didn't exactly stand up for myself during our marriage."

"Why not?"

"I was afraid. What did it say that I couldn't keep Will Sanders interested during the honeymoon stage of our marriage? And if I lost him…" She glanced away as she spoke, but Will reached out and touched her chin, guiding her head until their gazes met. The understanding in his eyes gave her the courage to finish her thought. "I would've been a big fat failure."

"He should've been the one afraid of losing you. You're worth a million Rich Lowells."

Definitely Rich Lowell, but maybe not Will Sanders.

Initially, while pretending to be Will, Lowell had showered her with cheap phrases, praising her beauty, how she dressed, making a point to tell her how sexy she was. She'd been too besotted to notice that he only pointed out what was on the surface.

By contrast, Will saw beneath her skillfully applied makeup and designer fashions. He glimpsed her flaws and didn't judge her for them. This allowed Megan to relax in his company and loosened her tongue.

"I'm sorry that I ever thought he was you."

"I'm not." And he sounded like he meant it. "We wouldn't be married if that was the case."

"We're not really married."

"Technically we are."

They stared at each other for a long moment, neither speaking. Megan's brain was scrambling for what to say next. A dozen replies reached her lips, but none passed. Each of them sounded too much like an easy, flippant retort.

But what if she put her cards on the table and he freaked? After all, he hadn't chosen her as his wife while she had fallen in love with and married Will Sanders. Granted it had been the wrong Will, but she'd enjoyed plenty of time to think about what she did and didn't want out of her marriage. And the truth was, after the fireworks of their courtship, marriage to Will's imposter was a low point in her life.

"Did you love him?"

Megan regarded Will, trying to determine what was at the heart of this question. Was he wondering if she still loved him? The simple answer was no, but she hadn't married Rich Lowell. She'd married Will Sanders. Or, at least, she'd thought she had.

"I wouldn't have married him if I didn't love him," she declared, still unsure what that said about her judgment.

Looking back she realized that Rich Lowell had been a poor man's copy of Will, lacking depth, character and compassion. So what had attracted her to him? Had she loved the man or who she'd believed the man to be?

Megan had no good answer and that bothered her immensely. Would she ever be able to trust herself to make the right decision when it came to love?

A muscle jumped in Will's jaw before he answered. "Of course."

Was Megan fooling herself to think she detected the slightest hint of disappointment in his manner?

"I promised you the truth," she said, "and saying that I loved him is a straightforward answer to a complicated situation."

Will nodded. "I imagine you have all sorts of crazy mixed-up emotions when it comes to Lowell."

Not just Lowell.

"Not when it comes to him." Megan traced the pattern of the pillow she held on her lap. "Our marriage wasn't all that great. He became a completely different person after the wedding."

"How so?"

"When we first started dating, he was the most romantic man I've ever known. He sent me flowers and called just to say he missed me. I got swept off my feet."

"Sounds like he was a better me than me," Will said with a self-deprecating grin. "I've never worked that hard to get a woman to like me."

"But you're Will Sanders. I'm sure most of the women you date don't require much encouragement to fall hard for you."

"Why? Because I'm wealthy? And easy on the eyes?" The corners of his mouth kicked up, but Megan noticed a hardness around his eyes. He was pretending to poke fun at himself. Pretending his experiences over the last year hadn't changed him.

"Don't forget successful in everything you do. Every guy wants to be you. Women want to be with you." Even as she spoke Megan realized he no longer took all those things for granted. How hard it must have been for him to come back from whatever he'd gone through in Mexico only to discover the man he'd thought was his good friend had betrayed him in every way possible. "And you're a good man."

"My psyche isn't all that fragile," he said and this time his irony appeared real. "You don't have to assure me I'm okay."

"I don't know," she replied. "You seem to be blaming yourself for things that aren't your fault."

"I can't get off the *what-if* merry-go-round." Green eyes steady and grave, he gave her an unrestricted look into his soul. "I spent a lot of time thinking while I was down in Mexico."

"What happened to you in Mexico?" she asked, emboldened by the whiskey and what she'd shared of her own troubles to step into uncharted territory.

Something haunted flitted through his gaze and then he was shaking his head. "That's not a conversation for tonight."

"Sure." She withdrew into herself like a spooked turtle. "I'm sorry I asked."

"Don't be." Will reached out and dusted his fingertips over her knuckles. "I'm still coming to grips with some of the things that happened, but I know I need to talk to someone about it. I'm just not ready."

"I hope when you are ready that you know you can talk to me."

"I appreciate the offer." He got to his feet and held out his hand, signaling an end to their exchange. "Are you ready to see your room and get some rest?"

His fingers were firm and warm against hers. As she rose to stand beside him, he gave just the tiniest squeeze, a comforting gesture that sent a spike of longing through her. The whiskey and conversation had lowered her defenses. More than anything she wanted his strong arms around her tonight. She'd expended all her bravery in her escape from Lowell and had none left to fight her attraction to Will.

But sleeping together again would be a mistake. The urge to lean on Will was so strong. She could fall for him too easily. But to pretend that they had any sort of future was dangerous. Physical attraction was exhilarating and great sex was addictive, but despite Will's claims that he'd *lusted* after her, he hadn't been interested enough to do anything about it. What made her think anything had changed?

Megan gave him a tired smile. "Lead the way."

As he led Megan through the sprawling ranch house, Will cursed his abrupt reaction when she'd asked about his time spent in Mexico. For a guy who wanted to get to know this beautiful, desirable woman much better, he was doing a terrible job of communicating. And as he escorted her to the guest room, he couldn't summon the right words to break through the palpable silence between them.

The charming, glib way he'd handled women in the past belonged to a different man. That guy hadn't been ready to settle down with just one woman when there was a banquet of beauties awaiting his attention. Old Will could afford to flirt and utter meaningless compliments.

Unsurprisingly, his thoughts had snagged on their one and only physical encounter after Jason's memorial service. He'd lost control. They both had. It had been rough and intense and sexy. She'd cried his name as he'd entered her and clung to him with rabid hunger as he'd pounded into her heat. She'd taken everything he'd given and asked for more. Begged for more. And when she came, her muscles clamping down on him, pulling him over the edge with her, Will had seen stars.

He would be a liar if he claimed that inviting her back to

the ranch had been an altogether altruistic move. Sure, he'd been primarily concerned with her safety, but he could've hired a team of security people to keep her safe from Lowell. In fact, whenever they shared the same air, he was gripped by a reckless, red-hot longing to have her back in his bed, and wondered if she felt the same way.

From the fireworks that had encompassed their lovemaking, he recognized that lust was a mutual thing, but was that all there was to it? Would a few weeks of hot, steamy passion fade into regret? She'd married a man thinking he was Will. By her own admission, she'd loved him. Will and Rich were as different as night and day. Would her passion for her husband translate to Will? Did he want it to?

Something was going on inside him. Something that jumbled his emotions and altered his needs. At the same time, he didn't want Megan's attentions because he looked like the man she'd married.

"Here you go," he pronounced unnecessarily, reaching into the guest room to flip on the light. Damn, he had grown awkward with women. No, not women. *This* woman. He cared—really cared—what Megan thought of him and he didn't want to screw things up with her. "You'll find the bathroom stocked with whatever you need."

"Nice." She nodded, her eyes flickering toward the large four-poster bed. "And the pajamas you promised me?"

His solar plexus took a hit at her reminder. He imagined her sliding naked between the Egyptian cotton sheets, the cool material raising goose bumps on her arms, her nipples pebbling as the soft fabric slid over them.

Damn.

"I've got a pair you can borrow." His voice sounded oddly calm considering the maelstrom of heady desire assailing him at the moment. And then he noticed the expression on her face as if she was trying hard not to smile. "What?"

"You don't seem…" Color flooded her cheeks. "That is… I'd be happy to wear your pajamas." She bit her lip as her eyes darted away from him.

"I don't seem…?" he prompted, eager to confirm he'd been right about where her mind had taken her. "What?"

"Pajamas." As if that single word explained everything.

Instead of prodding her again, Will waited in silence and hoped she'd fill in the gaps. Vivid color bloomed in her cheeks. The heat beneath her skin called to him. He remembered her silky, fragrant warmth as he'd stripped off her black suit and coasted his hands over her naked flesh.

"They don't seem your style," Megan said at last.

"No?" Had she thought of him in bed? He hoped so. After all, it was only fair considering how often he'd indulged in wicked fantasies of having her there. "I suppose you've imagined me wearing nothing at all?"

"I…" Her mouth hung open as she sought a retort. "Haven't." But she refused to meet his gaze and the flush hadn't left her face.

"Sorry to disappoint you," he rasped, "but I generally sleep in boxers and add a T-shirt in the winter." As much fun as it was to watch her squirm, he decided to cut her some slack. She'd had an eventful evening. "I can see you're wondering why I have pajamas if I don't sleep in them."

Her smile had a touch of gratitude in it. "You've piqued my curiosity." She relaxed a little before giving her head a rueful shake.

"They're a gift from Cora Lee. Every year for Christmas she gives me a pair. I don't have the heart to tell her I don't wear them."

"That's a lot of unused pajamas," Megan teased.

"I usually donate them, but didn't get around to it last year before…" Will trailed off as he remembered the reason. "Anyway, if they don't fit, I can raid Lucy's room to see if she has something."

"Raid? Couldn't you just ask her?"

"She's out of town for a few days and Brody is staying with Jesse and Jillian."

A micro widening of her eyes betrayed her surprise that they were alone in the house. Had she been hoping Lucy and Brody would act as chaperones? Was she now concerned that he would make a move on her?

"Well," she murmured, "I'm sure your pajamas will work out just fine."

"I'll go get them."

The pajamas were in the bottom drawer in his bureau, exactly where he remembered putting them two Christmases ago. He pulled them out then caught himself absently rubbing the material between his fingers as he retraced his steps to the guest room.

"You're frowning," Megan commented upon his return, meeting him in the doorway and taking the pajamas from his hands. "Is everything okay?"

"Everything is fine. These are from two Christmases ago. I was just wondering what happened to the pair that Cora Lee would've given to Rich while he was pretending to be me."

"We didn't spend Christmas with your family," Megan said, clutching the pale blue cotton to her chest. "I thought it strange that he wanted us to be alone on the holiday, but he claimed that he wanted our first Christmas together to be special." She shook her head. "I guess I should've guessed something was up from the way he avoided everyone, but he was so convincing and he made it all sound so romantic—" She broke off and buried her face in the pajamas, mumbling, "I was such a fool."

Will put his hand on her shoulder and gave a gentle squeeze. "You weren't."

And she wasn't the only one Lowell had tricked. He'd done a bang-up job impersonating Will, hurting a lot of people in the process.

Beneath a fringe of long, lush lashes, her piercing blue eyes were haunted. "I don't know why I'm going on and on about my own troubles when he turned your life upside down and then some."

"We've both been through a lot." Will knew it was a massive understatement, but she seemed to take comfort from his words. "Why don't you get some rest? I'm sure everything will look better in the morning."

Before he considered how she might interpret his actions, he cupped her cheek and bent to place a gentle kiss on her lips. He'd only intended the gesture to be one of solidarity, but she made a soft noise, fanning the desire that had been smoldering since he'd discovered she was his wife. Will couldn't have stopped himself from going back for a second taste even if he'd wanted to.

Her hand gripped his upper arm, fingers biting into his biceps as she swayed across the narrow space between them. The soft curve of her breast grazed his chest, sending his thoughts spiraling. Beneath his lips, hers parted, offering him the opportunity to take the kiss deeper. Unable to resist, he turned her with slow deliberation until her spine aligned with the door frame. Her trembling body tensed, as if bracing for that first steep plunge down a roller coaster. Will grazed his fingertips across her cheek, soothing her. Little by little, her muscles relaxed, and she coasted her palm up his shoulder and set her fingertips on his nape, awakening goose bumps up and down his arms.

Amazed at how easily she aroused him, he took his time exploring her mouth. Keeping the kiss light and flirty took all his willpower. Never before had he worked this hard to avoid making love to a woman. In the past he either wasn't interested or didn't think twice about letting mutual passion run its course.

The buildup of sexual energy in his body was neither slow nor joyful. Lust sank its claws into him like a ferocious feline and it was everything he could do not to howl at the ache that bloomed below his belt. This time he couldn't blame over a year of celibacy for the rush of passion. He and Megan had been together just a week earlier. Yet his yearning for her was even more sharp and unrelenting.

Will broke off the kiss and set his forehead against Megan's while his harsh breathing and pounding heartbeat filled his ears. This situation was beyond complicated. It wasn't just that they were married. Or letting the world believe they were. She'd fallen in love with a man pretending to be him.

One thing Will had never encountered was being a substitute for someone else. He wasn't oblivious to how golden his life had been. Until Rich had turned on him, Will had taken his money, power, success and relationships for granted.

Now, people who didn't know what had happened looked at him differently. With suspicion, indignation or hurt. As if at any second they expected him to do something vile or offensive. Acting as Will, Rich had harmed so many people. He'd killed Jason. Because of the ongoing investigation, the truth hadn't come out about Lowell's impersonation and Will was catching the brunt of the other man's evil doings.

"Are you okay?" Megan's soft voice disturbed the shadows that surrounded his thoughts, allowing him to break out of the darkness.

"I should've seen it," he replied in clipped tones, feeling powerless and hating it. "I should've seen through Rich's facade. I missed every sign that something was wrong with him and now so many people have had their lives ruined." Acid ate at his gut as he took a step away from her and raked his fingers through his hair. "He killed Jason."

"I know."

"Sorry," Will said, remembering too late that Megan had her own grief to deal with. She didn't need to take on his pain, as well. "This thing with Lowell is… He needs to be caught." Irritation sharpened his voice. "I can't move forward with my life until that happens."

"I guess we're both in the same boat with regard to that." Megan twisted her wedding ring around her finger. "We'll just have to make the best of things until he's locked up."

"Yes." But that wasn't how Will was used to living. "Sleep well. And tomorrow we will talk about how to keep you safe going forward. I don't want you going back to your house alone. And for that matter, I don't think you should go anywhere by yourself until Lowell is caught."

She looked ready to protest then apparently thought better of it. "Thank you for everything, Will. I'll…see you in the morning."

With a nod, Will shoved his hands into his jeans' pockets to keep from drawing her into his arms again and, with a final good-night, turned on his heel and strode away.

Four

It was a little after dawn when Megan showered, dressed and exited the comfortable guest room. Wearing minimal makeup and yesterday's clothes, she wasn't feeling at her best. If she'd been in a better state of mind the previous night, she could've taken Will up on his offer to swing by her place before heading to the Ace in the Hole.

Not that it should matter how she looked. She had no reason to impress Will. Yet she couldn't fight the longing to see his eyes light up with pleasure when he saw her. His approval fanned the yearning that grew stronger each time they were together. She had it bad for Will Sanders. The *real* Will Sanders. Shame flared as she acknowledged once again what a fool she'd been to fall for a cheap imitation.

Voices reached her as she made her way toward the kitchen, following the heavenly scent of fresh-brewed coffee. Instinct prompted her to pause as she neared the end of the hallway that led into the main part of the house. She wasn't skulking out of sight in a deliberate attempt to

eavesdrop, but something in the tone of the conversation
stopped her from barging into the scene.

"...sure having her here is the right thing?"

Megan recognized the speaker as Cora Lee and wasn't
surprised the matriarch had concerns. Because it had been
Rich and not Will that she'd married, Megan's relationship with her mother-in-law had been chilly and adver-
sarial. Several months after they'd eloped to Reno, Cora
Lee had confronted Megan about the way Will had dis-
tanced himself from the family, blaming the ever-widen-
ing chasm on Megan.

"Lowell attacked her in the parking lot of her company last night," Will explained in patient tones. "I'm not
about to have her fend for herself with that maniac out
there stalking her."

Cora Lee sniffed. "She's not your responsibility."

"She's my wife."

"She's Richard Lowell's wife."

A silence followed Cora Lee's declaration.

Megan's heart was pounding so hard she was surprised
it didn't give her away.

"The name on the marriage license is mine." Will's
firm tone brooked no further objections. "Besides, the authorities want us to continue acting as husband and wife.
It makes no sense for us to be living apart."

"That has been the case for months. Why all of a sudden are you trying to keep up appearances? Are you sure
you're not just using that as an excuse to have her around?"

"Why would I need an excuse?" Will asked mildly.

"I've seen the way you look at her. You're obviously attracted to her." Cora Lee made it sound like an accusation.

"And that's a bad thing?"

"It is if you start to think there might be more to the
relationship than a paper marriage."

"Funny. Before I left on my fishing trip with Lowell,

you were pestering me about finding a nice woman and settling down. Megan is a nice woman. She's also an accomplished businesswoman with a warm and generous spirit."

"Most people think she's cold."

Megan winced, knowing it was true. Growing up with two brothers like Jason and Aaron hadn't been easy. They'd been protective when it came to outsiders, but hard on her themselves. Coddled and bullied by turns, she'd resented and adored them in turn.

And now Jason was gone and she was finding it harder and harder to maintain the fortifications she'd constructed to hide her insecurities. His death had taken a sledgehammer to her defenses. Some nights she came home from work and sat in her kitchen, staring at Savannah's artwork on her refrigerator, wondering how any of them were supposed to go on without him.

"I happen to know different," Will said.

A pause and then, "I see." There was a world of judgment in those two words. "Well, you're an adult and obviously you think you know what you're doing."

Megan's stomach fell as she reasoned what Will's stepmother had construed from his defense of Megan. That they were sleeping together. This would only enflame Cora Lee's dislike and distrust, adding another obstacle between Megan and Will.

"Thank you for acknowledging that at thirty I can be considered an adult," Will remarked in a wry tone, sounding more like the man of old than the grim individual who'd returned to Royal a few short months ago. "And I'm not oblivious to the fact that my situation is complicated."

A pause. Megan's throat tightened as she waited for what was to come next. When Will spoke again, his low voice was troubled.

"I can't trust her feelings for me because I'm not sure she knows what she wants."

Megan winced as she absorbed the blow. He was right to be wary. Her feelings for him were crystal clear one second and mired in doubt the next. And all through her tangled emotions ran the sharp bite of physical attraction that knocked her off balance.

"But you're not going to back off," Cora Lee continued.

"Not about doing what's right for her. And that's why I want her to stay here with me until Lowell is caught."

From her hiding place, Megan nodded as the sensible part of her kicked in. If his family was actively counseling him to be wary of her, she might be running headlong into dangerous territory.

Yet even knowing that didn't stop her from longing to snatch whatever time she could get with Will. No doubt the odds were against anything developing between them. With Rich Lowell still at large, the dangerous situation they were in could awaken false feelings of affection.

Was she really ready to risk her heart again? Megan placed her palm against the treacherous organ and figured she had two options here. She could keep second-guessing what the future held or she could make something happen. The latter seemed the more empowering and attractive alternative.

While she'd been thinking, Will and his stepmom had stopped speaking. This was her opportunity to get that cup of coffee she so desperately needed after a restless night. She stepped out of the hallway and into the kitchen.

To her relief, Will was alone. He grinned upon seeing her and an electric jolt sent her heart into overdrive.

"Good morning." She gave him a bright smile. "I hope there's a cup of coffee with my name on it." While she advanced, he picked up the glass pot and poured dark liquid into a waiting cup.

"Do you need cream and sugar?"

"No, I like it black."

He nodded. "How did you sleep?"

"Really well once I drifted off." She inhaled the coffee fragrance before taking a sip. "Unfortunately that took me a while."

"I stared at the ceiling for a long time, as well. It's damn frustrating that Lowell is still on the loose after all this time. Especially with so many people looking for him."

"He's cagey." Megan took another sip of the coffee, appreciating the bracing dark roast. "He wouldn't have successfully impersonated you as long as he had if he wasn't."

"I never noticed that about him," Will mused. "I've been thinking about him a lot since…and I realize how little I really knew him. I don't know why I missed so much." Will fell silent. His expression grew thoughtful. "Maybe we weren't as tight as I believed. I completely missed whatever twisted thing caused him to hurt so many people. I should've seen it."

Megan considered her own failings and shook her head, absolving him of blame. Still lost in thought, Will didn't notice. She reached out, setting her hand on his arm, intending to offer comfort. His gaze flashed in her direction, emerald heat flickering to life.

"Can we not talk about Rich?" she asked, wanting instead to explore the attraction pulsing through her veins.

She longed for him to take the lead. To sweep aside her misgivings and kiss her like he'd perish in the next second without the taste of her lips. If he gave even the slightest indication that surrendering to desire was a good idea, she could follow his lead free of doubt.

At least for however long their passion remained hot.

"Sure." Will studied her for a long moment, his inscrutable expression awakening butterflies in her stomach. "Are you hungry? I think we have some cereal or eggs."

Megan shook her head. Lingering would only twist her confused emotions into tighter knots. She needed some time away from Will to ponder everything that had happened since last night.

"I'll grab something at home," she said.

"I spoke with Sheriff Battle this morning and there was no activity at your house last night, but he's going to leave one of his deputies there until you leave for work just in case."

"Thank you." Megan hadn't relished heading alone to her house. No matter what she'd claimed, she'd been spooked by Rich showing up last night and trying to make her go with him. "I guess I'd better get going."

"Listen, before you do, I want to talk to you about staying on at the ranch until Lowell is caught. As I've mentioned before, I think you would be safer here and I know it would be peace of mind for me."

Even though she'd expected the offer after listening in on his conversation with Cora Lee, hearing the words gave Megan a little thrill. She quickly tamped down the emotion and shook her head.

"I'll be fine. I have a good security system and the police will give me back my gun in a couple days."

Will made a face. "That doesn't reassure me. Lowell has demonstrated that he wants you and I don't think he'll stop until he gets his way."

"What makes you think he's even still around?"

"Believe me, I know," Will replied, his grave tone making Megan shiver. "And since it's only a matter of time until the bastard is finally caught, you'd only have to stay here for a little while."

"I'll think about it." But she already knew her answer needed to be no.

If she moved to the ranch, the temptation to jump into bed with Will would be too much. How could she ensure that she'd make sensible decisions about him with her hormones raging out of control whenever they were in close proximity? She wanted trust and emotional intimacy. Sex wasn't necessarily a conduit to those things.

Will nodded but looked unhappy to be put off.

Deciding it was time to go, Megan fetched her purse, and he walked her out to her car. She unlocked and opened the door, but before she could slide in, Will caught her elbow.

Her breath caught as his gaze flickered to her lips and held there for a heartbeat. She was on the verge of tilting her head in expectation of his kiss when he met her gaze.

"Call me when you get to work." His firm tone brooked no argument. "I need to know you got there safe."

"I'll be fine." Megan sighed in exasperation but saw he wasn't going to be put off. Before reason could prevent her, she set her palm against his cheek. Her thumb played over the rough stubble on his chin. "Okay, I'll call you."

And then he was stepping back with a satisfied nod, his features inscrutable. Megan got into her car, feeling slightly lightheaded at her boldness. Had he interpreted the gesture as mere fondness or could he read the yearning in her to connect with him?

With a quick smile and a friendly wave, Megan put her car in gear. Forty minutes later she pulled into the parking lot where she'd encountered Rich the night before. Her phone rang as she searched for an open space.

"Just checking to make sure you arrived at work okay," Will said.

"I'm parking even as we speak." Megan noticed she was grinning. Honestly, even talking on the phone with the man sent her emotions into overdrive.

"Did everything go okay at your house?"

"All was quiet and it didn't appear as if Rich had been there looking for me."

After Will's surprise appearance at his own funeral and Megan's discovery that the man she'd married was an imposter, she'd had all the locks changed on the house and her security system updated. Up until now, those measures had allowed her to feel safe in her home although sometimes the isolation led to her feeling much like a prisoner. And in a crazy way, she was a captive of circumstances.

"I'm sure he wasn't looking to take you on twice in one night," Will said.

Megan basked in the approval she heard in his voice. "Or he knew I'd go straight to the sheriff and that they'd have deputies looking out for me."

Or had he not bothered to head to her house because he'd known she'd stayed with Will? It wouldn't be the first time she'd wondered if Rich was keeping tabs on her. While they'd been married he'd been possessive of her time and attention, subtly cutting her off from family and friends until the two of them existed in their own little world.

"Given any more thought to my offer?" Will asked.

"A little."

Despite the September sun blazing down on the fifty or so cars lined up in neat rows around her, Megan noted a pang of anxiety as she parked her car in the first open spot she came to.

"And?"

"Honestly, I'm fine."

Automatically, she made a swift check of her mirrors as she shut off the car, refusing to be caught off guard again. All was quiet as she stepped out of the sassy red Porsche and strode toward her building.

"What if I tell you that I'm feeling the need for a bodyguard and I could use your services?"

"I'm hanging up now."

Her phone started ringing again as she neared the front sidewalk. She ignored a stab of disappointment as she glanced at the screen and spied Aaron's face.

"Hi," she said as she neared the building. "What's up?"

The glass door, emblazoned with the logo for Royals Shoes, reflected a smiling woman with long dark hair, wearing a gray-tweed business suit and electric royal blue pumps embellished with silver vines. Business on top, party on her feet.

"Are you kidding me?" Her brother's characteristic control didn't seem in evidence this morning. "Lowell attacked you at work last night and you didn't call me?"

Megan stopped dead in her tracks. She didn't want to have this conversation in front of all her employees as she walked the halls on the way to her office.

"I reported it to the sheriff's department," she explained. "How did you find out?"

"Will called me."

Megan ground her teeth together. "He shouldn't have done that."

"He's worried about you."

"I'm fine," she insisted.

"He said he wants you to stay with him until Lowell is caught."

"Oh, he did?" Megan blew out a breath in frustration. "And did he also mention that I said I'd be fine?"

"You were attacked last night."

"And I got away. Did Will also mention that I shot Rich?"

"Yes." Aaron growled. "When did you get a gun?"

"A few weeks ago. And if you recall, Daddy taught me to shoot. In fact, I was more accurate than either you or Jason."

"That was target shooting," Aaron reminded her. "Not shooting at a live person who is trying to attack you."

"And yet that's what I did last night." Megan pushed through the front door. "Look, I don't have time to argue this with you now. I'll talk to you later." And with a great deal of satisfaction, she hung up on her older brother.

Yet as she marched into her shoe company, some of Will's and Aaron's concerns began to undermine her confidence. Was she risking her safety because she was afraid of her growing feelings for Will?

Unbidden, the memory of the previous night's kiss rose in her mind. At least she'd been able to play it cool afterward. Still, he'd filled her thoughts for hours as she'd tossed and turned in the unfamiliar bed, longing to hear a knock on the closed door, or better yet, the turn of the doorknob followed by the quiet pad of his bare feet across the rug toward her.

Not that Will would ever sneak up on her like that. He understood all too well what she'd been through these last few months and would recognize she'd be opposed to any and all surprises.

Megan settled into her office chair and booted up her computer. It was only nine in the morning and yet fifty emails awaited her attention. She had no time to debate whether she would stay at her house and possibly endanger her safety or move to Will's ranch and put her heart in peril.

She'd worked her way through a dozen communications, either tabling or answering each email, before opening one that stopped her breath. It was a photo of her and imposter Will on their wedding day. She looked impossibly happy as she stared up at her new husband. Megan's throat ached as she stared at the photo and remembered that day.

There was no caption or message with the photo. Only a subject line.

I'm not giving up.

Megan picked up her cell phone and opened the messaging app. She sent a single line of text.

You're right. I'm safer with you.

Five

The sun was starting to slide toward the horizon when Will strode into the living room where Megan was watching a documentary about wild horses in France. They'd finished dinner a short time earlier and Will was feeling restless. It was the second night Megan would stay at the ranch and he hadn't yet settled into a routine with her.

If Lucy and Brody had been around, he might have gone to his office to catch up on paperwork or joined them to watch a little television. They'd all lived together for years and enjoyed a comfortable coexistence. With Megan, however, he couldn't decide if he was supposed to leave her alone or entertain her.

"What are you working on?" he asked, joining her on the couch.

She sat cross-legged on the soft cushions with a large sketch pad on her lap and several colored pencils nearby. When he leaned over to take a better look, their shoulders brushed.

Tonight she was wearing the same navy slacks and white blouse she'd donned to go to work that morning. The neckline gaped on the silky top as her hand drew lines on the paper, offering Will a peek at the upper curve of her luscious breasts. He felt like a lecherous jerk as his gaze traced the lacy edge of her white bra, but it was hard enough to keep his hands off her much less his eyes.

"Some sketches for next year's fall line," she explained, tipping the sketch pad his way so he could see what she'd done.

Although he had no idea if the designs were any good, her artwork demonstrated that she knew what she was doing.

"I didn't realize you were an artist as well as a businesswoman."

"Shoes have been my passion for a long time."

Will took the sketch pad and went through several pages. "These are quite good."

She regarded him with a trace of mockery. "I didn't realize you knew so much about women's shoes."

"I don't. I was talking about your artistic ability."

"Oh." She bit her lip and played with the pencil in her hand. "Well, thank you. I really enjoy this side of the business. And mostly these are just ideas. I have actual designers that take my concepts and turn them into gorgeous finished products."

"What does this mean?" He pointed to the word *gold* that she'd written and then drawn arrows toward the heels.

"Each season I try to have a theme. I've decided that all styles for next year's fall line will have gold accents. Either filigree embellishments or vines or snakes twisting up the heels. I'm envisioning it as my gold line."

"I'm sure it'll be very successful." Will handed back the sketch pad. "Feel like doing something a little different tonight?"

"What did you have in mind?"

Megan's eyebrows were raised in curiosity, but it was the enticing slant of her lips that had Will rethinking his proposition.

He had to clear his throat before he could answer. "I thought we might go for a ride. I know a great place to watch the sunset."

"I haven't been on a horse in years," Megan said. In a blink the smoky expression in her eyes vanished, leaving them sparkling with delight. "Sounds like fun."

Feeling glum, like he'd missed a prime opportunity for something wonderful, he said, "Go get your jeans and boots on."

Fifteen minutes later they were headed up a small rise to a place Will had often gone as a kid. Although he had grown up on the ranch and lived there now, he actually didn't own it. When his father had died, he'd made it clear he wanted Will's stepbrother, Jesse, to take over the ranch and for Will to run the energy company.

"From the start I think my dad recognized that Jesse had the passion for the ranch that I lacked," Will explained, answering Megan's question why Roy Sanders had divided the family holdings the way he had.

"But Jesse is your stepbrother and not related to you by blood," Megan said. "Did it ever bother you that your dad left him one of the largest spreads in Royal?"

"Never. One thing about my dad, he never considered Jesse or Lucy as his stepkids. He treated them like his own."

Megan was regarding him with a certain measure of awe. "How is it that you can be so fair when there's so much money at stake?"

It wasn't the first time Will had faced questions regarding his opinion on how his dad had doled out his fortune.

"It's only money," he said. "Why should I expect to

inherit everything when Spark Energy Solutions is all I need? Besides, by focusing all my attention on the business, I can turn it into a corporation the likes of which my father never dreamed possible."

"I don't know a whole lot of people that would agree with you. It seems like most would have a problem sharing such a huge fortune with stepsiblings. You're pretty amazing."

Will shook his head. "I was young when Cora Lee married my dad. Jesse and Lucy are a part of my earliest memories. As far as I ever knew, Cora Lee was my mom. Jesse and Lucy were my brother and sister. When my dad died, Jesse stepped right in and did a pretty good job filling Dad's shoes."

"You lost both your biological parents so young." Megan's expression grew sorrowful. "That's really tough. And yet you turned out to be this great guy with no issues."

"No obvious issues," Will corrected with a wry grin. "Although I have to say that Cora Lee was responsible for keeping us together as a family. The months after my father died were hard, but Cora Lee loved us fiercely and constantly reminded us how strong we were."

To Will's surprise, Megan reached out and placed her hand over his where it rested on his thigh. If it had been anyone else's hand, Will would scarcely have noted the touch, but with Megan, every look, each brushing contact with her body set his nerves on fire. After a too brief squeeze, she withdrew.

"She's really protective of you."

"Protective." Will chewed on his lower lip and mulled that over. "Is that another word for bossy and opinionated?"

Megan shook her head. "She's those things, too, but only because she worries about you."

"And how would you know that?"

"I heard you two talking this morning. She questioned the wisdom of me staying at the ranch."

Will thought back to the conversation, trying to recall what had been said. "And I suppose you heard her remark on how I'm attracted to you."

Megan nodded. "She didn't seem too keen on the fact. And she called me an iceberg."

"You're not. In fact, you're the furthest thing from one."

It was something he could attest to firsthand. The frenzy of her gyrating hips as he'd thrust into her. Her impassioned cries had an edge of near desperation to them as moisture had gathered between their straining bodies. He'd tasted the saltiness of her sweat as he'd licked his way up her neck toward her luscious mouth...

Noting a sudden tightness in his jeans, Will pulled off his cowboy hat and wiped sweat from his brow. Damn, the woman had gotten beneath his skin. He shoved the images of her from that night to the back of his mind. She was unloading her emotional baggage. He needed to listen so he could understand her better.

"Sometimes I feel as if I can't trust anyone," Megan said, the color in her cheeks high as if she'd read his mind and was also recalling their feverish lovemaking. "It's why I give off the appearance of being an iceberg. I keep my guards up all the time and push people away."

"Until Rich came along and broke through." Will couldn't stop the resentment coloring his tone. It bothered him that he'd been too dense or preoccupied to go after a woman as amazing as Megan.

"And look at what that got me."

"You can't blame yourself for taking a chance and having things turn out the way they did."

"Can't I?" She blew out a breath. "I get the point you're trying to make, but at the same time the fact that I was taken in by Rich makes it harder for me to trust again."

Will heard the echo of his thoughts in her words. "You can't live your life not trusting people." *Do as I say, not as I do.*

"I know," she said. "It's something I have to work on."

"You could start by trusting me."

"I could." She drew the words out thoughtfully. "What would trusting you entail?"

"I think you've already started. You told me how you felt about me in high school and that you overheard my conversation with Cora Lee. It would be nice if we could talk to each other about things that are bothering us."

"I guess I could do that." She paused and chewed on her lower lip. "As long as we start slow and small."

"Slow and small it is. You have been upfront with me. Let me return the favor." He released a ragged breath then went on. "That night we spent together after Jason's memorial service was a huge surprise to me. Not only was the sex fantastic, but being with you felt right in a way I've never known before." Speaking from his heart had never been harder, but Will felt that he owed Megan the truth. "That bothers me because I feel like I'm out on a limb, waiting for it to break."

The admission came out easier than he'd expected.

"You're not alone on that limb and there's no reason it has to break." She gave him a smile of heartbreaking vulnerability that nearly stopped his heart. "That night was wonderful for me, as well, but I think both of us recognize we're in a complicated situation and that how we feel in this moment might change once Rich is caught and life returns to normal."

Part of him resented her practical nature, but he knew she was right. That didn't stop him from wanting to haul her off her horse and make love to her beneath the stars.

"So what do we want to do?" he asked, then without

waiting for her answer, added, "I'd like for us to get to know each other."

"In bed or out?" She looked surprised that she'd asked the question.

He couldn't help it, a chuckle slipped out. With the laughter came a release of tension. Her features softened into a broad smile.

"Both." He might as well continue to be honest. "Pretending that I don't want to get you naked and make you scream my name again is contrary to learning about each other."

"Okay." She nodded. "And it's quite possible once we know each other…intimately…we will realize we don't like each other very much at all." Her teeth flashed in a flirtatious grin that belied her bleak statement.

"I hope you're kidding because I can't imagine what I could learn about you that would change my high opinion."

"I have all sorts of terrible traits."

"Name one."

She made a fierce face. "I expect you to be able to read my mind."

"That's pretty common in women," he said, his lofty tone earning him a scowl. "We'll work on it."

"I leave every drawer and cupboard door open that I touch. It makes my assistant crazy."

"My assistant use to complain that I acted as if she was the keeper of everything. As organized as I can be when it comes to my business, I never know where to find things like staplers or paperclips. It really drove her nuts when she'd told me several times where something belonged."

"I was tricked into falling for and marrying a man I thought was you," she muttered, her eyes on the horizon where the sun had fallen behind the clouds, painting the sky crimson, tangerine and gold.

Will couldn't let that hang out there without reminding her of his own failings when it came to Lowell. "My best friend tried to kill me and then took over my life, killing your brother and harming a bunch of people in the process."

They sat side by side on their horses as the day faded around them. Declaring their failures had dampened the mood, but also connected them. They were on equal footing in this debacle with Rich. What remained to be seen was whether that was a suitable foundation to build a relationship on.

"I guess neither one of us is perfect," Megan said, breaking the silence.

"I don't know if I'd say that," Will said, his gaze resting on her meaningfully. "There's not a lot about you that doesn't scream flawless."

Instead of smiling at his compliment or laughing it off, she grew silent and very still. Will immediately saw that he'd said something wrong.

"What did I say?" he asked.

"Rich use to say all kinds of over-the-top flattering things to me. Telling me I was beautiful and perfect." She sighed. "I fell for it. Pretty hard, in fact. I believed him because I thought it was you saying those things and they were exactly what I'd hoped you'd say to me all those years ago when we were in high school. Only, I wasn't beautiful or perfect in those days. I was skinny, awkward and at times my competitive nature got the better of me."

"I'm not Rich," Will said gruffly. "I'm not saying things to you with some hidden agenda. I'm not going to try to seduce you or sweet-talk you into my bed. I speak the truth." Far from being annoyed at being lumped into the same category as Lowell, Will appreciated that Megan had shared her concerns with him. "I promise I'll always be truthful."

"Thank you." Her fingers, which had tightened on the

reins, now relaxed. "I'm sorry if I jumped to the wrong conclusion."

"Don't apologize. You have legitimate concerns."

"I have issues." Megan rode in silence for a few moments. "Do you ever wonder if you'll be able to trust anyone again?"

"Yes… I do." Although he hadn't admitted that to anyone else, it seemed important to share with Megan. "You and I both have a lot more in common than you might think. We've both been through the ringer and it's not something we can easily bounce back from."

For a while the only sound was the steady thump of the horses' hooves and the rising symphony of insects as the sky deepened to a velvety navy blue.

"I'd like to trust you," Megan said at last.

Will smiled. "I'd like to trust you, too."

"Think we can?" She peeled her eyes off the trail ahead of them and met his gaze.

Although he saw hesitancy there, he glimpsed hope, as well, and nodded. "I think we can work on it."

Megan regarded herself in the boutique's three-way mirror. The luxurious decor, strategically placed lighting, glasses of wine and attentive store clerk had lulled her into a state of relaxation she hadn't felt since the night Richard had approached her. The outing was made even better because Dani had finally carved time in her schedule to come along.

Not that Megan needed to find a dress for Aaron and Kasey's engagement party this Friday. She had a closet full of expensive clothes. But she was attending the party with Will and that gave her the excuse to buy something new. Not just new, but different. Out of her comfort zone. And that was exactly how she'd describe the figure-hugging, black-lace dress she was currently wearing.

"That's the one," Dani declared, her lips pursed in a silent whistle.

"This is the one," Megan echoed, sliding her palms down the sides of the dress.

"Will is going to die when he sees you in it."

Although she told herself she shouldn't choose the dress for this reason, Megan couldn't lie to her friend. "I'd like that. It's been a long time since I've dared to be sexy and this dress makes me feel that way."

"How do you not look at yourself in the mirror every morning and say, 'Damn, I'm a sexy thing'?" Dani struck a sassy pose and pointed at Megan. "You're one of the most beautiful women in this town."

Megan grinned at her friend's antics. "Beauty isn't always about how you appear, but how you feel inside. And one thing Rich was really good at was destroying my confidence in a dozen subtle ways."

Dani sobered. "I get it. I'm sure every woman has that moment when she feels less than she is because of something someone says."

Megan gave her arms a vigorous shake, dispelling the somber mood. Setting her hands on her hips, she tried to match her friend's cocky attitude. "That's all behind me now. I am the new and improved Megan."

"You go, girl."

Inspired by Dani's cheerleading, Megan turned her attention to her friend. "Now, how about you? That bright blue wrap dress you tried earlier was perfect on you."

"I love it, but I don't know if it'll work with my new shoes." Dani had fallen in love with a pair of strappy red sandals with flowers from Royals Shoes' current collection, declaring that she'd loved the way the big, round petals let the foot peek through. And the bit of rhinestone in the center of each flower gave them the perfect touch of bling. "What about the black-and-white color-block dress?"

The simple sheath had black hourglass panels front and back with a strip of white running up the sides. The design gave the illusion that Dani had curves for miles. The red shoes would be a sexy pop against the dress's monochromatic palette.

"Cole's going to go nuts when he sees you in it," Megan said. "And in addition to looking fabulous, our dresses will complement each other." She paused, caught off guard by a sudden rush of emotion. "It's really been great having you back in my life," she told her friend in a shaky voice.

Dani came over to hug her. "I feel the same way."

With their fashion decisions made, the two women made their purchases before heading out. As soon as Megan heard the boutique door close behind her, she glanced around, scanning the street for any sign of Rich. Checking her surroundings had become a necessary habit. She thought she was being unobtrusive until she caught Dani's worried frown.

"He really has you spooked."

Megan didn't need to ask whom her friend was referring to. "When I first found out I'd married an imposter, I was more humiliated than concerned about my safety. But after learning what he did to Will and then to Jason, he's showed himself to be dangerous and unpredictable. And he's back in town." She'd kept the parking lot encounter to herself, but now she wondered if she'd done the right thing to come shopping with Dani. "He confronted me in my building's parking lot a few nights ago."

Dani's brown eyes went wide. "Why didn't you say something?"

"I didn't want to worry anyone."

"You didn't want to…" Dani shook her head in dismay. "What happened?"

"He said he wanted me to go with him."

"Go with him where?" her friend demanded.

"I have no idea. I think he's back to finish some unsettled business."

Picking up on Megan's anxiety, Dani began to scan the immediate vicinity the way her friend had done. "Are you sure it was a good idea for you to come shopping like this? Rich could jump out and grab you at any second."

Seeing her friend's alarm, Megan wished she'd kept quiet. "I don't think he'll try anything on a busy street in downtown Royal. If I thought otherwise, I never would've put you in any kind of danger."

"I'm not worried about me."

"I am. You have two beautiful boys counting on you to stay safe and a very formidable man who would be devastated if any harm came to you." Megan frowned. "In fact, maybe it would be better if this is our last solo outing until Rich is caught."

"You can't isolate yourself from everybody who loves you in an attempt to keep them safe." Dani looped her arm through Megan's in a display of solidarity and said, "Come on, let's go grab some lunch."

Despite being filled with misgivings, Megan nodded. Her throat constricted as emotion overwhelmed her. Having a good friend like Dani was priceless and she was more determined than ever to keep the mother of two safe. Even if that meant Megan had to keep her distance for the near future.

Once they were seated in a booth at the Royal Diner, Dani began to probe for details about Megan's encounter with Rich. Megan explained how she'd managed to get a shot off, possibly wounding the imposter.

"You are so brave." Dani regarded her in open admiration. "I don't know what I would've done in the same situation."

"I was terrified," Megan admitted without reservation. "And acting on instinct. I didn't consider trying to hit him, only scare him away." She released a quavering breath. "But now, and it's terrible of me to say, I think if he comes near me again, I could point the gun at his black heart and pull the trigger."

Although the confession shocked Megan even as she made it, she understood where the declaration came from. Long before Rich had killed Jason and threatened her well-being, he'd systematically targeted her self-esteem and psychologically tormented her. The love she'd had for him in the beginning had faded beneath long months of his subtle abuse after they were married. And yet she'd continued to play the part of good wife because she'd believed she was married to Will Sanders, a man she'd long admired. Once she knew she'd been fooled, it was easy to turn against Richard Lowell.

"If someone was out to harm me or my family, I'd be the same way," Dani said. "And Rich is a very dangerous man. You shouldn't have to think twice about doing whatever you have to do to protect yourself."

While Megan had never expected anything but support from her friend, she appreciated hearing Dani's input. Whatever shadows had darkened her psyche fell away for a time, leaving her feeling brighter and more optimistic than she had in weeks.

She blinked back the sudden moisture in her eyes and smiled. "Thank you. I needed to hear that."

Dani nodded. "So, I guess that explains why you are living at the Ace in the Hole? How is that going?"

"It's nice." Megan blew out a sigh.

"And spending so much time with Will?" Dani's voice took on a sly overtone. "Are you getting along?"

"Of course. He's wonderful."

Although they'd had dinner together at the ranch several times in the last few days, they hadn't returned to the camaraderie they'd achieved during the sunset ride. She wasn't sure if it was her fault or if he was holding back. Probably both of them were grappling with how far to advance their relationship and how fast.

They'd put sleeping together on the table, but as much as she craved his slow, deep kisses and the excitement of his hands gliding over her skin as he discovered all the places she loved to be touched, Megan didn't want only a series of sexual encounters, however incredible they might be.

So, maybe their lack of progress was her fault. Maybe she was giving off a vibe that was warning him away.

"And I'm sure he feels the same way about you," Dani said.

Megan sensed where her friend was going with the inquiry and made a face. "I wouldn't know about that, but he seems to be enjoying my company. At least, that's what he tells me."

"I'm just gonna come straight out and ask," Dani said with abrupt seriousness. "Are you two sleeping together?"

"No."

"Really?" Her friend looked crushed. "Because I know you were really attracted to him in high school. And the way he looks at you makes me think he's interested."

"It's too complicated." Megan ignored her rapidly beating heart. "And as much as I like him, I'm sure he sees me as the woman who married his greatest enemy."

"But he knows you were fooled. He also knows you married Will Sanders. That's got to give him a lot to think about."

Too much. Megan suspected Will had a lot of questions where her past decisions were concerned.

"I think he'll always wonder about my reasons for wanting to be with him," she said, recalling what Cora Lee had intimated. "What if he thinks all I'm interested in is being Mrs. Will Sanders?"

"Why would he think that? You have success and money in your own right. And you're certainly not the type to marry a man for position or wealth." Dani shook her head. "I don't think you're giving him enough credit."

Megan wished she could be sure Will's family wouldn't eventually convince him he was better off without her.

"And what about what happened between the two of you after Jason's memorial service?" Dani asked. She'd been delighted at the prospect of something good coming out of all the terrible things that had happened to Will and Megan. "Surely that's something you can build on."

"We were both hurting." Since it had happened, Megan had alternately dwelled on and shied away from thinking about the blazing-hot passion she'd felt in Will's arms. Could something so powerful be a mistake? Yet could she trust her own feelings any more in the wake of being fooled by Richard Lowell?

"And nothing has happened since?" When Megan didn't immediately respond, Dani pounced. "See that's what I'm talking about!"

"We haven't slept together again."

"So what *has* happened?"

"We might've kissed. But we've agreed not to take it any further."

Dani rolled her eyes in disgust. "Both of you have been dancing around your attraction for each other for far too long. Why don't you just tell him how you feel and see where it leads?"

"Because I don't want to create an awkward situation between us while I'm living at the ranch."

"But what if you two are meant to be together only you'll never know because you don't tackle your issues?"

"Maybe once Rich is caught, Will and I can have a conversation, but too much is up in the air right now. It's just too complicated."

Dani looked frustrated but nodded instead of arguing further. "I'll try to be patient, but don't expect me to let it go."

Megan recognized that her friend meant well and her eagerness for Megan to find happiness with Will was because Dani had reconnected with Cole and was madly in love. For a second Megan experienced a stab of envy. During those early days with imposter Will, she'd also believed herself in the best relationship of her life, but it had been one big lie. Not that Megan considered that Dani and Cole were anything except the real deal. There would be no startling revelations in their future. No breakdown of trust or respect.

"Just do me a favor," Dani continued. "Don't put up walls against Will. I know you're running scared right now, but I think he's good for you and vice versa. You two need each other for moral support. I'm just worried that if you put on the brakes too hard he might get the idea that you're not interested in him."

"I promise not to shut him down altogether."

Megan wasn't sure she'd have to worry about that since Will had behaved like a total gentleman since she'd moved in. Except for that first night, but how that kiss had come about was a little blurry in her memory. Had she encouraged him or had he taken the initiative? She only knew she had desperately wanted him to kiss her and so he had. And it had been mind-blowing.

"Wonderful," Dani said. "Now let's talk about what we're going to have for dessert."

Megan laughed. "We haven't even ordered lunch yet."

"Life is short. Eat dessert first."

Six

The night of Aaron and Kasey's engagement party, Will strolled into the Texas Cattleman's Club with Megan on his arm, all too aware of the glances being thrown their way. He wasn't sure what was to blame for the stir. Megan's stunning appearance or the two of them showing up together, looking relaxed and comfortable in each other's company.

While most of the party guests knew Richard Lowell had been impersonating Will for a year, the case wasn't common knowledge to the majority of folks living in Royal. Ever since Will had started showing up around town instead of being holed up at the ranch as he'd been through much of the summer, he noticed people that avoided him or regarded him warily.

From one peculiar conversation after another, he'd determined that Rich had behaved erratically while pretending to be him. Fortunately those who knew him best had attributed his short temper, secretiveness and occasional odd turn of phrase as a result of the injuries he'd suffered from the boating explosion. More than anything Will wished he could come clean with the people he'd known all his life and explain that Lowell had been impersonating him, but while Rich remained at large, the authorities wanted Will to continue the farce.

The only good part of any of it was spending time with Megan and pretending to be her husband, a role he grew into a little more each day.

"Have I told you how beautiful you look?" he murmured, guiding her toward the meeting room where Aaron and Kasey's engagement party was taking place.

At his compliment, her long black lashes fanned her flawless skin. With most women this behavior would be deliberate flirtation, but Megan was too genuine to toy with him. "Several times in fact."

Thanks to all the time he'd spent with her recently, Will now understood that she was wary of flattery. Yet it spoke to her growing trust that a half smile curved her lips, telling him she was pleased but reticent about showing how much.

"Too much?"

Her pale blue eyes glinted like sunshine on water as she met his gaze. "No, it's okay. I believe you mean it."

It continued to amaze him that a woman as beautiful and successful as Megan, with all she had going for her, remained locked in doubt. How could he not want to give her everything?

"Are you nervous?" he asked, noting a slight tremor in her slender form. "I promise not to leave your side."

"Well, that would be a change. I'm not sure that some of the people here will know what to make of you as an attentive husband." Pain lingered beneath her light tone. Almost as soon as the words were out, however, she squeezed his arm. "I'm sorry. I know it wasn't you and I shouldn't have said anything."

"No, I'm sorry." Regret sliced through him. Every time he faced his failure, it opened another wound on his soul. Some days the pain grew too intense to bear. "Damn it. If only I'd seen through him. It's my fault all this happened. Rich should never have had the chance to hurt anyone."

"Your logic is flawed," she said. "If we'd been married before the boating accident then I would have been married to him when he returned pretending to be you."

Will shook his head, not letting himself off so easily. "But you would've recognized the difference and called him out."

"He was pretty convincing," she reminded him. "He fooled your family and your friends."

"You would've known the difference," he insisted.

"What makes you so sure?"

Instead of entering the party, he detoured into the hallway that led to the club's offices. At this time of day, the narrow corridor was empty and Will exploited the isolation by backing Megan against the wall.

"This."

He leaned down and seized her lips with his, taking advantage of her surprised gasp to slide his tongue along her teeth and beyond. It wasn't a romantic kiss, full of promise and longing, but a deliberate claiming, meant to demonstrate his power over her senses.

She met the demanding thrust with equal fervor, a soft moan escaping her throat as she knotted her fingers into his hair and pulled him closer still. Her ardor made the kiss go hot in an instant. A shudder racked her form as he eased the hard planes of his chest and abs into her yielding breasts and soft belly. She moaned when he slid his leg between her thighs and made glancing contact with her most sensitive spot. The sound consumed him and he caressed his tongue down her neck, desperate for a taste of more than just her lips.

His willpower deteriorated with each desperate rasp of his breath. She smelled spicy, the scent more exotic than what she usually wore. It made him think of all the far-away places he'd like to make love to her.

He cupped his palm over her breast, feeling the tight nipple through the fabric of her dress. She flexed her fingers in his hair and pushed into the caress. Fondling her like this only added to his frustration as his erection pushed relentlessly against his zipper. The ache awoke him to their surroundings even as her teeth raked down his neck.

With a growl, he fought to bring himself back under control and was shocked at the difficulty. He didn't lose control like this. Well, once. And it had been this woman whose hunger had stormed his defenses and set him to devouring her.

Crushing his mouth over hers once more, he felt her melting beneath the hot caress of his tongue. Relentless, intoxicating desire pulsed through him, demanding release. It would take ten seconds to free himself, shift her under-wear aside and plunge into her. His hand was on the move to his zipper before the thought had completely formed in his mind. To his amazement, his fingers encountered her hand as it darted toward his belt.

"Megan." That was as far as he got as her fingers advanced too fast for him to stop and closed over his hard-on.

A groan ripped from his chest even as his hips bucked beneath her inquisitive touch. He still had his hand on her breast and her nipples peaked still harder. He plucked at them, and she cried out. The sound awoke him to their situation.

Almost too late, he realized that while the risk of discovery wasn't likely, they'd let themselves get so carried away the entire engagement party could've paraded past while they remained lost in each other.

With painful regret, he eased her hand away from his erection and pinned it beside her head, recalling the reason he'd dragged her to this isolated spot in the first place.

"Tell me if you would have been fooled by anything less than this," he demanded, dragging his lips across her cheek and down her neck, savoring the agitated press and retreat of her breast against his palm.

She trembled and her breath puffed out in a ragged chuckle. "No, I wouldn't have been fooled. Your kisses aren't like any I've ever known. In your arms I feel things… You make me crazy. Anything you ask I'd give you."

While part of him reveled in her words, another reminded him that lust was not love. The former they shared in abundance, but the latter was far trickier. Did he even know what love was? Will was pretty sure he could recognize it in others. Aaron and Kasey were a prime example of two people who were meant for each other.

Will had glimpsed the signs even before Kasey had moved into Aaron's home to act as a nanny for Jason's seven-year-old daughter after her father's disappearance. From the first, the intensity with which Aaron looked at Kasey broadcast that his interest in her was anything but professional.

At first Will had been an amused observer, enjoying the spectacle of the brooding, brilliant and driven businessman falling for his sweet and sassy administrative assistant. But soon Will had noticed the joke was on him as Aaron suddenly had it all, leaving Will to face how empty his life had become.

Which was when he decided his business successes weren't enough. He wanted a solid marriage. A family of his own.

"Megan—" He winced at his regretful tone and knew it was responsible for her sharp intake of breath.

"Don't you dare apologize."

"I'm sorry," he said, ignoring her command. "I shouldn't have done that."

"Damn you, Will Sanders! I bare myself to you and you apologize. You are the most frustrating man I've ever met."

"I know and I'm sorry."

"Stop apologizing." She smacked him hard in the chest with her clenched fists. "I wanted you to kiss me. In truth, I want even more. And I won't make excuses for that. It's good with you. It's better than good. It's fantastic."

"I feel the same way. You make me lose control and I don't want to do that with you." He pushed to arm's length and gazed down at her beautiful face, seeing that his clumsy words had hurt her. "You're misunderstanding me. The situation we're in isn't real. And it's dangerous. Were pretending to be something we're not and I think it might be causing both of us to take things where we wouldn't if circumstances were different."

"So you don't think we'd be attracted to each other if we weren't pretending to be married?"

"No, that's not what I mean," Will insisted. "I would be attracted to you no matter what the situation, but emotions get tangled up and I care too much about you to be anything but completely truthful."

"I get it. We're playacting. Pretending to be something we're not." She flashed a smile that curved her lips but brought no joy to the bruised blue of her eyes. "We're not married. And certainly not in love. Which means no one around us will question our behavior because I'm pretty sure fake Will and I weren't in love, either."

"Megan—"

"It's fine," she assured him, ejecting the two words in a way that convinced him she was anything but. "I'm going to detour to the ladies' room and fix my lipstick. I'll meet you inside."

Before Will could bumble another attempt to explain and cause even more damage, Megan slipped away from him and headed for the main corridor. He remained in place for a long moment, kicking himself and wondering when he'd become so inept when it came to talking to women.

Reapplying her lipstick became a trial as Megan's hand continued to shake in the aftermath of Will's passionate kiss and subsequent rejection. How dare he kiss her like that and then apologize! Especially after she'd followed Dani's advice and told him how he made her feel. It made her rethink her decision to stop retreating behind her defenses as she'd been doing since Will had first returned to Royal and she'd discovered she'd been married to an imposter.

But she couldn't keep bottling up her emotions. As she'd recently discovered, developing a thick skin hadn't prevented her from being humiliated. Nor was denying her growing longing for Will making her happy.

As she skimmed bright red lipstick along her bottom lip, she considered all that Will had said moments before. Was it fair to attribute mere sexual attraction to what was happening between them? Or was she kidding herself that the ache in her heart was real? Could her desire to be with him stem from proximity and pretending to be married?

I don't want to lose control with you.

Why the hell not? What was so wrong about letting go with her? Was he worried that she might fall for him? A ragged laugh tore at Megan's throat. She suspected it was a little too late to close the barn door on that one. Her fascination with Will was a decade old. From a time when her vulnerable heart jumped every time he slid into his seat in the AP Literature class.

The ladies' room door opened and two women swept in on a tide of laughter and perfume. Realizing she'd dawdled for too long, Megan dropped her lipstick into her evening clutch and headed for the door. To her surprise, Will hadn't gone into the party without her. As soon as she stepped into the hallway, he pushed off the wall and came toward her.

Dressed in a meticulously tailored charcoal suit and white shirt, he looked every inch a wealthy, successful man and her heart gave a great jolt at the dynamic power he exuded. Every cell in her body called for her to be his and it frustrated her to be denied.

"You didn't have to wait for me," she said, cursing her breathless tone.

"I didn't handle things very well a little while ago."

"I disagree." She headed toward the party and he fell into step beside her. "You spoke your mind and I appreciate your honesty."

"But you're not happy about what I said."

"I'm neither happy nor unhappy." Megan was amazed that she uttered the whopping lie with such equanimity. Fastening on a guileless expression, she took Will's arm as they crossed the threshold and entered the engagement party room.

"I want to explain where I'm coming from."

"We don't have time for that. Maybe later tonight we can discuss how to coexist peacefully until Rich is caught." The reasonable statement made her heart twist in agony.

"Coexist peacefully?" He gave a rough chuckle. "There's not an instant where I feel peaceful around you."

Confusion flaring, Megan shot a glance his way, but before she could do more than gather breath to chastise him for bombarding her with mixed signals, they were approached by Will's stepbrother, Jesse Navarro, and his beautiful wife.

"Jillian, that color is perfect on you," Megan gushed,

smiling as she took in the glamorous blonde's empire-cut dress in brilliant emerald that teased out the flecks of green in her hazel eyes. She'd pulled her long, wavy hair into a simple high pony to better show off the diamond dangles that hung from her ears. "You look fantastic."

"So do you," Jillian said, cuing in on Megan's black pumps, designed to look like ballet toe shoes with attached ribbons that wrapped around her ankle and then tied in bows. "Those shoes are stunning."

"Part of my winter collection. Text me your size and I'll send you a pair."

Megan wasn't being completely altruistic. Thanks to all the years Jillian had danced, her long, slender legs were toned and sexy. Having Jillian wearing her designer shoes would be great advertising.

"That would be amazing."

Jesse and Will watched the exchange in silence, neither seeming eager to weigh in on the women's love of all things strappy, stilettoed and bedazzled.

With niceties out of the way, the brothers settled into a conversation about an issue concerning the creek that ran through one of the Ace in the Hole's fields while the two couples circled the room in search of the engaged couple.

By the time they arrived at a cluster that included her brother and his soon-to-be wife, Megan realized any tension she'd been feeling at the start of the evening was long gone. Tonight for the first time Megan felt as if she and Will were a true couple instead of just two strangers pretending to be married.

She watched with admiration as Will navigated the guests with ease and confidence, remembering little details about each person they encountered so he could ask after their health, children, parents, ranch or business.

Megan also noticed how surprised people were that Will spoke to them at all. Richard Lowell had either avoided or alienated so many people during his time pretending to be Will that he'd done terrible damage to his nemesis's reputation.

As they navigated the party, the two couples added another pair to their group. Dani and Cole arrived late, looking mildly disheveled and unable to keep their eyes off each other. Catching Dani's eye, Megan quirked an eyebrow at her friend and was rewarded by a bright flush creeping into the younger woman's cheeks.

Remembering the steamy kiss she and Will had exchanged earlier and how the aftermath hadn't left her feeling giddy or satisfied, Megan felt a minor stab of envy. Her body continued to ache with sexual frustration even as her heart cried out to be heard. What she wouldn't give to be happily in love and free to show it. But what if Will wasn't ready for the sort of emotional journey she wanted to take with him? Could her heart survive being battered twice in less than a year?

At long last they reached the engaged couple, and Megan hugged her brother before turning to his fiancée.

"You look beautiful tonight," Megan murmured to Kasey, admiring the executive assistant turned nanny who'd captured Aaron's heart.

Petite and pretty with unique amber-colored eyes and caramel-highlighted hair, Kasey wore a lacy gold dress that shimmered in the overhead lighting. Megan was thrilled to welcome the beautiful and vivacious woman into the family. Not only was Kasey good for Aaron and Savannah, but Megan was looking forward to having her as a sister.

"So do you," Kasey said, her gaze dancing from Megan to Will. Then she lowered her voice and said, "You two make a gorgeous couple."

Like Dani, Kasey obviously liked what she perceived was happening between Megan and Will. Megan opened her mouth to dispel Kasey's assumptions, but decided once

Richard Lowell was caught the truth would come out on its own.

"Nowhere near as stunning as the two of you," Megan said, determined to keep the focus on the future bride and groom. "I don't know what you're doing to my brother, but keep it up."

To Megan's delight, Kasey blushed.

"It's more what he's doing to me. I've never known a man like him. He's great with Savannah. And so sweet and romantic," Kasey added with a heartfelt sigh. "Just this morning I woke up to a rose on my pillow and a note that said…well, let's just say it made me smile."

"Have you set a date for the wedding?" Jillian asked, joining the conversation.

"Not yet. We haven't settled on how many people to invite and that will determine how much planning we need."

Megan thought of her own wedding in a tiny chapel in Reno with no friends or family around. It had been a mistake she'd never repeat. "I imagine a big wedding could get out of hand pretty fast, but I would love to help you in any way I can."

"Thank you." Kasey gave her arm a friendly squeeze.

As she stepped aside to make room for Jillian to hug Kasey, Megan's gaze shifted to Will. The tangled emotions that enveloped her heart became complex knots as she caught his searching gaze on her. A line of fire streaked through her chest. He was obviously looking for answers, but the questions remained a mystery and his brief frown left her more confused than ever.

She longed to drag him into a corner of the room and demand he stop with all the mixed signals. What did he want from her? Friendship? Sex? Both? Or…neither? They were in this wretched situation together and she wanted to make the best of it, but wasn't sure what constituted *the best*.

When she was with him she craved his hot, searing

kisses, wanted his big, strong arms around her. When separated, she missed his smile and sense of humor. This seemed to prove her emotions weren't triggered by mere lust and proximity. She was falling for Will Sanders all over again.

In a far corner of the Texas Cattleman's Club parking lot, Rich sat in his truck and stared at the building's front door. He'd followed Will's Land Rover from the Ace in the Hole and watched as Will had escorted Megan in.

From his confident stride, Will looked like a man without a care in the world. And why not? He had his life back and the added bonus of a woman who obviously adored him.

Rich remembered when Megan used to look at him as if he directed when the sun rose and set. She'd been his to command. Especially after they got married. The things he'd done to her. What she'd been willing to do to him. He'd savored her passion because she'd belonged to him and not Will Sanders.

Well, he'd have her back soon enough. And this time Will would be around to witness Rich's triumph. He closed his eyes and let his head fall back while the sweetness of his impending victory filled him.

Rich's phone buzzed, disrupting the moment. He'd received a reply text about a meeting from a tech guy who knew all about electronic security and how to beat it. The FBI thought they were so smart, leaving his gold in place but setting up a surveillance net to catch him when he went back for his stash. They'd underestimated him from the start and continued to make one mistake after another. It had almost become a game to him, moving around the town of Royal unseen.

But his fun was about to come to an end. It was past time to get his gold, grab Will's girl and get the hell out of town. His only regret was that he couldn't be there to see the look on Will's face when he realized he'd been bested again.

Megan and Will hadn't lingered at the party after their friends had departed to relieve their babysitters. Earlier in the evening they'd agreed to make an appearance and leave early.

Now, humming along to a Taylor Swift song from her first album, Megan stripped off her finery and hung the black dress in her closet. Standing in just her underwear in heels, she caught a glimpse of herself in the dresser mirror. The black-lace bra and panty set had been an impulsive purchase and she didn't have to dig deep to locate her motivation for buying the peekaboo lingerie.

Her thoughts and decisions these days seem driven by her hormones. Lusty thoughts consumed her at the oddest times during the day. She might be staring at a sketch for a new shoe design and start to wonder if Will would appreciate her wearing the five-inch heels and nothing more than a smile. The thought increased her awareness of her skin and the hot blood bubbling beneath her surface. Before she knew it, an ache began to build between her thighs.

Never before had she struggled to stay focused on work. Well, that wasn't exactly true. She recalled fighting to keep her mind on her schoolwork in those high school classes she'd shared with Will. And those were the days before she knew what it was like to surrender to his feverish kisses and delicious lovemaking. What was a girl to do when she was living in the man's house?

Megan fetched the pajama top she'd worn that first night and slid her arms into it. She set her hands on her hips and posed in what she hoped was a seductive way. The mirror reflected her awkwardness. She had little practice acting sexy. Her marriage to Rich hadn't exactly awakened a lioness.

Most of the time her husband had come at her like a freight train. His passionate kisses had made her feel like a possession rather than a partner, leaving her unsatisfied and convinced there was something wrong with her. After all, she'd had years of being attracted to Will. She couldn't understand why, after he'd started to notice her, things had changed. In the days leading up to their wedding, she'd started to think maybe she was an iceberg.

Her phone buzzed, announcing a call. As she approached the dresser, Megan saw her reflection and realized she'd fastened most of the buttons on the pajama top, hiding her body and the sexy lingerie from view. Rattled by where her thoughts had taken her, she didn't check who might be trying to get hold of her.

"Hello?"

"So now you're living with him?"

Megan was so startled to hear Rich's sinister voice that her thoughts momentarily hit pause.

"How long have you been sleeping with him, Megan?" He sounded on the edge of rage.

"I'm not." But her trembling voice gave her away. "We're not." She spoke the second denial with more heat.

"Such a pretty liar. Do you know what happens to pretty liars?"

"Leave me alone." Her skin prickled as if a hundred needles peppered her flesh.

"You're my wife. I'm not ever going to leave you alone."

The truth of that statement flattened her like a steamroller. He wasn't going away. And he wasn't getting caught. How much longer could she stand to be looking over her shoulder every second of every day? She considered how many years he'd hung around Will and pretended friendship while taking advantage of everyone around him. And given the way he'd eluded capture these long months, could Megan expect to ever be free?

"I'm not your wife. I never was. Leave me the hell alone."

No matter how many times she spoke those phrases, Megan knew it made no difference. Rich wasn't going to give up and go away. She disconnected the call and threw the phone onto the bed. She'd only just covered her face with her hands when the phone began to ring again. The strident tone ricocheted off the walls of her lonely bedroom. When the noise stopped, she snatched up the cell and blocked the last incoming number. Hands shaking, she set the phone on the dresser and stared at it.

The sheriff would want to know about this contact, but Megan couldn't bring herself to pick up the phone again. Not even to call the authorities. Instead, she fled the room, leaving the phone behind, and went to find the man who could make everything okay again.

Seven

Megan burst into Will's room, not stopping to think what she might find. He had shed his suit coat and tie and was standing at the sliding-glass door staring into the night, dressed in shirt and slacks.

"Will."

He spun around at her voice and his eyes narrowed as he surveyed her, taking in her panicked expression. "What's happened?"

"Rich called me. He's not letting me go. He knows I'm staying here with you. And he doesn't like it."

Three long strides brought him across the room and into her space, but although his voice sought to comfort, he didn't touch her. "You're safe here."

"Am I?" Megan punctuated her question with frantic arm gestures before grabbing her hair and tugging. "He's going to get me. I just know it."

"He's not going to come anywhere near you. Stop." Will grabbed her hands and eased her fingers free of her hair before drawing them against his chest. "I won't let anything happen to you."

"You can't stop him," she proclaimed, wanting badly to believe he could keep her safe. "Jason tried and look what happened to him. Rich killed him."

"Lowell caught Jason off guard the same way he did with me on the boat. That's not to happen again." Will softened his voice and spoke as if to calm a terrified child. "It's okay. You're going to be fine. We all will."

Megan sought calm in the promises but adrenaline pumped hard and fast through her body, making her heart thunder in her chest. "I want to believe you, but he scares me."

"You've already beaten him once," Will reminded her.

"I caught him by surprise. He's not likely to make the same mistake again."

"Well, if he tries anything, he'll have to go through me."

And that was part of what Megan was afraid of. She knew Will would put himself in harm's way to protect her.

"I don't want you to get hurt," she choked out.

"We need to call Special Agent Bird and Sheriff Battle and let them know what Lowell is planning."

Will loosened his hold on her wrists and made as if to back away. But the shock of hearing Rich's threats had struck a match to her emotions and although her fear was fading, her nerves continued to spark with energy that needed an outlet. With one hand, she grabbed his shirt to keep him in place.

"Make love to me." She used her free hand to tunnel her fingers into Will's thick black hair and tugged hard enough that he winced. "I need you."

His bright green eyes raked over her features as the air between them sizzled with electricity. "What you're asking…"

Megan met his questioning stare with one eyebrow raised in challenge and debated how far she was prepared to go.

"I'm not asking." Her hand moved down his body, feeling hard muscle bunch and ripple beneath her palm. Whatever it took, she would do. Megan was not sleeping alone tonight. "Don't speak. Don't think. Just act."

"What you're asking…" he ground out, shaking his head, his eyes already glowing with intent. "Is this really what you want?"

"You're all I've ever wanted."

The words came from a secret place deep inside her. Strangely enough, she'd never admitted this fact to imposter Will and he'd professed to love her. Why then did the confession slip so easily from her lips with a man who'd done his best to keep his distance from her?

"I don't deserve that or you."

"You deserve all of it and more."

It seemed that Will's head was at odds with his hormones because even as he tried to warn her off, his big body was easing into the empty space between them.

"I promised myself…" he rasped, whatever he meant to say fading as his hands stroked over her rib cage and came together at her spine.

This is what Megan had been waiting for and she rocked into his beautiful, powerfully male body. Every button of his dress shirt imprinted itself on her skin, and the metal of his belt buckle went from cool to hot an instant after it came into contact with her flesh.

Rubbing herself against the hard thrust of his arousal, she brought her lips to his, driving her breasts against the unrelenting planes of his chest and arching her back to better savor the heat pouring off him. A whimper gathered in her throat as he slid his palm down her back and cupped her butt, lifting her onto her toes. The move put her off balance but she welcomed his taking charge. It proved he wanted her.

His tongue plunged into her mouth and she met the thrust eagerly. The kiss was electric and growing hotter by the second. Why the hell had they been fighting this? Her thoughts were swamped by need and the joy of the hard crush of his muscular arm as Will tightened his hold on her. Being unable to breathe had never felt so thrilling.

His lips dominated hers, awakening a quaking in her muscles that left her without strength or balance. She needed neither because Will was the rock she could build her life upon. In his arms she was safe and drowning in pleasure that outmatched anything she'd ever known.

The taste of him intoxicated her as did his need. She reveled in the bite of his fingers as he pulled her into him, intent on eliminating even the suspicion of distance between them. The texture of his hair tickled her fingers even as the mild scratch of his beard raked down her throat as his lips trailed fire across her skin.

Part of her recognized that tonight might be a one-shot deal. As determined as he'd been to keep things casual and play it cool, she suspected he had no interest in being tied down. After all, their marriage was a mistake. He hadn't chosen her. He'd inherited her like a box of oddities gathered from a dead relative's house. No doubt as soon as all the legal stuff was cleared up, he'd be quick to part ways.

Which was why it was crazy for her to want this moment, to lose herself in him and surrender everything that made her strong. Yet in the months since he'd returned from Mexico, she'd grown attached to him, to the way he made her feel.

Maybe it would have been different if he hadn't treated her so gently…if his kindness hadn't been a balm to her soul after her difficult marriage to Rich. Maybe, if he hadn't tried to connect with her, looking at the photo album of their wedding, sympathizing with her shame at being fooled, she might have been able to keep her distance.

Marrying imposter Will had reawakened all the longing to be loved by him. Was it any wonder that when the real Will appeared and he was as charming, handsome and desirable as ever that her emotions were thrown into a chaotic storm? Still, after what had happened following Jason's memorial service, she'd promised herself that she wouldn't open herself up again. And yet only a short time had gone by and here she was, begging the man to do whatever he wanted to with her. As much as she'd tried to deny it, the truth was that she craved his taste against her tongue and the hard weight of his body possessing hers.

Will broke off the kiss and rested his forehead on her shoulder. His hands bracketed her waist while he breathed with the same ragged intensity gripping her. His breath puffed against her skin, calming her frantic heart while his stillness awakened a deep fear. As panic infiltrated the fog of passion surrounding her at his inactivity, her body continued to pulse and throb with need. Yet a second, discordant rhythm began as her mind questioned what could be wrong.

Did he not want her? Was he gripped by regrets? Maybe she wasn't good enough. Pretty enough. Desirable enough.

And just as she reached a crisis of insecurity the likes of which she hadn't felt since high school, he grabbed the lapels of her pajama top and ripped it wide-open. She gave a sharp gasp. The abrupt move held desperation and shocked her to her toes. But the sight of his dilated pupils and flared nostrils quieted her brief spike of anxiety.

"Will?"

"Dear Lord, what are you wearing?"

Despite the paralyzing self-doubt she'd been feeling moments ago, her lips twisted in a wry smirk. "Your pajamas."

"Not those. I'm talking about this." His fingertips

dusted across the lace covering the upper swell of her breast, setting her skin to tingling. "Have you had this on all night?"

Megan couldn't help herself. She let loose a breathy laugh. "Yes. You didn't seriously think I put it on so I could come in here and seduce you, did you?"

"A guy can hope." He tore his attention from her breasts and met her gaze. One corner of his lips kicked up.

"Well, okay," she conceded. "Maybe I had you in mind when I got dressed tonight."

He hummed in appreciation. "Tell me more."

"You make me feel sexy all the time. It's not anything I'm used to and I don't really know what to do about it."

"I guess then we're even because I'm taking cold showers at least twice a day." He cupped her face in his hands. "And I don't know what to do about it, either."

"Maybe we should stop fighting and go with it."

"That sounds like a great idea to me."

She tugged at his shirt, freeing it from his waistband, desperate to run her palms along his bare skin. He shuddered as she skimmed her fingers along his abs, riding the waves of hard muscle, and she smiled as his teeth nipped at the sensitive joining of her neck to her shoulder. She gulped in air, her protesting lungs warning her that long moments had passed where she'd forgotten to breathe.

Will skimmed his hands up her rib cage, claiming each bump and dip until he reached the underside of her breasts. Megan was almost afraid to move. She certainly wasn't going to speak. But a small noise rumbled in her throat, a moan of need and longing she couldn't contain. As if that tiny sound was all he'd been waiting for, Will eased his fingers over her breasts and claimed them.

Megan pushed into his hands, driving her lower half into him, rocking against the hardness restrained by his zipper. Words were beyond her, so she used her body to communicate everything she was feeling.

Will's mouth found hers again. His tongue plunged deep before retreating and diving back in once more. At the same time he bent and gripped the back of her thighs, hoisting her off her feet and moving her deeper into the room.

Megan wrapped her arms around his neck and let her knees fall open so that by the time he settled her on the bed, his erection was tight against where she needed him most.

Mindlessly determined, her hands stroked over him, plucking at his shirt buttons, tugging at his belt, needing him naked. Steely muscles tightened and relaxed beneath her ministrations. Everywhere she touched him drove her longing higher.

When they'd made love the last time, they'd come together in a raw, frantic coupling that had been about loss and the need to offer solace to each other. This time Megan's hunger didn't feel any less frenzied but, having spent these weeks with Will, she wanted more than a quick tumble into his bed followed by a banquet of recrimination.

Almost as if he sensed where her thoughts had taken her, Will once again eased away. His fingertips, firm and even a little rough on her flesh until now, trailed sweetly down her cheek and across her passion-bruised lips.

"Will?"

Megan stared at his face, desperate to discern his thoughts, but found his expression inscrutable. A muscle jumped in his jaw, mirroring the tension in his body as his gaze moved over her features with a fondness that drove a spike through Megan's heart. She wanted to cry out, demand that he not look at her like that unless he meant it, but feared that her words might push him away. Instead, she brushed aside the narrow straps of her bra and reached behind her to unfasten the hooks.

The black lace fell from her breasts, igniting emerald fire in Will's eyes. She thrilled that he wanted her and at this moment didn't care if she was merely a convenient woman in his bed.

"I need to taste you," Will murmured, lowering his lips to her neck.

"Oh, please do."

If she thought she was turned on before, Megan was about to discover how badly she'd misjudged because as Will stroked his tongue over her nipple, she went up in flames.

As he drew Megan's nipple into his mouth, Will's muscles contracted, his body tightening with need that pushed him to the brink of pain. He guided her backward, easing her down until her spine rested on the mattress. All the while he danced his fingers over her flesh, forging a trail for his mouth, divesting her of the blue pajama top.

She quivered beneath his touch, her hands busy with an exploration of his shoulders and face. Chest heaving with each ragged breath, Will marveled at her luscious form. All too often in the last few days he'd found himself struggling to maintain his distance. Tonight that wasn't going to be a problem.

"You are gorgeous," he growled. Mouth dry, he guided black silk over her hips as his lips grazed the flat planes of her belly.

Damn, she was incredible. Her smooth skin was a beacon for his lips, hands and tongue. He couldn't wait to taste every inch of her. Before hooking his fingers into her panties and stroking the fabric down her thighs, he molded the curve of her hip with his palm, thumb skimming along the sensitive skin beside her belly button. She gasped and trembled, her eyes squeezing shut as she tipped her pelvis, pushing into his touch.

"I love the way you respond to me," he said, playing his fingers over her torso.

She shuddered, her breasts shifting with each quavering breath. "Your touch makes me feel things I've never known."

Her words intensified the ache that always assailed him whenever she was near. Will leaned down to brush his lips across her inner thigh. The scent of her drove him wild. An intoxicating blend of feminine arousal and the signature floral scent that incorporated shampoo, lotion and perfume. It spoke to a primal part of him.

"You haven't seen anything yet," he promised, drawing his tongue along her skin, delighting in every impassioned whimper issuing from her parted lips.

"I can't wait," she replied, throwing her arms above her head in an overture of surrender. The move stretched her lean body, thrusting her breasts forward as she yielded like a willing sacrifice.

Will was happy to accept all she offered and pledged that no woman would be as sweetly plundered as Megan tonight. As fast as he was able, Will divested himself of the rest of his clothes. Dipping into his nightstand drawer, he pulled out a handful of condoms and scattered them across the mattress. Megan had lifted onto her elbows to watch him strip and now arched an eyebrow.

"Ambitious," she remarked, her gaze chasing the foil packets as they bounced and skidded in all directions.

He merely answered with a bold grin as he stepped out of his boxer briefs before easing onto the mattress and between her legs. He kissed the inside of her knee and trailed his tongue up her inner thigh, noticing her shaky exhale as he skipped past her hot center and deposited a series of kisses around her belly button.

Her beautiful breasts begged for his attention and he obliged, lashing his tongue over her hard nipples and making her moan. Ever since their night together, he'd been dreaming of sucking the tight points into his mouth and delighting in the telling hitch in her breath.

Fierce, frantic emotions spilled through him. Excitement. Arousal. Fear. Longing. Each raced beneath his skin, the tumult making him growl. His gaze raked over her naked body, devouring her tempting curves then returning to her flushed face. Her eyes were open, lids heavy as she watched him.

"What are you thinking?" he asked, meeting her smoky gaze.

She smiled dreamily as he palmed her breast and rolled her tight nipple between his fingers, tweaking gently to make her pant. Her hips rocked and her thighs shifted restlessly.

"That you know how to drive a girl crazy."

"How crazy?" He wanted her desperate and needy.

"To the point that it hurts, I ache so bad for you."

He liked the sound of that and trailed his fingers down her body. Skimming across her hip, he cupped her butt in his hand and lifted her until she rested tight against him.

"I ache for you, too," he declared, ignoring the relentless need building with each second.

"Then what are we waiting for?"

"I need to taste you first."

"So taste."

Her impatience made him smile. He set his mouth on her again and savored her muted moans that washed over him as he swirled his tongue against her slick, heated core. Her fingers dug into his shoulders as her breath shifted into a faster, irregular rhythm. Sucking hard, he grazed the perfectly groomed strip of hair above her sex and then curved his hand and slipped his fingers into her slick, feminine heat.

Hot and wet.

It was the sweetest torture to listen to the soft, impassioned noises she emitted and try to maintain his tightly coiled restraint.

"Will." She huffed out his name and tipped her hips to facilitate his intimate touch.

Her body strained as he slipped his fingers through her wetness, bracing for the instant he made contact with her clit. He shifted higher on the mattress and brought his mouth into contact with hers. He pushed his tongue past her lips even as he slid one finger inside her. Her tight, wet walls closed around his finger as he stroked in and out, driving her close, so close. She shuddered and rocked into his hand, writhing for him, pleading, panting.

"Make me come."

"Not yet."

"Please... Will. Please."

Her body grew to bow-string tautness and he played her like a master. Any second and she would come apart for him. Only this wasn't how he wanted her to climax. He had a much different plan for that.

Slowing his pace, he kissed his way down her body, feeling as well as hearing her groan of dismay as he eased her back from the brink of an orgasm.

"Patience," he commanded, sliding his shoulders between her thighs and opening her wide.

Using his thumbs, he spread her folds and inhaled the scent of her. Hot, slick heaven awaited him, but he took his time adjusting his breathing, listening to her agitated pants as she anticipated what he intended to do.

"What—?"

He interrupted her question by applying a small amount of pressure to her clit. She bit down on her hand, blocking a cry even as her hips bumped forward, eager for more contact. Gathering her butt in his palms, he drew his tongue along her center, holding her tight as her hips jerked in reaction.

Incoherent words spilled from her lips as he set the flat of his tongue against her clit, feeling it twitch as he licked her. Last time they'd been together, he hadn't had the chance to get to know her like this, plying her with varying flicks and strokes to see what she liked best.

Her head was thrashing side to side, hips moving restlessly as she rubbed herself against his mouth. Her actions turned him on, drove him on. Too hard. Too fast. Before he realized what he'd done, her breath stopped as she reached the brink. And then she exploded. Shaking, keening, rocked by the pleasure he'd brought her, Megan climaxed with all the power of a sun going nova.

And Will watched it all happen, humbled and enthralled that she'd given herself over to him and to the gratification he could provide.

"That was amazing," she murmured as he came to lie beside her. "I've never…"

"Never?" he teased, his body screaming for release. Will stroked a damp strand of hair away from her face and smiled down at her.

"Well, yes, I mean, I've done that before. But it's never felt like *that* before."

He chuckled as he reached for a foil packet. To his surprise, she sat up and plucked the condom from his hand, sliding it on him with eager dexterity. Sheathed, he rolled her beneath him and kissed her deeply. She bent her knees and shifted so he lay between her thighs, his erection pressing against her soft core.

Tongues tangling, Will stroked his fingers over her body, starting the process of arousing her all over again. She was quick to respond, her teeth nipping at his lower lip, hand reaching between them to caress his hot, hard length. He ground his teeth to stop himself from slamming into her.

"I need you with me," he said.

The last time they'd come together, it had been wild and hot. They'd both been in search of oblivion, fleeing pain and loss. He was looking for a connection this time.

"I'm right here."

"Not just your body." He set his hand beside her shoulder on the mattress and pushed his weight off her. "But also your mind. Be here, in the moment."

Her hands came up to cradle his cheek while her eyes met his in soft understanding. "You're crazy if you think I'm anything less than one hundred percent yours." Her voice wavered in a manner that told him the admission frightened her and, by the last word, fell to a mere whisper as she finished, "There's no one else."

Satisfied that she meant every word, he leaned down and sucked her lower lip between his, running his tongue along the delicate flesh. Their breaths blended and quickened as they gave themselves over to desire.

He entered her in a long, smooth thrust that claimed her inch by torturous inch. The prolonged slide of flesh against flesh, as her snug inner muscles slowly enveloped him, challenged his mastery of the situation. Yet even as his nerves screamed at him to slam into her as deep as he could go, Will resisted the frenzy assault on his willpower.

But as her inner muscles clamped down on him, he felt his emotions tearing free beneath the onslaught of pleasure. He clenched his jaw and held tight to his slipping restraint. Her tightness and heat felt so good around him. The wet friction made his steady withdrawal torturous. Worse was her shattering response, the delicious keening torn from her lips, as he pushed forward with another full-length thrust into her impossibly tight body.

"Yes," she moaned as he drove hilt-deep, his body claiming hers. "Again."

As if he needed encouragement to repeat the mind-blowing movement.

Mine.

The thought popped into his head even as he pumped forward once more. She bore his name. Belonged to him. No matter that she'd fallen for Rich's masquerade.

Her lips parted as she panted in pleasure, body quaking as she climbed higher. She clutched at his back, her nails driving into his skin, communicating her hunger.

The minor pain drove him on. He changed the angle of his thrusts, taking himself deeper. His pace quickened as need seared his body. He didn't grasp that he'd closed his eyes until a wild sound burst from her lips and he realized he was no longer watching her reaction. Recognizing the flush and focused tension in her face, he knew she was close.

"Come for me, sweet Megan," he crooned, tangling his fingers in her hair and tugging until her lashes lifted and her wide blue eyes locked with his. "Come hard for me."

And then she was going off like a rocket, her release a thing of beauty that inspired his awe like nothing had ever done in his life.

"Will." His name on her lips was part exultation, part prayer. "Oh, Will…"

As much as he wanted to be with her at this moment, Will held back so he could watch and savor. He continued his steady strokes, drawing out her climax as wave upon wave of pleasure shattered her. Despite his own need pulsing insistently inside him, Will waited until he'd wrung every last thread of pleasure from her body before he let himself go.

Eight

Flat on his back, heart thundering in the wake of their explosive passion, Will rolled his head in Megan's direction in time to catch her knuckling a tear from the corner of her eye.

"What is it?" he demanded, searching her expression. "Did I hurt you?"

She buried half her face in the crook of her arm before replying. "No."

He tugged at her arm, needing to see her whole face. "Then why the tears?"

"You can't possibly understand what it's like…" Her voice had thickened with each word until speech failed her.

He noticed her throat working and wondered what had gone wrong in the seconds between her climax and this moment. "Help me understand."

"I'm just so happy right now."

At her words, Will's emotions soared and then dipped.

"Most people smile when they're happy," he said, pulling her closer, striving to keep his tone light.

Despite her assurances, his chest ached. He kissed salty wetness from her cheeks, unsure how to reassure this beautiful, complex woman.

"It scares me," she said.

"Being happy scares you?"

She burrowed her nose against his shoulder, once again hiding her expression. "I'm not afraid of being happy, but of how I'll feel when it stops."

"Why does it need to stop?"

"We live in complicated times."

Her reluctance to let him glimpse her face warned him there was more to her fear than her tone revealed. She had something important to tell him, something that was eating away at her. Earlier that night they'd confronted their playacting and agreed that the danger they found themselves in had led to confusion about what was real.

Now that Megan was echoing his earlier concerns that their current intimacy had an expiration date, Will found himself all the more determined to tread carefully. There was no reason to think they couldn't enjoy each other's company both in bed and out of it as long as they both understood that it might not—probably wouldn't—go anywhere.

Megan rolled onto her stomach and propped her chin on her hand. Her long lashes shadowed her blue eyes as she regarded him. "I hope you realize what just happened wasn't about Rich calling me."

He hadn't. But now that she'd brought it up, Will wondered why she'd felt compelled to point that out.

"Okay."

"I came to you tonight because I needed comfort and support," she said, her blue eyes taking on a poignant intensity as she spoke. "And because I needed to feel like a normal woman instead of a victim."

He reached out and swept a strand of hair off her cheek, tucking it behind her ear. The gesture sparked a flood of tenderness so he leaned over and kissed her softly on the lips.

Faster than he could've anticipated, the kiss turned hot and wet and needy. The suddenness of it set fire to his nerve endings. Breathing heavily, he pulled back.

No matter how heavily his mistakes over the last year weighed on his soul, losing himself in Megan calmed him.

Being with her felt like a beautiful dream. With all that had happened sometimes he wondered if he deserved to be happy.

"Maybe we should agree that we're both in need of comfort," he said.

She reached out and boldly trailed her fingertips over his chest before venturing lower. "And that we shouldn't feel guilty about being there for each other in any way we can."

A sigh formed on Will's lips the way his body stirred back to life. "So for the moment we are going to let our passions get the better of us and not question if it's the right thing to do?"

"That works for me." With a full-blown grin lighting up her face, Megan suddenly pushed to her knees and strad-dled him. Her long hair swung forward and framed her face as she raked her nails over his nipples, causing him to expel a breath in a rough exhalation. "It's going to be a lot more fun around here if we go with the flow instead of having to fight this attraction between us all the time."

"I'm all for going with the flow," he growled, any lin-gering tension melting out of him as he reached up to cup her head and draw her down for a deep, satisfying kiss.

Three days after Aaron and Kasey's engagement party, Megan was adrift in a golden glow following the many passion-filled hours spent in Will's arms. They'd gotten lost in a seductive bubble of hot showers, whispered sexual fantasies and creative positions. Never had she felt such heady desire or learned so much about her body in such a short period of time. Will had tricks up his sleeve she'd never imagined and she'd lost count how many times he'd made her come.

She'd even skipped work yesterday so they could take advantage of their final day of privacy before Lucy and Brody returned to the main house. It seemed as if once they'd settled the issue of their expectations when it came to their sexual relationship and what it might mean in the future, they were able to enjoy each other's company without the dreaded *what-ifs*.

"How was your day?" Will asked, accepting the glass of whiskey Megan extended in his direction. Eyeing the level of amber liquid in her glass, he arched an eyebrow. "Or shouldn't I ask?"

"Frustrating." She exhaled wearily as she carried her drink to the couch. "One of our suppliers didn't deliver on time, which puts our production behind schedule. If you haven't figured it out yet, I hate being late for anything."

"You are definitely the most prompt woman I've ever met," Will said drily as he checked his cell phone before pocketing it.

"It's frustrating having our production happening out of state," she grumbled, "because I have to rely on other people to manage the operations."

"What can you do about it?"

"I've considered locating a plant in Royal, but it's a huge capital expense and I'd have to balance the operating costs to see if it makes sense." Kicking off her shoes, she drilled her thumbs into the arch of her left foot.

"If you want to run some numbers, I'd be happy to take a look."

"I'd appreciate that."

Will joined her on the couch and set his drink on the coffee table. Reaching down, he pulled both of her feet into his lap and slid his warm palms across her weary soles. The massage she'd enacted on her feet couldn't compare to the robust combination of strength and heat of Will's long fingers as he hit a particularly sensitive spot and a lusty moan rolled from her throat.

"Damn," he murmured heatedly. "I love it when you make noises like that."

A familiar flutter started up in her body and she regarded him from beneath her lashes. "Keep up what you're doing and you'll hear plenty more."

In recent days they'd reached a level of comfort with each other that Megan had never known with Rich. At the same time, they weren't venturing anywhere near the tough topics that could've shattered the harmony. And there were plenty of them, starting with whether it was wise to keep tearing up the sheets when the relationship had nowhere to go?

Will smirked. "Any idea how much time we have before dinner?"

Pleasure arrowed from Megan's foot straight to her core. Heat surged through her, driven by her slow but insistent pulse. The man's hands hadn't moved beyond her feet but desire had awakened like a hungry cat.

"Enough time for a shower, I think," she replied with a scorching glance at him from beneath her lashes. "I'm feeling a little dirty at the moment."

"If you like my foot massage, you'll be amazed at how well I can scrub your back."

"I'm looking forward to a thorough demonstration of your prowess."

Bubbles seemed to have filled her veins because as Megan raced toward Will's master bedroom with him seconds behind her, her feet barely seemed to connect with the wide-planked pine floors.

An hour later Megan emerged from Will's bedroom, satiated and relaxed, her insides warmed by a glow of contentment. They'd made leisurely love in the shower, luxuriating in the soapy slide of fingers over skin while hot water poured over them.

Megan marveled that as often as they'd surrendered to temptation in the past few days he continued to be able to surprise her.

Lucy and Brody were finishing up an apple cobbler dessert as Megan and Will made their way into the kitchen. Because Megan was in the lead, she got the full brunt of Lucy's arched eyebrows and knowing grin.

"I wasn't sure when you two were going to make an appearance," Lucy said, "So we went ahead and ate without you."

"Sorry about that," Megan murmured. "We were talking about business and got sidetracked."

"Sure." Lucy's voice dripped with irony. "You two are just a couple of workaholics."

"I can't get enough of Megan's figures," Will said, winking outrageously at his sister. "They're just fascinating."

"I'm sure," Lucy retorted.

Will and Megan loaded their plates with roasted chicken, potatoes and salad, and carried them to the dining table where they sat in adjacent chairs and leaned into each other's space. To prove to Lucy that they often discussed business over dinner, Megan shared her latest business troubles and Will spoke of the latest ventures into solar energy his company was making.

Lucy and Brody finished dessert and made their escape while Will explained how he approached his position as CEO of Spark Energy Solutions with an eye toward innovation. In addition to the company's original energy resources of oil and coal, he was avidly pursuing various ways in which to generate energy, including geothermal power.

Megan smiled at Will's passion. For nearly an hour as he'd regaled her with one tale after another, she'd been riveted both by the topics and his boyish enthusiasm. "Are you looking to move Spark Energy Solutions into that sector?"

"At the moment I'm not ready to expand our current operations." A shadow passed across his features. "But it's something to investigate for the future."

Megan reached out and touched his hand. "I imagine you've got a lot on your plate at the moment."

She didn't know what sort of shape Rich had left the company in, but she wouldn't be surprised to hear he'd neglected the business.

"We have several key relationships that I'm working to repair," Will admitted. "That and many other issues are monopolizing my focus at the moment."

"You haven't talked much about how Rich left things at SES, but it sounds like he made a mess there, as well." Megan hoped Will took her up on this offer to listen.

For the last few months Megan had been overwhelmed by shame at being fooled and that had led her to shy away from talking in-depth to anyone about her sham of a marriage. Was Will similarly afflicted by doubt when it came to trusting after being nearly killed by a friend? She imagined he was kicking himself for being fooled the same way she was.

With Jason being dead, she wasn't sure whom Will was talking to these days. Her throat tightened at their mutual loss. She didn't always appreciate her brothers' bossiness when it came to her, but she loved them fiercely. And Jason's death had left a big hole in her life.

They both needed to share their stories with someone. Why not each other?

"As you know, there's money missing," Will admitted, his tone stark, expression flat. "A lot of it."

"So it wasn't just the Texas Cattleman's Club that he stole from." Although no one had spoken of Will's financial losses, Megan had assumed Rich had helped himself to Will's fortune.

"No. I think he intended to spread his thievery around in order to avoid anyone getting suspicious. But whatever accounts I had access to, Rich siphoned off what he quietly could and converted the funds to gold, which he's stashed outside Royal."

"But wouldn't gold be impractical?" In this day and age, with shell companies and off-shore banking, surely Rich would've done better to hide his stolen money. "Why not just set up accounts in the Cayman Islands?"

"Maybe he was worried that after he faked my death, he couldn't be able to access the funds or that the electronic trail would be discovered." Will shook his head. "I've given up on trying to figure out Rich's logic."

"But gold?" Megan imagined Fort Knox, the gold reserves with stacks and stacks of bars that stretch for hundreds of feet. "How much would he have?"

"A gold bar weighs four hundred troy ounces. That's around twenty-seven pounds and, at today's rate, it's worth a little over half a million dollars."

"How big is that bar?" Megan screwed up her face as she tried to picture where Rich would store the gold.

Will held his hands about six inches apart. "This long. It would fit comfortably in my hand."

"So the bricks would fit in a duffel bag. That wouldn't be hard to hide."

"Hide, no. The weight would be the issue. Just a dozen

bars would be over three hundred pounds. You can't exactly get on a plane carrying it."

"What about driving across the border into Mexico?" Megan asked, remembering how Rich had spoken of places he'd visited and how he could see himself living like a king there.

"That's what the FBI speculates he will try to do."

"So where is the money?"

"Safe with the authorities."

That was a relief, but Megan sensed there was more to the story and, given the way Lowell had come after her, that she might have a part to play. "So, if they have it, why hasn't Rich left the area?"

"Two reasons. One, they left the stash in place, substituting the real gold bars for gold-covered tungsten. And they're keeping surveillance on the cabin for when he comes back." Will paused and gave her a searching look. "Second, I think he's been pretty clear that he wants you."

Anxiety rose at Will's somber declaration but she deflected her fear into bitter reflection. "I can't imagine why. He wasn't too interested in having me before you returned to Royal," she said, recalling how her frustration had built in the months following her honeymoon. "Rich was gone a lot while we were married and, even when he was in Royal, it's not as if we spent quality time together."

Her stomach ached as she revisited those hollow, lonely days and the steady leaching of happiness from her marriage. Not to mention the persistent erosion of her self-esteem. Maybe if their courtship hadn't been so intense and uplifting, her disappointment might have been easier to bear.

"Do I need to remind you that he confronted you in your company's parking lot and tried to get you to go with him?" Will pointed out, frowning at her.

"I've had a lot of time to think about that and I'm not

sure that was as much about me as you." Megan shook her head to forestall Will's argument. "He took over your life after trying to kill you. Now that you're back, the authorities want us to continue pretending to be married. Maybe he doesn't realize our closeness is part of the operation to bring him to justice and wants to take me away from you in order to hurt you."

"Is that how you see our closeness?" Will asked, his tone deceptively mild. "As part of an operation to capture him?"

"Of course not."

She believed what was happening between them went way beyond playacting. But how far, she wasn't ready to confront. Megan recognized that she and Will had mutually agreed to enjoy each other's company without making things complicated by trying to define what they were doing or to dwell on the lasting repercussions.

"I'm glad to hear you're not faking any of this," Will said, reaching for her hand.

He absently played with her fingers while staring into her eyes before bringing her palm to his lips. Goose bumps broke out as he nipped at the fleshy part of her thumb before whisking a kiss along her love line.

"Not hardly," she replied as her insides turned to mush, unsure what exactly he meant by *this*. "Everything you make me feel is absolutely real and impossible to fake."

While this was a scary admission to make, Megan recognized that she continued to play it safe. Not knowing what the future held or how their feelings for each other might change once Rich was caught and her "marriage" to Will was dissolved, she continued to hold back when not in his arms.

Ironically, as difficult as it was for her to speak the truth of her heart and risk his rejection, she gave herself over to him completely when they made love. He brought something out in her during those raw, vulnerable moments that she'd never known before. She'd discovered a surprising strength in letting go.

Unfortunately, when passion faded, so did her confidence.

"Good."

Without releasing her hand, Will got to his feet, tugging her out of her chair and up against his body. His other hand coasted down her back and over the swell of her butt, coaxing her hips into contact with his. His lips drifted down her neck.

"Now, are you ready for apple cobbler?" He nibbled on the cord in her throat, sending an electrical charge through her body. "Or should we see what else we can find for dessert?"

Nine

On the morning of Cora Lee's harvest barbecue at the Ace in the Hole, the matriarch had staff and family scrambling this way and that at her bidding. Although the weather report had predicted clouds, the blue sky wasn't having any of it. The sun blazed down on Will's shoulders as he and Megan arranged picnic tables covered in red-and-white-checkered tablecloths on the expansive lawn beside the main house. The centerpieces consisted of tin buckets filled with bright yellow sunflowers and hurricane lanterns with votive candles that could be lit as darkness fell.

The food would be served buffet style. Since the day before, Cora Lee had been supervising the smoking of fifty pounds of brisket slathered with her secret barbecue recipe. The aroma wafting out of the smoker was making Will's mouth water. The smells brought back memories of so many wonderful parties growing up. He'd spent many a night while in Mexico dreaming of Cora Lee's cooking and of home.

A hand on his arm brought him back to the moment. He looked in Megan's direction and noted the questions in her eyes.

"I was just thinking how good everything smelled," he explained, not telling her the whole truth. He hadn't talked to anyone about his time in Mexico, but that compulsion to keep mum was stronger with Megan. He didn't want to damage the growing trust between them. She expected him to be the same Will Sanders that existed before the fateful fishing trip and he hated to disappoint her.

Megan glanced toward the black, drum-shaped smoker. "Cora Lee makes the best brisket in the county. I imagine a whole lot of people will be loading up their plates today."

The invited guests were family and a few close friends as well as ranch staff and their families. In the case of those closest to him, Will expected a number of the conversations to surround the manhunt for Lowell and the general frustration over how long it was taking to catch the guy.

"Good thing there's going to be dancing later," Will said, hoping she'd take a turn on the floor with him. "We're going to want to work off some of the feast."

A second later he found himself wondering if she'd enjoyed dancing with Rich. Will cursed himself for letting the question come up. Every time he pictured her with Lowell was another instance where Will validated Rich's purpose in choosing Megan. The last thing he wanted was for anything like that to come between them.

Will put his hand on Megan's back as Cora Lee approached them, feeling the stiffness in her body and wondering why Megan always tensed around his stepmother.

"Any further tasks you like for us to do?" he teased Cora Lee, hoping to ease the hostility between the women.

"I think I have everything in hand," his stepmother said. "Why don't you to go get ready so you can be here to greet the guests as they start to arrive."

"Sounds like a plan."

As they crossed the grassy expanse toward the big house, Megan glanced up at him, her brow furrowing in consternation. "It almost sounds like she wants us to play host and hostess. Doesn't she realize people are going to be wondering what's going on between us if we do?"

Inwardly, Will winced at her concern. He had similar questions about their situation. For days now he'd been delighted at their ever-increasing closeness even while waging an inner battle over what the future held in store for the two of them.

"Most everyone coming knows our situation and that the authorities have asked us not to dissolve the marriage. I don't think it'll be a problem."

Yet he could tell from her expression that she remained troubled.

"I suppose you're right. I just didn't want to answer a bunch of questions about why I'm staying here. I'm so sick of talking about Rich and the manhunt."

Will suspected that was only part of her discomfort. Just as likely she was frustrated by the rampant curiosity about their relationship that he'd been deflecting more and more of lately. No doubt people speculated whether she'd married Rich Lowell the man or Will Sanders the millionaire rancher. It was natural to be curious. When he'd first returned home, the same question had crossed Will's mind several times.

"Just stick with me and I'll shut down all questions. We'll concentrate on eating too much and having fun today."

"I'd like that." She reached down and took his hand, giving it a little squeeze. "You always know how to make me feel better."

"It's easy." He lifted her hand to his lips and dropped a sizzling kiss into her palm, holding her gaze as he did so and letting her see the heat in his eyes. "When you're happy, I'm happy."

"I'm happy," she breathed.

Two hours later that sentiment was proved true over and over as they strode through the party, chatting about upcoming baby showers and engagement parties, talking up Cora Lee's barbecue and keeping the conversation away from anything relating to Richard Lowell.

Megan came out of her shell as they welcomed guests and shepherded people toward the buffet. She was smiling more than Will had seen her do since he'd popped into his own funeral. It lightened his heart to see her shed the worry of these last few months. Although he'd initially viewed it as a prison, more recently the ranch had proved to be a good sanctuary for them both, offering privacy and security. He could honestly say that he and Megan had stopped being awkward strangers and were slowly moving toward something not yet defined but with great promise.

Her perfume hit his nose at the same time she gave a little snort of laughter in response to a story Dani Moore was sharing about a customer at a restaurant she'd worked at. Will liked the pretty executive chef and approved of the affectionate glances she cast at Cole Sullivan, former Texas Ranger and the PI he had hired to investigate Jason's disappearance.

Will winced the way he always did when he thought of the danger he'd put Jason into. If not for him, Megan's brother would still be alive.

"Is everybody done?" Cole asked, getting to his feet and glancing around their small group. "I'll get rid of the plates and bring back dessert."

Will got to his feet, as well. "There's pecan pie, chocolate cake, cookies, bars." He was peering at the buffet table. "Any preferences?"

"Or we could bring a sampler and share," Cole suggested.

The two women exchanged delighted smiles before turning their attention back to the men. For a second Will was struck by their similarity. With their long, brunette hair and similar builds, they could've been sisters. Today Megan wore snug jeans, a sleeveless blouse in white lace and cowboy boots. Dani had chosen a tank top emblazoned with Eat Like A Texas Girl, cutoff denims and boots.

"A sampler it is," Will said.

After he and Cole gathered an appropriately large sample of sweets, they returned to the table only to find Dani sitting alone.

"Megan went to get some more drinks," the executive chef said by way of explanation.

"I'll go see if she needs help," Will replied.

Refreshments had been placed in a variety of locations, offering everything from water to punch to beer to harder forms of alcohol. While Will might switch to something stronger later, he was following Megan's lead and drinking water at the moment. Off to one side of the buffet table sat a brand-new watering trough of galvanized steel filled with ice, soft drinks and water. Figuring that was where Megan had gone, he headed toward it. From the table where the two couples had been sitting, he had to circle a large oak tree to reach the beverages. As he approached the oak, he heard Megan's voice.

"There's nothing serious going on between us," she said, her tone breezy but firm. "And I'm not interested in any sort of a relationship at this moment."

All day long Will had stood at her side, deflecting all talk of their current living arrangement and personal relationship. Now he paused while still out of sight, caught off guard that Megan intended to have this conversation without him.

"You two look awfully comfortable with each other." The voice belonged to his sister, and Will's concern eased somewhat. "It wouldn't surprise me if, with all this time you're spending out here on the ranch, something might blossom."

Stunned that his sister would go there, Will was on the verge of making his presence known when Megan spoke again.

"We're friends." Her sharp tone sliced right through Lucy's attempt at matchmaking. "That's all there is between us."

"But you married him. You must have feelings for Will even if it's confusing."

Apparently he wasn't the only person grappling with what to make of Megan's decision to become Mrs. Will Sanders and what it meant now that she knew she'd married an imposter.

"I married a man pretending to be him. It's not the same."

"No, I suppose not," Lucy conceded. "I can't believe none of us wondered what was going on with Will after he came back from Mexico," she added. "I never liked Rich. He was just awful."

"Not to me," Megan murmured. "I mean, not to me when he was pretending to be Will."

"Several times since Rich came home pretending to be Will," Lucy said, "I've often wondered why you married him."

"Because I was in love," Megan declared with a poignant dose of heat.

The admission struck straight to the heart of what often bothered Will. Of course she'd fallen in love with Rich. She never would've married him otherwise.

"It had nothing to do with the Sanders money or the power your family wields around Royal if that's what you're insinuating," Megan continued.

"I believe you," Lucy replied in a soothing tone. "But don't you think you could fall in love with the real Will?"

"Everything has been so mixed up and complicated lately. I'm not sure how I feel about Will and it just wouldn't be right to stay married to him," Megan said, not answering Lucy's question. "He deserves to be happy and so do I. More than anything, I just want to be done with the whole situation so I can get on with my life."

Megan's declaration went through Will like an ice storm. Of course she wanted to move on. Lowell's capture would put an end to what had been a very difficult time in her life. She'd been fairly candid about her marriage and the troubles that had surfaced from the beginning. What she hadn't shared was how much she blamed herself.

Before his own life had taken a radical turn, he'd formed an opinion about Megan primarily based on what her brothers had said of her. She was a hardworking perfectionist who took setbacks personally. From this and some observing of his own, Will suspected she was doing a good job beating herself up for being duped by Rich.

"Will?" Megan had left her conversation and encountered him while returning to their table.

"Dani said you were getting some more drinks. I came to help."

"That's really nice of you."

Nothing in her manner suggested she was upset by the indelicate discussion she'd just had. Nor did she seem suspicious to find him lurking within earshot.

Will badly wanted to confront her about what she'd said, but had no idea what purpose it would serve. They were two strangers brought together by circumstances. No need to add stress to an already tension-filled situation.

They returned to the table in silence and he strove to put the incident behind him but found his thoughts returning to her words over and over. It was pretty obvious where she stood. He needed to rein in his wayward attraction and be prepared to let her go when Lowell was caught.

But when he made good on his earlier promise to get her out on the dance floor, curbing his body's reaction to her was harder than he'd expected. And it wasn't even because he got to hold her in his arms and sway to romantic music.

The evening started with young and old jumping onto the dance floor for a series of foot-stomping, quick-turning line dances that got the heart pumping. Through song after song, he and Megan danced side by side. Their bodies never touched, but Will took hit after hit from her enthusiastic grin, the laughter in her beautiful blue eyes, and the uninhibited sashay of her slender hips in time with the beat.

Her joy in the music and the camaraderie of friends affected him as strongly as a dozen kisses. Which just went to show that his attraction for her was rooted in both lust and affection.

After an hour or so, the music settled into a series of two-step swing songs. Will noted Megan's smile when he chose her young niece as his partner for the first dance. Then he partnered Cora Lee, Jillian and Dani before putting out his hand once again to Megan. She came willingly into his arms. Not, he suspected, because she was eager to be close to him but rather because he'd proved himself a capable partner.

Yet even as they shuffled and twirled through a series of songs, Will couldn't shake his concern at what Megan had told his sister. These last few days with Megan had brought him to a place he'd never known before. They'd seemed to have reached a level of intimacy both in bed and out that had him thinking about the future.

He'd imagined asking her to stay at the ranch long after

Lowell was caught. He'd pictured them sharing business ideas and dreams, and knew his life would be richer and more satisfying with her in it. He'd believed Megan was his reward for the months of pain and terror he'd endured in Mexico.

To hear that she was only biding her time until she could get back to her regular routine had dashed his hopes in one fell swoop. It hurt more than he cared to admit that she didn't share his vision for them.

With a concerted effort, Will came to terms with his concerns. A lot about their current situation was up in the air. Lowell continued to elude capture and his continued presence threatened Megan's peace of mind. Of course she wanted it all to be over.

Will knew he should just focus on the here and now and let the future sort itself out. In the meantime, he and Megan were enjoying the benefits of living beneath the same roof. Why, just that morning she'd...

"Are you okay?" Megan asked, her voice barely rising above the sound of the applause as the band took a break.

"Perfectly fine." Which wasn't completely true, but this was not the time for a serious discussion.

"You seem distracted."

"Do I?" He compressed his misgivings about the future into a tiny package and stuffed it into the back of his mind. "Feel like sneaking off somewhere so I can demonstrate what I've been thinking about?"

"There'll be plenty of time for that later," she teased, taking his hand and smiling up at him as if she was completely happy living in the here and now.

Will responded with a smile of his own. Maybe he should follow her lead and live in the moment. Why steer into a storm when the boat ride was way more enjoyable beneath clear skies? Yet for the first time since he'd come home to Royal, Will found himself hoping the manhunt for Lowell stretched out indefinitely.

Taillights disappeared down the driveway as the last of the guests headed out. Megan strode beside Will on their way to the main house.

"Lucy and I had an odd conversation this afternoon," she said, broaching a subject that had been nagging at her on and off all evening.

"How so?"

"She wondered if she should move out."

Will glanced her way. "Why would she want to do that?"

"She seems to think she and Brody are in the way." Megan hoped her tone was neutral enough to give nothing away. "Of us…being together."

"They're not. I'll talk to her."

When Will asked no more questions, Megan cursed his lack of curiosity. Why couldn't he just ask her what had prompted Lucy's offer? Now he forced her to steer the conversation back to what she and Lucy had discussed.

"It seemed odd to me that she would believe she was in the way," Megan said.

"I don't know why. There's more than enough room for all of us in the main house."

She sighed. "Yes, but she…seemed to think there was something going on between you and me." These last few words came out in a breathless rush.

Now she'd captured his interest. One eyebrow lifted as he peered at her. "What did you say?"

"That you are only trying to keep me safe." Megan paused and held her breath, hoping he would jump in and say that was not all there was to it. "Then she questioned whether I plan to stay married to you."

"And you told her we were divorcing as soon as Lowell is caught?"

His question startled her. Was that what they were doing? Since her first night at the Ace in the Hole they'd avoided all mention of the future, preferring to live in the present and pointedly not label or question what was growing between them. Maybe that had been a mistake.

"I told her I was looking forward to moving forward with my life," Megan said, choosing her words carefully. "Maybe we should consider the sort of signals we're sending out."

"What sort of signals do you mean?"

"Like maybe people are picking up on the fact that there's some attraction between us."

"And that's a problem for them?" Will opened the back door that led from the yard into the mudroom and motioned for her to precede him. "Or for you?"

"Maybe a little of both." Megan emerged into the kitchen and turned to face him. "I don't want your family to think I'm trying to stay married to you through manipulation. Or that I have any interest in your money or hope to gain from your position in the community."

In the low light of the under-cabinet lighting, Will's face displayed blank astonishment for a long moment. Then he began to laugh. "I'm pretty sure you're the least manipulative woman I've ever met. And don't forget this attraction is a mutual thing."

He took her hand and pulled her close. When her thighs bumped against his, Megan caught at his biceps to maintain her balance. He dipped his head and nuzzled her temple, his hot breath warming her skin.

Relaxing into the soothing sweep of his palm up her spine, Megan said, "Just so we're clear that living together and being attracted can lead to trouble down the road."

"What sort of trouble?" Will's lips moved over her ear,

sending a cascade of shivers across her skin. The slightest pinch of teeth on her earlobe and Megan's breath hitched as he continued. "We're two consenting adults. It's our business and our business only what we do."

Megan nodded, wishing she could speak her true concern. Will had no idea what a difficult man he was to resist. Or to read. Was he was thinking of her as a roommate—possibly one with benefits—while her susceptible heart was falling for him a little more each day?

"You're right." She put her palms on his chest and shoved herself away from his tempting body. Summoning a bright smile, she fake yawned then said, "Well, it's been a long day, and I really need some rest. See you in the morning."

"Oh, no, you don't," he growled, wrapping his arms around her. "Let's give my nosy sister something to talk about."

What followed started as a friendly but rousing hug that made Megan's pulse skip. The intereaction quickly evolved into a sizzling kiss that wrapped her in longing. Every point of contact between their bodies heightened her arousal until all she could do was hold on while her knees weakened and her fingers crept into his dark hair.

With heat sizzling along her nerve endings, she moaned piteously as he lifted his lips from hers. She wanted him so badly. It was on the tip of her tongue to demand he take her hard and fast against the nearest wall when she glimpsed wariness in his eyes. Immediately, Megan felt exposed and, reacting like a skittish deer during hunting season, she retreated rather than let herself be hurt.

"I don't think your sister's anywhere around," Megan whispered past her raw throat.

Will's arms relaxed their hold but he didn't set her free. Instead, his palms skated over her rib cage, following the curve of her waist to the flare of her hips before starting a return journey up her spine. The caress both soothed and invigorated her. She shivered as his warm breath played across the skin just below her ear, leaving her aching with hunger only he could satisfy.

His lips moved over her collarbone, thumbs coasting along the lower curve of her breasts, making her nipples tighten. "Megan…"

She was never to know what he intended to say because from somewhere deep in the house came the sound of the door slamming and a little boy shrieking. The ravenous tension went out of the moment like air from a popped balloon.

With a huge sigh, Will set his hands on her hips and stepped back. "Obviously she's occupied getting Brody ready for bed. I guess that was all for nothing."

If Megan had had a skillet in her hand she would've clobbered him. How could the man whip up her emotions with so little effort and then act as if nothing happened? A better question might be how could she stop it from happening over and over?

"Is that all you were doing just now?" she demanded, her body awash in conflict. "Making a point to your sister?"

Will frowned down at her. "Are we okay?"

His question was the last thing she expected. "Of course. Why wouldn't we be?"

"I just want you to know that having you at the ranch has been great."

"Thank you." Megan wished she had some idea where he was going with this. "I've enjoyed being here and appreciated getting to know you better."

"I'm glad we're both on the same page."

And then, before she could sort out what he meant by that, Will swept her off her feet and began to move with purpose toward the master suite.

Megan's motor was redlining by the time he set her on her feet in his bedroom, and she pushed up on her toes, meeting his descending lips with a greedy moan. They wasted no time with words—it was just teeth and tongue, lips and hands, sighs and moans as they kissed and clawed at buttons and buckles. Seams tore. Buttons flew. Hooks parted. Each time his tongue plunged into her mouth Megan grew more frantic with need. Blind to anything but the craving to glide her fingers over his warm skin and take his erection into her hands, she fumbled with his zipper.

She'd never known such all-consuming hunger until Will had touched her for the first time. With his mouth on hers, erection buried deep inside her, it was as if the entire world spun away and it was only Will's tongue sliding against hers, his hard body crushing her beneath him.

For a few blissful hours, she could pretend that her life was without danger. That her brother wasn't dead. That she hadn't made an enormous mistake by falling for a cheap imitation of Will. That love was real and trusting someone was possible again.

A growl broke from his throat as she freed him. Something primal and raw burst free inside her as she took him in hand and ran her fingertips along his swollen length. He was huge and powerful, and she craved the taste of him. Dropping to her knees, she ran the tip of her tongue around his velvet tip. His cry of pleasure cut off abruptly as if his lungs had stopped functioning. But he was quick to demonstrate his gratification by digging his fingers into her skull as she slid her mouth over him.

Each shudder of his body and incoherent groan fanned her own desire. Just when she thought he'd let her take him all the way to orgasm, Will drew her back to her feet and claimed her lips in a fiery kiss that left her lightheaded and gasping.

And then a whimper broke free from her throat as his hands slipped between her thighs and found her hot and wet for him. His touch was perfect. One finger dipping between her slick folds to drive her mad.

Even as her knees buckled, he was scooping her off her feet once more. He lay her in the middle of his bed and dug into the nightstand for protection. Sliding it on, he joined her on the mattress. His lips and tongue coasted over her skin, leaving a damp, sizzling trail of fire from her neck to her navel. She quaked beneath the electric shock of each new sensation as he devoured her body and set her heart free.

Lost in Will and her hunger for him, Megan plunged into voracious need and incendiary desire. She surrendered to the heavy longing deep in her womb and the sharp ache of arousal between her thighs. Will would take care of her as he always did and she would do the same for him.

"Megan." Her name on his lips was so filled with desperate longing that she could do nothing but smile. "Open your eyes and see that it's me," he murmured, an edge to his soft command. "See the man who is making love to you."

Although her eyelids felt impossibly heavy, she couldn't deny him. Her lashes came up. Her gaze collided with his as he filled her in a single, deliberate thrust that shattered her world. This was what she'd longed for. The heat. The absolute rightness. As their bodies found a perfect rhythm, Megan knew this was the man she'd waited all her life for.

He cupped her butt and lifted her to the angle she liked, driving into her with smooth, unrelenting thrusts that she welcomed over and over. She wrapped her arms around his neck and slid her lips over his damp skin, tasting salt and aroused male. The blend poured rocket fuel on the fires already burning out-of-control inside her and she sank her teeth into his shoulder, nails biting into his back.

Hips moving like pistons, he bent down, nipped her neck and murmured, "Come for me."

A combination of the command and his hot breath caressing her ear and Megan's body began to thrum with a familiar pressure. He seemed to know exactly what was happening because he started to roll his hips, unleashing a maelstrom inside her. She felt herself coming apart and wondered if she'd ever be the same again.

Yet within every aftermath she discovered a stronger, better, more confident version of herself. Will did that for her. Each time they made love. She became new and improved.

Her climax bowled into her then. Her body arched as she cried out. Taking this as his cue, Will's thrusts increased in intensity until he possessed more than her body. He laid claim to her soul. It felt so incredibly good that a second orgasm ripped through Megan and she exhaled a slow, lingering breath as the last wave of pleasure shuddered through her.

Moments later Will collapsed onto her, having found his release, and Megan's hands coasted over his sweat-slicked shoulders, loving the weight of him pressing her into the mattress.

"I love that you're so good at that," she murmured, too spent to keep her eyes open.

"Anything to keep you happy." His breath puffed against her neck as he shifted to lie on his back, pulling her limp form snug against his side.

He kissed her shoulder, sliding his lips into that sensitive spot near the hollow of her throat. A smile tugged at her lips as tingles sped across her nerve endings. Despite her exhaustion, she shivered in reaction, but it had been a long day and her body was sated and lethargic.

"You make me happy," she told him, hypnotized by the slow sweep of his fingers up and down her back.

What he replied, if he replied, she never knew.

Ten

In the days following Cora Lee's barbecue and the revelations about how Megan viewed the state of their relationship, Will tried to adjust his own perception. This was easy during the day as he sat in his big office at Spark Energy Solutions and poured over the contracts Rich had signed in Will's name, looking for potential legal exposure. But when he came home and Megan greeted him with a kiss and a smile, his heart and body took over.

Sometimes they spent the evening hours walking around the ranch hand-in-hand, talking about their past successes and failures, views on social issues, anecdotes about her niece and his nephew, and a hundred other things lovers shared.

Other nights they skipped dinner and feasted on each other, satisfying their appetites with mouth and hands, driving hunger away with endless kisses, frenzied sex and blistering, blissful orgasms.

Will felt as if he'd tumbled into an alternate desire-filled world of perfect pleasure and there was no way he was leaving without a fight.

And with each hour in her company it became clearer that he was falling in love with the woman his archenemy had married.

"It's moments like this—" Will said, air leaking from his lungs in a contented sigh. Presently, he was smack-dab in the middle of his big bed with a disheveled and very naked Megan sprawled beside him "—that I marvel at how damn lucky I am to be alive and back home."

Megan drew circles on his shoulder with her fingertips. "Do you think Rich planned all along to kill you and take your identity?"

Will stared at the ceiling as he recalled how shocked he'd been to show up in Royal and discover what Lowell had done.

"I've thought about that a lot in the months since I returned from Mexico and what I've decided is that his attack was an impulse. Which is in part why it failed."

"I've talked to Jillian about how she was trying to contact you," Megan said. "Those of us who'd been tricked by Rich have formed an informal club."

Will hated the pain underlying Megan's wry tone. "I blame myself for so much of what Lowell did in my name." The imposter had a lot to pay for and it frustrated Will that the bastard was still at large. "When I started getting phone calls and emails from Jillian Norris, I never should've simply assumed I was the victim of identity theft and put off dealing with it till after my trip to Cabo San Lucas."

"But at the time how could you know Rich had gone to Las Vegas, pretending to be you?" Megan asked. "You thought he was your friend."

This last statement made Will wince. "That doesn't say much about my ability to judge a person's character."

"How did he come to attack you?"

"While we were hanging out on the yacht, drinking beer and fishing, I started talking about how Jillian had contacted me and her insinuations that I had gotten her pregnant." Will paused and shook his head. "So there I was, going on and on about someone running around pretending to be me, all the while not paying attention to Rich's reaction until he referred to Jillian by her name. It was then that I realized I'd never identified her."

"Did you call him on it?"

"I never got the chance to. One second I'm trying to wrap my head around Rich knowing Jillian's name and the next he's coming at me, fists swinging, murder in his eyes."

Will wasn't proud that Rich had gotten the drop on him. But the situation had deteriorated so fast and without warning.

"What happened then?" Megan's blue eyes seemed larger than ever as she gazed at him, completely wrapped up in the story.

"He came at me like a defensive end, head down, shoulders driving forward. He hit me in the gut and I went backward toward the rail. I got in a couple good punches, but he had momentum on his side and I was off balance both physically and mentally."

"Is that when he pushed you overboard?"

"No. I managed to twist to one side before he did and got a little space between us." So many of the details from that day were fuzzy because of his head injury and the speed with which the incident had taken place. "I'm pretty sure I asked him what the hell was going on, but he never answered and rushed me again." Will blew out a breath. "I threw a punch and managed to land a hit to his throat. It slowed him down, but he just kept coming. I've never seen anything like it. I've known the guy for over ten years and this was a side of him I'd never seen before."

"Sounds like he snapped. It's amazing you survived."

"I've been accused of leading a charmed life and, after what happened on that boat, I'm pretty sure that's the case."

"So what happened after he charged you?"

Will paused for a second to sort through his recollections about the day before resuming the tale. "He picked up one of the empty beer bottles that we hadn't thrown away yet and chucked it in my direction. It hit me on the head. The impact was just enough to daze me and, without much room to maneuver, when he came rushing at me again, I wasn't ready for him."

"I just can't believe all this happened."

"It's pretty much what I was thinking as he bounced my head against the railing. I blacked out after that because some time had passed when I heard the sound of a boat motor and smelled fire. I managed to get to my feet and saw Rich heading out in the inflatable we'd been towing."

"He left you on the burning boat?"

"From everything I've gathered since coming back to Royal, I think he realized if I died, he could become me."

"Rich used the boat blowing up to explain his scars and said it was an accident, but do you think he started it?"

"I do. It was a new boat with no electrical or mechanical problems. It wasn't an accident that it caught fire or that it exploded. He needed to get rid of all evidence of foul play."

Megan nodded. "How did you survive?"

"At first I went looking for the source of the fire to see if I could put it out, but I smelled gas and got the hell out of there. On the way to the rail, I grabbed a life preserver. I was swimming and trying to put on the life preserver when the boat blew." Will trailed off as he relived those frantic moments as he'd swum away from the burning boat. There'd been nothing but water from horizon to horizon and the sound of the receding inflatable growing fainter by the second.

"The explosion was something. I wasn't far enough away from to escape the blast and I blacked out again after something hit me in the back of the head. I don't remember getting the life preserver fastened, but I must've done a decent enough job because I survived long enough to be picked up."

"And you were in Mexico all that time? Why didn't you call anyone and let them know you were alive?"

This was the tricky part of his story. Will wasn't a man who was used to being at anyone's mercy and his months with the Mexican cartel were some of the most difficult he'd ever endured.

"Here's what I haven't told anyone," Will said, knowing he was taking a risk unburdening himself to Megan. "The people who found me were drug runners. They were on their way back to Mexico, and when they heard the explosion, they detoured to see what was going on."

Megan's eyes went wide. "I'm surprised they rescued you."

"So was I. I can only assume that, given the size of the boat, they believed I might be worth something to them and they intended to ransom me back to my family."

"Why didn't they? You would've been home."

"These were seriously deranged people. I didn't trust them. It wouldn't have surprised me if they received the money and then slit my throat."

Megan shuddered. "You must have been terrified!"

"Honestly? If I had let myself dwell on it, I might have been. Instead, I focused on my fury at Rich for gaining the upper hand and leaving me to die."

"So how did you keep the drug runners from ransoming you?"

"Well, at first I was in a coma, medically induced because of the brain injuries I'd suffered when the boat blew up. When I woke, I suffered with amnesia for several months. As my memories came back, I realized what a bad situation I'd landed in. So, I kept pretending to have amnesia while I tried to figure out how to get out of my predicament. Since I didn't have any ID on me, they had no idea who to contact. And because technically I wasn't missing, no one was looking for me."

"If they were as bad as you say, why would they take care of you? I can't imagine that a comatose guy they'd dragged out of the Pacific Ocean would be worth their time."

"Luckily, I bore a resemblance to the head of the cartel's dead son. She was the one who decided to keep me around while I recovered." He still couldn't believe he hadn't been killed and his body dumped. Members of the gang had bragged about dealing with several tourists that way and constantly threatened to do the same to Will if he stepped out of line.

"So what kept you from returning home after you recovered?"

"I was closely watched," Will explained. "The Mexican government is doing their best to capture or kill the cartel leaders operating there and this has led to the splintering of major trafficking organizations. Elena was particularly paranoid about maintaining her power while keeping drugs and money flowing. Several of her gang thought I was a US agent, but the circumstances of my rescue made that seem pretty farfetched."

"You're lucky to be alive, aren't you?" Megan mused, nibbling on her lower lip as she regarded him.

"Very. If Elena hadn't taken a fancy to me, I doubt I would've survived. Most of my time with the cartel I spent with her in the family compound. Still, she trusted me only to a point. I had no access to a phone or a way to communicate with anyone outside.

"Eventually, I talked her into letting me go out on some of their drug runs." He released a breath. "On one of them, I was able to make it to a phone and called Jason. He didn't pick up, but I started to leave a message then realized that Rich was still out there and that if anyone knew I was alive, they might become his target." And he'd been right. Will was convinced Jason was dead because he'd confronted Rich after suspecting he'd had something to do with Will's disappearance.

"Did you tell Jason where you were?"

"No. Too late I realized that I couldn't involve him in a rescue attempt. If I was going to get away, I was going to have to do it on my own."

"How did you escape?"

"We got into a pretty nasty gun fight in Los Cabos and I saved the life of one of the cartel gang. It bought me some cred and a few weeks later they took me along on a drug run to the US. I started to put a plan together and on one of the runs I was able to slip away."

"But you still didn't contact anyone once you made it to the US?"

"I tried contacting Jason, but couldn't get through. That was a few days before I returned home to Royal."

Megan pressed her lips together and blinked rapidly. "Because he was already dead, only none of us knew it yet."

Seeing her sorrow, a slow burn kindled in Will's gut. "Rich has so much to atone for," he growled, bile rising at all the terrible things Lowell had done while pretending to be Will. "I'm going to make sure of that."

Megan sauntered into Will's office and found him sitting on the leather sofa near a wall of bookshelves. Several documents lay scattered on the cushions around him. He looked up as she neared and the line between his dark eyebrows vanished as he spotted her.

"Well, this is a surprise," he said, setting aside the document he had been reading.

"I came by to see if you'd like to take me to lunch."

Before he could get to his feet, Megan skirted the coffee table and lowered herself onto his lap. Encircling his neck with her arms, she drew his head to her, depositing a lingering kiss on his mouth. His fingers closed over her waist and thigh as he met the exploratory thrust of her tongue with matching passion.

Megan was breathing hard by the time she lifted her lips from his. Although his hand had only walked partway up her thigh, heat pounded through her in anticipation of where his fingers might go next.

"I don't suppose we dare lock the door so I could have my way with you," she said, only half joking.

They were both flushed, and Megan recognized the sensual cant of Will's lips as she'd seen it often over the last few days right before he swept her into his arms and carried her to the bedroom.

"As much as I'd love to take you up on that tempting offer—" His fingers drifted over her belly and curved as they pressed between her thighs, wrenching a gasp from her. Sighing, Will gave his head a reluctant shake while his eyes flickered toward the open door and his assistant's desk beyond "—it's probably not the best idea since I'm trying hard to restore my reputation after Lowell's antics. As it is, my return has proved confusing for any number of people as my behavior has returned to normal."

"And normal doesn't include a midday tryst in your office." Megan gave his tie a sharp tug as she returned the knot to center. "Even if the woman involved is your wife."

Will looked pained. "It would be one thing if it were

generally known that Lowell had been impersonating me for over a year, but most of my employees are suffering a case of whiplash."

"I imagine they are." Megan deposited a kiss on Will's cheek before gazing around. "I think my office is bigger than yours," she teased, hoping to see him smile again. "Although your desk is much more grand than mine."

"It belonged to my great-grandfather." Six feet long with beautifully patterned veneers and carved, scrolling columns, the desk lent an atmosphere of gravitas to a room dominated by Impressionistic landscapes, white walls and cream carpet.

"I have to say, this isn't exactly what I pictured for your office."

Will looked surprised. "You sound like you haven't been here before."

"I haven't." Megan tunneled her fingers through Will's thick, dark hair. "This is my first visit."

"How is that possible? You were married to Rich for almost a year."

Megan glanced away from his keen green eyes, trying to summon the words to explain how she'd stayed married to a man who'd kept so much of himself and his life away from her. Her gaze fell on the document Will had set aside when she'd entered.

"What is that?" she asked, pointing to the pages. She leaned forward to get a better look and gasped as the text became clear. "These look like settlement clauses." She leaped off his lap and snatched up the document, giving it a more thorough read. When she reached the end, she flipped back to the beginning. Heart clenched in dismay, she gripped the paper hard enough to crease it. "Why are you preparing divorce paperwork?"

"My lawyer has been working on our situation for a while now."

Her throat tightened painfully. "How long?"

"Since I came back and found out we were married." He held out his hands in a soothing manner that had no possible chance of calming her anxiety. "Look, it's just in case…"

Megan couldn't believe what she was hearing. So all those nights while they'd made love and slept entwined in each other's arms, he'd been making plans to divorce her?

"In case of what?"

A muscle bunched in Will's jaw before he answered. "When everything is said and done and Lowell is caught, we no longer have to stay married."

Although Megan could tell Will wasn't happy to be discussing the dissolution of their marriage, his actions in having legal paperwork drawn up showed that he'd been thinking about severing ties.

"We haven't talked about this in weeks," she reminded him, barely able to speak past her raw throat. "Not since I moved in with you."

"I know." He rubbed his eyes. "I want you to know that this time with you has been fantastic."

Nothing in his manner or tone told Megan he spoke anything except the truth, and waves of betrayal buffeted her. "If that's true, then why…?"

He made a grab for the legal document, but missed as she swept it beyond his reach. "We've been existing in a vacuum, hiding out at the Ace in the Hole, ignoring this situation we find ourselves in."

Each one of his words lashed at her heart. "That's all this is? A *situation* we find ourselves in?"

"No, of course not. I care about you."

"I care about you, too." Suddenly it became hard for Megan to breathe. She couldn't seem to get any air into her lungs, and as darkness swallowed her vision, she felt as if she was smothering. "So why can't we go on like we are?"

"What are we?" Will's voice took on an edge. "Husband and wife? You didn't choose me."

It was a backhanded way of saying he had not chosen her. "So we're going to get divorced?"

"I don't know." But in his eyes she could see he did know. "It kind of makes sense that we should."

"I can't believe this is happening." Megan's heart twisted, making her lungs seize. How had she let herself be fooled into falling in love with Will Sanders a second time?

He got to his feet and took the document out of her hand, dropping it on the coffee table before taking her upper arms in a firm grip. "Look, we don't need to talk about this right now. Let's just get through the next few days and then we can consider our options."

"Options?" Megan echoed dully, wondering why she'd let Will into her heart these last few weeks. Given what she'd learned today, it was pretty obvious that he planned to extricate himself from their relationship as soon as he could. "Are there really any options?"

"Once things get back to normal, we can make decisions then."

"Sure." The smile Megan offered up came from pain and disappointment, not joy, but Will didn't seem to notice because he smiled back in reassurance. "I guess I better get going."

"You don't want to do lunch?"

"I guess I'm not as hungry as I thought I was."

Megan sidestepped, and Will's hands fell away from her arms. As she was turning away, her eyes began to burn. She absolutely, positively, would not cry until she'd reached the privacy of her car.

"I'll see you later at the ranch," Will said as she passed the threshold.

To Megan's relief, she navigated Spark Energy Solutions' halls and reached the front door without bursting into tears and making a huge fool of herself. Nor did she start to cry when she reached the safety of her car. Instead, the emotions rising in her were first humiliation and then anger. At Will. And at herself.

Was he right? Had they been existing in a cocoon, isolated from reality? Maybe for him. In her case, Will had become her reality and the way she felt around him was her strength. Now to discover it had all been a lie...

Megan drove through the streets of Royal with no destination in mind. She'd set aside a couple of hours to go to lunch with Will and the thought of returning to work while consumed with heartache held no appeal. Nor could she claim any appetite. Maybe what she needed was a little retail therapy. She would go buy a baby gift for Abigail who was due in the coming month.

Abigail had briefly worked at Spark Energy Solutions as imposter Will's assistant and had been seduced by him. The brief affair had led to her getting pregnant. As with Jillian Norris, in the aftermath of being taken advantage of by Rich, Abigail had found true love. The new man in her life: trauma surgeon Vaughn Chambers.

Leaving her car near Main Street, Megan strolled past several shops, letting herself be distracted by the window displays. She loved how this historic section of downtown Royal housed trendy boutiques beside antique stores and service shops, and wondered why she'd never thought to open a Royals Shoes store here.

She was a few doors down from the baby/children's boutique, where she loved to shop for Savannah, when she suddenly realized she was no longer alone on the sidewalk. All the hair on her arms rose as a shadow fell across her.

"Miss me?" came a familiar voice near her ear as her purse was jerked from her grasp.

The rough action spun Megan around and she tensed

as she stared at the man who'd accosted her. Rich Lowell. "Not for a second," she snapped, making a wild grab at her bag.

Lowell easily swung it beyond her reach and sneered at her. "Too busy playing wife?" he asked. "It figures that you'd fall into bed with Sanders since he's the one you've wanted all along." Rich took a step nearer, his eyes narrowing. "It must drive him crazy that I got there first. Every time he makes love to you, I bet he remembers that you belonged to me before you ever climbed into bed with him. Every kiss reminds him I was there first. When you call his name as you come it reminds him that I was your husband the whole time he was gone. He can't touch you and not think of my hands on you."

Rich's words pummeled Megan, driving to the heart of her insecurities regarding her relationship with Will. She dug her fingernails into her palm, refusing to answer, unwilling to give Rich the satisfaction of seeing her angry or upset.

"You might have had my body, but I was never yours." Although her last encounter with this man had ended with her getting away, Megan wasn't confident that would happen this time, but that didn't stop her bold words. Nor was she about to let him see her fear even when he seized her arm in a biting grip. "I never loved you," she went on brazenly. "I loved who you were pretending to be—Will Sanders. And after we were married, you showed the bastard you really were."

"You loved me," Rich growled, his fingers tightening further as he forced her along the street and into an alley between two buildings.

"It doesn't matter how I felt once," she said, scrambling for a way out of this predicament. "You killed my brother and I despise you."

He jerked her to him and put his arm around her.

Megan resisted as best she could, twisting her body right and left, but his strength outmatched hers. Still, she fought until he shoved her against the alley wall. She hit it with enough force to drive the breath from her lungs. Before she could recover, he yanked her hair, dragging her head back until her face was tilted to his. Seconds later his mouth came down on hers, his breath stinking of whiskey and cigarettes. He bit at her lower lip, causing her to cry out, then plunged his tongue deep into her mouth. Out of breath, with panic starting to rise, Megan fought his hold, but he was too strong.

Still, she struggled, kicking at his shins and pounding his arm, but to no avail. When at long last he lifted his lips from hers, his cruel smile sent a wave of terror through her. The authorities had returned her gun, but it was in her purse and Rich had taken that from her. She had only her wits to use against him.

"You're mine," he snarled. "I'm going to make you remember that."

His ominous words shredded Megan's bravado. "What are you planning to do to me?" she demanded in a breathless rush, her imagination taking her to terrible places.

"We're going on a little trip."

The last thing she needed to do was to let him get her into a car. "What sort of trip?"

"I have something to pick up and then we are heading south to Mexico."

Anxiety tightened Megan's stomach into knots. Will had talked about the likelihood that Rich would take refuge in Mexico. It would be easy for him to disappear, and her with him. She couldn't let that happen.

"You'll never make it," she cautioned. "There's a huge manhunt underway for you."

"You don't think I know that?" He laughed, and the sound grated along her nerves.

Despite her fear, Megan kept her voice from trembling. "It will be that much worse if they think you've taken me with you."

"That's where you're wrong. Why do you think I need you to come along?" A mirthless smile formed on his lips. "You are going to tell everyone that I'm Will Sanders, the love of your life."

"And when we get to Mexico? You'll let me go?"

"Sure." Rich caught her face in his powerful fingers and squeezed. "Right after I make sure Will won't ever want to touch you again."

Seeing that he meant what he said, Megan was even more convinced she couldn't go anywhere with him. But how could she stop him? She had to tip someone off.

"I'm supposed to be having lunch with Dani in fifteen minutes," she lied, quickly formulating a plan. "If I don't meet her, she'll know something's wrong and contact the authorities. Sheriff Battle and the FBI will come looking for me and you won't be able to get away."

Rich stared at her for a long moment while Megan held her expression as earnestly as possible, praying he wouldn't suspect she was lying.

"So text her and let her know you can't make lunch."

Megan shook her head, pretending to resist. If he had to force her to contact Dani, he might miss that she was trying to trick him. She never saw the blow coming, but suddenly there was a blinding pain in her cheek and the coppery tang of blood in her mouth. While she regained her balance, Rich rummaged through her purse until he found her phone and then handed it to her.

"Send the text and be quick about it. And make sure you show me the message before you send it."

Megan unlocked the phone and, while her cheek throbbed, formulated what she could say to Dani that would alert her without the text arousing Rich's suspicions.

Can't make lunch. Call with K Cole about fall line is happening now. Text you later.

"Let me see."

Megan showed Rich the text, holding her breath while he read the message. "Is it okay?"

"Who's K Cole? And what's this 'fall line' you're talking about?"

"Kenneth Cole, the world-famous fashion designer," Megan replied coolly, masking her nerves beneath impatience. "He's interested in collaborating with me next year. It will be huge for my company."

"Delete the 'text you later' line. You won't be texting or calling anybody."

Praying that her friend would understand and contact Cole and Will, Megan sent the text. As soon as it was gone, Rich snatched the phone from her hand, dropped it to the pavement and crushed it with his heel.

"Hey," she complained, feeling as if her lifeline had been cut. "You didn't have to do that. I could've just turned it off."

"They can track you with the phone. This way nobody will know where you are."

"You've bought us a couple hours at the most," she said. "My assistant will be expecting me to return after lunch."

Rich gave her a rough shove toward the end of the alley away from the main downtown street. "Then I guess we'd better get going."

Eleven

Will paced in front of the large desk in his office, the argument with Megan playing over and over in his head. The arrival of the divorce papers this morning had thrown him for a loop. So much had happened since Megan had moved into the Ace in the Hole that had compromised his original intention to divorce her. But while he'd reviewed the legal documents, he'd recalled the conversation he'd overheard between her and Lucy. Megan had made it pretty clear that once Lowell was apprehended she wanted to move on with her life. Will figured that meant ending her marriage to him.

While reviewing the settlement, he'd grown more and more depressed. Was he really prepared to just let her go? It's what she claimed she wanted, but the emotions that had developed between them these last few weeks seemed to contradict that. Surely there was a way for them to start over. Or just start.

So, why hadn't he told her that he wanted them to stay together once this business with Lowell was through?

His cell phone rang and he glanced to where it sat beside his keyboard. Cole Sullivan's face filled the screen. Frowning, Will leaned over and picked up the phone, queuing the answer button.

"Hey, Cole. What's up?"

"Dani just called me. She got a really odd text from Megan and now Megan's not responding to text or answering her phone."

"What sort of odd text?" Wills gut twisted. "What did it say?"

"Something about not making lunch and that she was taking a meeting with K Cole about her fall line."

Will recalled that she'd come to SES to have lunch with him. "Was she having lunch with Dani?"

"No, and I'm wondering if the Cole she's referring to is me. But what's the part about her fall line?"

"I saw her sketches for next year. She was planning to feature a lot of gold in the designs." A part of Will applauded Megan's cleverness even as the ramifications electrified him. He was out of his chair and grabbing his keys before Cole arrived at his own conclusion.

"Gold like Lowell's stash at the cabin."

"He's got her and is planning to make a run for his gold."

Cole cursed. "I'll call Sheriff Battle. The cabin is under surveillance."

"While you do that, I'm going up there."

"That's a bad idea. Why don't you let the sheriff and the FBI take care of this?"

"Given how slowly they've mobilized in the past, I'm not going to sit around and let Lowell get away again. That's my girl he's got. I'm heading out to rescue her."

Knowing that Cole would take care of contacting the

sheriff, Will slid behind the wheel of his Land Rover and burned rubber out of the parking lot. He focused on the road and traffic as he headed out of town, ignoring the voice in his head that reminded him he had no plan. Not accurate. He had one plan. He would trade himself for Megan.

His phone rang as he bumped along the dirt road leading to the cabin. A brief glance at the screen showed him Cole was calling back. Will ignored it. No doubt Cole would try to talk him out of what he was about to do. He didn't have the energy to spare for such a ridiculous debate.

When Will rounded the last curve, he spotted the cabin dead ahead and wasn't surprised to see a late-model pickup backed up to the cabin porch. He let the Land Rover roll forward until it stopped within ten feet of the truck. He shut down the engine and got out. A quick scan of the area showed no sign of Rich or Megan. Could he have been wrong?

Then the cabin door opened and Megan stumbled onto the porch with Rich at her back. Her dark hair hung in limp tangles against her bruised cheek. Rage filled him as Will noted her split lip and swore he would make Lowell pay for hurting her. She was carrying one of the fake gold bricks. From her stiff posture and movements, Will suspected Rich was threatening her with a knife or a gun.

"Lowell," Will called, "this is between you and me." It took all his willpower to keep his attention locked on his nemesis and off Megan's frightened face. "Let her go."

"Not likely. She's coming with me."

"She's not what you want," Will replied, glad his voice reflected none of his anxiety over Megan's safety.

"Well, you're right about that. But she's what you want and so that's why she's coming with me."

There was no way Will was letting that happen. "Take me instead."

"Will, no!"

Megan's impassioned cry tore at him. It was a struggle to keep his hands loose at his sides and his attention fixed on Rich.

"We can take my vehicle," Will continued. "I'll help you get across the border and you can disappear in Mexico."

"I could take you both. Dump you in the desert and take her with me."

"But there's no way you can control both of us. And Megan has already proved that she's smart enough to best you." Will let a small grin form. "Whereas you kicked my ass down in Cabo."

His feint worked as he'd intended. Rich relaxed and returned Will's smile. "I sure did. Turns out you're not the winner everyone thinks you are."

"But you're a winner, aren't you, Rich?" Will shifted forward another half step. "Or you will be if you get away from here with the money you stole. But time's ticking. Make up your mind before there's a gauntlet of police cruisers between you and the border."

"Fine. We'll do it your way." He shoved Megan forward, and she nearly pitched off the porch, the heavy gold brick in her hands disrupting her balance. "Put the gold in the truck, Megan."

Now that she was away from Rich, Will could see that he was indeed holding a gun. Megan's gun. Despite the pistol's small size, the pink grip was a beacon for Will's attention.

At the moment, the barrel remained aimed at Megan. Will intended to change that. As soon as she'd stepped off the porch, Will began walking forward, determined to put himself between her and the gun. Rich licked his lips as he watched his gold disappear into the pickup bed and his distraction allowed Will to get within fifteen feet of him.

The gun barrel swung in Will's direction. "Stop right there."

Megan had frozen, as well, but she was edging away from the truck and toward the corner of the small cabin. With his attention fixed on Will, Lowell didn't notice she was getting away.

"We need to leave now," Will said, his hands in the air, showing no resistance. "The FBI has the cabin under surveillance. They will be here any minute."

Megan was almost to the edge of the cabin, but still too close. Any sudden movement on her part and Rich might decide to put a bullet in her.

"Aren't you wondering why they haven't arrived yet?" Rich sneered, gesturing with his gun. "I knew they were keeping an eye on the cabin and got a buddy of mine to loop the video stream. They've been watching cactus grow for the last forty-five minutes."

Will frowned. That would explain why he'd arrived ahead of them. "The sheriff knows you're here and is on his way."

"Then I guess we better get going." Without taking his eyes off Will, Rich called, "Megan, baby, get in the truck. We're going now."

"No!" Will shouted.

Only, Megan had faded around the corner of the building and was out of range. Seeing that she'd vanished, Rich took several steps in that direction.

As soon as his gun and attention came off Will, he charged across the distance and launched himself at his nemesis.

Everything that Will had endured in the last year and a half came rushing at him as he dashed toward the man who'd stolen his life. It was the fight on the boat all over again. Only this time Will wasn't stunned by his friend's vicious attack or reeling from what he'd learned Rich had done. This time Will operated with focused determination and a fury that strengthened his muscles.

He ignored the part of his brain that recognized charging an armed man was the heart of stupidity, but he couldn't let anything happen to Megan. She was the most important person in his life and without her he might as well be back living with the Mexican cartel without any hope of escape. His future was a vacuum without her in it.

"Run, Megan!" he yelled.

Two steps and he was on Rich, tackling him from behind, letting his weight drive the other man to the plank floor. A rotten board cracked beneath them and their impact with the hard surface jarred the gun from Rich's hand. The pistol skittered out of reach, but Will only peripherally noticed it was out of play before Rich shot his elbow back and connected with his ribs. Pain flared in his side as Rich heaved his body up and to the side, gaining enough space to scramble out from beneath Will. Lowell levered himself onto one knee and before Will made it to his feet, drove his shoulder into Will's midsection. The move put Will on his back. He blocked several blows before driving one of his own into Lowell's jaw.

The months Will had spent with the Mexican cartel had been one long fight to stay alive. Although he'd been under Elena's protection, that hadn't insulated him from being tested by several members of her ruthless gang. In a culture of violence, he'd had to demonstrate that he wasn't weak and that had involved some nasty scuffles. Most of the fights he'd come away battered and bruised, but as the months had gone on, he'd learned to give as good as he got.

While Lowell reeled back from the punch, Will got to his feet and prepared to charge his opponent again. Too late, he realized that their fight had carried them toward Megan's gun. Rich tripped over the Sig and nearly fell, but maintained enough presence of mind to scoop up the pistol and point it at Will.

Will braced himself, knowing the distance between him and the gun was too far. He'd never reach Lowell before he pulled the trigger.

"Don't do this," Will said, knowing words wouldn't delay the inevitable.

Lowell laughed. "You forget this isn't my first attempt to kill you. This time, I'm going to make sure you're dead."

Will saw Lowell's finger tighten on the trigger, but when he pulled, nothing happened. Rich's eyes went wide as he stared at the gun. Will couldn't quite believe he was still alive and realized that Rich had neglected to disengage the safety. From handling Megan's Sig, Will knew it had a frame-mounted safety that Rich probably hadn't noticed.

In the split second of Lowell's distraction, Will raced toward him. Although his adversary couldn't fire the gun it didn't mean it wouldn't make an excellent bludgeon at close range. Lowell delivered a vicious swipe and the pistol connected with Will's temple, stunning him.

The seconds it took for the fog in his brain to clear, Lowell headed for the truck's cab, jumped in and started the engine. Without weighing the intelligence of pursuing the thief and murderer, Will stumbled to the pickup's tailgate, grabbed the cold steel and threw his leg up and over. He almost missed landing in the truck bed as Lowell hit the gas and the vehicle lurched forward.

Panting, the pounding pain in his head making thought difficult, Will slid from side to side as the truck fishtailed, wheels spinning on the gravel road as Lowell accelerated. Flat on his back, staring up at the blue sky, he scrambled to formulate a plan for how to stop Rich. If Lowell reached the highway, the speeds he could reach would make it dangerous to stop him.

Another curve and Will slammed into something hard.

The gold-wrapped tungsten. He picked up a bar, testing the heft before getting his feet under him and making his way forward. Although he worried that Lowell would see him coming, Will reached the cab and swung the brick toward the driver's-side window. The glass shattered beneath the weight of the twenty-seven-pound brick and the momentum carried the brick into the side of Lowell's head.

Almost immediately the truck began to spin as Rich lost control. Will looked up in time to see an electrical pole in their path, but the obstacle was lost from view as the vehicle's erratic movement threw him to the opposite side of the truck bed. Without anything to hang on to and the steel beneath his feet bucking and shifting like a bronco, Will lost his battle to stay upright and began pitching toward the railing and the hard earth beyond at speeds above anything he could expect to survive.

Megan returned to the cabin when she heard the truck speed away. She'd only gone about fifty feet or so into the brush and headed back the way she'd come at a jog. Will's Land Rover sat where he'd parked it. Rich's truck, loaded with all the gold, was nowhere to be seen. A dust cloud marked the direction the vehicle had gone. Megan wanted to scream. Rich had gotten away again.

But where was Will?"

She headed toward the Land Rover, her gaze scouring the area for any sign of him, but he was nowhere to be found. She spun in several circles, growing more concerned when it was obvious she was alone. Had Rich taken Will prisoner after he had offered himself up in trade for her? She thought about what Rich had threatened to do to her once he'd made it to Mexico and knew he wouldn't hesitate to kill Will once he was no longer useful.

A sudden rush of dizziness swept over Megan, and she put her hand on the Land Rover to steady herself. She needed to get help, but Rich had destroyed her phone and she couldn't find the keys for Will's SUV. Then she remembered that law enforcement was watching the stash. Surely they would contact the sheriff's office and FBI. Maybe they were on their way already. Unfortunately, Megan was still stuck there until they arrived.

After what seemed like forever, a single vehicle appeared around the bend in the road. It wasn't the police, but rather Cole Sullivan. She ran to him as he got out of his truck. The look on his face made her stumble, and he caught her before she could fall.

"Where's the sheriff?" she demanded, scrutinizing his expression and not liking what she saw. "And the FBI? Rich was here. He got the gold. And I think he took Will. They have to stop him."

"Megan." The break in Cole's deep voice and the pain in his blue eyes told her more than words that something was terribly wrong.

She dug her fingers into his arm. "What happened? Is Will okay?"

"There was an accident. We're not sure what happened, but the truck containing the gold flipped." He hesitated. "The scene was pretty confusing. Do you know who was driving?"

"Will told me to run. I was behind the house when I heard the truck start. When Rich brought me here, he made me drive. I'm assuming he did the same with Will." Cole glanced away from her and Megan's heart began to pound. Why did you ask me that?"

"The driver was pinned in the cab. The firefighters were working to free him when I left to find you, but he was bleeding out and they couldn't..." His voice broke. "It wasn't looking good."

Megan wanted to shriek, but forced herself to be calm. "Was it Will?"

Cole's head slowly moved back and forth. "I don't know."

"What about the passenger?"

"Thrown from the truck before the crash. From the skid marks, it looked as if the truck was swerving. Maybe they were fighting for control."

"So he's alive?"

"Bloody and banged up. I don't know how serious his injuries were. The paramedics were working on him when I drove up here to find you. I have to be honest with you, I don't know if either man is going to survive." He glanced down at his phone. "A friend of mine was on the scene. He promised to keep me updated."

"But no one knows which man is which?" The pitch of Megan's voice sharpened as panic built.

"Like I said, the scene was pretty confusing. You're sure you don't know who was driving?"

Megan shook her head. "You need to take me there. I can identify Will."

Cole eyed her swollen cheek and split lip. "Maybe I should take you to the hospital."

Was he serious? This was a life or death situation concerning the man she loved and Cole was worried about her.

Megan waved away his concern. "I'm fine."

Except she was anything but fine or okay. In fact, she was nearly hysterical. If she lost Will...

No. She would not think that way. He would survive. He had to. She absolutely, positively could not lose him twice.

Cole's phone buzzed. He glanced down at it and she didn't think she'd ever seen a man's face go so ashen.

"What?" she demanded, suddenly terrified to hear the news.

"They're pretty sure the driver was Will." A pause while Cole's Adam's apple bobbed. "He didn't make it."

"No!"

A wave of dizziness swept over Megan as she screamed her denial, and then the landscape around her and Cole's face started to grow fuzzy. The next thing she knew everything went dark.

Twelve

"I have Megan. I don't think she's hurt, but she's out cold."

Megan heard Cole's words as she came to. Her body swayed as the vehicle she was in bumped over rough terrain. She grabbed at the seat belt strap stretched across her chest and opened her eyes.

"I'm taking her to the hospital," Cole continued. "I'll meet you there."

"What's going on?" she murmured, her throat raw and scratchy.

"Are you okay?" Cole's brows knit together as he glanced her way. "You passed out."

"Will didn't die," she said fiercely, her initial shock fading. Somehow her heart knew that everyone had it wrong. "Have you heard any more from the sheriff or FBI?"

"No, that was Cora Lee. She heard about the accident and is going to meet us at the hospital."

"Why are we going there? I need to go to the accident site."

"You've been through a traumatic experience." He glanced at her swollen cheek. "And I think you should get checked out."

"I'm fine," she said impatiently. "I need to know for sure what happened to Will."

"Hospital first," Cole said.

Megan noted his stony expression and realized there was no use arguing. "Can you at least call someone and let me talk to them?"

"I've already tried and got nowhere. The investigation is ongoing and they're not going to tell us anything until they have definitive answers."

"Will just can't be dead," she muttered, more determined than ever that she was right.

When Cole didn't respond, Megan subsided into silence and fumed. From the blur of scenery moving past her window, Cole was driving fast. His hands on the steering wheel clenched and relaxed as he concentrated on the road ahead.

Cole's phone buzzed and he glanced at it. "I called Dani to meet us at the hospital. She's just arrived. I figured you'd appreciate the company."

Although Megan wanted to thank him for his kindness, she couldn't summon the words. It was crazy to blame Cole for what had happened to Will. After all, it was her text to Dani—a text that was supposed to warn Cole—that had prompted Will to come running to her rescue. So, if anyone was to blame for what had happened to him, the finger should be pointed straight at her.

They'd reached the outskirts of Royal and Cole navigated toward the hospital with near reckless speed. As familiar landmarks flashed by, Megan's emotions fluctuated between despair and hope that everyone was wrong and Will had somehow miraculously been the one who'd survived the accident. If he was dead, wouldn't she somehow know it?

"Megan?"

Cole's voice roused her out of her reverie. She realized
they'd arrived at the hospital's emergency entrance. Dani
was coming toward her side of the car. Cole disengaged
the locks, allowing Dani to open Megan's door. She practically fell out of the car and into her friend's arms.

"Oh, Dani. It's all so awful. Have you heard about Will?"

"Just what Cole told me. I saw Special Agent Bird go by
a while ago. Apparently the passenger survived."

"Was it Will?"

"I don't know." Dani's expression was sympathetic as
she squeezed Megan's arm, offering whatever comfort she
could. "Agent Bird wants to talk to you as soon as you're
checked out."

The lack of clear information about the situation was
making Megan frantic. "I want to talk to him now," she
declared. She couldn't wait for answers, needing to look
the FBI agent in the eye to see if he really couldn't confirm who'd survived the wreck. "Cole, please see if he can
come talk to me."

"I'll park and go find him."

"Is Cora Lee here?" Megan asked, leaning on Dani,
needing both physical and emotional support as anxiety
continued to batter her. "Cole said she was coming to the
hospital, as well. Maybe she's heard something about Will."

"I haven't seen her yet. The whole situation is really
confusing." Dani looked close to tears as she scrutinized
Megan's battered face. "Can you walk?"

Megan wiped the back of her hand beneath her eyes,
clearing the tears that had rolled onto her face. "I'm fine."

Regardless of Megan's declaration, Dani slid her arm
around her friend's waist and the two women began walking toward the emergency entrance.

"Cole said you passed out."

"It was just… I was overwhelmed at hearing about the accident." Megan gripped her friend's hand. "He just can't be dead."

Dani nodded but said no more. Nor did either woman speak while Megan checked in at the reception desk and waited to be called into an examination room.

From where she sat, Megan could see outside and it appeared as if a couple news crews had assembled near the hospital's entrance.

No doubt word had spread that a member of one of the town's most prestigious families with deep roots in Royal had been involved in a fatal crash. How long before the whole story came out? Megan braced herself as she realized the press would want to talk to her and that as the wife of the imposter, she would come under great scrutiny.

While people came and went, Megan sat with her hands balled in her lap, her gaze roving constantly as she searched for Cole or one of the FBI agents. Someone. Anyone who could tell her if Will had survived.

Inactivity and the day's taxing events began to take its toll on Megan's endurance. Bile rose in her throat and her head began to spin. As the edges of her vision began to darken, she gripped her chair's wooden armrests to keep herself upright.

"Are you okay?" Dani asked, gazing at her sharply. "When was the last time you ate?"

Megan frowned, her memory blurry. Had she eaten breakfast? "Dinner last night, I think."

Dani clucked her tongue. "I'm going to get you something to eat and drink."

Megan nodded, and Dani headed toward a bank of vending machines. While she fought fatigue and paralyzing fear, Megan glanced around the waiting area, wondering where Cole and the FBI agents were.

She spied the other FBI agent involved with the Richard Lowell case exiting the elevator. Determined to get answers, Megan got to her feet and headed straight for Special Agent Marjorie Stanton.

Megan had heard that the redhead was six months' pregnant and eager to close the manhunt before going on maternity leave. Still, she didn't look particularly happy as Megan approached her.

"Have you heard anything more about Will?" Megan began, searching the special agent's expression for answers. "Cole told me…" She couldn't speak the words. "Please tell me he's not really dead."

"Will survived the accident," Agent Stanton said, her eyes softening slightly as Megan cried out in relief.

Dani had reached Megan in time to hear this last bit and put her arm around her friend, lending her support. Will was alive! But he'd arrived at the hospital in an ambulance. How badly had he been injured?

Megan had to know, but it was as if her lungs had seized. She couldn't gather enough breath to voice the questions swirling in her mind. An incoherent noise rattled in her throat as she struggled.

"Is he going to be okay?" Dani asked for her.

"Looks like it. He's pretty banged up, but should recover. I was told he has a head injury and a dislocated shoulder in addition to potentially several broken ribs. He's being examined and no doubt they'll keep him for several days to monitor him. You don't want to mess with brain injuries, especially when he's suffered trauma before."

Abruptly Megan's voice returned. "But he's okay?" She didn't wait for the agent to answer before she rushed on. "When can I see him?"

Stanton glanced at the emergency room entrance where more reporters had gathered. "You'll have to speak to his doctor. Excuse me."

Overwhelming relief exploded in Megan, unleashing a fresh wave of tears. Dani folded her friend into a soothing embrace.

"That's great news. He's okay," the executive chef said, her arms tightening as Megan was battered by sobs. "You're both okay."

Megan leaned on Dani for several minutes, unable to catch her breath or to quell her shaking as everything she'd been through caught up to her. It was all over. Lowell was gone and both she and Will had survived. They might have been dealt serious wounds to body and soul, but if they had each other, they could heal.

"I never believed he could be dead," Megan said when she was finally calm enough to speak without breaking down. "I just couldn't. What if I'd never had the chance to tell him I love him?"

"But now you can and everything is going to be okay."

It wasn't until Megan was upstairs in a small lounge, waiting for Will to finish with a series of tests to determine the extent of his injuries that she remembered what had happened between the two of them in the hour before she'd been kidnapped. The confrontation in his office about their future split after Rich's rein of terror was over. She'd fled without speaking her heart and wasn't sure Will even wanted to hear that she'd fallen in love with him.

At Megan's urging after finding out that Will was going to be okay, Dani had headed off to take care of her twin boys. Left by herself as the events of the day caught up with her, Megan scooped her feet up beneath her and leaned against the arm of the couch, promising herself she'd only close her eyes for a few minutes.

When she woke, the sunshine that had painted a corner of the room had gone and the sky had grown dark. She rubbed her eyes and glanced around, wondering why no one had awakened her. Seated in a chair a few feet away was Cora Lee. The older woman looked as tired as Megan felt.

"How's Will? Is he in his room?"

"He's doing okay for a man who was thrown from a speeding pickup truck." Cora Lee leaned forward and peered at Megan. "How are you doing? You've had a traumatic day, as well."

Megan noticed Cora Lee staring at her bruised cheek and shook her head. "I'm fine."

"You should go home and rest."

"I want to see Will."

Cora Lee's eyes shifted toward the hallway that led away from the waiting area and toward the individual rooms. "I don't think this is the best time."

"What do you mean?" Cora Lee had no right to keep her away, but this wasn't the moment to defend herself against the allegation that Megan wasn't good for Will. "I need to see him. To make sure he's okay."

"He's resting and shouldn't be disturbed."

"Disturbed?" Megan's temper spiked. "I'm not going to disturb him. Why are you trying to keep us apart? I'm his wife. I should be with him."

"You're not—" Cora Lee broke off and pressed her lips together. With a gusty sigh, she continued. "He doesn't want to see you right now."

"What?" Every bit of fight went out of Megan. "Why not?"

"He didn't share his reasons with me. He simply asked that you give him a couple days before you come back."

"A couple *days*?" Megan had no idea what to say. "But I can't wait a couple of days to tell him how I feel."

All at once Cora Lee got to her feet and came over to sit beside Megan. "How do you feel?"

"I love him. I want to spend the rest of my life with

him." Megan's throat tightened. "I made a mistake when I married Rich, but the only man I've ever wanted was Will."

"I believe you." Cora Lee squeezed Megan's icy fingers, her own hands offering much needed warmth. "And I'm sure Will does, as well. Just give him a little time."

Megan nodded dully but couldn't help but worry that the more time it took for Will to make up his mind, the more likely it would be that he'd decide he no longer wanted her around.

Staying apart from Megan these last few days had been one of the hardest things he'd ever had to do, but he'd needed to do some thinking and to come to grips with what the two of them needed to discuss. The end of their pretend marriage. There was no more putting it off. He had to set her free.

But first she deserved to know the truth he'd been foolishly keeping to himself. That being married to her was the best thing that had ever happened to him.

Will dressed in jeans and a white button-down shirt. Easing his arms into a caramel-colored sport coat, he slid on his favorite boots and checked his reflection in the mirror. Aside from a few bruises and the tension around his mouth from lingering aches and pains in his head and ribs, he looked presentable enough.

A glint of gold on his left finger caught his eye, and he spun the wedding ring around and around. Despite the all-clear from the authorities, giving him permission to end his pretend marriage, Will hadn't been able to bring himself to take off the symbol of his union with Megan. While the wedding ring was as much of a pretense as their marriage had been, his instincts told him by taking it off he'd signal that he'd given up. And he couldn't bring himself to do that.

The sound of a door closing came from the front of

the house, followed by Cora Lee's voice calling his name. Leaving off staring at his reflection, Will exited his bedroom and headed into the great room. He found his stepmother in the kitchen, pouring herself a cup of coffee.

"How are you feeling this morning?" she asked, running a critical eye over him. "You look dressed to go somewhere. Are you sure that's a good idea?"

"I have to talk to Megan."

"Well, it's about time. I don't understand why you wouldn't speak to her in the hospital."

"I didn't know what to say."

"You could start with 'I love you,'" his stepmother offered, her voice, like her famous lemon bars, a blend of tart and sweet. "Or are you going to continue to behave like a thickheaded idiot?"

Amusement surged through Will at her blunt words. "If I was less thickheaded, I might not have survived the crash."

To his surprise, Cora Lee's eyes grew bright with unshed tears. "Don't you ever scare me like that again."

Will came around the large island and wrapped his arms around her sturdy form, squeezing her until his ribs shrieked in protest. "I will do my best going forward to stay out of trouble."

"Wonderful." She freed herself from his embrace, wiped all moisture from her cheeks and gave him a no nonsense nod. "Now to the reason why I came here today."

She stepped over to her purse and reached inside. While Will looked on with interest, she pulled forth a ring box and held it up between them with all the flourish of a magician pulling a rabbit out of a hat.

"You brought me a ring?"

"I brought you my ring."

Will regarded the small square box in surprise. Cora Lee had stopped wearing the large diamond ring after his father died, claiming the flashy thing had never suited her, and he'd assumed it had been in her safe-deposit box all these years.

"Would you like me to put it in my safe for you?" he asked.

"No." She gave him a disgusted look. "I want you to give it to Megan. You both need a fresh start and she can't keep wearing Lowell's ring."

When he made no attempt to take the ring, she gave a huge sigh and took his hand. Her grip tightened fiercely as she set the small box against his palm and closed his fingers around it.

"I want a fresh start," he mumbled, feeling the bite of the box's velvet-covered corners against his fingers. "I'm not so sure Megan feels the same way."

"But you're going to ask her to marry you." Cora's bright eyes remained locked on his expression for several seconds before she nodded. "You two so obviously love each other... After everything you've been through, don't let Lowell win."

"He can't win. The bastard's dead." Yet wouldn't his former friend's ghost linger between Will and Megan as long as they didn't speak their true feelings? "I'm on my way to see her now."

Cora Lee nodded in approval. "Take the ring."

He shook his head, thinking back to her concerns when he wanted Megan to move to the Ace in the Hole and wondering when his stepmother's opinion of his relationship with Megan had transformed. And did it really matter if Cora Lee gave him her blessing when Megan wanted to move forward with her life sans Will Sanders?

"I'm not sure she wants to stay married to me," he said.

"Take the ring," Cora Lee repeated in that all-knowing, bossy way she had. "It will be better if you're prepared."

Prepared for what?

* * *

Will turned Cora Lee's words over and over in his mind as he drove to Royals Shoes. When he'd made the decision to approach her today, the last thing he'd imagined himself doing was sliding an engagement ring onto Megan's finger. She'd claimed she wanted to be done with this wretched situation they found themselves in. Yet her reaction to seeing the divorce settlement he'd been working on had told a different story. Maybe there was hope for them after all.

At Royals, Will followed the receptionist's directions and headed down the hallway that would take him to Megan's corner office. He'd called ahead and spoken with her assistant, Lindsay, confirming that she had no meetings scheduled before noon. Having a deeply personal conversation at her company might not be the best idea, but now that he'd decided on a course of action, Will couldn't wait to get everything off his chest.

He slowed as he approached Lindsay. "Did the flowers arrive?"

"They did," Lindsay said, her eyes glowing with approval. "And it's a gorgeous bouquet."

With a satisfied nod, Will stepped into his wife's big, elegantly appointed office and agreed with her estimation that she had more square footage. To his left, an enormous bouquet of brightly colored flowers dominated the conference table and scented the air. Although the beautiful arrangement contained some of Megan's favorites, Will regretted that he hadn't sent red roses instead. Despite Megan's aversion to them, nothing said *I love you* like two dozen fat scarlet blooms adorning long stems.

Megan sat at her desk, her back to him, her gaze fixed on the small patch of green outside her window. He quietly closed the door and advanced ten feet into the room, unsurprised by the way his heart hammered relentlessly against his ribs, rendering him short of breath. The sheer destiny of the moment immobilized him. He was madly in love with his wife, an outcome that he'd been marching toward since he'd set foot in Royal and found out he was married.

And yet, thinking about it now, maybe it had been coming a lot longer and he'd just been too foolish to notice a good thing when it was right in front of him.

"Hi," he said, his voice lacking his usual crisp confidence.

Megan swung her chair around and faced him. Her wide-eyed gaze swept over him. "When did you get out of the hospital?" she asked.

"Late yesterday."

Pain flared in her eyes. "Why didn't you call me? I would have come to get you."

"I had some thinking to do." He shoved his hand into his jacket pocket and felt the hard edge of the ring box.

"Is that why you refused to see me until now?" Megan got to her feet and slipped out from behind her desk. She strode toward the conference table and eyed the flowers he'd sent her.

"I wasn't ready to have this conversation," Will said.

She crossed her arms over her chest and her lips drew down at the corners. "What conversation is that?"

Will fingered the box. "The one where we agreed to dissolve our marriage."

"Why wouldn't you want to have this conversation?" she demanded, her voice raw and angry. "Isn't that what you've been waiting for? After all, you were drawing up a settlement agreement even after I told you I wasn't interested in your money."

"Look. You married me—"

Megan interrupted, "I married someone pretending to be you."

Irritation flared. "You married Will Sanders and deserve something for your trouble."

"My trouble?" She looked ready to breathe fire. "Being married to you wasn't a hardship."

He'd believe her if she wasn't glaring at him. "But you were tricked and lied to."

"That was Lowell, not you." Suddenly she deflated. "I liked being married to you."

His heart jerked. "I liked being married to you, too. In fact," he continued, "in a weird way, Lowell did me a favor." Not that this had stopped him from wanting to see the guy pay for all the lives he'd wrecked. "Before I left on that fateful fishing trip, I wasn't thinking in terms of marriage and family. Everything that had happened in my life up until that point had been easy and that made me take too much for granted. Family and friends. My business success. And except for when my dad died, I'd never known heartache or loss."

"And now?" Despite her luminous expression, a trace of shadow lingered in her eyes. "That's changed?"

"I'm a completely new man. And I've been thinking a lot about why Lowell chose you. He suspected that I was attracted to you before I'd admitted it to myself and that's why, after I disappeared, you were the one he targeted. He wanted everything that was important to me. Especially you."

"But you never said anything." Megan looked as if she wasn't sure she believed him. "You never gave me the slightest hint."

"What can I say except that I've been a jerk?" Will gave her a sheepish grin. "Jason kept me apprised of your personal life. If any guy had made a move, I would've been there to cut him off."

Megan arched an eyebrow. "That's awfully arrogant of you."

"I never claimed to be perfect."

"Neither of us is."

"So how do we move forward?" Will swept a lock

of hair behind her ear, savoring the softness of her skin against his fingertips. "I came here today intending to say I'd understand if you wanted to move on. No hard feelings. We can dissolve the marriage and part as friends."

As the words poured out of him in an agonized rush, he gauged her reaction. Letting her go was the last thing he wanted, but she'd been through so much and he did not want to put pressure on her.

"What do you want to do?"

The time had come for him to open his heart to her. Come what may, he couldn't let her go without at least telling her the depth of his feelings. "I want to stay married."

"You do?" She looked hopeful.

Will nodded. "I think we've discovered in the last few months that we're good together, don't you?"

"Yes. But…"

"But what?"

"You are an honorable man. I don't want you to stay married to me because you think it's the right thing to do."

Seeing her doubts and understanding the reason why, he took her hands in his. "Being married to you is the best thing that's ever happened to me."

"Oh, Will." Her blue eyes grew watery as they scanned his expression. "That's how I feel, too."

"I love you," he declared, shocked and humbled by the dramatic change in his fortunes from this morning until this moment. "I can't imagine my life without you. And I'll take you anyway you want. Friends. Lovers. Wife. Whatever makes you happy."

Megan reached up and tangled her fingers in his hair, giving a slight tug. Her voice when she spoke quivered slightly. "I love you. More than anything, I want to be your wife and the mother of your children."

Will had no words, but the situation called for none. He hauled her against him and brought his lips to hers. With a happy cry, she kissed him back, communicating her joy in the most elemental of ways.

"You have no idea how happy I am right now." Will deposited feverish kisses on her eyelids, nose and cheeks.

"Hopefully, I can make you even happier," she replied, peering at him from beneath her lashes.

He glanced toward her closed office door and raised an eyebrow at her, remembering the conversation they'd had in his office. "I'm game if you are."

She laughed joyfully while her arms banded around his tender ribs in a fierce hug. Despite the pain, he couldn't bring himself to complain, but something must've showed in his expression because Megan released him with a whispered apology.

"I don't think you're in any condition for that," she teased.

Will chuckled. "I'm *always* in condition for that."

"Maybe you should sit down." She waited until he'd gingerly lowered himself onto the couch and then straddled his lap. Cupping his face in her hands, she deposited a series of tantalizing kisses on his cheeks, nose and chin.

Frustrated by her gentleness, he slid his hand into her hair and brought their mouths together. With slow lashes of his tongue, he devoured her with deliberate care while her fingers trailed over his shoulders and nape. Her fragrant skin warmed beneath the slide of his lips along her neck, and she purred in pleasure. The sound awakened a nearly ravenous hunger.

Earlier, in order to straddle him, she'd had to hike her skirt up, baring her long, lean thighs. Now, as she sensuously rocked against the erection thickening beneath her, Will's palms coasted up her legs until he encountered the elastic on her panties. Both of them gasped in unison as he slipped his fingers beneath the fabric and delved into her slick heat.

Crying out in pleasure, Megan threw her head back,

closed her eyes and thrust her breasts forward. In moments like these she stole his breath. Hot color flushed her cheeks as she tightened her thighs on either side of his.

The exquisite sight of her grinding on him with such utter abandon made him groan in sheer joy. He punched his hips upward, driving himself against her. The move sent a shaft of pain lancing through his ribs, stopping his breath. To avoid further discomfort, Will froze. This alerted Megan that something was wrong. Her eyes snapped opened and fixed on his expression, seeing the pain he fought to conceal.

"I'm so sorry," she exclaimed, obviously mortified. "I didn't mean to hurt you."

He shook his head and gently coaxed her mouth to his, saying against her lips, "The only way you could ever hurt me is by leaving."

Abruptly, her eyes brightened with unshed tears. She set her forehead against his and scanned his features while a ragged breath slipped free.

"I can't believe I almost lost you a second time," she murmured, her voice a raw agony. "I couldn't bear it if that happened."

"With Lowell dead, you don't ever have to worry about that again. I'm not going anywhere."

This time Will didn't even feel the pain as he hugged Megan. They were going to stay married. Be a real family. It had been so long since he'd felt a part of something like that. "We're going to be so happy," he said, conscious of a very goofy grin spreading across his face.

"The happiest," she agreed, putting out her left hand so Will could slide the ring onto her third finger. "And I think after all we've been through, we both deserve it."

Will couldn't agree more.

Epilogue

Putting a huge wedding together in less than a month might have daunted most brides, but Megan had been denied a huge ceremony surrounded by family and friends because Rich had insisted they run off to Reno, and she'd had a pretty good vision for her dream event. They were holding the ceremony at the Ace in the Hole, and had invited over two hundred people to be witnesses as Megan and the real Will Sanders said their vows.

After Lowell had died from injuries he sustained in the car accident, the background on the investigation and everything that had happened after he'd returned from Mexico pretending to be Will had been well and fully covered not only by the local news, but nationwide. The story had a scandalous twist that the media had eaten up for nearly a week until breaking news out of Austin had sent the reporters scrambling to cover a juicy sexual harassment allegation against one of the state senators.

Megan had given one interview to the local paper and

avoided the rest. She hadn't wanted her personal life poked and prodded, nor did she relish the possibility of seeing her words sliced and diced to make the story a more salacious read. Instead, Megan kept her talking points simple, emphasizing her shock in finding herself married to an imposter and confessing that she'd been in love with Will Sanders since they were in high school, but that she'd barely had any contact with him during the ensuing years.

"A bride is supposed to smile on her wedding day," Will said, lifting their entwined fingers so he could kiss her knuckles.

They were strolling into the Texas Cattleman's Club where their wedding reception for four hundred would soon be under way. Organizing such a large event in a short period of time might've been a daunting task if so many hadn't pitched in to help. Megan had been overwhelmed by the support she'd received from new friends and old, but especially the women harmed by Rich. These women had showed their community spirit by organizing the catering, flowers, wedding cake and decor.

"Wasn't I smiling?" She couldn't imagine how this wasn't the case. Since Will had confessed his love and said that he wanted to spend the rest of his life with her, Megan's days had become one long series of happy moments. Except for one thing. "I guess I'm just wishing Jason could be here to share this day with us."

Will's gaze locked with hers, and the pain in his eyes made Megan's heart clench. Maybe she shouldn't have mentioned their shared loss on what was supposed to be the happiest day of their lives, but since she and Will had found each other, she'd been aware of an ever-growing sense that her brother was smiling down on the union.

"I think he'd approve of us being together," Will said, echoing her own thoughts.

"I do, too."

And that was all the time they had to talk. A second later they stepped into the club's largest ballroom, and applause erupted from the hundreds of guests. Seeing the semicircle of people standing closest to the door, Megan found her throat closing up as emotion overwhelmed her.

Four months earlier she'd sat in a room with four of the women waiting to greet her, stunned by the loss of her husband and confused by the damning tales several of those women had had to tell.

The first person Megan hugged was Selena Jacobs. Despite the years of anger since they'd fallen out in high school over something stupid, Megan and Selena had recently put aside old hurts. The healing had begun after Megan had discovered that Will's marriage during college to the gorgeous cosmetics entrepreneur had been to help her out, not because they'd been in love. Now, Selena was madly in love with Knox McCoy and had confided to Megan earlier that the couple was expecting a baby girl they planned to name Carmela.

Standing beside Selena was Abigail Stuart, another of Lowell's victims. She and Vaughn had become parents to their little girl a few weeks earlier. Megan hugged the new mother and thought of the future children she hoped to have one day.

She and Will accepted well-wishes from Jillian, now her sister-in-law, Allison Cartwright, now Gibson, and the men they'd fallen in love with. It amazed Megan that a little over four months ago most of these people had been strangers. Now, she felt as if they would forever be a part of her life.

"Well, Mrs. Sanders," Will began as they moved deeper into the room. "What do you say to getting this party started with a dance?"

"Isn't it traditional to eat dinner first?" she teased as he pulled her into his arms on the dance floor. There would be a band later, but for now a sound system in one corner of the room played softly in the background.

"I think we left traditional in our rearview mirror a long time ago," he replied, grinning down at her.

"I guess you're right." And as circuitous as the path that had lead to this moment had been, Megan would do it all over to be this happy.

"I love you." Will dipped his head and dropped an affectionate kiss on her lips. "Forever and always."

"I love you, too." Megan framed his face with her hands as her heart expanded with joy. "Always have. Always will."

* * * * *

COMING SOON!

We really hope you enjoyed reading this book. If you're looking for more romance, be sure to head to the shops when new books are available on

Thursday
9th August

LET'S TALK
Romance

For exclusive extracts, competitions
and special offers, find us online:

f facebook.com/millsandboon

◎ @millsandboonuk

𝕏 @millsandboon

Or get in touch on 0844 844 1351*

For all the latest titles coming soon, visit
millsandboon.co.uk/nextmonth